Stage Effects

J WILCOX

Grosvenor House
Publishing Limited

The right of J Wilcox to be identified as the author of this
work has been asserted in accordance with Section 78
of the Copyright, Designs and Patents Act 1988

The book cover is copyright to J Wilcox

This book is published by
Grosvenor House Publishing Ltd
Link House
140 The Broadway, Tolworth, Surrey, KT6 7HT.
www.grosvenorhousepublishing.co.uk

This book is a work of fiction. Any resemblance to
people or events, past or present, is purely coincidental.

A CIP record for this book
is available from the British Library

ISBN 978-1-83615-092-3

Also by J Wilcox

A Rather Cryptic Crime
Missing But Not Missed

Coming soon

Where There's A Song *(Preview on page 283)*

For new publications and other book news, follow me on -
Facebook: J.Wilcox
Instagram: J.Wilcox_author

For John

1997, a dancing show,
The Beck, stage right, and Cupid raised his bow.
And now, as swift years fly, of this I'm certain,
I'm glad you smiled at me around that curtain.

Acknowledgements

Once again, my thanks go to Jonathan for reviewing the drafts, giving feedback and laughing in all the right places; to Lynne for reviewing, and for the culinary and crossword contributions; to Sally for her crossword clues; to Toby for his very helpful feedback; to Mary for her beautiful artwork; to Jasmine for her invaluable help with the publication process, and to Harry, my unofficial sales and media manager!

Acknowledgements

Prologue

The final curtain closed to fervent applause, and *The School for Scandal*, competently presented by The Lymeford Amateur Dramatic Society, was over. As the actors took their bow, the audience members who had come to support them cheered with enthusiasm and breathed a secret sigh of relief that their partner, relative or friend had got through without a hitch.

The loudest applause, however, came for that local celebrity and doyen of the West End, Roland Rawlison, as he pranced onto the stage to the delight of his fans. Rawlison had reached that point in his career when an appearance to shore up the local am-dram society was as welcome to him as it was to them, but the whoops and cheers of the whole audience, not just his supporters, proved he had not lost his touch. Even a group from the local school, conveyed there by an eager performing arts teacher, joined in the enthusiastic applause, though none of them had been born when Rawlison was a household name.

The members of the cast were elated; the drudgery of learning lines and the hours of fraught rehearsal were all forgotten. The technicians and theatre staff were also in good humour; the production had gone through without disaster which was the best they ever hoped for with an amateur show.

In short, everyone within those theatrical walls was happy. And none more so than one individual who had murder in mind and had just seen exactly how it could be accomplished.

1

"Oh, do say you'll do it, Leslie," begged Gloria, through a mouthful of fruitcake. She dabbed up the crumbs from her plate with her finger and popped them in her mouth before fixing him with her most imploring look. "We're simply relying on you to step in; I just don't know what we'll do if you say no. And anyway, think how much more fun it will be if we're both in it."

Leslie knew from experience that Gloria was difficult to resist once she was set on a purpose, but he stood his ground bravely. "I'll need a few days to decide," he said. But catching her pleading expression he added, "Well, perhaps if I look at the script tonight, I could let you know tomorrow."

"Oh," she sighed, "I didn't think to bring the script; how stupid of me. But you'll love it, I know you will. I say, this cake is very good."

Taking the hint, Leslie cut another generous slice which she accepted with rapturous appreciation.

"It's called *Who Will It Be*? and it's a very clever play," she said eagerly, heaping two spoons of sugar into the coffee. "And you're so absolutely perfect for the role of Sebastian Bancroft. As soon as I heard about Frank's accident, and even before they put out a plea for a replacement, I knew the part was for you. And it couldn't be more convenient with the rehearsals in the village hall, here in Dartonleigh."

Leslie refilled the coffee cups and Bennett, still only a couple of bites into the first slice of cake, gave him an amused smile. So, Bennett was not against the idea.

They were in the sitting room of Leslie and Bennett's cottage, with the French windows open, and the September sun sending its lazy warmth into the room. While Gloria was engrossed in her cake, with crumbs and fruit bouncing off her substantial bosom, Leslie weighed up the pros and cons of her invitation. Unquestionably his first reaction was to decline. True, he had enjoyed treading the boards in the past, and it was in a light operatic society that he and Bennett had first met, but that was years ago, and he was highly dubious about the wisdom of trying to rekindle the old thespian passion.

Gloria had finished her cake, and dabbed her mouth politely with her napkin, sending a further shower of crumbs to the floor. Oblivious, she sighed wistfully. "They've had such bad luck with this play. I'm only in it, as you know, because the lady who was originally cast for the part fell ill. The church hall in Lymeford, where they usually rehearse, is shut for renovation and none of the other ladies in the company would travel out this far, even though it's less than five miles. You know what they're like in these parts, it might as well be Exeter that you're asking them to go to. Then, just when the rehearsals were starting to come together, Frank had the car crash and has ended up in hospital with his leg pinned in three places."

Leslie could feel himself giving in. After all, he had nothing very pressing to fill his days just now so he might as well spend them learning lines. Cooking, his great love, and village life were enough to occupy his time, but they could hardly be an excuse for not obliging a friend. Similarly, his garden offered endless possibilities for pottering about in, but there was nothing urgent that could justify a refusal. It might even be a welcome distraction from the impending horticultural show for which he had no produce worthy to enter this year. He could not even plead he wanted to spend the last few weeks of long, mild days out on his favourite Dartmoor walks. It was no pleasure to go out without Bennett who, much to Leslie's frustration, rarely left the cottage these days. Since his heart attack Bennett rarely bestirred himself, even though that was now some time ago and he had made an excellent recovery, and despite Leslie begging him to take exercise. Leslie could not account for it, but then there was so much about Bennett that, even after twenty years, Leslie could not account for.

Gloria fixed her friend with an expression of earnest entreaty. Leslie, recalling the experience of having to remember lines and perform in front of an audience, said, "Is there really no one else connected with the company who could do it?" It seemed extraordinary that a theatre company, even a small amateur group, should need to resort to an outsider.

"But it can't just be any old person who plays Sebastian," Gloria replied. "They must be able to sing, too. As I told Kara—she's the director—you were made for the part. You've got everything: a wonderful voice, you're an old hand on stage, I know you'll fit in with everyone, and you're so clever, I know you'll be able to pick it up quickly."

"That's very kind of you," said Leslie, unconvinced by Gloria's flattery which, though meant sincerely, he knew to be misplaced. "But—"

"It's on in a month," interrupted Gloria, "so you don't have to commit yourself to it for very long."

Leslie tried one last appeal. "But I genuinely don't know if I could manage it," he said. "It's such a long time since I've been on a stage, and I've no idea if I could learn the lines anymore."

"Bosh," said Bennett suddenly. "When do you ever have problems memorising pieces for your choir? You can do it on your head." He turned to Gloria. "It might stop him pestering me to go out for a walk every five minutes or fretting about the autumn flower show."

"Well, why don't you volunteer for the part?" Leslie retorted, indignantly. "You've got just as much experience as me on stage and your voice is a hundred times better than mine."

Bennett simply peered over his glasses with an inscrutable expression.

4

Ignoring this last exchange, Gloria said to Leslie, "There now, I knew you'd be up for it. And the thing is," she added, playing her trump card, "I've been rather naughty and told Kara I'd take you to see her tomorrow. At eleven o'clock. So, it would be a tiny bit awkward to cancel now, though of course I will if you really won't do it."

**

And so, the next day Leslie found himself clambering into Gloria's little red convertible and speeding away, roof down, towards Kara's house which was in a hamlet just outside Lymeford. It was a beautiful golden day with the first hint of autumn in the air and, in principle, just the day for a spin. But Leslie knew there was little chance of appreciating the verdant hedgerows, the glimpses of vast, purple moorland and the various streams and quaint cottages along the way as, if Gloria's driving was true to form, they would pass in a blur.

Gloria kept up a stream of chatter, mostly about the company members, throughout the journey. It was fortunate she did not seem to need much response, as Leslie could only manage a few stifled replies through gritted teeth as they swung round the lanes.

"Kara's a bit of a character," she said, changing down several gears at once as they flew round a sharp bend and were suddenly yards away from the back of a tractor.

"Really?" said Leslie, once they had slithered to a near halt, horribly close to the tractor's rear. Although he was familiar with Gloria's unique driving style, it did not make it any easier to endure.

"Oh, I'm sure she doesn't mean anything by it," she said airily. "But you know what these theatricals are like. They're all a bit highly strung."

Dirt spiralled off the tractor's huge, mud-clogged wheels, spattering the windscreen and showering the little car with muck. Leslie pulled up his jacket hood and crouched low in the seat.

"She's got a good excuse for being snippy now, of course," continued Gloria, oblivious to the pieces of straw clinging to her hair and chiffon scarf. "Frank, the man you're standing in for, is Kara's husband. So, not only is she directing the play and having to recast you in Frank's part, but she's got all the worry of him being in hospital as well. I'm not surprised she's rather stressed."

This sounded ominous, but Leslie said nothing as Gloria went on.

"Then there's Terry, he fancies himself as a bit of a lad. He's the society's chairman, or whatever the person in charge is called. It's through him I got involved, of course."

Leslie had already heard this story. Earlier in the year Gloria had signed up as a volunteer usher at the theatre in Lymeford, throwing herself into the role with great enthusiasm. There, she met Terry who was a volunteer of many years standing, and she had been charmed by his personable manner. She had shown a friendly interest when he spoke about the amateur theatre company of which he was the proud chairman, but she was highly surprised when, later, he asked if she would stand in for a cast member who was suddenly indisposed. Greatly flattered, Gloria agreed, and was now part of the production.

Even when Gloria had first told him this story, it had struck Leslie as odd that they could not find someone from within the company to take on the role. He had seen a number of the productions put on by the Lymeford Amateur Dramatics Society (or LADS as they styled themselves) and they seemed to have plenty of good amateur performers to choose from. In his experience, the casting of a play inevitably left plenty of disappointed members who would eagerly snap up the chance to step in if the opportunity arose; why would LADS be any different? He had discussed it with Bennett who had taken the same view. And now Leslie himself, a complete outsider with no connection to the company, was being brought in. It seemed very strange, and the explanations Gloria had given did not seem to ring true.

They were still trundling along behind the tractor, which now belched out diesel fumes in addition to filth, and Leslie brought his attention back to the present.

Gloria was still chattering on about the members of the cast. "Roland Rawlison's in the play, too," she said. "They cast him in all their productions if he's available because he's such a big noise. I mean, I don't think he's been on the telly or in the West End or anything like that for years, but he's still remembered and loved round here and brings the audience in. I haven't seen him yet. Apparently they've written a cameo part into the play especially for him, so he doesn't have to rehearse much with the main cast. He's got a house somewhere near Lymeford but someone said he lives in London most of the time."

At that moment, the tractor pulled up before swinging into a wide gateway and Gloria braked sharply and then, with nothing now to impede her, she lurched forward at speed. Leslie gripped the sides of the seat and did not open his eyes until Gloria said, "It's along here somewhere. She told me to look out for a house with a big yew hedge and lions on the gateposts. Oh, I think that was it!"

She executed an emergency stop and then shot the car backwards down the narrow lane for twenty yards, exclaiming with triumph, as she pulled up, that they had arrived. The journey had left Leslie in no fit state for anything; he was covered in mire and his nerves were in shreds. He removed himself from the car without delay but Gloria, beaming cheerfully, said she thought it might be better if she stayed in the car. Deciding not to ask why, Leslie took off his soiled jacket, shook it out, and folded it neatly on the passenger seat then turned his face towards the fine house.

The stately lions atop the gateposts were not the only feature of grandeur at the property. The tall black and brass gates were ornate and electrically operated, so Leslie had to press a buzzer and announce himself into a grille before they swung open with a buzzing noise. Despite this imposing entranceway, the gravel drive was barely large enough to accommodate three cars, and the house, though detached, was smaller than Leslie's initial impression. However, it was fronted by an imposing porch with columns in what Leslie believed was the Queen Anne style, and a row of clipped topiary bushes in ceramic pots.

While Leslie was choosing between the bell pull and the enormous brass knocker, the door swung open. He half expected a maid in uniform to bob a greeting to him but instead he was met by a stout woman in her late forties with a great cloud of black curly hair.

"Oh, yes," she said and looked him up and down. "Come through."

Leslie had not expected the director, if this was she, to fall on his neck with gratitude, but it was disconcerting to be received with quite such indifference. But Leslie was well-mannered to a fault, and so he followed the lady into the living room and waited courteously until invited to take a seat.

A tall, dark-haired man appeared through a doorway at the far end of the room and nodded a greeting to Leslie. Since he bore no signs of injury, let alone a leg pinned in three places, this was clearly not husband Frank, but no one troubled to introduce him. Flashing Kara a smile of dazzling white teeth, he said, "Shall I do coffee, Kara?"

The lady looked up from a pile of papers which she had started giving her attention to, and said, "Oh, yes, I suppose so." Then, as he disappeared, she said to Leslie, "That's Terry, the chairman. He's going to read through with us. We'll have to wait for him before we start. Here's a script. And the rehearsal schedule."

Leslie received them with his customary politeness. Kara picked up her own script, heavily annotated with highlighter pen and sprouting fluorescent marker strips, and thumbed through the pages in silence, as though Leslie was not present. This was so far beyond ordinary rudeness that Leslie felt intrigued rather than offended. He opened the copy at the first page, took a pencil from his pocket, and awaited the arrival of the coffee and its maker.

There was plenty of time for Leslie to take in his surroundings. He had already noted, as he had stepped through the front door, a gilt-edged chaise longue and a tall Grecian-style urn filling the small hallway. The room they were now in, which ran the full length of the house, was dominated by two glittering chandeliers, undoubtedly impressive, though surely intended, thought Leslie, for a much higher ceiling. From the patio doors at the rear hung full-length, royal blue velvet curtains, tied back with thick plaited gold cords and with a heavily brocaded pelmet above. The carpet was also strikingly blue and very deep. About the room stood an assortment of vintage-style chairs and footstools, and some little tables displaying diverse vases and ornaments. An ornate gilded carriage clock and two candelabra adorned the mantlepiece, and on the chimney breast hung a huge family portrait of Kara with a man and a girl, presumably the beleaguered husband, Frank, and a daughter. It had been painted by an artist who knew how to please the customer. A large grand piano occupied the top of the room, and Leslie was trying to decide if the bust on the plinth beside it was of a composer or a Roman emperor, when Terry returned bearing the coffee on a tray. He certainly seemed at home here.

Flashing another glittering smile at the world in general, he poured from a steaming cafetiere, and Leslie was relieved to note it smelled as good as the coffee he would brew at home. The absence of biscuits or cake was a disappointment, especially as Kara looked like a lady who liked to indulge.

"Shall we get down to business, then?" Terry said brightly, looking at Kara.

"You've done this kind of thing before?" said Kara abruptly, without looking at Leslie.

"Yes, sort of," said Leslie, "but not for many years, and mostly light opera. And I've never seen this play, I'm afraid; in fact, I've never even heard of it."

All he knew about the work from Gloria was that it was a Victorian farce, full of mistaken romantic intentions.

Kara ignored Leslie's comment, and there was a short silence until Terry said, "I think you wanted to look at act one, scene three, Kara," adding, to Leslie, "It's on page twelve."

Leslie found the page and got his pencil ready.

"Act one, scene three," Kara repeated mechanically, finding it in her own copy. "Oh yes. This is a *really important* scene with Bella—she's the female lead. Bella is being played by my daughter, Pippa. It's *really important* you get this scene right; the rest of it should be OK. It's *really important* that you play it right and don't upstage her."

Leslie suspected that he was getting a glimpse of Kara's creative vision for this play: any scenes with her daughter in were really important, and everything else was secondary.

"It's really upset Pips that we've had to have a change of cast. I was all for postponing it until Franklyn had recovered, but Terry said we can't cancel at this stage. That's why we've had to bring you in." She shot the two men a poisonous glance.

"The show must go on, and all that," said Terry, with a forced laugh.

Leslie had arrived at the house feeling nervous, worried he would not be up to the job, for LADS had a good reputation, as amateur companies go. But he knew that in the am-dram world success was precarious, and the main ingredient for triumph or disaster was, in his experience, the director. He looked pessimistically at Kara.

"Well, let's get started, then," she said with sudden impatience. "You're playing Bancroft, by the way. Terry is playing Sir Harold, and I'll read in as Bella, and any other parts."

Without giving Leslie a synopsis of the play, the context of the scene, or any notes about the characters, Kara launched in with Bella's opening lines and they read through to the end of the scene without stopping. Terry played the role of an aristocratic but henpecked husband rather well, and Leslie felt a faint flicker of optimism. However this was offset by Kara, who played his lovelorn daughter, Bella. She was unbelievably melodramatic, and Leslie wondered how he could possibly risk upstaging Pips if she played the part in the same style. Leslie, sight reading his lines, made little effort at dramatization since he knew nothing at all about his character.

"Well, that should do, if you play it like that," said Kara as the scene concluded. "I still think we should wait until Franklyn's better, but if we can't—"

"Great, great," said Terry hastily. "You'll soon get into the part when you meet the rest of the cast at rehearsals."

Papers were gathered, and Terry started to collect the coffee cups.

"Don't you want to hear me sing?" asked Leslie. He had spent hours the previous evening picking and rehearsing a solo which he could sing, if necessary unaccompanied, without disgracing himself. In fact, he and Bennett had had a most enjoyable time, and gone on to all their old favourite songs afterwards, but Leslie was still rather put out when Kara said:

"That woman, what's-her-name, said you could sing, so I'm sure it'll be fine. I have to finish now as I've things to do before I go and see Franklyn later. I've given you the rehearsal schedule. You can't miss any of the sessions as you've started in so late."

"You go and do what you need to do, Kara, love," said Terry, "and I'll see Leslie out."

He escorted Leslie into the hallway, shutting the door behind him. "Thank you so much for coming, you'll be great, absolutely great," he said effusively. "It's so good of you to step in at short notice like this; wonderful. I know you'll be marvellous.

Kara's under a hell of a lot of pressure at the moment, so if she doesn't seem quite, you know… Well, she's got a lot on her mind. If you've got any questions about anything, the part or the rehearsals, or anything at all, probably best you speak to me first. I'll give you my number. I'm trying to help her out at the moment while everything is difficult, you know, taking the pressure off her a bit. I'm the chairman and I've been with LADS for twenty-odd years, so there's not much I can't find my way around."

Including Kara's house, Leslie thought to himself.

2

"Are you going ahead with it?" asked Bennett over lunch, when Leslie had regaled him with an account of the meeting.

"I don't feel I can really get out of it," Leslie replied, as he collected up their empty plates.

"You don't owe them anything."

"I know that," said Leslie, rather on the defensive, as this had touched on one of his weaknesses. "But when I expressed my reservations on the way home, Gloria was so desolate I more or less promised. Did I tell you she's coming for dinner later and going through the script with me?"

Bennett put down his coffee mug and, muttering something that included "glutton for punishment", he pushed a piece of paper across the table towards Leslie.

The sheet bore five words in Bennett's inimitable writing: *Loud and soft and hard.*

"Five letters," said Bennett.

"Loud and soft and hard." Leslie said the words over a few times as he loaded the dishwasher. "Loud will be 'F'. Does it start with F?"

"It does," said Bennett.

Leslie topped up the cafetiere from the kettle, muttering, "Five-letter word starting with F."

"I'll need a clue," he said at last.

"The last letter's T."

Leslie sat down, picked up Bennett's pencil and wrote: F _ _ _ t. "Fight... Fought... Front... First... No, there's too many. Go on, what is it?"

"Flint," said Bennett, and there was just a trace of triumph in his voice. He drained his coffee cup and went back to his library, leaving Leslie frowning over the paper.

***

A little while later, Leslie headed across to the shop to buy a couple of items he needed now that Gloria was joining them for the meal. The weather was still glorious. Leslie loved the village at any time of the year, but today the great square-towered church looked particularly majestic under the golden sun, and the assortment of houses, cottages and shops that clustered round it were at their most charming. Leslie and Bennett lived in one of these; a whitewashed, thatched cottage. It was designated a cottage because of its thatched roof and quaint appearance, even though it was a large double-fronted property, tastefully modernised inside and very comfortable. Leslie still felt as fortunate as he had done when they moved there just over six years previously.

His mind did not dwell for long on his pleasant surroundings, however, as he was already thinking of the evening meal. Exactly how he served the caramelised tomato tart he had set his heart on depended on whether there were any anchovies on the shelf, or new potatoes which would be the perfect accompaniment. Much as Leslie loved the village shop, there had been many times when, cursing, he had been forced to change his menu plan because a vital ingredient was not available. The shop was a co-operative, owned by several wealthy residents, most of whom had taken early retirement and moved to the village from the Home Counties, and it had the air of an up-market delicatessen rather than a functional store. The shop's stylish ambiance was very popular with visitors and day-trippers, it was true, and as most of the village's residents drove out to the big supermarkets or had their main shopping delivered, they put up with the fickle availability of basic items. The anchovies on his shopping list were probably a safe bet; it was the potatoes that may not be available.

Today, Leslie was lucky, and he was soon picking through a tub of good quality Jersey Royals. He put a jar of anchovies in his basket and a roll of puff pastry from the chiller cabinet; although he made almost everything from scratch, he was no martyr. He had just selected a packet of local butter when Janet came through from the storeroom.

"How are you, Leslie, dear?" she said, leaning on the counter. "And how's Bennett?"

They exchanged a few polite enquiries while Leslie was deciding between double and clotted cream for the dessert. Guiltily he put both into his basket; since the heart attack he tried to avoid such fat-laden extravagances, but as they had a guest, he told himself that he could make a concession.

"I hear you're to be in the theatricals," said Janet, prodding her finger at a poster displayed at the counter. Leslie saw, at once, that it was a flyer for the LADS production of *Who Will It Be?*

As Janet was speaking, another of the local ladies, Vera, stepped into the shop and, spotting Leslie, said, "Aye, aye, it's Sir Lawrence Olivier!"

Leslie knew that in Dartonleigh news travelled faster than the speed of light, but even by village standards this was impressive, especially as the amateur dramatic society was based five miles away. He looked at both the women in astonishment and it went through his mind that Gloria must have called in at the shop when she dropped him off earlier. She lived in the neighbouring town in the opposite direction to Lymeford, but she was fond of their little shop in Dartonleigh. However, it seemed he was wrong.

"It's all right, I haven't got second sight,' laughed Vera. "My daughter-in-law, Tracey, does the costumes for the LADS and she rang me up to ask if I knew you; she wanted to know if she'll have to alter the costume. It's a double-breasted jacket, genuine vintage style of course, and a shirt and cravat; you wear your own trousers. Tracey's going to bring along some bigger jackets to the next rehearsal as poor Frank, who you're replacing, is a forty-inch chest and I said as I thought that might not do for you."

Leslie was not prepared to admit that he would not fit into a forty-inch jacket even with the aid of a genuine vintage gentlemen's corset, but he had no need to reply as Vera was still speaking.

"And look at this." She stabbed her finger at the poster. "Directed by Kara Anderton. Kara, indeed. She's Karen to me. She grew up on the estate outside of Lymeford, and I worked with her mother," she added to Leslie. "Her husband made a pile of money somehow, they bought a swanky house, and she started calling herself Kara. They're all a bit peculiar, the whole family."

There seemed to be no one that Vera did not know, even outside the village.

"It's lucky for them that you agreed to it," she went on. "I don't know what they'd have done otherwise. No one else from the company will be in it with Karen, or 'Kara', directing it this time. You wait until you hear her at the rehearsals. Rude? I'll say! Tracey said that last time Karen was director, half the cast walked out the week before dress rehearsal and they had to pull the show. That was years ago, and they haven't let her direct any of their plays again since. Apparently, it's bad enough when she's just in the cast."

"I wonder they've let her do it again," said Janet. "But perhaps she's mellowed over the years."

"Not a bit of it!" Vera leant across the counter and continued in a conspiratorial whisper, "It's the chairman's doing, he got the committee to agree. And why? Because he's carrying on with Karen. She's got him under her thumb. And they're saying that he's spent more time at her house than at his own since Frank's been in hospital."

"You don't say," said Janet, mildly. "But people do like a rumour. You don't want to believe everything you hear."

Leslie broke up this unsavoury, though fascinating, conversation by placing his basket on the counter.

"I do hope you'll be all right, Leslie, dear," said Janet. "It doesn't sound quite your cup of tea."

"I bet you didn't know you were letting yourself in for that," chortled Vera.

"It's only for a few weeks," said Leslie, carelessly, though he was secretly wishing he'd been furnished with this information before he'd agreed to the role. "And I've got quite a thick skin when I need it."

With this lie on his tongue, for Leslie was far from insensitive, he paid for his goods and left the shop. He had plenty to fill his mind as he crossed the road towards The Daffodil Tea Shop. At least he now understood why, first Gloria, and now he, had been drafted in to fill the gaps. But it sounded as though he was in for a few unpleasant weeks, and he wondered what the other members of the cast, those who were prepared to submit to Kara's rudeness, would be like.

The Daffodil Tea Shop was one of Leslie's favourite locations in the village. Its cosy atmosphere and superb cakes were matched by the warm welcome he always received from Annie, the café manager, and her staff. And because The Daffodil also acted as the village bakery store, selling homemade bread, rolls, cakes and desserts to take away, hardly a day went by when Leslie did not find an excuse for calling in. At peaks in the holiday season, the café and the tea garden were often full, and it was not unusual to see a line of hopeful diners, who knew of its reputation, queuing up outside. Today it was not so busy and the customers occupying the tables were finishing off their lunches; the afternoon-tea brigade had not yet started arriving.

"Hello, Leslie, love," said Annie. "What perfect timing you have. I'm just grabbing myself a quick sandwich. Come and join me. Laura, be a dear and bring a pot of tea for Leslie. Camomile? And a sandwich?" She looked enquiringly at him.

"I've just had my lunch, thanks," said Leslie, "But a cup of tea would be very nice."

They went to a table in the corner of the café and Leslie's camomile tea was brought in an elegant teapot with matching cup, and three dainty shortbread biscuits on the saucer.

"Now, is it true that you're to be in the next LADS production?" Annie asked. "Vera told me just now, but she's such a fearful old gossip that I never believe a word she says until I've heard it from someone more reliable."

"It's quite true," confirmed Leslie, taking a nibble from one of the biscuits. "Though the rumour seems to have gone round before I'd even been asked about it, let alone agreed. Between you and me, I don't know if I've done the right thing."

Annie was a good friend and could be trusted, so he told her the whole story, including the unpleasant meeting at Kara's house and what Vera had been saying about the company.

"I wouldn't normally take any notice of Vera, as I said before, but I've heard a few things about LADS, myself. As you know, I hear a lot of things working in here," said Annie. "Apparently, they're rather a lecherous lot and there seems to be more drama off stage than on."

Laura reappeared, unasked, to top up their drinks and present them with a very tempting selection of cakes.

"I really shouldn't," said Leslie ruefully, thinking of the vintage-style, double-breasted jacket, but he helped himself to a small slice of lemon cake all the same. When Laura had moved away, he said to Annie, "If it wasn't for Gloria, I'd back out. They'd be sure to find someone else."

"Oh, go on with you, you'll be fine!" said Annie encouragingly. "With Gloria in it you're guaranteed to have some entertainment. She'll be resolutely cheerful, even if there's murder and mayhem going on all around her. But you must promise to come in and tell me about the rehearsals, I want all the details."

Annie could not linger over her lunch, so it wasn't long before Leslie was strolling home, full of cake, tea and reassurance, and carrying the sourdough loaf he had originally gone into the café for.

3

The agreeable task of cooking promised to be a happy distraction for the rest of the afternoon. Beginning with the dessert, Leslie carefully cored three large cooking apples, picked from his own tree, plugged each base with a plump, dried fig then pressed in a mixture of dried fruits, crystalised ginger, and soft light brown sugar. Arranging the apples in an oval ceramic dish, he doused them with ginger wine and set them aside to marinate, thinking with pleasurable anticipation of soft apple, flavoursome fruits, sweet gingery syrup and decadent clotted cream.

He was slicing a tomato when Bennett, who had finished his work in the library, ambled into the kitchen and sat down at the table, as was his custom while Leslie was cooking. Normally he would bring the paper to read, but today he had Leslie's script in his hand.

"Have you had a look at it?" Leslie put the slices of tomato into the heavy pan on the hob and sprinkled them with salt and sugar. "What do you think?"

"A curate's egg," declared Bennett, propping the document up against the bag of new potatoes.

"As bad as that," said Leslie, his mood plummeting.

"Let me be more accurate," said Bennett. "I've only given the play a swift glance, and from the bits I read, there are some cracking good lines in it." He hesitated thoughtfully, with an expression that Leslie could not read.

"But?" said Leslie. He tore up a few fresh basil leaves and tossed them dejectedly into the pan with the tomatoes.

"There are also some clumsy parts. Every now and then I felt as though I'd turned over two pages at once or picked up the page of a different script. If they've written in a cameo part for Roland

Rawlison, as Gloria told you, I suppose that might account for it. It may be a good original play, with some amateurish alterations."

"Is that allowed?" asked Leslie. "I thought you weren't supposed to change a single word in a published work."

"If I remember rightly, it depends on how long ago the author died," said Bennett. "Or if you have official permission to make changes, of course."

"If Kara's rewritten it, I'm not surprised it's not very good. I don't believe she knows what on earth she's doing. I'm sure she's only directing it to guarantee her daughter a starring role." Leslie sighed heavily. "I hope it's not going to be a disaster. I wonder how Roland Rawlison will react to having poor material."

"He'll probably make it up as he goes along," said Bennett. "I read somewhere that he's got a reputation for going off script. Probably due to the booze."

"I'd forgotten about his drinking. I suppose that's why he's now reduced to panto in the provinces once a year and bolstering up Lymeford's productions from time to time. He used to be brilliant, do you remember? I saw him in a few things in the West End, donkey's years ago. He was in *When We Are Married*; I think it was on at the old Strand Theatre. It was hilarious, one of the best things I've ever seen."

"Not the first actor to have a fine career cut short by the demon drink," said Bennett. "On which subject..."

He went out to the drinks cabinet to select something for the evening meal. He returned a few minutes later with a bottle of Riesling.

"I wonder where they found this play," he said, as he put the bottle in the fridge. "As far as I can see from a cursory search, there is no record of it having been staged anywhere. And the playwright, Cora D. Lewis—a completely unknown name."

"If it's a Victorian farce, as Gloria said, there can't have been many women scriptwriters about. I wonder if that's why we haven't heard of it; no one thought a play written by a woman was worth looking at."

"Perhaps," said Bennett. "I did find one reference to the work in the publisher's archive, but that's all. And this script you've been given isn't a published copy, surely, not even an online publication. It's got the publisher's details typed on the front sheet, but it looks like it's been printed off from someone's computer, not from an official source."

"Isn't that illegal?" said Leslie, feeling even more disconcerted. "All the amateur companies we've ever been involved with have always been sticklers for keeping on the right side of the copyright law. Think of all those numbered librettos that had to be paid and signed for."

"I suppose it depends on where they got the original copy from," said Bennett.

"I'd rather not know any more for the time being," said Leslie, hastily. "Let's wait until Gloria arrives."

It was difficult to talk on any other subject than the play, so they fell silent for a time, Bennett flicking through the script and Leslie engrossed in the tomato tart under construction. He rolled out the sheet of pastry to fit his square baking tin, which he lined with a generous piece of baking parchment, occasionally checking the tomatoes which were still cooking slowly in the pan. Once the pastry was in the oven, he loaded up the dishwasher and then, retrieving the bag of potatoes, which was acting as Bennett's temporary book stand, he set about scrubbing them, peering through the glass into the oven every couple of minutes. As the last potato went into the saucepan, he grabbed the oven gloves and took out the pastry. It had swollen into a pleasing, lightly golden cloud and, after pausing briefly to enjoy the aroma, he took a long-tined fork and pierced it before taking the edges of the parchment and flipping over the now deflated square.

Bennett was watching this procedure and, when Leslie looked across, he cocked his head enquiringly.

"It prevents a soggy bottom," Leslie explained, arranging the cooked tomatoes on the pastry base, and topping it with anchovies and rosemary.

In due course, Bennett was dispatched to lay the table before going to get changed. Although they were not dressing for dinner, Leslie would have complained about Bennett's threadbare cardigan and fraying shirt at the dining table, even if they had been eating alone.

Gloria's timekeeping was famously erratic, and more than once Leslie wondered at the wisdom of having chosen cheese souffles as the starter as he did not dare to put them into the oven until she arrived. But it was a particular favourite dish of Gloria's and, hopefully, it would be worth the wait.

He was slicing sourdough bread ready for toasting to accompany the souffles when, from the kitchen window, he saw the little, red open-top car pass the cottage and draw up into the lay-by where Gloria prised herself from behind the steering wheel. Bennett let her in, and she burst straight into the kitchen, a kaleidoscope of colour. She was dressed in a kaftan-style dress of canary yellow and peacock blue, with several yards of coloured beads decorating her magnificent bosom. A flowing scarlet and gold wrap was draped across her shoulders, and there was a matching swathe of chiffon losing its battle to tame her hair. She held an enormous multicoloured floral bouquet which she bestowed on Leslie with greetings and thanks which were equally florid. Leslie was quite exhausted by the time Gloria had been shepherded towards the sitting room, and he instructed Bennett to keep her company while he put the souffles in the oven and dealt with the flowers.

As soon as Leslie joined them, Bennett passed him a restoring glass of dry sherry, and Gloria said:

"I was just telling Bennett what a scream the play is. I didn't get the humour of it when I read it through first, but when it's acted you can see how funny it's going to be. You've probably realised by now that it's about a girl, Bella—she's played by Kara's daughter, Pippa—who wants to marry the local doctor's son. The son is James and is, by coincidence, played by a boy called James. It's very confusing because one of the other men is also called James, so when Kara says, "James," you don't know if it's the character James she means, or James who's playing James, or James who's playing Gibson, the art master." She finished this enigmatic summary with a peel of laughter.

Leslie realised that he would not be relying on Gloria's baffling synopsis, and he looked across at Bennett who raised an eyebrow. Oblivious to this, Gloria went on:

"Actually it doesn't have to be that difficult; the older James, playing Gibson, doesn't mind being called Jim, but Kara never remembers that." She took a sip of her drink. "Where was I with the plot? Ah yes! Bella, that's Pippa, comes from an aristocratic family, so James, the suitor, played by the young James, is not good enough for her. Not good enough in the mother's eyes, anyway. The mother is Lady Charterhouse. The father, he's Lord Charterhouse, obviously. He's weak and will give the girl her way in anything."

Defeated, Leslie's mind had drifted off to the dinner, and he was just calculating how much longer he dare stay away from the oven when Gloria said:

"The mother is played by Kara, who is also coincidently Pippa's mother in real life, as you know, and the father is played by Terry."

"But Kara is the director. Is she playing a part as well?"

"Oh, didn't you know?" said Gloria. "I thought it was strange, too, so I asked her about it. She said that, because no one would come into Dartonleigh for the rehearsals, she'd had to double up and take the part. But," she said lowering her strident voice a tone or two, "I don't think that's the real reason. I believe it's because she can't bear not to be on the stage, even though she's directing. Wait until you see her in action, and I think you'll agree with me."

Leslie recollected the more convincing version of the boycott, which he had heard in the shop just a few hours earlier, but he thought better of mentioning it. In any case, it was time to replace the souffles with the tomato tart in the oven and direct Gloria and Bennett to the dining table.

Before long, Leslie returned carrying a tray bearing a plate of warm sourdough toast slices and three ramekin dishes from which towering golden-brown crusts erupted.

"Oh my," gasped Gloria, eyes wide.

A hush fell over the room for a time as, apart from a flurry of activity when Gloria's wide sleeve caught a piece of toast and sent it to the floor, they gave the food their reverent attention. At length, Gloria broke the silence.

"I think that was the most delicious thing I have ever tasted," she said. "Utterly exquisite. That wonderful light, crispy crust but perfectly squidgy inside."

Though not, perhaps, the first choice of adjective for the souffle's creamy centre, Leslie took the compliment in the spirit in which it was undoubtedly intended. The main course was equally successful, and they tucked into the tart, potatoes and green beans, which had been dotted with sea-salted butter, with no interruptions other than an occasionally appreciative, "I say!" and, "So delicious!" from Gloria.

"Are these home-grown, Leslie?" Gloria asked.

"Yes, but by Brian Masterson." It was impossible for Leslie to keep the chagrin from his voice, for Gloria had touched a nerve. Events earlier in the year had prevented him from his usual horticultural activities and these beans had been given to him by the winner of the summer horticultural show, and his great rival.

"Oh him!" sniffed Gloria, who knew all the affairs of Dartonleigh. "He probably bought them from the farm shop at Lower Stretton. Everyone knows what a cheat he is."

Bennett topped up their glasses and they sat for a while enjoying a welcome pause between courses. Whether it was the magic of the meal, or just Gloria's natural caprice, she suddenly became more lucid.

"I didn't finish telling you the plot," she said, putting down her glass. "In a nutshell, Lord Charterhouse, the father, decides to make Bella's suitor, James, seem more agreeable to his formidable wife, by persuading three less suitable men to woo their daughter, before he breaks the news that he has already given marriage consent to James. The three men are Bella's singing teacher—that's you, Leslie, her piano tutor and her art master. Unfortunately, Lord Charterhouse fails to explain his scheme clearly to any of them, or to Bella or James, and the play is full of hilarious misunderstandings. Finally, there is a scene where James, not realising it's all a ploy in his favour, challenges his rivals to fight it out with him, whereupon Lady Charterhouse intervenes and instantly gives him consent to marry her daughter. She had really objected to him because she thought him lily-livered and weak, and his show of strength revealed that he was worthy. There now!"

Gloria's enthusiastic, and much clearer, rendition of the storyline gave Leslie a little more confidence in the plot, but other objections had materialised.

"The age difference will be impossible," he said, "if I'm supposed to be wooing the character played by Kara's daughter. I know that in am-dram there's a lot of licence, but for a girl to be wooed by a man who is nearly old enough to be her grandfather looks so sordid. It's different if all the juvenile leads are played by middle-aged actors; it may look ridiculous, but it's not seedy. How old are the others?"

"James, the one playing James the real suitor, is about the same age as Pippa, early twenties. I expect that's why he was cast in the role, as he's not got what you'd call a big personality. You're the singing tutor, as you know, and Roland Rawlison is the music maestro. I haven't seen him at rehearsals yet, but he must be older than you, Leslie, surely? Jim who is playing the art master is in his forties, I should think." Seeing the dispirited look on Leslie's face, she said, "Don't even give it a thought; it's artistic licence."

"Age-blind casting," said Bennett. "It's all the rage, I believe."

"There now!" exclaimed Gloria in triumph. "I should have known there was a fancy theatrical term for it —age-blind. And pretence is what the theatre's all about, after all. Believe me, the audience will hardly notice."

Leslie was not convinced but he did not pursue it and retreated to the kitchen. Unfortunately, misfortune met him there, as well. The baked apples had exploded, and the bowl contained a mush of sticky pulp. Leslie rarely had disasters in the kitchen, but was resourceful nonetheless and, after cursing silently, he carefully picked out the split skins and served up the remaining mixture of apple puree, dried fruits and syrup as elegantly as possible into the dessert bowls.

He carried them through without explanation or apology and when Bennett, who had seen them cooking, peered into his bowl and looked up with raised eyebrows, Leslie fixed him with a 'don't you dare' expression. In the centre of the table, he placed the two bowls of cream and a plate of thin ginger snaps which he had decided to make at the last minute.

Gloria helped herself to a generous serving of both double and clotted cream, her necklace trailing into her dessert bowl as she leant forwards. Giggling a little, she carefully licked the apple mixture from the beads and then took a ginger snap from the plate which Leslie offered her.

"I say, this is simply heavenly," she said, after the first spoonful. "Unbelievable. What is it called?"

"It's my own recipe," said Leslie, in perfect truth.

The dessert was indeed a most delicious accident and Leslie made a mental note to add it to his recipe book. The tartness of the apple balanced the ultra-sweetness of the syrup; the texture of the cooked, dried fruits made an excellent contrast to the apple puree, and the clotted cream, melting into the mixture, was the perfect indulgent topping. The ginger snaps had been worth the trouble of making, too, judging by Gloria's rapturous exclamations as she bit into one, oblivious to the crumbs she was scattering.

At length, they retired to the armchairs in the sitting room and Leslie brought in coffee. "Who are you playing?" he asked Gloria. "And are there any other characters? I haven't had chance to look at the script yet."

"I'm Griselda," she replied, "Lord Charterhouse's sister. He confides in me, and my role is to make sure Lady Charterhouse is in the right place to witness the unsuitable men wooing her daughter. But thankfully I don't have too many lines to remember. There's only one other character in the play and that is Bella's governess. She comes into the story because she is 'affianced', as they call it in the script, to the art master, so when he starts making eyes at Bella, she is distraught. It's being played by Caroline who is actually very good at being distraught. She bursts into tears whenever Kara is short with her, which is quite often, unfortunately. I've got an excellent lavender oil for her which I'm bringing to the next rehearsal."

Gloria ran an alternative therapy business and had a remedy for every occasion. Not wishing to get diverted onto this topic, Leslie passed her a chocolate mint and said, "We've been wondering why the play isn't better known."

Gloria unwrapped the mint, put it in her mouth and rolled the foil wrapping into a little ball thoughtfully. "Someone else asked that very question when we were reading through at the start of rehearsals," she said. "And we were told that when it was first published, and someone tried to stage it, it was immediately censored. This was well over a century ago of course, and the relationship between two of the male characters was thought to be a little—um— ambiguous, apparently. But there's no evidence that the author really had any *intentions* in mind." Gloria gave the word 'intentions' a meaningful emphasis. "And then when the play was unearthed in more recent years, it was thought to be unsuitable again, but this time because it had rather out-of-date attitudes. Racial issues, you know." She lowered her voice to a whisper, quite unnecessarily in the privacy of Leslie and Bennett's sitting room. "The N word. More than once. They've had to rewrite those parts."

"Interesting," said Bennett. "First the play was censored for being ahead of its time, and then for being behind the times."

"Hold on a minute," said Leslie, suspiciously. "These two characters, the ones with this so-called ambiguous relationship. Who are they?"

"I don't think anyone said who they were," said Gloria earnestly. "And in any case, Kara said that's not how she is interpreting the characters."

Leslie looked at Bennett and was infuriated to see amusement on his face.

"Why on earth go to all this trouble for an unknown play that seems riddled with complications?" said Leslie, unable to disguise his irritation.

"Well now," said Gloria, "there was some gossip—I don't know if it's true—that Kara chose it because she had been searching for a play that Pippa could star in as the leading lady, but not have to do too much. And in this play Pippa doesn't actually say a great deal but even then, they've taken out most of her lines."

"Whatever's the matter with this Pippa?" asked Leslie. "She wasn't at the house when I was there, and Kara read her part. It seems rather stupid, and unfair on the girl, to give her a prominent role if she's going to struggle with it."

"Oh, there's nothing the matter with her, I don't think," said Gloria. "It's just that she doesn't seem to have her mother's enthusiasm for the stage."

More discouraged than ever, Leslie drained his glass and thrust it out to Bennett for a refill. Bennett passed him the replenished glass and said, "So this play has had a cameo role written in, some racist material written out, and the leading lady's lines cut. It's a wonder there's any of the original left."

"Oh, I don't think they've changed all that much. And it's very good, and so funny," persisted Gloria. "You'll love it. Why don't we go through the scenes you're in now, Leslie, and I can give you all the notes and stage directions we've had so far?"

Leslie opened his script, filled with misgivings of every kind.

4

It was late when Gloria finally left, and Bennett poured Leslie a glass of Madeira.

"You knew, didn't you?" Leslie rounded on Bennett, free to show his annoyance now that they were alone. "You'd spotted—what did Gloria call it—the ambiguous relationship between two of the characters. And my part is one of them, isn't it?"

"Those are the cracking good lines," said Bennett, evenly. "If the whole production was like that, it would be a masterpiece. You've got the best scenes in the production, if you play it like the writer obviously intended. There's nothing very ambiguous about it to my mind."

"What do you mean?"

Bennett picked up the script and flicked through the pages. "Here you are," he said, passing the script to Leslie. "Act one, scene five. There's a love song in it where the piano tutor and music teacher sing alternate lines to Bella and to each other. When they sing to Bella, the stage directions state: 'As if reluctantly wooing her'. When they sing to each other, the directions indicate that the lines are delivered 'with comic effect'. I can see how that would seem to leave room for interpretation. But the verses of the song are Shakespeare's *Sonnet 36*, one of the sonnets well known to have been written by the Bard to a young man. The writer hasn't chosen that by accident, not when you look at some of the other dialogue between the two characters."

"I'm sure Kara wouldn't have spotted that," said Leslie, feeling slightly more relieved. "So, I hope Gloria's right about Kara's interpretation of the play. I wouldn't have gone into it if I thought I was going to be involved in a parody."

"You can hardly expect to avoid parody in a farce," said Bennett, with irritating logic. "But I suppose you don't mind if it just parodies old ladies, awkward young men and lovers?"

"All right, I get the point," Leslie replied. "But I'm clinging to the hope that they don't turn it into a complete send up."

"With Roland Rawlison playing your foil?" said Bennett, making no effort to appease Leslie's qualms. "He'll milk it for all it's worth. You know what his act is like. I found a picture of him playing Widow Twankey at Eastbourne. Here." He reached for his phone and found the shot.

"That's it, I'm pulling out of it," said Leslie and he stamped off upstairs to bed.

***

At twenty past seven the next evening, Leslie was walking across to the village hall, feeling as apprehensive as if he was about to sit an exam. It was still light, although there was the hint of a rosy sunset in the sky, and he could think of a hundred and one things he would rather be doing. Sitting in the garden with a glass of wine came top of the list at that moment, and he said so to Gloria.

"But just think what a favour you are doing us," said Gloria, who had called for him at seven o'clock, in time for a quick bracer before the rehearsal.

The hall, which was only a minute's walk from the cottage, was the venue for most of the events that happened in the village, from coffee mornings to quizzes, committee meetings to film nights. Leslie had crossed its threshold hundreds of times, but never with such trepidation, not even to await the judging of his produce at the horticultural show.

As they approached, they could hear loud music blaring and, going in, Leslie could see that a fitness class was in progress in the main room, led by an energetic young woman in pink and black Lycra. He caught a glimpse of a few less athletic-looking ladies, red in the face and puffing heavily.

"I wonder if she'll turn the volume down this week," said Gloria ominously, as they turned into the smaller room opposite.

Across the room, Kara was taking papers from her bag and thumping them down on a table; Terry was struggling to push an upright piano against the wall, and two other men were stacking chairs. Leslie supposed that they were James and Jim. A young woman, about twenty years old, was seated in the corner engrossed in her phone and, by her resemblance to the portrait on Kara's chimney breast, she could be none other than Kara's daughter, 'Pips'. No one took any notice of Leslie and Gloria but, unabashed despite being a newcomer herself, Gloria made straight for Kara.

Kara glanced up, ignored them, and turned to Terry. "You'll have to go and say something," she said angrily. "What's the point of coming all the way out here to this godforsaken place and be stuck in this rabbit hutch of a room, if we have to compete with that godawful racket?"

"It's another ten minutes before we start, love," said Terry soothingly. "Let's see if she turns it down then. She probably will, after last week."

"She won't, you know she won't," snapped Kara. "Can't you just do it now, for God's sake? I want to start on time, not waste half the rehearsal arguing with that stupid cow again. You booked this place, you sort it."

It was years since Leslie had witnessed such arrant rudeness, and even Gloria was taken aback.

"I say," she whispered, and stepped back to allow Terry to pass. As he went by them, he raised his eyes as if to say 'Women!' but Leslie wondered if this was to save face, as surely he could not be that crass.

The music immediately fell silent, presumably while Terry and the fitness instructor had their conversation, and Kara took advantage to call everyone to order.

"Where's Caroline?" she said. "Late every damn week."

"It's only twenty-five past," said the older of the two men who had been stacking chairs. "And I think that's her now."

The door banged and an anxious-looking woman rushed in.

"We're waiting for you," said Kara, untruthfully. "Seven-thirty is when we start, not turn up."

The new arrival flung her jacket down and scrabbled for her script and pen from a canvas shoulder bag. She was small and probably in her mid-thirties and dressed in black trousers and a shapeless navy sweatshirt. Gloria's description of Caroline had been faithful, for she did indeed look as though she might cry at any moment. Caroline glanced across at Terry who, returning from negotiations with the fitness teacher, had also come into Leslie's line of vision. Terry winked at her, and when Leslie looked back at Caroline she had blushed to the roots of her hair.

The music started up again in the hall opposite, but considerably more quietly and Terry walked to the front looking smug.

"We were going to start with act two, scene one," said Kara to the company, now assembled in front of her, "but that is your scene with Roland." She nodded at Leslie as she spoke, clearly having forgotten his name. "Roland's let us down and won't be coming tonight so we'll have to leave it. Probably just as well, as it happens, with that racket going on next door, as that scene's got a song in it. And without Roland, we'll cut rehearsing act one scene four and five as well."

Leslie's heart sank. Because they were on the rehearsal schedule, he had spent most of the day reading through these scenes, and he had barely looked at the ones that Kara was now announcing. She raced through the new schedule for the evening, with everyone scribbling feverishly.

As soon as Kara had finished outlining the timetable, and before she could say anything further, Terry interrupted her with a beaming smile.

"Just before we kick off, as chairman I'd like to welcome Leslie to LADS for our production of *Who Will It Be?* As you all know he's standing in for Franklyn who, you'll be pleased to hear, is getting along splendidly in hospital. I'm sure we're all very grateful to Leslie for stepping in at short notice."

There was a ripple of applause and Leslie wished, more than ever, that he had said no to Gloria at the outset. Terry seemed about to say something else but before the clapping had even a chance to subside, Kara called everyone to order for the second time, and the rehearsal began.

Leslie found that the change of schedule worked in his favour, as he had very little to do in the rehearsal, and he could observe the proceedings with more detachment. They began with a scene that mainly concerned the relationship between the governess and the art master, played by Caroline and Jim, or 'old James', as Kara had taken to calling him. Caroline was crippled with nerves and Jim was terribly wooden. These traits were not improved by Kara impatiently barking stage directions at them and failing to clarify or apologise when Jim intrepidly pointed out that they were different to the ones given at a previous rehearsal. Caroline dared say nothing at all beyond her lines and looked as though she was grateful to have got away without a flogging.

Next came a scene where the main protagonists were Gloria and Kara, and they were just getting underway, Gloria waving her arms expressively as she recited her lines, when the door opened, and a lady put her head into the room. It took Leslie a moment to realise that it was the fitness instructor, now in outdoor clothes.

She looked round until she spotted Kara, then said with a jeer, "I'm sorry to hear you're menopausal. Have you thought about HRT?"

She vanished, and there was utter silence. Leslie caught sight of Terry burying his face in his hands, and Kara with the most murderous expression on hers. There was no time for any further reaction as the silence was broken by a great crash and some rich expletives coming from the doorway. Several people, led by the unmasked Terry, rushed across to see what had occurred. It transpired that the fitness instructor, beating a hasty retreat, had collided with a lady who was arriving with armfuls of costumes. At length, the wardrobe mistress, who Leslie remembered was Vera's daughter-in-law, Tracey, was ushered in complaining bitterly.

"I spent all afternoon pressing these and look at them now!"

"Oh, for God's sake, can't you even bring a few costumes into the room without stopping the entire bloody rehearsal?" Kara screamed. "How many more bloody interruptions are we to have?"

Tracey, who had coloured and was looking very fierce, was drawn hastily aside by Jim, who whispered something to her, and she withdrew to the corner, giving Kara a furious glare. Leslie cringed at Kara's offensive behaviour, but Gloria, at whom some scathing comments were now being addressed, appeared completely unperturbed. Wondering what everyone else made of it, Leslie looked around the room. Pippa and James, both redundant, were occupied with their phones, as if they had nothing at all to do with the proceedings, Caroline was huddled in the corner behind Tracey who was busy with the costumes, and Jim was watching the rehearsal with minimal reaction. There was no sign of Terry, which was not surprising after his ruse had been uncovered.

Terry had evidently taken refuge in the kitchen as he reappeared at the tea break, bearing a tray of steaming mugs, and with his usual self-assurance restored. Tracey took Leslie aside for a fitting and, to his relief, no tape measure was produced. After trying on two or three jackets, they settled on a navy, double-breasted blazer with a paisley cravat, which were possibly not authentic for the period but were rather dashing.

Leslie sighed. At least he would enjoy wearing the costume, even if everything else went wrong.

5

They got through the rest of the session without further incident. Leslie now discovered it was customary for those who had attended rehearsal to repair to a pub at the end of the evening to restore themselves. Lymeford, where they were normally based, offered a choice of watering holes, but Dartonleigh had only one. Fortunately, The Woodman was excellent—quaint, cosy and serving an excellent range of beers, wines and spirits, and with very good food if required.

They crowded into the snug at the front of the pub which, despite the mild weather, had a cheerful fire flickering in the huge inglenook fireplace. Kara had refused to join them and stomped off home, taking Pippa with her. No one had made any effort to persuade her otherwise, especially not Terry who had clearly been keeping out of her way. The younger James had also taken himself off, perhaps to some other more conducive social activity.

Terry had joined Leslie and Gloria at their table and insisted on buying the round of drinks. As he returned from the bar, Gloria suddenly exclaimed something about lavender oil for Caroline and, excusing herself, squashed in at the next table with the others.

"Sorry you didn't get too much to do this evening, Leslie," said Terry, once he had refreshed himself with a few mouthfuls of white wine. "You've probably realised that you play opposite Roland most of the time, you lucky chap, and it's a shame he couldn't make it tonight. And the thing is, he's given me his availability at last; it seems he can't make any of the scheduled rehearsals until the technical run. We love Roland to bits, but you know what these pros are like; you have to work around them,

I'm afraid. Between you and me, he has a cameo part because this isn't the first time we've had this issue. I haven't broken it to Kara, yet; Roland's not in her good books at the moment." He raised his eyes with another of his 'Women!' looks. "But if we can get a couple of rehearsals fixed up just between the two of you, then it will all be hunky dory."

He scrolled through the messages on his phone then read out some dates.

"As far as I know, I'm free at all those times," said Leslie, writing them neatly on the back of his script. "But I'll check on my calendar at home and let you know if there's a problem." There wasn't, in fact, a single engagement that was not meticulously entered into Leslie's phone calendar, but he did not like being put on the spot.

"That's super," said Terry, "and I'll see when the village hall is free. You'll love working with Roland, I know you will. You'll be fine."

These unsolicited words of reassurance were given with such emphasis that they had exactly the opposite effect, and all Leslie's misgivings resurfaced. He suppressed his concerns, and the two men fell into rather laboured small talk for a while. Leslie was not sorry when Terry, draining his glass, said that he must be on his way. He bid an effulgent farewell to the others on the next table, as if bestowing largesse upon them, and made for the door. But not before Leslie caught sight of him surreptitiously patting Caroline in the small of the back as he passed her, and of Caroline blushing scarlet.

Leslie's plan to make a quiet exit behind Terry was thwarted by Gloria loudly insisting that he join them at their table, and when he protested that they were already too crowded, the two tables were pushed together. Leslie found himself seated between Jim and Gloria.

"I'm driving," said Jim, indicating his glass of diet cola, and grimacing.

"Me, too," said Gloria, who had a cup of frothy latte on the table in front of her. "But I don't mind too much as they give you biscuits with coffee." Giggling, she picked up one of the little amaretti from the saucer and popped it into her mouth appreciatively.

"Shame old Rawlingson didn't turn up," said Jim.

"Roland *Rawlison* never comes until the play's nearly on the stage," said Tracey, emphasising the correct pronunciation of the actor's name. "I don't know why they ever schedule him in earlier."

"I'll be glad when I've had a chance to start rehearsing with him," said Leslie anxiously. "I hate leaving things to the last minute."

"I shouldn't worry. Old Rawlingson likes the stage too much to let anything go wrong," said Jim.

Leslie felt only slightly reassured by this, but the conversation moved on to other things. Before long, Gloria resumed her absorbing discussion with Caroline and Tracey about the virtues of various herbal remedies, and Leslie fell into conversation with Jim. After a little small talk, they came back to the subject of LADS.

"They're not a bad crowd if you forget Kara," Jim said.

Leslie made a noncommittal reply, saying that, apart from Gloria, Terry was the only person he'd had much to do with so far.

"Terry's not a bad bloke," said Jim. "Talks a load of bullshit of course, if you'll pardon my French. Gave me a lot of guff about my being perfect for Gibson the art master, even though it was completely obvious that I'd only got the part because everyone else was boycotting this production." He lowered his voice and leant forward. "And nobody could pretend that old Caroline would have had a part under normal circumstances. She only joined LADS a few months ago and Terry talked her into it before she realised what was going on. You know why Gloria's in it, don't you? When the woman who was originally cast for

Griselda got cold feet at the last minute and pulled out, pretending she was ill, Terry rang round every female in LADS and not one would do it. They all stuck together."

"What about yourself?" Leslie could not restrain his curiosity. "You didn't join in the boycott?"

"Only chance I'll ever get for a main role," said Jim shamelessly. "I've been in LADS for over ten years, and I've never had a speaking part. I'm only ever cast in a crowd scene. I can see their point; they've got some damn good actors and a good reputation to keep up. So, I wasn't letting a chance like this go by, and I don't give a stuff what the others think." He took a drink of the cola and screwed up his face again. "As for that witch, Kara, she's a psychopath, as far as I'm concerned, and I just ignore her. I keep telling Caroline to take no notice of her rantings."

Leslie was in awe of such armour-plated insensitivity, but knew it was beyond most people and certainly the fragile Caroline. He glanced round to see if she had overheard any of this but her place was empty. Gloria and Tracey had been listening to the conversation.

"Caroline's powdering her nose," Gloria said to Leslie, evidently having read his thoughts. "I say, you're a tough nut, Jim. I couldn't help hearing what you were saying. I think we should all take a leaf out of your book."

"Jim's right; it's the only way to deal with Kara," said Tracey. "I'm glad I don't have much to do with her. She's a nightmare to even fit for a costume; nothing's ever right."

"Terry doesn't seem to be fazed by her," said Gloria. "But I suppose he knows her quite well."

"You could put it like that," said Jim with a vulgar laugh. "He's got to know most of the women in LADS quite well over the years."

"Oh, I say, I didn't mean to imply anything," said Gloria, flushing. She lowered her voice to what, for her, was a conspiratorial whisper. "He's not married, is he?"

"Divorced," Tracey replied, also in a lowered tone.

"His ex was an actress," said Jim, as though that explained it.
"Well, that was what I heard, but it was before my time in LADS."

"It's a sore point," said Tracey, "and no one ever mentions it."

"Oh, of course," Gloria replied earnestly, but with a look in
her eye that suggested to Leslie she was hoping to extract further
details.

However, Caroline reappeared at that moment and the subject
was dropped.

***

"I don't think there can be anything going on between Terry and
Kara, do you?" said Gloria. "I'd heard the rumours about it, of
course, but she behaves as though she loathes him."

"She seems to act that way to everyone," said Leslie,
considering the matter. He remembered Terry's familiarity with
Kara's house, but also her hostile manner to him. He then thought
about the rather dubious little exchanges between Terry and
Caroline.

Gloria had managed to contain herself until the front door of
the cottage closed behind them before picking up this topic. They
went into the sitting room and Bennett, who had been reading,
looked up and raised an enquiring eyebrow.

Leslie went straight through to the kitchen, and by the time
he returned with coffee and some plates stacked generously with
cheese and biscuits, Gloria had supplied Bennett with a full
account of the evening.

There was a lull in the conversation while coffee was poured,
plates passed around, cheese cut, crackers taken, and pickle spooned
out. Gloria was always the most gratifying of guests as Leslie was
sure that her effusive appreciation was completely sincere.

"I will have just a teensy bit more," she said, in response to
Leslie's offer. She lent forwards and cut a formidable wedge of

gooey brie. "This cheese is just so delicious, and I suppose the chutney is home-made?"

Before Leslie could confirm this, Gloria capriciously switched topic.

"I suppose a man like Terry would be miffed if his wife divorced him," she said. "No wonder he doesn't want it spoken about. A bit of a dent in his pride, don't you think?"

"Is that what happened, then?" said Leslie. "He didn't leave her?"

"Oh, I don't know, actually," said Gloria. "I just assumed she got fed up with his philandering, if what we've heard is true." She licked apple and walnut chutney from her fingers and sighed. "It's such a shame. He's so charming as chief usher at the theatre, and everyone loves him. It seems that LADS brings out another side to him, and not a very pleasant one. But, despite it all, I'm not sorry to have got involved with the play. It's always good to try something new, and I think I've got myself a couple of new clients. Well, Caroline at least—I'm not so sure about Tracey. She seems interested but I have the feeling she might just be humouring me."

And, having alighted on her favourite subject, she talked on about valerian, lemon grass and lavender oils until it was time for her to go home.

***

"I think I'm developing an unhealthy obsession."

Bennett looked up from buttering a slice of toast. "Roland Rawlison?" he enquired, with his knife poised above the bread.

Leslie had tried, without success, to convert Bennett to olive spread since the heart attack and would normally have had a pang of guilt or apprehension when he saw the thick layer of butter that Bennett plastered onto his toast, but today he had other thoughts on his mind.

"Yes," he admitted sheepishly. He loaded the cereal bowls into the dishwasher.

It was two days since Terry had given him the date and time of his rehearsal with Rawlison and, since then, Leslie had spent hours looking up information about the actor.

"If you get bored when the production is over you could write his biography," Bennett suggested.

They had both already known that Rawlison was a native of Lymeford, for he was the only famous son the town had to boast of. It was also common knowledge and pride locally that although he lived mainly in London, he still owned a house in the town, hence his connection with LADS, who had been quick to adopt him when his professional work started drying up. But over the last two days Leslie had become an authority on the actor's entire career, piecing together every detail that had ever been published of the man's life story.

Rawlison, he found out, had been the only child of the town's sweetshop owners. Amassing the pennies, threepenny bits and sixpences from the sales of barley sugar and sherbet dip-dabs, they saved up enough to send their rather unconventional son to RADA. He started out as a stage actor, quickly finding roles in the National Theatre Company and then in the West End. He had early success, was very well regarded, and even nominated for various awards. But then his private life started to intrude and soon eclipsed his thespian accomplishments. Rawlison did not keep his numerous male associates a secret and, although by then these relationships had long been legal and were relatively unremarkable in the theatre, his lifestyle in general attracted negative publicity. His indiscretions and misadventures, usually fuelled by alcohol, increased and there was a gradual decline in the serious productions in which he was cast.

"I was right," Leslie had said on the previous afternoon, looking round the door into Bennett's library for the third time that hour. "He was in *When We Are Married*, but it was at

The Aldwych not The Strand; I knew it was somewhere round there. I remember now I saw him in *Twelfth Night*, too, which was on the following year. He disappeared from view for a long time after that, and it was reported that he'd gone completely off the rails and had to go into rehab."

Bennett had looked up from his work but made no reply, and Leslie had gone back to his research.

Rawlison, Leslie discovered, had eventually returned from his exile into a steady trickle of TV work with a few theatrical roles, but sadly his stage career never fulfilled its early promise. He developed a one-man show, touring the regional theatres, which lasted for a few seasons. His act and his persona became increasingly camp and, although the critics loved it, his show lacked a wide audience appeal. As reports about his drinking increased so his popularity waned. Several bizarre incidents then occurred which the press suggested were desperate publicity stunts as Rawlison tried to make a comeback. On one occasion, he had apparently attempted to drive away a sports car which had been left running at a petrol station, and he claimed he had mistaken it for a friend's car. Months later it was reported that he had married one Stephie Sweetcroft. This anomalous situation had been short-lived as she died from cancer six months later, leaving Rawlison a rich man, and giving the press a different set of motives to speculate about.

"I wish now that I'd never found out anything about him," Leslie sighed, pouring out two cups of tea. "He sounds a most unprepossessing person."

"You can make up your own mind later today," said Bennett, for the rehearsal was at five o'clock that afternoon.

"I suppose so," said Leslie despondently. "At least Kara won't be there, that's one thing to be thankful for."

Kara was apparently unavailable, and Terry was to be in attendance instead, explaining that since "Roland is inclined to do his own thing," the absence of the director would not make much difference. Leslie's own need for direction seemed to have been completely overlooked but he supposed that Terry would take on that function. This was not to be, however, for just after lunch, Leslie received a call from him, crying off, too.

"It's just me and Roland Rawlison tonight, now," said Leslie, looking round the library door. "It seems that Terry has to work late and can't get here. All that he was worried about was opening the hall, but I told him that there are half a dozen people I can get the keys from. I'm dreading the rehearsal; I can't say I like Terry, but at least he's the devil I know."

"You might find out that you're better off with the devil you don't know," said Bennett, and he turned his attention back to his work.

6

Leslie was in the hall more than half an hour before the rehearsal was scheduled, in case, he told himself, the key did not work, or the room needed rearranging, or he had forgotten something and needed to go home for it, or the room was double booked. In truth, he was feeling so intolerably anxious that he knew he was driving Bennett to distraction and was better out of the house.

In the event, it took him only a few minutes to open the room, arrange the chairs, and shove the piano away from the wall, take off its cover and unlock it; he was feeling particularly nervous about rehearsing the song. He had just lifted the lid and confirmed with relief that the instrument was in tune, when a peel of recorded music struck up from the main hall opposite.

Leslie had been aware of noises in the corridor and the arrival of some children but, preoccupied with his own concerns, he had not given it much thought; activities in the other rooms were to be expected in the village hall at this time of day. But he now realised that they would have to compete with what sounded like a children's dancing class. He was more thankful than ever that Kara was not joining them and hoped that Rawlison was more forbearing than the director.

Leslie walked across the room and looked through the door's long glass panel, into the crowded corridor. He could see a couple of latecomers being hurried into their lesson, and half a dozen waiting mothers were propping up the walls, chatting to one another while some other small children swarmed about in perpetual motion. He withdrew, lest his behaviour be misunderstood, and hoped fervently that the dancing class would be over before he had to attempt to sing.

Leslie sat down and tried to put his mind to the script but every few moments there would be a disturbance in the corridor, and he would jump up anxiously in case it was Roland Rawlison arriving, but it was invariably the waiting children. Towards five o'clock the noise increased to a near cacophony and Leslie realised that another group of children was arriving; presumably a changeover of dancing classes was due.

At five o'clock precisely, Leslie heard a click and this time when he looked up, the door opened a crack and a man, unmistakably Rawlison, slid in through the gap. He shut the door swiftly and pressed his back to it with his arms spread wide behind him, as though barricading himself in. He gave a quick glance over his shoulder and said, in mock accusation, "Who told my fans I was coming here today? Was it you? I had to fight my way through them."

He turned towards the door and Leslie realised that he must have said something to the children as he came in, as there was a crowd of little faces peering in through the glass. He stepped back and, to their obvious delight, performed some exaggerated and effeminate ballet moves, then he reached up and briskly lowered the blind on the door.

By this time, Leslie was also laughing with genuine amusement and Rawlison, having given him a brief appraising look, broke into a most engaging smile.

"What an entrance," he sighed dramatically. "So, you're the unlucky beggar standing in for Frank. But just you keep laughing at my gags, and we'll get on famously."

He walked across the room and the two men shook hands. Rawlison was a trim, dapper man, a little shorter than Leslie and older but with an enviably full head of hair, grey and immaculately groomed. His walk was steady and his handshake firm, but Leslie detected a distinct aroma that suggested the actor was not currently on the wagon. Whisky, Leslie thought.

The two men had only just introduced themselves, with Leslie invited to call the actor Roland, when a blast of cheerful music struck up again from the room opposite, along with the voice of the teacher rhythmically urging the participants to "Skip and skip and skip and skip and higher and higher and higher and higher."

Roland uttered an expletive and asked if Leslie knew how long 'Dame Ninette' was going on for.

"I'm afraid I don't," said Leslie, who felt irrationally guilty about the situation. "I'm really sorry about this. It's been pretty much continuous for the last half an hour."

"What did you say?" shouted Roland, with his hand cupped to his ear, though in truth the noise was no more than mildly distracting. He gave another exaggerated sigh. "I suppose it's to be expected with am-dram, but God knows how we'll rehearse the song."

"I don't know if it would help," said Leslie tentatively, "but I live just across the way, opposite the church. It's very quiet and we have a piano which is well tuned. It's a grand, and better than this one. But if you don't think—"

There was a crash behind the door, followed by a wail and the sound of scolding.

"Oh, lead me to it," pleaded Roland, melodramatically.

Leslie quickly cleared up and locked the door behind them. As they squeezed past the waiting parents and children, Roland said over his shoulder, "I'll give you my *Sugar Plum Fairy*, sometime."

In a few moments they were walking past the church in the pretty village centre.

"I'd forgotten how quaint this old place is," said Roland, stopping and looking around. "I haven't been here for years. Lovely spot, but I can't understand why they've put the rehearsals out here."

"We are rather off the beaten track," admitted Leslie apologetically. "And no one from the company seems keen on coming here."

"Don't believe that old tale. It's a strike against the director, no one will work with her. I thought twice about it myself but," Roland gave a deep sigh, "you can't disappoint your public, can you?"

The last comment had been said light-heartedly, but Leslie fancied that the man was not entirely joking.

"Well, Terry seems to be holding the production together," Leslie replied.

"Don't talk to me about that tosser," said Roland, with sudden and surprising vehemence. "Misogynistic bastard."

Leslie was at a loss for a reply but fortunately Roland moved off again and, with a complete change of subject said, "What's the pub like these days?"

They had just drawn level with The Woodman and they paused to look down the sloping path towards the picturesque, thatched inn where, as usual on a nice day, visitors and dog walkers were sitting at the wooden tables outside, refreshing themselves before or after their rambles.

"Oh, it's very good," said Leslie, "and always popular, as you can see."

"What about the food?" said Roland.

"It's got a good reputation, but we rarely eat there, living next door as we do."

"There's only one place in Lymeford where I can dare to eat. I've a gastric ulcer, you see," said Roland, and his hand went instinctively to his stomach. Then he laughed apologetically. "Excuse me; there's nothing more unappealing than the description of someone else's insides. So, this is your place, is it? Lucky man."

Agreeing about his good fortune, Leslie opened the front door, and they went inside.

Bennett was reading in the lounge, and he looked up at Leslie and cocked his head enquiringly. But when he saw Roland, he unpeeled himself from the chair and shook hands. On this, the only occasion that they had ever entertained a celebrity, Bennett would be wearing threadbare brown cords, his most shapeless cardigan and the worn-out carpet slippers with a hole in the toe. But Bennett would be Bennett and he probably would not think twice about his appearance if he was granted an audience with the King.

Tea, coffee and food were all declined by the guest in deference to his stomach complaint although a small glass of brandy was accepted, with a roguish insistence that it was purely medicinal.

"The piano's through here," said Leslie, leading the way into the library.

Bennett remained in the lounge but, after a few moments, he was called to read in the parts for the missing actors.

As soon as the rehearsal was underway, Leslie forgot that he had ever felt nervous. Whether it was the familiar environment of his own home, or Roland's clever and comic rendition of the piece, he relaxed and started to enjoy himself. It was immediately obvious that when Roland was on stage, he would be the one everyone would be watching, which was most reassuring.

The actor gave Leslie few directions; by and large it was unnecessary, as whatever Leslie did, and however he delivered his lines, Roland's response, sometimes by the slightest look or gesture, made the piece work. However, he did say:

"Now, regarding the love interest between us, dear boy, we'll understate it at the start; just enough to keep the audience guessing. I know that will be difficult, well it will be for me, anyway," he said teasingly, and gave Leslie a smouldering smile. "That fool Kara seems to think this can be played as two straight men; God knows why you'd want to. She's completely missed the point and I don't intend to pay any heed to her."

"Won't she kick up about it at the rehearsals?" asked Leslie.

"She's incapable of noticing innuendo," said Roland, "and, anyway, we can play it down during rehearsals. Once we get to the performances and the curtain goes up, there's not a thing she can do about it."

Bennett, normally languid, entered into the rehearsal with a gusto that would have surprised most people who knew him. He adopted a winsome falsetto when reading Bella's part and a bluff heartiness for Lord Charterhouse which was, in Leslie's opinion, even more entertaining than Terry's interpretation of the role. At one point, when his two characters were in an extended dialogue, Bennett suddenly and quite deliberately exchanged the voices, with a ridiculous effect, and the scene collapsed in laughter.

"Dear God," said Roland, wiping his eyes. "What a scream. Why aren't you in it, man? Too smart to get involved, I suppose. I haven't had such a good laugh since Kara dried on stage. Did you hear about that?"

When Leslie said that they had not, Roland sat back in his chair with the satisfied look of a raconteur with an audience.

"It was a few years ago now, and it was a terribly naughty thing to do in front of an audience. I'd never have done it to anyone else, but Kara had been such a cow to everyone, and so up herself, that I simply couldn't help it. She had a line right after mine, but I'd started ad-libbing, having a bit of fun with the audience, and it threw her right out. I fed her some line or other, and she could easily have come back in, but she stood there opening and shutting her mouth like a bloody goldfish. If it had been anyone else, I'd have helped them out of it, of course, but instead I turned the thing into a send up. I really went to town and by the end of the scene the audience, and the rest of the cast, were doubled up. I thought she was going to kill me! As we came off stage, she swore she'd get even with me, but God knows what she thought she could do. Needless to say, since then she's never been my biggest fan. She wouldn't have had me in this production, I'm certain, if Terry hadn't insisted. Not that there's any love lost between me and him, I can tell you; he just knows that I bring in most of the audience."

Making himself quite at home, Roland reached across and topped up his glass; he was now on his third brandy and Leslie hoped he had not come by car. The actor took an appreciative swig then said, "I would have pulled out myself, long ago, and gladly never have seen any of the LADS bastards again. But it's my only chance of playing to my home audience these days, and I don't like to desert them."

Leslie suspected that this was another way of saying it was one of his only chances of getting on a stage these days, but naturally he kept his thoughts to himself.

"I'm glad now that I didn't stand down," he said, eyeing Leslie with a mock roguish expression. "No, really, you're damn' good and it's obvious you've put the work in. You know the play inside out. And it hasn't escaped me," he turned to Bennett, "that you've just done both those parts without a script in your hand."

"He's infuriating," said Leslie. "He has an extraordinary memory. We've been through it dozens of times together; he was word perfect in all the parts after about the second read through, and I'm still struggling to remember just my lines. And I'm terrified that my mind will go blank on stage."

"It won't, it won't," said Roland reassuringly. He was starting to develop a glazed look in his eyes, and he leaned across and patted Leslie's arm. "Listen, dear boy, I won't let you dry. I'd never do that to anyone except Kara, especially not you. Though I can't promise I won't go a bit off-piste at times. Especially if I come on a bit *piste*. No, seriously, I'll be as sober as a judge. Anyway, you know the gist of the thing, and we can always fall back on rapport."

Roland imbued the word 'rapport' with a hint of ardour, but Leslie was more concerned by the implication that he might be required to ad-lib. However, he followed Roland to the piano, where the actor had gone declaring that it was time to rehearse the song.

They began by singing the piece straight through, with Roland at the keyboard. He was clearly one of those great all-round entertainers: actor, comedian, singer and musician. Having admired the piano and complimented Leslie on his voice, he said, "As you know, we're supposed to be reluctantly trying to woo the girl, under the supervision of the father who is hovering in the background. So, we must look as though we're only pretending to compete with each other for her affections."

Leslie felt doubtful of his abilities to capture this portrayal and Roland, perceiving this, said, "Look, there's no acting involved. She's a girl and less than half your age; just think how you would really feel if you had to pretend to flirt with her. And for our lines to each other, just let that build naturally through the song."

After that, it was not so difficult. Leslie all but squirmed with embarrassment when he sang to the, currently absent, Bella, to which Roland muttered, "Spot on, spot on." For their lines to each other, they started with subtlety, but as the song progressed, the amorous exchanges between the two men became increasingly overt and humorous. Here and there, Roland threw in an ad-lib comment, often with nothing to do with the play. Between the last two verses he played an extended introduction and, casting a furtive glance in Bennett's direction, hissed, "He's not the jealous type, is he?"

Leslie drew himself up and replied, as if affronted, "I wouldn't know, sir. I have never given him cause."

"Brilliant, brilliant," laughed Roland. "We'll be able to have some fun with this."

They sang it through once more, with Roland adding a quite different set of asides this time, and he then pronounced that they had all done enough for the day.

"What about our other scene?" said Leslie.

This was a scene, immediately after the interval, where the music master and singing teacher reprise the song but this time, they are alone on stage and sing it entirely to each other. The music teacher, Roland's character, then declares that he will not take part in the falsehood of wooing a girl he does not care for and, taking his departure from his clandestine lover, he makes his exit from the stage, and the play. Leslie had not been looking forward to this, and he feared he would be cringing with mortification.

"Ah, yes," said Roland. He picked up the script again and peered at it with closer attention. "Odd having this scene after the interval, don't you think? It would be so much more natural to finish act one with this song. I bet you that old cow, Kara, moved it so that I couldn't have a bevvy in the break, or bugger off home."

If that was the case, Leslie thought it was probably the only sensible thing that Kara had done, judging by Roland's current condition.

"Shame she's mucked about with the script at all; it's damned good in places," he went on, and stifled a yawn, clearly ready to finish. "I don't think this scene need detain us too long."

Bennett, not needed any further, drifted from the room, and Leslie opened his script at the relevant place. There was a short piece of dialogue and then the song. Roland began the opening lines, capturing a quite different mood to the comic rendition in the previous scene. He went into the duet with such evident pleasure that Leslie could not help but enjoy himself too. Roland infused his performance with such wistfulness that it was rather moving and not at all tasteless or mawkish as Leslie had feared. Leslie sang his part without any affectation, enjoying the harmonies.

Roland delivered his parting speech and then, barely pausing, said, "Perfect. We're not doing that again, old lad, it could only get worse. I knew you'd get it the first time through. It's going to be splendid. We'll make 'em laugh before the interval and cry after it." He stood up wearily and collected his papers with some deliberation, like a man who was accustomed to functioning when he had a surfeit of alcohol on board.

"I don't know," said Leslie tentatively, "if you'd like to have something to eat with us? It's only chicken soup, though; we don't have a big meal every day. I made it earlier as I didn't know what time we'd be finished and it's something that Bennett can heat up for himself if I'm late. But you've probably made other arrangements…"

There was a hesitation and Leslie added, "It's home-made so I know it's not heavy or greasy, if you're worried about your stomach."

Bennett had appeared from the sitting room. "Soup is cuisine's kindest course," he quoted vaguely.

"I've got no other plans, and if you're sure I'm not taking food out of the mouths of orphans and widows?" said Roland.

Leslie assured him that there was plenty to go around and went to the kitchen while Bennett took Roland through to the sitting room. Leslie suddenly felt tired and, for a moment, regretted inviting Roland to stay. It was not the first time he had rued his impulse for hospitality which, at times, felt almost involuntary.

When Leslie went through to announce that dinner was ready, the two men were standing by the French windows, and it was evident that Roland had been complimenting the décor and the garden.

"It's all Leslie's work," he overheard Bennett saying. "I wouldn't know where to begin."

Gratified, as always, by the slightest compliment from Bennett, Leslie's weariness lifted considerably, and he returned to the kitchen in a buoyant mood.

In no time, they were seated at the dining table with the deliciously steaming bowls in front of them and, as so often happened at Leslie's table, a reverent hush fell for the first few minutes of the meal.

Bennett poured glasses of wine, but Leslie was relieved to see that he was pouring small measures and had placed the bottle out of Roland's reach.

"Did you really make this yourself?" said Roland, at last. "It's divine, really heavenly. And these cheese scones? How did you know they're my favourite?"

"I was worried they may be too heavy for you."

"Heavy? My dear boy, they're as light as a powder puff." Roland turned to Bennett. "The man's a god; he can sing, act, cook, and create this idyllic home and garden. Where did you find him?"

Bennett paused with his spoon midway from the plate. "I think he found me," he said, dripping soup onto the tablecloth without noticing.

That was the problem with Bennett and soup, and Leslie normally avoided serving it when they had guests. Roland, now bleary-eyed, seemed not to notice and changed the subject.

"It's been wonderful rehearsing here. It's going to be a different matter when we have to run it through at Kara's place," he said, suddenly truculent. "I wish to God we didn't have to. It's bound to be a nightmare."

Leslie was not looking forward to that particular rehearsal either, but it was rather unreasonable of Roland to complain. It was being held at Kara's house because it was the only date that Roland could make, and the hall was not available, according to Terry who had told Leslie about the arrangements.

"She'll be worse than ever on her home territory and that prize arse Terry will be there. I won't bore you with the history, but LADS is full of treacherous, philandering bastards; just remember that."

From what Leslie had read of Roland's past, this might be a case of the pot calling the kettle black, but naturally he did not say so.

Roland supposed that it was time he ordered a taxi home and, as usual for the village, there was a long wait before the soonest one could arrive, so they had time for more of Roland's anecdotes. Luckily, he kept off the contentious subject of LADS and, instead, treated them to tales about his life in the theatre. It was a fascinating narrative and Roland shamelessly name-dropped all the famous stars he had ever worked, and sometimes slept, with.

When the actor eventually drew breath, Leslie ventured to say that he had seen him perform in London. "It was *When We Are Married*, he said, "at The Aldwych. It was wonderful—one of the best things I've ever seen. I'm not just saying it, ask Bennett, he'll tell you that I mean it. And there was *Twelfth Night* as well, I've never forgotten either of them."

Roland, who was noticeably inebriated, leant across and took Leslie's hand in both of his, his eyes brimming with tears. "That means a lot to me, it really does," he said in a quavering voice. "You don't know how much."

He hiccupped loudly and looked as though he may start sobbing at any moment but fortunately, they were saved by the arrival of the cab.

"Did I tell you that I'd been in two minds about taking on this production?" he slurred in a confidential tone. "They're all such bastards. But it's different now I've got an ally. Someone on my side." He gripped Leslie's arm, as much for balance as anything. "You are on my side, aren't you, dear boy?"

Leslie replied rather awkwardly, "Oh yes, of course, Roland."

"Call me Roly, dear boy. Please. It's Roly to you."

As Leslie escorted Roland from the room, he caught Bennett's eye, and Bennett gave him a very satirical smile.

"Of course—Roly," said Leslie, ushering him through the front door and into the waiting taxi.

The cab pulled away and Leslie hurried back to the sitting room where the two men collapsed in helpless laughter.

7

For the next couple of weeks, Leslie was consumed by the play. He was confronted by posters all over the village—they were on display in the window of The Daffodil and the neighbouring antique store, in the post office, on the village noticeboard, in the village hall and, of course, at the counter in the shop. The production was the first thing that anyone mentioned, everyone assuring him that they had bought tickets. If he stayed indoors, he was plagued by his lines and the song, which went round in his head until he thought he would go insane. There was no respite even at night, for he seemed to dream about nothing else. On one occasion, he awoke with a hideous sense of impending doom after a nightmare in which he was trying to leave the stage, but was glued to the spot, unable to move his legs, and knowing that something terrible was about to happen if he did not make his exit.

It was the morning after this sinister dream that, looking through the kitchen window, he saw Gloria pulling up in her car. They had not been expecting her, but she was given to arriving unannounced, and Leslie automatically clicked on the kettle as he went to the front door.

"I wasn't really calling in for a coffee, but perhaps I will just have a quick one," said Gloria, following him into the kitchen and eyeing the cake tin. "I'm on my way to Lymeford for the hairdressers—I have to look my best for the production—and I thought I'd stop by and see if you'd like to have some lunch out. It's not the same lunching on one's own, so do say you're not busy with anything."

The thought of Gloria's driving, and a recent surfeit of her company, might have been enough for Leslie to think up an excuse to decline, but today a trip out might be a welcome distraction, given his ominous mood. While he was hesitating, Gloria gave a little giggle and said:

"Actually, I've been a little bit naughty. I was so sure you'd say yes that I've already booked my favourite table in the window of The Lemon Drop."

Leslie recognised that this was manipulation rather than a confession, but he knew when he was beaten and, to Gloria's unfettered delight, he agreed.

As soon as the coffee and cake were finished, they set off in the car and Bennett, who would not be persuaded to join them, was left in peace.

They arrived in Lymeford without incident, if one disregarded the occasion when Gloria's erratic mode of driving resulted in furious hooting, and Gloria made for the hairdressers while Leslie set off for his favourite shops. The centre of Lymeford was a crisscross of narrow streets, unsuited to the traffic that passed through, and Leslie retreated down a quieter side street to a row of independent food stores. He bought some calves liver and oxtail in the butchers, and then called into the greengrocers for celery, onions and a selection of root vegetables for the stew which he was now contemplating with pleasurable anticipation. He blenched, somewhat, at the prices, but Leslie liked to support the local businesses when he could and the quality was very good, or so he told himself as he paid the steep charges.

The time sped by and soon, with two heavy shopping bags, Leslie made his way to The Lemon Drop for his tryst with Gloria. As he approached the café he suddenly saw a familiar figure appear from a footpath on the other side of the road. It was Terry and, having no desire to be seen by him should he look back, Leslie stepped aside into the doorway of the hardware store that he was passing and affected interest in the plastic storage boxes that were stacked to eye level outside the shop. He had a perfectly good view of Terry and saw him go into The Swan, just a few yards along. Leslie was glad that he had secreted himself, as he fancied that Terry glanced up and down the street before stepping inside.

Predictably, Gloria had not arrived at the café when Leslie got there, but he was shown upstairs to the window table which she had reserved and, a little ashamed of his insatiable curiosity, chose the seat which gave him a good view down to the entrance of The Swan. There was no reason why Terry should not be popping into a local pub in the middle of the day, but there had been something in his manner that had piqued Leslie's interest.

It was lucky that Gloria had booked as, even though it was well past peak tourist season, The Lemon Drop was, as usual, busy. Some snippet of information about the café had been niggling at Leslie's mind all morning and, as he picked up the menu, which had a line drawing depicting the street in an olde-worlde style, he remembered reading that this was originally the sweetshop where Roland Rawlison had grown up. The café's name was, presumably, a nod to its origins. He looked around and tried to picture the place as it might have been then and imagine the family living above the shop in these very rooms—it seemed impossibly small.

He glanced out of the window, musing on how different things were in yesteryear, when he was snatched back to the present by the sight of the hunched figure of Caroline scuttling along the pavement opposite. As she reached the door of The Swan she paused and, although Leslie could not see her face from this angle, her mannerisms were decidedly furtive as she looked cautiously around and sidled in, as though she was entering a house of ill repute and not a high street pub. It was impossible to imagine that she had not gone in to meet Terry, and Leslie was filled with forebodings for poor Caroline's heart. He sighed; it seemed to be impossible to escape from the play and its off-stage dramas, even when he was on an innocent lunch out.

It was another five minutes before Gloria burst into the café and up the stairs, her hair now a mass of ringlets. She exclaimed with delight as soon as she saw Leslie, gushing with loud apologies for her tardiness and drawing the attention of everyone in the place. However, all the staff, and even some of the customers, seemed to know her well and as she had already decided what she was going to eat, their orders were taken without delay.

It was a pleasant leisurely lunch; Leslie's salmon and cream cheese bagel was very tasty, and Gloria declared the French toast which she had ordered to be delicious, though not a patch on anything that Leslie made. He had now taken up the menu, and, thinking about his vintage style waistcoat, was trying to talk himself out of a dessert, when he glanced through the window. Terry was emerging from The Swan, and walking briskly along the pavement.

Leslie had not mentioned his sighting of Terry and Caroline to Gloria, as it seemed like the kind of cheap gossip that he was wont to complain about in others, though he had been sorely tempted. With a continued effort of will, he now made no reference to Terry outside in the street. Of course, if Gloria were to look out of the window now, she would be able to see him for herself, but the waitress had just arrived, and she was absorbed in an order for banana pancakes. Leslie ordered mango sorbet, justifying it to himself on the grounds of keeping Gloria distracted, and telling himself that a sorbet could not do too much damage to his waistline.

A few minutes later, Caroline appeared through the pub doorway and Leslie had a good view of her face, flushed and with a rather wild expression.

This time, Gloria realised that Leslie had spotted something and, swivelling around, said, "I say! It's Caroline. Doesn't she look wound up. I must invite her to join us for coffee, there's plenty of room at our table." She started to rise, though Leslie could not tell whether she meant to hurry down the stairs or possibly rap on the upstairs window, which was just the kind of thing Gloria would do.

"I think perhaps not," said Leslie hastily, adding more quietly, "I think she was meeting someone in the pub, and she might be embarrassed if she thought we knew."

Forced to abandon his earlier discretion, he explained what he had seen and Gloria, who had resumed her seat and was leaning forward with gratifying interest, whispered, "I say! An assignation!"

"They can hardly have got up to very much in The Swan," Leslie pointed out.

"Maybe not," said Gloria, "but it's what it could lead to." She drew out a handkerchief from her bag and mopped her face which was now crimson. "We know that Terry has quite a reputation, but Caroline! Who'd have thought?"

"I think Terry started paying her attention to make sure she didn't drop out of the play," said Leslie casting his mind back to Jim's comments. "And she might not be the sort of person who suspects an ulterior motive."

"Yes, rather an innocent, poor dear," said Gloria. "Someone really ought to warn her."

"Perhaps so," said Leslie, uncertainly. "But I'm not sure I'd like to try it."

Gloria looked thoughtful but at that moment the desserts arrived, and conversation inevitably stalled.

8

There were now only three more rehearsals at the village hall, and the first two went off much the same as before. Leslie had little to do as his scenes with Roland were omitted and, to his relief, Kara ignored him, as she did young James who always played his part with sufficient competence to avoid notice. Kara seemed rather nonplussed by Gloria, who met every reproach with cheerful ebullience. When Kara barked at her to "Stop waving your arms around, you're not a ruddy windmill," Gloria burst into a rhapsody of laughter, exclaiming, "A windmill, oh, I say! Oh, I say! A windmill!"

Kara saved her worst venom for the permanent members of the company. She was merciless to Jim who let it all wash over him, and utterly vile to Caroline, who Leslie twice saw weeping on Terry's shoulder in the kitchen, which was worrying. She snapped and snarled at Terry, who took it with hearty forbearance, and one could only wonder at what he was really thinking. Kara's only sympathy was with Pippa who, despite Kara's coaxing, cajoling and flattery, seemed resolutely bored by the whole thing. Leslie had never had much to do with young women or girls, but Pippa seemed to him more like a teenager, permanently engrossed in her phone and only looking up to scowl at everyone, including her mother. He wondered why on earth she had agreed to participate.

After the rehearsals, they withdrew to The Woodman though Kara, Pippa and James never joined them, and Terry only ever had one token drink before escaping. Once he had gone, they became quite a cosy and confidential group and Gloria was wonderfully encouraging.

"I don't know how you remember all those lines, Jim," she said, "I know I never could. I think you're simply marvellous."

Jim swelled with pride at such unaccustomed praise.

"And Caroline," she went on, "you play Constance brilliantly, totally convincing. I do wish you'd take no notice of Kara; we all know she's not quite right." Gloria tapped her temple with one finger to clarify what she meant. "I know it's not easy, but just block her out and believe in yourself, dear."

"I'd have given the whole thing up," said Caroline shakily, "if it wasn't for Terry."

Jim raised his eyebrows and Gloria said, hastily, "Yes dear; well, we're all here to help and support each other. Let me give you the dates of the meditation sessions I'm running at my shop, and I've a new valerian tincture which has had very good reports. You must try it and tell me what you think of it."

Once started on her pet topic, Gloria was apt to monopolise the conversation until it was time for everyone to go home.

After the rehearsals, Gloria strolled back with Leslie for a night cap and Bennett was regaled with the details of the evening. It was after the penultimate rehearsal in Dartonleigh, and while Leslie was bringing in the cheese and biscuits, that Gloria said, "I've managed to find out about him at last."

"Who do you mean?" Leslie pushed a small table closer to Gloria and put a table mat and then a plate onto it.

"That young James. I asked him directly."

Leslie had seen Gloria talking to James during the break and guessed that she had imposed herself on him, as he usually melted away into a corner and warded off conversation by fixing his eyes on his phone screen.

"I asked him how he had come to be involved with *Who Will It Be?* and he said that Kara had invited him. He was at school with Pippa, and he'd had parts in some of their school productions so Kara knew that he could act, and even though he left school over two years ago, Kara tracked him down."

Gloria had just speared a silverskin onion on her fork and, holding it like a trident, she lowered her voice for dramatic effect. "He said that he wasn't keen as he hadn't done any drama since school and he had a lot of college work to do, but that he needed the money. At that point he went bright red and said he wasn't supposed to tell anyone about the money." She sighed, popped the onion in her mouth and munched it thoughtfully. "Fancy them having to bribe someone to be in the play. I promised James I wouldn't tell anyone, but you don't count."

"That does explain it," said Leslie. "He gives a perfectly competent performance, but he's completely disengaged from the production as a whole."

"I think he's a little shy, rather than standoffish," said Gloria.

"Perhaps I should make more of an effort to be friendly," said Leslie guiltily.

"Leave the poor boy alone," said Bennett. "He's probably perfectly content to turn up, earn his money and go away again without having to make conversation with a lot of old fogeys."

Leslie was about to make a token protest at this label, but Gloria interrupted.

"Yes, he seemed quite happy with the arrangement," she said. "Unlike poor Caroline. If the production doesn't give her a breakdown, I think this business with Terry will. I do hope she'll come to my group. Did I tell you that I'd started meditation classes at the shop? I'm quite convinced it will help her."

Anxious not to get drawn into Gloria's latest venture, Leslie said, "Yes, I believe you did."

"Mind you," said Gloria, "I think she's in for a hard time. I was doing a reading with her, and she drew out the rhodonite crystal. That's not bad in itself, but when she placed it on the mat, it had its flawed side showing. That's a broken heart, for sure, I thought as soon as I saw it. I didn't put it quite like that to her, of course."

65

Leslie held his breath lest Bennett should let out a snort of derision, but fortunately he was busy with his cheese and biscuits. Gloria had more to say.

"Actually, I'm wearing an amethyst at the moment."

To Leslie's dismay, Gloria plunged her hand into her considerable cleavage.

"Here!" she exclaimed, plucking out a glittering purple stone which Leslie could now see hung from a long silver chain round her neck.

"It's for good luck. So much negative energy around at the moment." She paused with her lips pursed, and then continued. "I wasn't going to mention it, as I didn't want to worry you, but now that the subject has come up, I feel I ought to. Yesterday, when I was doing my own daily reading, I drew out the *black diamond*." She spoke the last two words with great emphasis, leaning forward dramatically, causing the amethyst to rattle against the cup she was holding. "The black diamond. Do you remember? It's the crystal of bad omen."

***

Before the final rehearsal at the village hall, there was the practice at Kara's house to be endured. The scene to be rehearsed was the one which Leslie and Roland had practiced at the cottage, when Bennett read in the parts of Bella and Lord Charterhouse. Gloria was also required for this scene, so she arranged to pick Leslie up on the way.

Leslie had offered to take a turn and give Gloria a lift for a change, but she would not hear of it, insisting that she could collect him en route, whereas Leslie would have to drive out of his way to pick her up. Neither of them alluded to the fact that Leslie and Bennett's vintage Rover was rarely brought out of the garage these days, as it was wholly unsuited to the country lanes, and Leslie detested driving. Sometimes he resolved to shake off his reticence and take to the wheel again, especially when he had just been Gloria's passenger, but he never did anything about it.

After another alarming assault on Leslie's nerves, which surely not even Gloria's valerian tincture could relieve if he was to try it, the drive was over and they drew up alongside the yew hedge, narrowly missing a taxi which was just pulling away. Roland was standing at the big iron gates and, spotting Leslie in the open top car, he waited for them. To Leslie's astonishment, Roland seized him by the shoulders and kissed him on each cheek, continental style. He seemed sober enough but there was more than a whiff of whisky on his breath.

"My dear boy, so good to see you. And your lovely companion." This was to Gloria who, overawed by this introduction to the celebrity, was speechless for once, and she flushed scarlet as Roland took her hand and, bowing slightly, kissed it gallantly.

Roland had apparently already announced himself into the grille by the gates, as they had opened and the three walked up the path together to the front door, which was open, revealing Terry at the threshold. He welcomed them very cordially, but Leslie detected a decided frostiness in Roland's manner and, having admitted them, Terry subtly retreated to the far end of the sitting room.

The furniture in the room had been rearranged and the grand piano turned around, which must have been quite a task on the thick pile carpet. The settee had been repositioned and Pippa, who was lounging on it, did not look up when they came in.

Leslie and Gloria stood politely to one side, but Roland strutted impertinently about the room, peering at the pictures and ornaments.

After a couple of minutes, Kara stalked in and said, impatiently, "Well, let's get on with it, shall we? That's the front." She flapped her script towards the wall with the portrait on it.

"'Downstage', darling," smirked Roland who had taken on an affected air that Leslie had not seen before.

He was obviously being provocative and would probably have ridiculed Kara if she had been the one to use the term 'downstage' in a sitting room. Kara glowered and ordered everyone to their starting positions.

"Pips, darling," she said, her voice suddenly ingratiating, for her daughter was still sprawled on the sofa.

"Yeah, give me a minute," the girl replied, without looking up from the phone which she was tapping away at. "It's not seven o'clock yet."

Everyone looked at the clock on the mantlepiece where the hands were, indeed, pointing at one minute to seven.

"The sooner we get started the sooner we can stop," Kara said, as though coaxing a child.

Pippa showed no signs of bestirring herself and, ignoring her passive defiance, Kara moved away, announcing that they would start with some notes for the scene. She peered at the script and Leslie had the impression, not for the first time, that she was not entirely conversant with it. She made some general comments relating to the entrances and positions of the characters in the scene. Her obvious design was to ensure that Bella was literally and metaphorically centre stage, though Pippa, who had just arisen and joined them, shuffled about indifferently.

Leslie's spirits were depressed. This scene had the potential to be one of the funniest in the play, but this was entirely dependent on timing, and everyone on the stage had to get it right. With just this rehearsal, and with Kara in charge, it did not seem possible.

Then Kara made what was, perhaps, the only sensible suggestion that Leslie had heard from her.

"Roland, I think you had better take us through the directions for the song. You've rehearsed this already with, er, Bancroft." She waved her hand at Leslie. "There's no point reinventing the wheel."

"No, indeed, darling," said Roland. "You might get a flat tyre."

Kara looked livid and Roland, taking up the invitation with feigned conceit, strutted across to the piano, and played some elaborate phrases that had nothing to do with the show. "Let's have you all in position for the song. Lady C and the gorgeous Griselda upstage left, peering in the room through the window."

Gloria and Kara took up their places behind the settee which had been positioned for that purpose, Kara scowling and Gloria beaming, like a couple of method actors registering anger and joy. Roland graced them with a supercilious smile.

"Lord C, seated downstage left, obscured from the two ladies by a screen, and looking like you're trying not to be seen."

Terry perched obediently on a footstool.

"Bella, centre, unaware of your mother and your aunt looking in at you through the window. And the distinguished Mr Bancroft, stage right, the other side of the piano."

Leslie moved across to the instrument and Pippa apathetically positioned herself in the middle of the room.

Satisfied that everyone had taken up their places as best they could in the limitations of the long, narrow sitting room, Roland continued.

"The success of this scene hinges on focus," he said. "In simple terms, where you are all looking, and when. But it's not difficult—even for you, darlings. When Bancroft or I are singing to Bella, you look this way towards the action. When we are singing to each other, you look away from us. I don't care what you look at, but it must be decisively not over here. And do try to make it look natural. Let's give it a go."

As Leslie had feared, it was ambitious attempting to perfect this scene in one rehearsal, and Roland became increasingly irascible as the time went on. Terry was much better than everyone else but Roland insulted him with condescending little compliments, while his comments to Kara and Pippa became ever more withering. To compound the offense, he treated Gloria with tactful respect, even though her acting was execrable and her timing worse, and to Leslie he said nothing at all, but cast him an occasional conspiratorial wink. This was most unwelcome to Leslie who felt very uncomfortable. But he was also bemused by Roland's attitude. Whatever Roland thought of them all, it seemed insane to foster such hostility, and risk sabotaging the scene that he was to star in. Then Leslie noticed a telltale hand tremor as Roland was fumbling irritably with the script and realised that he was probably badly in need of a tipple. This, he thought, would account for at least some of his antagonism.

Against all Leslie's expectations, the scene eventually came together. Terry's capable rendition was no surprise, but Pippa was considerably better than he expected once she exerted herself and followed Roland's directions. Although Kara and Gloria were positioned behind him, there was a huge, ornate mirror on the wall in front of the piano in which he had an excellent view of their performance which was reminiscent of a couple of pantomime dames. They were hilarious, though unintentionally so—it was just the stuff that am-dram was made of and would be relished by the audience.

***

"I ought to feel better about the production, now," said Leslie to Bennett. "But I don't."

It was later the same evening. Gloria had finally gone home, and the detritus of supper had been cleared away. Bennett poured a glass of port and passed it across.

"I'll be so glad when it's over," Leslie continued, taking a sip. "It feels like an ominous cloud hanging over me. The production itself isn't too bad, but there's such a wretched atmosphere between them all and it's playing havoc with my nerves."

"Given that you were recruited because there had been a mass boycott, it was always destined to be tense," said Bennett with irritating rationality.

"But I didn't know about all that when I signed up," said Leslie crossly. "I really can't understand why they went ahead with the production under those conditions. It's all wrong. In an amateur company, the rehearsals are part of the raison d'être. If no one wants to be in it, why bother doing it? I've been in enough shows to know that people sometimes fall out, and there can be a bit of jealousy or backbiting here and there, but this is in a different league. They can't go on like that without something going bang."

***

Leslie thought that the explosion had come on the day of the final rehearsal in the village hall a few evenings later. He walked across with Gloria in good time, and almost as soon as they had left the cottage they could hear a row. Outside the hall there was an unusual number of people milling around and they could hear the sound of angry voices.

"Oh, I say, what's going on?" said Gloria. "Who's that man and whatever is he carrying? It looks like a box of beetroots."

Leslie was suddenly able to make sense of the situation. The autumn horticultural show was due to start the following day and members were coming in to set up. It soon became apparent why this was causing such a commotion for, as they pushed their way inside, they saw that the small hall, supposedly booked for the LADS rehearsal, was full of produce waiting to be set up for display in the main room. Trestle tables were covered with every kind of fruit and vegetable, to say nothing of elaborate flower arrangements, and there were four giant pumpkins by the piano. The floor was littered with leaves, and bits of string, straw and soil, all being trodden in by the volunteers who had been in the throes of setting up.

"We won't be rehearsing in there tonight," said Gloria and, before Leslie could reply, she turned and hurried through the door.

Everyone seemed to be talking at once. In the hallway, Kara was practically doing a war dance and was using a lot of bad language. A small man, whom Leslie knew to be the organiser of the event, was attempting to respond and phrases such as 'mix up' and 'communication error' could just about be made out above the background noise of irate voices all trying to have their say. Terry was doing his best to pacify Kara, but she was having none of it, and rounded on him to vent her spleen. To curtail this public dressing down, he turned and walked away, and for the first time Leslie saw him let his guard down, for he wore a very angry expression.

It certainly was an ugly scene. Leslie knew almost everyone there, either from his involvement with the horticultural society, or because they were neighbours who had gathered to enjoy the spectacle, and he was mortified in case he was somehow associated with Kara's outburst. Jim, Caroline and James were hovering about outside, but Pippa had made herself scarce. Tracey was standing in the hallway, incongruously clutching an armful of costumes ready for the final fitting, and her mother-in-law, Vera, was beside her, bearing a basket of very fine-looking plums.

"Keep your hair on, Karen," Vera smirked. "It's not our fault if there's been a cockup with the bookings. Well, if you're not the image of your mother when you talk like that!"

Kara looked as though she was about to knock the basket out of Vera's hands, but at that moment Gloria burst back in through the door, scarlet and perspiring, and exclaiming loudly, "It's all right, it's all sorted." This interruption was so loud and unexpected that everyone fell silent. "We can have the back room of The Woodman for our rehearsal. I've just been in there and arranged it. It's a very good room," she said, and added, for Kara's benefit, "we sometimes use it for our mahjong club. Follow me!"

It was indisputably the best solution, and such was Gloria's self-confidence that Kara, Tracey and Leslie trooped out behind her without question, and a round of applause went up from the bystanders. They were joined by their LADS colleagues and Leslie hung back to keep out of Kara's way as, rather than expressing any gratitude or relief at the solution, she was laying into Terry for the double booking. Leslie could not avoid hearing snippets of their conversation.

"It must have happened when I was changing around the dates to try and fit in with Roland," said Terry who was back to his old suave manner, and firmly fixing the blame onto the absent actor. "The woman who does the bookings must have made a mistake."

"Roland bloody Rawlison," hissed Kara. "I'll kill him before this production's over, I swear I will."

9

The week of the production finally arrived. There were to be three performances: the opening night on Friday, and a matinée and evening show on Saturday. Before this, was the technical run on Thursday, with the dress rehearsal on Friday afternoon. But the whole thing kicked off with the 'get in' on Wednesday, which everyone was expected to help with.

Gloria and Leslie arrived at the Lymeford Arts Centre in good time on Wednesday morning and they waited in the foyer where they had been instructed to assemble. Leslie had been to numerous productions and events at the arts centre so he was familiar with his surroundings, but it was strange to see the reception desk shuttered, and the coffee counter and bar closed.

When he had first moved to Dartonleigh this had simply been Lymeford Theatre, but recently the foyer had been enlarged and modernised, and the venue denominated an arts centre. The big central space in the new foyer was now frequently arranged to make room for groups of musicians to perform, or for art displays, but it was set out today with tables and chairs, café style.

"I usually sell programs at the top of the stairs," said Gloria, indicating the grand staircase in front of them which led to the upper areas of the auditorium, its wide expanse currently roped off by a thick maroon cord. The funding to update the venue had stopped short of the actual theatre itself which retained its traditional, if shabby, elegance. "Some of the ushers can't manage the stairs all that well but I don't mind, and in any case, I love watching everyone milling around in the foyer below. You can't see anything from the bottom entrances." She waved her hand towards the passageways on either side, past the reception on one side and the bar on the other, from which the lower rows of seating were accessed.

Gloria greeted various members of staff carrying out domestic duties as they went past, and they waved cheerfully back—she was obviously known to them all—and the house manager came over and had a friendly chat with them.

"Gloria is one of our star ushers," she said to Leslie. "Always cheerful, always ready to help; exactly what the patrons need."

"And Louise is our favourite manager," Gloria replied. "We always have a good show when she's on duty."

Before this exchange of lavish compliments could go any further, Terry appeared, and Louise returned to her work.

On seeing them, Terry said in his most affable tone, "Ah, here already! Jolly good, there's plenty to do."

Leslie was a veteran of amateur productions and knew that one may be required to help with anything from stacking chairs, sweeping the stage, and making the tea, to constructing a piece of scenery that could not be finalised until it was on stage.

"You can help unload the van," Terry announced. "Follow me."

He strode past the reception desk on the left and along the corridor he had just appeared from, and Leslie and Gloria hurried to catch him up. They passed the lower entrance into the auditorium and reached a private door which Leslie, as an audience member, had only ever seen shut. Terry tapped in a code, and they all went through.

One could tell immediately that they were now in a part of the corridor which was officially the 'backstage'; the unpainted walls and concrete floor were telltale signs. There were two more pass doors with code locks like the one they had just come through, one straight ahead, and one to their right. The doors were badly knocked about and they were held open with a red fire extinguisher and a stage weight. On their left was an emergency exit, also propped open, and they could see a service yard outside.

They stopped, and Terry waved his hand at this external door, announcing grandly, "This is the stage door."

Leslie presumed that it was dignified with this title as members of the cast and crew used this route to sneak in and out, avoiding the foyer. As if to confirm this, Tracey came through it, carrying a couple of bags she had unloaded from her car, which was parked immediately outside.

"Do you need any help?" Terry asked. "We're on our way to unload the van but if you need a hand—"

"No thanks, I've taken everything else down." She crossed in front of them, going through the open door to their right, and descending some stairs which evidently led to the dressing rooms.

"Leslie is not to lift anything heavy, Terry," said Gloria firmly.

For one uneasy moment Leslie thought Gloria might launch into a detailed account of the events which had led to the shoulder injury which still sometimes troubled him, but fortunately she seemed focussed on the present.

"If he dislocates his shoulder again, we'll have no Bancroft for the production," she said. "I'm relying on you to make sure he behaves himself." She wagged her finger at him in mock rebuke.

Terry looked a little bemused but, maintaining his near perfect composure, said, "Health and safety first, of course! There are plenty of lightweight things which I'm sure you can both manage."

Ignoring this, Gloria turned to Leslie. "Give me your bag and I'll stow it downstairs in the dressing rooms. I'm going to help Tracey sort out the costumes." Without waiting for a response, she took Leslie's bag and clambered down the flight of stairs into the bowels of the earth.

By the time Leslie looked up again, Terry was heading through the pass door ahead and, after following him up half a dozen steps, Leslie found himself, as if by magic, on the side of the stage. He picked his way through the wing, stepping carefully round a coil of rope, a box of tools and other miscellaneous items lying about, and caught up with Terry who had paused to wait for him. On stage, work was going on up a tall scaffold tower and the man at the top was carrying on a loud conversation with a woman at the foot, while several other people bustled about. It did not take much deduction to work out that they were the theatre technicians.

"The van's behind the scenery dock on the other side of the stage," said Terry, pointing across to the far back corner.

He shouted to the woman at the base of the scaffold tower "Is it OK if we come across?" adding, to Leslie, "Sue's a stickler for safety."

He was given the all clear and they crossed the stage to the wing opposite. This opened out at the back into the scenery dock, which was rather like a small warehouse. A huge shutter was open, through which Leslie could see the van which had reversed up on a concrete ramp and stood with its rear doors open.

Leslie paused in the wings and was conscious of a sharp thrill of pleasure. It was years since he had been in any kind of a show, but the buzz of excitement was reignited. He breathed in the unique backstage atmosphere and, putting out of his mind the travail of the last few weeks and the guaranteed slog of the next two days, he allowed himself a brief 'roar of the greasepaint' moment.

Noises from the van brought him back to reality and turned his attention to the mundane chores that were needed to make the miracle happen. A large man, clad in a scarlet jumper, was standing in the back of the van, clutching a box. Terry said something to him, and then disappeared.

The man, who had an impressive white beard and an even more impressive girth, turned to Leslie. "Welcome," he said, peering over the box with a most friendly smile. "I'm Keith."

Before Leslie could introduce himself, Jim appeared, calling out, "Hey up, it's Santa Claus!" He clambered down the ramp, took the box from Keith and carried it into the back of the scenery dock.

"Cheeky devil," laughed Keith. "Still, I don't mind what they call me if they help with the unloading. We're short-handed this year."

Jim reappeared, this time with James in tow, and they got either side of a large piece of scenery. Leslie and Keith retreated into the scenery dock until they had gone by.

"I'll give you the task of sorting the props, if you don't mind," said Keith, as they returned to the van. He turned to a huge wooden trunk in the back of the van and fumbled with a key. "God knows why Terry's put them in this great cask of a thing, or why he's bothered to lock it," he added, placidly. "Just to give us something extra to do, I suppose! Let's get these boxes out and I'll show you where they go."

The trunk, with its brass hinges and lock, put Leslie in mind of a pantomime treasure chest, and he wondered if it was a repurposed stage prop. It contained two cardboard boxes, which they extricated with some difficulty as Terry had made a thorough job of packing them in with some thick plastic sheeting.

Carrying a box each, Keith led the way through a door at the back of the wing. "This is the quick-change area," he explained helpfully, though Leslie could deduce for himself, from the hanging rail and long mirror, that this was the place where costume changes happened when there was no time to get down to the changing rooms.

"And this is the props table," Keith added, putting his box down on a white trestle table set up along the wall. "Bring yours over to stage right."

They made their way along the narrow passage behind the stage to the other side where there was an identical changing area and props table, on which Leslie put his box. He was given the job of marking up the tables and laying out the stage properties according to the instructions on a sheet, so they could be easily located during the performance. It would not, he knew from experience, prevent some absentminded actor from carrying their props back to the dressing room, but at least a gap on the table would show that something was missing, and a search could be instituted before the next performance.

He began with the props on stage right, marking the place for Lord Charterhouse's pipe; the embroidery frame which was to be cast to the ground in despair by the dejected Bella; the brightly coloured fans which would be wafted energetically by Lady Charterhouse and Griselda at every possible opportunity, and half a dozen other items. The table on stage left, the other side, held mostly props that were required in rapid succession for a scene in act two. It was supposed to be very funny but rehearsing it had been misery. The only two people with the necessary skills to achieve the comedic effect were Roland and Terry and neither of them was involved in this piece of action. As Leslie marked the place for the pink bowl and the mink stole, he recalled, painfully, Kara's denunciations and Caroline's tears. Kara had threatened to scrap the stunt entirely since it was purely for humour and did not contribute to the plot, but Terry had been insistent that they could make it work and in the end he was right. But whether they would pull it off on the night and, even if they did, whether it was worth the suffering, Leslie had his doubts.

Despite these recollections, sorting the props was an agreeable job and Leslie shamelessly spun it out for as long as possible. When he had put the final object—a jewelled lorgnette—into place and labelled it clearly, he wandered back to the scenery dock where he found Keith grappling with a bookcase. From even a short distance away it looked like a solid piece of furniture, and it was only as Leslie approached that he realised that it was two- dimensional, a piece of cleverly painted scenery. Gratified by Leslie's admiration, Keith admitted to it being his own workmanship.

"Not bad, though I say so myself," he said. "Now we just need to get an A-frame on it, and all these other flats, so that they'll stand up. Are you any good with a drill? I've marked them out and the screws are in that tin."

"I should be able to manage," said Leslie. "I can put up a shelf if called upon, though I'm not really into DIY. Cooking's my thing."

"Is it really?" said Keith in a reverent voice. "Eating's mine!" and he patted his midriff good-naturedly. "Here, have this drill, the cordless one, it's quite light."

They chatted cordially between the intermittent whirring of the tools. After a little while, Leslie said, "Is Kara here? I haven't seen her." He tried to sound nonchalant.

"She won't be here before lunch," Keith laughed. "It's all right, you can relax and enjoy yourself until then! Don't worry," he added, for Leslie was looking embarrassed at having given himself away, "we all know what she's like. Normally everyone would be here for the get-in today, whether or not they're in the production, most of them getting in the way, of course. But, as I expect you know, there's been a walk out."

"I did hear a bit about it," said Leslie.

"We normally have a whole crew on scene shifting, but this time it'll be just me and one of the theatre techies getting all this lot on and off the stage."

Keith made a wide sweeping gesture at the scenery which surrounded them. It seemed an impossible undertaking.

"How many technicians will there be at the production?" asked Leslie—he could not quite bring himself to refer to them as 'techies'.

"We've got that lad, Jezza, in the sound and lighting box and Brad on the side of the stage doing the curtains and scene shifting with me." He lowered his voice. "I wish it was the other way round; Brad's a right misery. We've also got Sue but she's acting as stage manager, so she'll be stuck at the control desk."

He nodded towards some technical apparatus on the side of the stage.

"We usually have someone from LADS as stage manager, one of the experienced ones," he added. "We could do with Sue to help with scene shifting but we'll just have to manage."

It seemed to Leslie absurd that they had chosen to put on the most complicated and labour-intensive production when they had the fewest people to help, but he supposed they had not anticipated a boycott when they decided on the play.

Keith continued his discourse. "There's always been a whole team of ladies on make-up, and a separate group on costumes. Normally no one wants to be left out; we have a running joke about how many names we can get on the programme! We usually even have a couple of people in the sound and lighting box to help the techie, though they're not really needed there. I've done it myself; it's a great experience. Even Kara did it when we put on *Journey's End* because there weren't any women in the cast. It was bliss! But I pitied the poor techie who was trapped in the sound box with her." He laughed mischievously, then reverted to his original topic. "This is a real skeleton crew, but we'll have to manage."

No one could have described Keith as a skeleton, but Leslie kept the joke to himself. Instead, he said, "It must have been a relief to Kara and Terry that you didn't pull out."

"Life's too short," said Keith. "I know how to mind my own business. I never get involved in their politics or arguments or affairs."

Leslie wondered if Keith was referring to amorous affairs, given the rumours he had heard and, if so, how he could dismiss it quite so lightly. However, before he could think of a way of satisfying his shameful curiosity, the conversation was interrupted by Terry calling from the loading bay entrance.

"Can I have a couple of you chaps to bring the backcloths in?"

At the same time, the technician, Sue, shouted out, "Clear the stage, everyone, so that we can bring the bar down."

This resulted in a surge towards the van and Leslie was relieved to see Jim and James stepping forward to help.

Apart from a few odd coils of rope and some bottles lying around, all that was left in the van were three huge plastic sacks, tied at the top with draw cords. Terry snatched up a large glass bottle as Jim and James dragged the first two bags to the rear of the van and, between them, heaved each one out, staggering under the unwieldy weight in the awkward space.

As they returned for the third and final bag, Leslie turned his attention back to his carpentry. There was a sudden exclamation from Terry and a great smash as the bottle fell from his hands and onto some solid object on the floor of the van. A few choice words were uttered from among the throng and the distinctive reek of turpentine advertised the contents of the broken container. There was a moment of chaos as the men, dodging and sidestepping the broken glass and the lake of turps that had formed, bore the backcloth into the scenery dock.

In his customary tactless manner Jim said, "What possessed you to have a glass bottle in the van?"

"I didn't expect anyone to barge into me," Terry replied acerbically, and turned away in search of something to clear up the mess.

As Jim dragged the bag towards the stage, Leslie overheard him muttering, "Bloody cheek, it was him who barged into me."

Gloria was suddenly at Leslie's side and after an, "Oh my, what a mess," under her breath, said with loud and buoyant cheerfulness, "Who's for tea and who's for coffee? It looks like I've come at just the right moment."

10

By the time Gloria was back with the drinks and plate of biscuits, the worst of the glass and turps had been cleared up, and they all retired into the auditorium for their break, away from the fumes. Terry joined them a few minutes later, his usual geniality restored.

Before long, they returned dutifully to their tasks and Leslie could see just how much scenery there was, now that everything had been unloaded. He still had several pieces to complete work on, and he was not sorry because the alternative was to join Jim, James, Terry and Brad, the dour technician, on stage where they were on their hands and knees tying the first backcloth onto the bar.

It looked a fiddly and uncomfortable job. Brad seemed to be of the same opinion as, after a while, he got up and stomped moodily into the wings, where Sue was busy at the equipment Keith had referred to as the control desk. Leslie overheard snatches of Brad's complaint. "Three cloths? they're having a laugh, aren't they? … Amateurs and their bloody backcloths."

Keith, who had also heard this, stopped what he was doing and sighed. "They don't like the traditional stuff anymore; it's all projection and special effects now. Even LADS is going that way. We haven't done anything on this scale for years; even *Lady Windermere's Fan*, and *School for Scandal* were pared right back." He sank into a brief reverie, evidently thinking of the good old days. "Terry's the worst, always wanting to modernise and, as he's the chairman, what he says, pretty much goes. I've told him that I think he's trying to put me out of business. I guess he must have agreed to the traditional set this time because Kara wanted it, and she goes ballistic if she doesn't get her own way. Whatever the reason, I'm glad. You can't replace this with illusions, to my mind." He swept a hand round, encompassing the beautifully painted scenery and innumerable pieces of traditional furniture and ornamentation.

While Keith was talking, Gloria had joined them again.

"Oh, you're so right," she said enthusiastically. "Since I've been ushering here, I've noticed that if ever the curtain opens on a lovely backcloth and scenery, there's always an "aah!" from the audience. You don't get that with a bare stage and a few flashing lights or moving pictures on the—*Cyclorama*." She pronounced the last word self-consciously, obviously proud of her grasp of the lingo.

Keith looked pleased to have his views corroborated. "It'll come full circle, I dare say," he said, nodding sagely.

There was some bustling about on the stage and everyone moved into the wings while the bar, complete with the first backcloth, was hoisted up, and the second bar lowered. Terry was clearly in charge of the process.

"These two go on the same bar," he was calling out. "Make sure you've got them on the right side—the correct side, I mean. Cloth two, stage right, cloth three, stage left."

"I say, Terry's very proficient, isn't he?" exclaimed Gloria, some of her old admiration apparently reignited. "I can't believe it; he's marvellous as head usher, and such a good actor, and now he seems to be able to organise all this. Is there anything he can't do?"

"Oh, Terry's what you call a good all-rounder in the theatre," said Keith. "He can turn his hand to most things. Perhaps not the make-up! But then he is a fanatic. Most of us learned what we know on the job, so to speak, but he's done a lot of courses. Acting, writing, the technical side, you name it."

"The technicians don't seem to mind him getting so involved," said Leslie, "even when he's telling them what to do."

"He's been attached to this theatre for years," said Keith. "Probably since before that young Sue there was born, and he often lends a hand backstage as a volunteer. That's when he's not ushering. They're all used to him and glad of the extra help, I should think."

"My goodness that is keen," said Gloria. "I didn't realise he did so much."

"And all unpaid," said Keith. "It's a shame really, he tried to get into professional acting, but he didn't start early enough in life. It's something he'd always wanted to do, but boys were expected to get what was called a 'proper job' back then. Years later, when he could afford to try, he'd left it too late. He's a good actor, but not good enough to break in professionally, or not lucky enough—one or the other."

"Such a pity," sighed Gloria. "Everyone should be able to follow their dream."

"And when he knew he could never make it as an actor," went on Keith in a low voice, "he tried to start up his own theatre company, a professional one, not an amateur set up like this. But it all fell through, and I think he lost quite a packet. It was at the same time his marriage fell apart, so don't mention it, will you? It's not something anyone talks about."

"Oh, I wouldn't dream of it," said Gloria earnestly.

"What does he do for a living?" Leslie asked. "He seems to be able to devote a lot of time to the company."

"He's an electrician," said Keith, "self-employed. He's really good. If you ever need any work doing, I'd recommend him to anyone, and everyone in the company uses him. He fits his work around LADS and his volunteering here at the theatre. He puts in a hell of a lot of hours for both."

"What you'd call a labour of love," said Gloria.

"Talking of labour," said Keith, taking up his drill, "we'd better get these finished."

Presently, Keith and Leslie finished their carpentry, and at the same time the backcloths were all winched up, and Terry called lunch break. Gloria and Caroline appeared with more mugs of tea and coffee, and a plate of home-made cakes which Leslie had supplied. Everyone perched themselves in the auditorium again, most of them conversing in little groups, though James spoke to no one and looked out of sorts. Leslie had seen his figure hunched over the backcloths earlier and hovering round the van to help, but he had not noticed anything particular about his mood. Now, he could see he looked thoroughly disgruntled, and Leslie wondered who had upset him. Not Jim, surely, as although he was apt to be tactless, he wasn't one to actively give offence. Nor Terry, as he took great pains to keep everyone on side. Perhaps it was the technician, Brad, who looked quite capable of offending anyone.

Whoops of joy went up when the plate bearing Leslie's baking was passed around and even James cheered up and mumbled, "Ace brownies, thanks," through a mouthful of cake. But before long his morose mood had returned and Leslie's heart sank when Keith said, "Will you and James have a go at painting that extra flat, to go behind the drawing room window? I'll set you up in the scenery dock."

Leslie took pity on the boy when he turned to see him scuffing along disconsolately behind him a few minutes later and remembered how difficult he had found it to disguise his own feelings as a young man.

"Have you had to take time off to help with this?" said Leslie once they were set up, hoping that he was essaying a neutral question.

"Sort of," James replied. "I'm at college but we don't have any classes on Wednesday or Thursday. I'll have to skive off on Friday afternoon."

Dipping his brush into the tin of green paint, Leslie was about to ask what he was studying when the boy continued in a sullen tone.

"But now I wish I hadn't bothered."

"Has someone been making themselves unpleasant?"

"No," said the boy in a voice of deep gloom. "Not here, anyway."

Leslie painted on, wondering if he was going to get the rest of the story without a prompt. He did not have to wait long before the saga began to unfold.

"There's a big party on Saturday evening. If I'd known about it before, I'd never have agreed to do this. Now my girlfriend has said she's going without me."

"It isn't something you could go onto afterwards?" Leslie asked in his most tactful voice. "We'll be finished here well before ten-thirty."

"That's exactly what I thought. I don't have a car, but Jen does, and I thought she'd watch the show and then we could go on to the party after. But she says it's not worth going that late and, to be fair, she's probably right as it's miles away. And in any case, Jen doesn't want to drive, so she's going in a cab with the others at seven. I can't possibly afford a cab on my own, my mum doesn't drive and my dad's away, though I could hardly have asked him to get me to Paignton at that time of night, in any case, could I?"

"Perhaps she'll have second thoughts," said Leslie, reloading his brush with paint.

"Oh, I doubt it," came the bitter reply. "She's been arsy about me doing this from the start. It's because she found out that I went out with Pippy for a bit when we were at school. I only told her because I didn't want her to hear it from someone else, but now I wish I'd never mentioned it. It was nothing anyway, it only lasted a term and there's certainly nothing between me and Pippy now. Pippy's fixed up with a guy called Gareth; Jen knows that, but she still keeps making stupid comments."

He made a few moody brush strokes on the canvas before continuing his lament. "I haven't dared even talk to Pippy in the rehearsals, just in case anything got back to Jen. I think that suits Pippy, too, what with Gareth being on the scene. It was never serious, and she didn't even tell her mum she was going out with me. She always told her she was out with a girlfriend. I didn't get it at the time but now I've seen her mum, well, she's mental, isn't she? She'd do your head in if she was your mother. I feel sorry for Pippy, really; she's like a different person here. I don't know if she's changed or if she just acts up around her mum. Pippy's OK really, she was a good laugh at school. Mind you, she's got a side to her if she doesn't like you. She put some really disgusting stuff on social media about a girl from school. That's why we split up actually, because we had a row about it."

Having got that off his chest, they painted on amicably for a while and the conversation turned to James's college course which was business studies, and where he had met his current girlfriend, Jen. Little buzzing noises from his phone interrupted him from time to time at which he would pause to make a one-handed reply, the paint dripping off the brush in his other hand onto the newspaper below. It was after one of these messages that he swore vehemently and slammed his paintbrush down, causing an eruption of paint spots, some of which caught Leslie's trouser leg. James apologised morosely.

"Trouble?" Leslie asked, picking up one of Keith's rags and dabbing his trouser leg. He had worn old clothes for the occasion, but this was a large splash of paint, and he was particular about his appearance.

"I've just heard from someone that Jen's ex is going to the party now as her 'plus one' and he's going in the cab with her." James's voice was filled with suppressed fury.

"I think it's time we had coffee," said Leslie. "I'll go down and get this paint off my trousers and bring us back a cup each."

As he left, Leslie glanced back and James was messaging furiously, looking very wrathful.

In each of the quick-change areas was a set of stairs which was obviously the route between the dressing rooms and the stage—several people had passed up and down that way while

Leslie had been working there earlier. He made his way to one of these stairways now and made a cautious descent, opening a door at the foot of the stairs into a subterranean world. He found himself in what seemed to be a rabbit warren of corridors, but fortunately he could hear ladies' voices and then an unmistakeable peel of laughter. He called out Gloria's name and she immediately appeared from round a corner, followed by Tracey and Caroline, the latter looking more cheerful than he had ever seen her.

Gloria and Caroline attended to the coffee request while Leslie followed Tracey along a passageway to the laundry, which was a dungeon of a room, containing a huge sink, a couple of washing machines, ironing boards, and rows of hanging rails.

The paint mark presented no difficulty to Tracey and, before long, Leslie was back with James, sipping coffee and, in Leslie's case, resisting the temptation of another cake. His costume was already a snug fit. Showing no such restraint, and with his mood temporarily improved, James helped himself to a second brownie which he declared to be "awesome."

They resumed painting without returning to the subject of James's blighted love life but ten minutes or so later, just as they had finished the canvas, the younger man uttered a very impolite term. Leslie wondered if he had received another message with further bad news but, looking up, he saw that the cause of his invective was on stage.

Kara had arrived.

Mumbling another thank you to Leslie for the "amazing brownies", he quietly took himself away. Leslie did not resent James disappearing just as it was time to clear up—he was sympathetic to the young man's feelings and, in any case, he knew he could tidy everything away much better on his own.

Leslie kept his head down and tried to remain inconspicuous as he had observed that Kara was prowling round with an unpleasantly confrontational glint in her eye. She seemed rather in awe of Keith and his team and left them alone; with this in mind

Leslie hid behind the scenery both literally and metaphorically. He could hear Kara making peevish comments to Sue and Brad, who fobbed her off with various technical replies and, once she was out of earshot, abused her heartily. Leslie cleared everything away with remarkable speed and was about to see if Keith needed him for anything else when Gloria materialised at his side, once again, announcing that she was going to show him around downstairs.

"It's quite a maze until you get your bearings," she said.

Leslie was relieved to get out of Kara's way and gladly followed Gloria through the quick-change area down the little flight of stairs again. When he had come down here earlier, he had been immediately borne off to the laundry, and he had not had much time to take in his surroundings. Now he could see that this region, far away from public scrutiny was, to use an apt term, the Cinderella of the theatre when it came to funding. The mushroom-coloured walls were grubby and the whole place looked as though it had not been decorated for decades. However, framed photographs, some of them signed, and posters of productions from yesteryear, hung from the walls and leant a certain kind of charm to the environment.

"There are some dressing rooms along there," said Gloria, indicating the narrow, low-ceilinged corridor straight ahead of them. "But they're only opened when there's a show with a big cast. On the left is the laundry and also some rooms used by the technicians, but unless you get paint on yourself again, I don't suppose you'll need to go down there."

She turned right and, pausing to show Leslie a small galley kitchen which held evidence of their earlier refreshments, made her way to the duplicate door which led up to the opposite side of the stage.

"If you carry straight on, there are some showers and *the conveniences*." Gloria lowered her voice and mouthed the last two words, heedful of the indelicacy of the subject. "And these are our dressing rooms," she said with a proud flourish of the hand.

Leslie paused, trying to get his bearings. The layout was not as confusing as it first seemed. There were two parallel and identical corridors of dressing rooms—the one which was shut up and this one which they were using. At the end where they were currently standing was the kitchen and two sets of stairs up to the backstage area, with the showers and laundry room leading off from either side. At the far end was the set of stairs which Gloria and Tracey had used when they had first arrived that morning. The dim lighting, narrow corridors and low ceilings made it rather disorientating nonetheless, and it would certainly be no place for a claustrophobic.

"Oh look!" Leslie said, suddenly, indicating the framed poster on the wall beside him. It was for *The Importance of Being Earnest* and clearly dated back many decades. Gloria peered at it.

"I say! There's Roland," she exclaimed, for his was among the photographs of those starring in the production. "It's a long time ago but he hasn't changed very much, has he?"

Before Leslie could reply, a muffled sound of women's voices, and then a burst of laughter, could be heard.

"That's our dressing room," said Gloria. "We're in number five at the end. It's really just me and Caroline in five, but Tracey's in there with us. She's been put in the laundry with the spare costumes, but there's plenty of room in five with us. Now, let's begin our tour here." She indicated the first dressing room.

"Dressing room one is for Kara," she announced, somewhat unnecessarily, as a laminated sheet bearing Kara's name had been fixed to the door. "And opposite, in dressing room two is Pippa. They're the only ones who get a room to themselves. As you can see, you and Roland Rawlison are here in number three. Terry, James and Jim are in four. We put these names on the doors. In fact, we had to do it twice as there was a mix up."

She had opened the door to number three while she was speaking and they stepped into a little room which contained all

91

the features of a traditional dressing room: mirrors surrounded by a frame of light bulbs above a counter that had once been white, hanging rails, an old-fashioned wash basin, and a decrepit shower cubicle. It was very shabby, but Leslie thought it enchanting.

Gloria obviously shared Leslie's feelings as she gleefully pointed out the features of the room and then switched the lights around the mirrors on and off, like an excited child. "As I was about to explain," she continued, having exhausted the demonstration, "Terry had given us a list of who was in each dressing room and the names to put on the doors, but when Kara arrived, she gave us a different set and made us change it all. Caroline told Kara that we had been following Terry's instructions and Kara was very nasty to her. Poor Caroline—we'd been having such a lovely day down here until then."

As Gloria paused for breath, the sound of feet could be heard and what sounded like someone going into the adjacent dressing room.

"That's her," mouthed Gloria. "Kara. I recognise her footsteps and that's her dressing room next door. Shall I finish showing you around, or do you think we should wait until she's gone?"

Leslie had no desire to encounter Kara, so they stayed where they were. Almost immediately, they heard another set of footsteps, brisk and striding, which stopped abruptly just outside, and after the briefest pause, Terry's voice was heard saying:

"Hello? Who's been messing about with the dressing rooms?"

The door of dressing room one clicked open, and Kara said, in an icy tone, "The dressing rooms had already been arranged. I had no idea that you were going to interfere in it."

"I wouldn't dream of interfering, Kara, love." Leslie thought Terry's agreeable tone of voice sounded rather forced. "I always arrange the dressing rooms. It's not something I would expect the director to have to take on."

"Well, this one has taken it on."

"The thing is," said Terry, in his most ingratiating manner, "Roland always has dressing room one, on his own; he'll go ballistic if he doesn't."

"Let him," said Kara with an air of finality. "He's hardly in the damn play. He's got a bit part, let's be honest. It's about time everyone recognised he's a has-been. I'm in dressing room one this time; you can't expect me to share if I'm acting and directing. And dressing room two is promised to Pips. She's not going in with those two... females."

"Oh, I say!" gasped Gloria at this affront, and she looked as close to outrage as her unshakably benevolent nature would allow.

Terry had not given up. "Come up to the auditorium and let's talk it through. I've got a bottle of wine. I'm sure we can come to a compromise." His voice was now oily with persuasion. "It would be the end of our productions here if we lost Roland. Whatever you or I might think about him, you know as well as I do he fills the auditorium."

"I don't care if he fills the London bloody Palladium. I'd rather we hired that poxy Dartonleigh village hall than pander to Roland bloody Rawlison for one minute longer."

There was a pause, then Terry said, in a strained voice, "God knows, it might come to that."

11

Bennett was still working in the library when Leslie arrived home and he did not look up when Leslie slumped himself into a leather armchair and began recounting the events of the day. Quite soon, however, Bennett clicked the keyboard decisively, the printer whirred, and he went across to the bureau and took three newly printed sheets which he passed to Leslie.

"What do you think?" he said, when Leslie paused for breath.

There was a grid on each sheet of paper which, at first, looked like partially completed crossword puzzles with their clues beneath. Reading the instructions, which were written with Bennett's customary clarity, Leslie found that he was looking at a new type of crossword in which the answers were all anagrams. The clues were unnumbered, so that in addition to solving the anagrams, one had to work out where they fitted in the grid, horizontal and vertical, blocking out the unfilled squares which also conformed to a pattern. Some answers had already been entered; the first and easiest puzzle had the most answers already filled in while the third had only one line completed.

"Ingenious," said Leslie, trying to inject enthusiasm into his response. "Is it really a new concept? I can't believe it hasn't been done before."

Bennett raised a quizzical eyebrow but then his expression changed.

"Yin!" he said. "I've been looking for a name for it. Y.I.N; Yes, It's New. Perfect; short and with a suitably oriental feel. I just need to sell the idea to an editor now."

The two men got up and Bennett wandered into the sitting room while Leslie went to the kitchen to put the cottage pie, which he had prepared the previous evening, into the oven. He felt very weary after the day's efforts and, after slicing some green beans to go with the meal, he went through to join Bennett.

"*The Armed Man*—Karl Jenkins," he said, as he sat down. The music which Bennett had selected was instantly recognisable, not least because Leslie's choir had sung it quite recently.

The Kyrie was playing and the two men sat without speaking, Bennett staring into the middle distance and Leslie with his eyes closed. It was one of his favourite pieces and, counting himself fortunate that Bennett hadn't chosen something obscure, as he might have done, he settled back to enjoy it. However, by the time the Agnus Dei was starting, he silently cursed Bennett for not picking something shorter, or that was not so impossible to interrupt. With a rumbling stomach, he hurried into the kitchen and turned the oven down low. When at last the achingly beautiful Benedictus was over, Leslie wished heartily that Bennett had chosen a few Strauss waltzes, a Rogers and Hammerstein overture or even a blast of modern jazz.

"Honestly, Bennett," he complained when he was eventually serving out the dinner, "you might think twice before putting my soul through the wringer, after a day with LADS."

Bennett shook his head in mock penitence but made no apology.

"And delaying dinner, more to the point," Leslie went on. "I'm starving."

His morale was restored by the cottage pie and, by the time they were enjoying stewed plums and Greek yoghurt, with a splash of port, he felt sufficiently recovered to continue with his account of the day. He related the argument they had overheard about the dressing rooms and, having laughed about Gloria's response to Kara's insult, Leslie said, "I wonder what Roly's reaction will really be to having had his dressing room usurped by Kara. Terry seemed disproportionately concerned about it."

"Roland will be ecstatic that he's sharing with you. Terry could have saved himself a lot of anxiety. He obviously hasn't noticed that Roland has taken a shine to you," said Bennett.

"Oh really, do you have to?" Leslie protested.

He cleared away the dessert bowls and started to make coffee.

"You'd have thought Kara would have put Terry in with Roly, given his seniority," said Leslie. "I suppose she knows that Roly doesn't like Terry, though with the mood she's in, that would probably cause her to put them together for the hell of it."

"She sounds like the sort of person," said Bennett placidly, "who might think it better to put the two old queers in together."

"I hadn't thought of that, but you're probably right," Leslie replied in disgust. He carried the tray of coffee through to the lounge and then flopped gratefully into an armchair. "It's certainly the most elaborate production I've ever been in," he continued. "It's all very professional. There were three technicians from the theatre there today: Sue who's acting as stage manager, and a young chap who they call Jezza. We didn't see much of him because he's doing the sound and lighting from the back. And then there's a miserable chap, Brad, who's on curtains, scene shifting and the other side-of-stage stuff. He looks as though he despises all amateurs."

Leslie pushed the plunger down on the cafetiere. "We only have Brad until the matinée, thank the Lord," he went on. "I heard him say that he's off after that and someone else takes over for the Saturday evening performance. Goodness knows how the replacement will manage without a rehearsal. But fancy getting three technicians for a production, in any case. Think of some of the things that we've been in, Bennett, in church halls where they hired in the equipment and no one knew how to work it."

They fell into a reverie remembering the theatrical successes and flops of the past, and Leslie poured out the coffee. "And you should see the set. Masses of scenery and there are three backcloths. Three! It seems completely over-the-top for an amateur production. I hope we can do it justice."

"Perhaps the director's not as daft as she seems," said Bennett. "A lavish set covers a multitude of sins."

"I suppose so, but it's a lot of effort and there's a huge amount of scene shifting during the play. Not surprisingly, there was no sign of Kara there to help with the menial work, not that anyone wanted her. It was quite a nice atmosphere this morning before she arrived, if you disregard Brad stalking about and poor young James fretting over his love life. The minute Kara arrived the atmosphere was about as toxic as it could get. And that was without Roly there; naturally he didn't turn up for the donkey work."

"It sounds like the fun is just starting," said Bennett wryly.

"I've got a dreadful feeling of foreboding; I don't know when I've ever felt such an undercurrent of ill will." Leslie sighed. "I expect I'm just tired and nervous. Still, it'll soon be over, and I'll be glad to see the back of it."

12

The cast had a one o'clock call for the technical rehearsal the following day, but Leslie and Gloria arrived early while the scenery was still being set and the technicians were sorting out an issue with the lighting. Terry and Keith had just positioned a Victorian-style settee on the stage, and Leslie, who was standing in one of the auditorium aisles with Gloria, was wondering whether he should offer his help.

Suddenly, Sue hurried onto the stage. "I'd no idea that wing was to be completely obstructed, Terry," she said, sounding very anxious as she surveyed the painted scenery that depicted the wall of a drawing room. She waved a document at him. "It's not at all obvious from the stage directions, and you must see that it's a fire hazard. You know that the actors have to be able to leave the stage from both sides in an emergency."

Leslie and Gloria sat down quietly to watch this dramatic interlude unfold.

"It's OK, Sue," said Terry in his most reassuring tone, and moved towards the offending scenery. "This door here opens." He performed a demonstration, opening the scenery door and stepping through into the wings.

"But that doesn't count as a fire exit," said Sue, uneasily. "It's not what you could call a clear escape route."

"It's fine, Sue, honestly it is," Terry replied with an air of finality. "The other wing is clear the whole time and there's never more than nine of us on the stage, even for the bow. Nine people could easily get off the left wing all at the same time, and there are fire exits front and back from there."

"Not much good if there's a fire on the left side," Gloria whispered to Leslie.

Sue hesitated, and Terry went on, smoothly. "I can't help it if it wasn't picked up sooner. You can't possibly expect me to redesign the set at this late stage; we're hours behind as it is." Although he spoke in his usual genial manner, there was a subtle undertone that was both accusing and patronising.

A master manipulator, thought Leslie.

Brad's voice could now be heard off stage calling out something in his usual disagreeable tone.

"Well, just make sure there's absolutely no obstructions stage left, at any time," Sue said, rather lamely, and she turned and walked away looking unhappy.

Tracey came into the auditorium and directed them down to the dressing rooms to collect their costumes and wait until called. Leslie was hanging the double-breasted jacket and trousers on the costume rail when Roland came in.

He let the door close slowly and, looking round in mock disbelief, said, "I've never had to slum it in dressing room three before. They were too cowardly to warn me; I didn't know until just now. I believe they thought I wouldn't turn up if I knew I wasn't in number one as usual. Terry seems obsessed with the idea that I might walk out on the production. That's why he's all over me this time, for a change, nice as pie. It's all a ruse to make sure I stay; they know how much they need me." He sighed with mock conceit, but once again Leslie thought that behind the parody, he meant it.

"To be honest, when I went to dressing room one and saw Kara's name, and Pippa in dressing room two, I nearly did turn around and go home. But then I saw I was sharing with you, darling, and I knew that it was meant to be." Roland shot Leslie an amorous glance which was humorous but nonetheless disconcerting. "But fancy having to play second fiddle to Cruella De Vil and her little tart of a daughter."

Roland put his bag down on the counter under one of the two mirrors. "I'll take this one if you've no preference," he said. "Closer to the door so I can make a quick escape if it all gets too much. Don't worry," he laughed, "mere jest, I don't mean it. I wouldn't leave you in the lurch. Not that the rest of them don't deserve it. You've seen how little I'm in the play. Cameo role, be damned. I'm effectively reduced to spear carrier."

Roland sighed dramatically, but before he could expand on this theme, there was an unpleasant electrical clicking and crackling sound from the speaker above the door, and a disembodied voice said, "Cast to the auditorium in fifteen minutes, cast to auditorium in fifteen minutes."

"About ruddy time, too," said Roland. "Mind you, it's always the same. They have a touching faith in the techies and when they say they'll be ready at one o'clock, everyone believes them. I'll be jiggered if we're on stage by three."

Sure enough, an hour later they were still in the auditorium waiting to start. Leslie and Roland were sitting a few rows from the front, and Roland consulted his watch ostentatiously and at regular intervals with smug satisfaction, while keeping up a running commentary of sarcastic or wry observations about the proceedings. He seemed in an unusually docile mood, adopting a manner of resigned martyrdom, though Leslie wondered if he had some mischief up his sleeve. He also feared that his temper might change once his alcohol level started to dip.

Caroline had latched firmly onto Gloria and sat next to her in the centre of the front row, keeping up a whispered conversation. A few seats along, Jim and James were sitting together, although James was, as usual, engrossed in his phone, and Jim seemed happy enough staring into space.

Mercifully for everyone, there was no sign of Kara or Pippa, and Terry was running around on the stage assisting with the setting up. He certainly was at home with the theatre staff and, far from objecting, they seemed quite accustomed to his involvement, as Keith had explained earlier. However, having seen the recent exchange between Terry and Sue, Leslie wondered if his interference really was as welcome as it seemed.

The stage was now fully set for the first scene, and it was undoubtedly charming, even with the scaffolding tower still in the centre while the final lighting adjustments were made.

"This damn bracket's loose again," Brad shouted down in his usual irascible tone. "Pass me up an adjustable spanner, Sue."

Sue searched through the pockets of the tool belt round her waist without success. "It must be on the side," she said. "Give me a minute." She disappeared into the wings and returned saying, with uncharacteristic irritation, "Where the hell has it gone? I can't find it anywhere."

Leslie wondered if her earlier altercation with Terry still rankled.

"For God's sake, you'd lose your head if it wasn't screwed on," said Brad.

"Hey, what d'you mean?" she retorted, craning her neck to look up at him.

"Come on!" taunted Brad, "you can't deny it. Your phone, the big screwdriver, the adaptor lead. Even a set of theatre keys."

"This is good," said Roland to Leslie, rubbing his hands together in glee. "When's the fight scene?"

"You're not still going on about those keys, are you?" said Sue, angrily. "I didn't lose them, they were taken. I left them on the bench for two minutes and when I came back, they'd gone."

"Oh yeah, it was the theatre ghost, I suppose," said Brad.

They were interrupted by Jezza's voice calling out, "I hate to spoil your fun, guys, but could someone get Brad an adjustable or we'll be here 'til midnight."

Everyone turned round. At the back of the auditorium, behind the last row of seating, was a large glass window into the sound and lighting box where the audio and lighting effects were controlled. The technician had slid back the glass and was leaning out. He gave them all a friendly wave.

"Will this do the job?" said Keith appearing from the side of the stage.

At the same time Terry appeared from the other wing carrying a box of electrical cables, seemingly oblivious to the recent squabble. He descended the temporary steps at the front of the stage and trotted past them up the auditorium stairs, calling out, "Thanks for your patience, folks; won't be long now," in his suave manner.

"Smug bastard," said Roland, in a loud voice. "Thinks he's Harold ruddy Pinter."

Leslie watched Terry taking the steep stairs like a man half his age and he did, indeed, seem to exude a most irritating self-satisfaction; it was enough to provoke animosity in anyone. Jezza took the box of equipment from him. He selected one of the cables, momentarily disappeared from view then reappeared with a thumbs up sign.

Leslie turned back to the stage as Brad, from the top of the scaffold tower, shouted to his colleague, "OK, Jezza? Ready? Bar one, can fourteen."

The stage was flooded with a pinkish purple light and Brad called out further instructions. Spotlights and floodlights of varying colours came on and off in turn as the scaffold tower was moved about the stage, with Terry and Brad consulting and calling instructions to Jezza. Sue had vanished. In any other circumstances Leslie would have thought it strange that Kara, as director, was not taking a hand in this, but he guessed that Terry had somehow diverted her, knowing that she had nothing constructive to add to the process and would only upset everyone.

Whether or not Leslie's surmise was correct, when at last the scaffolding was wheeled off the stage, Kara came prowling in, with Pippa slouching along a few yards behind, and the calm and orderly atmosphere was replaced by palpable tension.

"Only two hours behind schedule," Kara snorted, sarcastically. "We're running this through to the end, if we're here until midnight."

"My God," said Roland. "Enter Lady Macbeth, stage left." Roland stood up and Leslie was afraid that there was about to be a confrontation, but he turned and walked out of the auditorium, in the direction of the dressing room stairs.

"For God's sake!" exclaimed Kara, only noticing Roland's departure as he passed through the door. "Where the hell has he gone? Just when we're ready."

"Let's get everyone on stage for their mics," Terry called out, hastily. "Roland will be back in a minute, I'm quite sure."

Fortunately, everyone started moving to the stage so there was no further discussion about Roland's movements. Leslie suspected that he had gone down to the dressing room for a swig from the bottle he had seen protruding from Roly's bag.

"Which one of you's got orange, number one?" shouted Jezza from the sound box.

"What does that mean, please?" called back Gloria, with perfect equanimity. She ignored Brad's derisory exclamation as he started to stomp towards her. Fortunately, he was intercepted by Sue who said:

"There's a coloured dot and a number on the battery pack— that's the block clipped to your waistband."

Everyone scrabbled for their battery packs.

"Ah-ha, not me! I'm purple. Number one," Gloria announced.

"It's me," squeaked Caroline, as though she was confessing to a crime.

"Who are you?" shouted Jezza, leaning out of the sound box.

"Caroline," she called out nervously.

"There's no Caroline in the sound plot," Jezza shouted back after a moment's consultation.

"Oh, for God's sake, it's your character he needs to know. He doesn't care who you really are," snorted Kara. She shouted up to the figure leaning out of the sound box. "She's Constance. Constance—er—something-or-other."

After the others had each identified themselves, and their microphones, Jezza shouted down, "Orange mic one. Constance. Can we have a sound check?"

Poor Caroline was frozen to the spot.

"Just say something, for God's sake," Kara snarled.

"A nursery rhyme. Or count," said Terry, encouragingly.

"One, two, three," Caroline muttered.

Jezza shouted, "I'll need a bit more than that."

"Say some of your lines," barked Kara impatiently, "or we'll be here all night."

There was the shortest of pauses and then Caroline burst forth, "I don't know how you can be so beastly to me. If you had any proper feelings, you would be ashamed."

It took Leslie a second to realise that this was, indeed, a line from the play that Caroline had, by some Freudian impulse, selected to blurt out. There was a stunned silence by everyone at the aptness of the quote and the unprecedented passion and conviction with which she delivered the lines.

The deathly hush was broken by Roland who had returned unnoticed to the stage and said, with a smirk, "Good girl, what a delivery."

He was quickly interrupted by Gloria saying, brightly, "Now who's next? Is it my turn? I'm purple, number one. Griselda."

Roland was the last for his sound check and when Jezza called down, "OK, let's have Hugo Merryman," he swept past Leslie, breathing whisky fumes, and stood centre stage. There was a perfect pause, and then:

"I have had a most rare vision. I have had a dream past the wit of man to say what dream it was. Man is but an ass if he go about t'expound this dream. Methought I was—there is no man can tell what. Methought I was, and methought I had—but man is but a patched fool if he will offer to say what methought I had. The eye of man hath not heard, the ear of man hath not seen, man's hand is not able to taste, his tongue to conceive, nor his heart to report what my dream was."

It was a masterpiece of elocution, and when he had finished there was a spellbound silence. With evident gratification, Roland surveyed the faces staring at him: Caroline with admiration, Sue with deep respect, Gloria with unaffected awe. Even young James looked impressed. Jim stared, open mouthed, then said, "Blimey!"

Roland's eye alighted on Pippa, the only blank face on the stage, and he said, with a wistful sigh, "Midsummer Night's Dream. Stratford, with Dame Judi. You should have seen my Bottom."

Everyone laughed except for Pippa who said, "Gross," and Kara who exploded:

"For God's sake, I've bloody well had enough of him."

"The old ones are the best," sighed Roland with great complacency as he strutted back to the group and, since his mic was still on, everyone heard him and there was another ripple of laughter.

13

The technical rehearsal for act one went through relatively smoothly and some lost time was made up. Act two started well, and once the first scene was over, Roland announced that he was going home as he had no further part in the play after this, apart from the final bow. Kara declared that he was going nowhere in case they wanted to re-run any of his scenes, but then contradicted herself by saying, with a sneer, that it wasn't likely he would be needed as he was in so little. Roland walked away, without responding, before she had even finished speaking, leaving Kara seething at his mutinous rudeness. However, Leslie suspected that she, along with everyone else, was rather relieved at his departure, and they all moved quickly into place to begin the next scene.

This was the part of the play that featured the stunt with a multitude of props being handed in and out of the wings, and a costume change for Bella that was followed immediately by the most complicated set change involving scenery and backcloths. Leslie had been very relieved that he was not in this scene, but in the end everyone who was not on stage was clustered in the left wing with some job to do, other than Terry who was orchestrating the whole.

Consequently, Leslie found himself clutching a mink stole, and elbow to elbow with Brad who had the unenviable job of manipulating the backcloths. This was a complex and exhausting task. Within a short space of time, a garden cloth had to be pulled in front of the drawing room cloth, which was replaced by an old-fashioned street scene, which was then revealed when the garden cloth was 'wiped', as Brad called it, a few minutes later. By the third attempt to co-ordinate this with the action, the props and the equally complicated change of the set, Brad was puce and perspiring.

"Jesus," he hissed. "If anyone ever puts this play on here again, I'm on holiday, believe me." He glared accusingly at Leslie. "Only a madman would set something like this. There are a hundred better ways of doing it. Using projection, for a start."

Leslie was excused from responding as this was his cue to thrust the mink stole at Caroline in exchange for a pink bowl.

Leslie thought, not for the first time, that the complexity of this play would certainly have put off most amateur groups. Perhaps that was the real reason why it had never, apparently, been staged before, rather than the purported inappropriate content.

***

Leslie awoke early the following morning to the unwelcome discovery that he could remember none of his lines. It was as though his brain had been wiped clean overnight, and he struggled even to recall the names of the characters. This did not cause him quite as much panic as might be supposed since it had happened on previous occasions, when it had always been temporary. But it was unnerving, nonetheless. It was also accompanied by an inability to eat anything, the only time, other than illness, when his appetite ever faltered.

He was sitting at the kitchen table, hunched over a cup of camomile tea when Bennett came down to breakfast.

"Got The Forgetters, have you?" he said.

"I'm afraid so," said Leslie disconsolately. He barely noticed the cornflakes which Bennett, with imperfect aim at his cereal bowl, broadcast liberally across the table, or the puddle of milk left on the worktop.

"It'll come back," said Bennett. "It always does."

"I hope you're right," said Leslie, rising in search of his script. He was always in dread that there would come an occasion when the condition was permanent.

By the time Gloria arrived, they had been over and over Leslie's lines until he was as confident as he could be that he was word perfect. Annie ran across from The Daffodil in her apron to tell Leslie that she was looking forward to seeing him on stage later.

"I've got tickets for tonight and tomorrow night," she said. "I know that it's going to be so good that I'll want to see it twice. If it wasn't for the tea shop, I'd have come to the matinée as well."

Leslie was about to say, doubtfully, that he hoped her optimism was not ill-founded, but Gloria cut in.

"You won't be disappointed," she said. "The play is hilarious. It's a wonderful stage set, Roland Rawlison and Leslie are a scream, and I think the rest of us do jolly well, too, for a bunch of amateurs."

"Well, I can't wait," said Annie, "and, break a leg."

It was quite a squeeze in the little car as Bennett was also going along and, despite having left their costumes at the theatre, Gloria and Leslie seemed to have bags galore. Leslie had been very touched when Bennett had requested tickets for each of the performances, especially given his usual disinclination to budge from the cottage. It had been agreed that he would travel to the theatre with Gloria and Leslie; he would be in no one's way in the foyer with his book during the dress rehearsal. He clambered into the back seat, resolutely refusing Leslie's offer of the front even though his long legs were crooked round at an awkward angle.

Conversation was more or less impossible as they sped along in the open-topped car, but that did not stop Gloria from keeping up a lively monologue the whole way. Leslie ventured a few vague responses, but Bennett said nothing other than calling out, on one occasion when they had taken a corner practically on two wheels:

"It's all right, Gloria!"

As Leslie looked round, he saw Bennett glance over his shoulder then shout out again, "It's all right, Gloria, you've shaken them off!"

***

At the theatre, Gloria made for the stage door, but Leslie went in through the foyer with Bennett, arriving at the same time as Roland Rawlison.

"Parting is such sweet sorrow," quoted Bennett as he moved towards the padded chairs in the corner where he proposed to install himself for the next couple of hours.

"You're not going to sit out here, are you?" said Roland, calling him back. "No, come into the auditorium. We could damn well do with some intelligent feedback. And you can keep me company. I'm barely in the second act and I don't intend to fester in the dressing room."

"Surely Kara won't allow a visitor in the audience?" said Leslie. Knowing Roland's opinion of the director he added, hastily, "I'd hate Bennett to be involved in an embarrassing scene."

Leslie could not recall a single occasion when Bennett had ever exhibited the slightest sign of embarrassment, but it was the only way he could think of averting the row that would probably result.

After the briefest consideration Roland said to Bennett, "You must watch. Come in through the top doors, just as the curtain is going up, and sit near the back. You can't be seen up there from the stage when the auditorium is in darkness and the stage lights are on. I'll tell that girl, Sue—she's acting as stage manager—that you're sitting in to give notes, so that the crew don't bother you."

This seemed to settle the matter, though Leslie could not guess if Bennett intended to fall in with Roland's plan.

"Look, the bar's open," said Roland. "Let's have a quick one before the rehearsal, we've got ten minutes. Don't worry, I'll only have one. And I've brought nothing with me today, I vow, not so much as a hip flask."

Roland's promises were probably of doubtful value but there was no point in arguing with the man.

"Well, here's to a bad dress rehearsal!" said Roland raising his glass. "But actually, for once I don't think we need a barrel load of luck to get us through. Here's to a script that's got some damned good material, once we've had our way with it, and a cast that's got at least two decent actors."

The implied compliment to Leslie was flattering, but he feared Roland was rather recklessly tempting fate. He had no chance to say so as the actor was in a garrulous mood.

"I don't mind telling you that when I first read the script and found out I was playing opposite Frank, my heart sank. There was no way that he could have carried off the part. Ham? He's pure luncheon meat. He couldn't pick up a comic line if you handed it to him. He's usually in the backstage crew and was obviously forced into the part by Kara when everyone else walked. Funnily enough he has a good singing voice which was the only saving grace when I was going to play opposite him. Not in your league, of course; he's more of a karaoke man, and I'd been wondering if we'd manage any of the harmonies. But now it's all worked out fine; that accident really was a bit of luck. Frank's a nice enough bloke, and how he got ensnared by that baggage, Kara, I'll never know."

"Turned round and found the gate locked, perhaps," said Bennett.

"Exactly," Roland laughed. "That was about the measure of it."

"Do you know Frank outside the company?" Leslie asked, falling prey to his natural curiosity.

"Oh yes. I've known him for as long as I can remember. He's a local man like me, and our families knew each other back

in the day. He's a couple of years younger than me, of course."
He gave a humorous little cough to acknowledge the
understatement. "I went off to the big city while he was still
in short trousers, so we didn't grow up together, but we ran
across each other often enough. One day I bumped into him in
The Swan, it must have been a good twenty years ago. We got
talking and he asked if I'd support their LADS production.
I happened to have a few weeks free and it's good to help these
little amateur companies. And the locals always make such an
appreciative audience."

"I didn't realise you got involved through Frank," said Leslie.
"For some reason I thought it was Terry. I suppose it's because
he's the chairman."

"Him!" said Roland, venomously. "He was nothing back
then, and still is nothing, in my opinion. I could tell you a few
things about him, but I won't bore you with it now. I don't want
anything spoiling what's going to be a belter of a show."

He put his empty glass down with a sudden bang. "I know!"
he said. "We must have a picture together, Leslie and me. You
don't mind, do you?"

This was clearly a rhetorical question and without waiting for
an answer Roland sprang to his feet and steered Leslie across the
foyer, calling over his shoulder to Bennett, "You don't mind
taking it, do you?"

Bennett ambled in their wake and Roland selected a well-lit
spot in front of a plain, plum-coloured wall. "Oh damn!" he
exclaimed, pulling his phone from his pocket. "I think it's out of
juice."

"I'll take it on mine and send it to you," said Bennett, pulling
out his own phone and focussing it on Leslie and Roland.

Roland threw his arm round Leslie's shoulder and said,
"What a partnership, what a duo. We could be the next *Flanders
and Swann*."

"*Hinge and Bracket*, you mean," said Leslie.

111

Both men laughed and Bennett took the picture. Suddenly, Leslie was aware of Kara, across the foyer, glaring at them, and he wondered how long she had been there. There was no reason he should not have a photograph taken with Roland, but it was just the kind of thing that would annoy Kara. Leslie wondered if Roland had seen her there and set the whole thing up just to provoke her.

14

They had only just got into the dressing room when they heard the now familiar electrical crackling which indicated that the speaker system had been switched on, and they were given their fifteen-minute call.

A knock at the door proved to be Tracey. "You two chaps haven't had your make-up done, have you?" she said, as though they were a couple of tardy schoolboys.

"Make-up? For the dress rehearsal?" said Roland incredulously. "Whose damn fool idea is that?"

"Sorry, it's practice for me, I've never done it before," she said.

"You can practice on someone else," was Roland's pugnacious answer.

"Suit yourself," she replied jauntily, and set off with Leslie trotting meekly after her through the maze of corridors to the laundry.

"It's been a big learning curve for me, this show," said Tracey, dabbing and spreading foundation on Leslie's forehead. "I've only done the costumes before. But there are lots of videos on stage make-up, and I've even tried it out on my hubby and the kids at home. It's not as hard as you'd think. Turn your face this way now."

She worked the foundation systematically round Leslie's face and, if she had not told him, he would have thought she was experienced at the job.

"Janice is normally on make-up but, like all the others, she's totally refusing to help. Petty, I call it. I know they can't stand Kara—well, who can? But to leave everyone in the lurch is just mean. They're obviously trying to sabotage it."

113

"That does seem a bit extreme," agreed Leslie, as Tracey manipulated his head to yet another angle, and daubed him with a dun-coloured sponge.

"Kara's made herself an enemy of everyone, one way or another," she said. "There was a massive walk out a few years ago, so most of the company don't go back all that far, but she doesn't take long to get on people's nerves, as you've seen. I think she's got one of those, what d'you call it, personality disorders. It can't be anything else, so I don't take it personally. If I help, it's for the show—for you and Jim and Caroline and Gloria, not Kara. Or that dickhead Terry."

Fortunately, Leslie could not reply as Tracey was, at that moment, carefully applying something to his lips with a thin brush, but she chattered on without need of a response. Tracey's precision work seemed to depend on a stream of continuous talk, just like so many barbers that Leslie had encountered.

"Kara's had to put me on prompt too, something else I've never done, because there's no one else. They're all coming to watch though because they're expecting it to be a flop. They think that if Kara's had to resort to putting Jim in a main part it must be utterly dire. Of course, they don't know how good you are; you and Roland Rawlison will bring the house down. And old Gloria's just perfect for Griselda, isn't she? Terry's always good. Kara, though a cow, will be word perfect, and I think even Pippa and James and poor Caroline will have a good shot at it once they're on the stage. Nothing like a costume and a bit of slap for letting the inhibitions go."

This was just the pep talk that Leslie needed and he felt considerably more positive as he made his way back to the dressing room, just in time to hear the disembodied voice give the five-minute call.

The first act went through without stopping. Despite the adage about a good dress rehearsal, Leslie allowed himself to feel quite hopeful about the evening performance. He wondered if Bennett had watched and, if so, what his verdict would be. Roland was right, it was impossible to see anyone beyond the first few rows of the auditorium when the stage lights were in operation.

They were called to the stage for the act one notes. Brad and Sue fussed round, adjusting a headset here and an amplifier there, while Kara addressed them like an imperious general. A couple of costume malfunctions were acerbically remarked on. Caroline's skirt was too long, causing her to catch her heel repeatedly in the hem and forcing her, on one occasion when she could not extricate it, to limp awkwardly into the wings. Jim's moustache had half detached itself and fallen over his mouth, fluttering like a trapped moth every time he spoke. Both hitches would have drawn a joyous response from an audience, albeit not the comedy intended. Other than these points, Kara was forced to admit, grudgingly, that it had not been too bad.

As they were waiting in the wings to start act two, Roland said to Leslie, "We're moving the song reprise onto the apron. It's unaccompanied so I don't know why we were stuck at the piano. It needs to be further forward. Just follow me."

"It's too late to make a change now, surely," said Leslie desperately. "Won't it cause problems?"

"Just follow me."

They took their places, and the curtain went up. Sure enough, as soon as they moved forward, stepping out of the pool of light which had been set to illuminate their duet, there came the reaction which Leslie had feared.

Kara, who was watching the scene from somewhere in the middle of the auditorium, bellowed, "Where the bloody hell do you think you're going?"

"Moving to the apron for the song," Roland replied equably.

Brad had materialised at Kara's side, and they appeared down the aisle. "The apron isn't lit at this point, you know it's not," he said impatiently.

"Well light it, dear boy, light it," replied Roland, casually.

"But it's not programmed in," he snapped back, referring, Leslie gathered, to the computerised system which Jezza was in charge of. "The whole thing will have to be reset."

"You can override," said Roland, with irritating nonchalance. "Just like you would for impro. You have heard of impro?"

Brad glared at him angrily. "No one asked us to programme that kind of override feature," he said through gritted teeth. "You have heard of programming?"

"Ooh, touché, darling," replied Roland, giving Brad an arch smile.

It could not have been scripted better and Leslie laughed despite himself. Others were equally amused and there was an involuntary ripple of laughter. Brad, who looked as though he thought he was being made a fool of, muttered some strong expletives under his breath, and Kara rounded on him with quite unjustifiable wrath.

"Temper, temper, children," said Roland under his breath, but he still had his mic switched on and Leslie suspected that he knew it.

Terry appeared from the wings and called out, "Jezza, cut the head mics for a minute. Everyone, we'll take five, then start at the top of the act."

The lights came up on the stage and there was some general murmuring.

"You'll regret this, I'll make sure you do," growled Brad to Roland, but Sue had appeared by now and she ushered him away.

Terry drew Roland to one side and, having tapped his own mic to check it was dead, said in a low voice which only Leslie, letting his curiosity get the better of him, could overhear.

"Look, Roland, you're a pro, a great pro." Terry's voice was at its most emollient. "But have a heart; have pity on us amateurs. I know ad-lib and impro are your thing. I don't deny it goes down a storm, but these guys"—he made a sweeping gesture taking in the cast, crew and entire theatre—"they need things rehearsed. They haven't got your flexibility, and they need to work to the stage directions."

"Bugger the stage directions," said Roland. "We're taking this as far downstage as we can go without falling off."

While Leslie was eavesdropping this conversation, he could not help hearing a row that was going on simultaneously, and very much louder, between Kara and Brad. Brad was declaring, with much invective, that he'd a good mind to leave the lighting as it was—they could sing in the effing pitch dark for all he cared,—and that he would charge double time if they insisted on resetting anything now. Kara's vituperative reply was less coherent, but the general gist was that she intended to get Brad the sack if he tried it on.

By some miracle of diplomacy, Terry eventually managed to cool everyone down and announced that act two was restarting.

As Leslie and Roland moved back into position Roland said, with great complacency, "Always work on the apron, old man, if the stage has got one, that's my motto. Then, no matter what you do, they can't pull the curtain on you."

***

There were no further incidents, and they got to the end without stopping, although it was horribly strained, and the comedy entirely lost in tension. The cast gathered on stage for the notes, and the earlier contretemps was not referred to. However, as everyone scurried silently away, Leslie heard Kara call Roland back. He flapped a hand dismissively at her and said:

"In a minute, in a minute. I have to see what Bennett thought of it." With this, he headed for the auditorium and as Leslie glanced back, he could see Kara on stage looking apoplectic.

With the rest of the cast, he descended the stairs into the dressing room area, and conversations started to break out, with Gloria's perennially lively voice over the top of Jim's low, booming monotone. Leslie felt relieved to have a few minutes alone to restore himself with peace and quiet, but this was not to be his portion. The speakers had been left on and, as he shut the door and sat on the chair at his place in the dressing room, he could hear Kara's voice loudly and Roland's faintly behind the electrical crackles. It was impossible not to listen, especially as the conversation was becoming clearer as Roland evidently rejoined Kara on the stage.

"He'd no business watching... I don't give a damn what he thinks. I'm the director of this production and I'm about to tell you what I think for once."

"Director?" Roland's sneering laugh came from the speakers. "Terry Wiseman's puppet, more like."

"You listen to me." Kara's voice was rising to shouting pitch.

"You can say nothing to me worth listening to," Roland interrupted. "If you start ranting at me, as you do to the others, I might just walk out on the production, like everyone's been saying I will. Then you'd be stuffed."

"You wouldn't dare."

"Wouldn't I? I'd be through that door in a jiffy, if it suited me." Roland's voice was filled with provoking insolence.

Kara let rip with an outburst of abuse, her voice coming over the speakers in a tinny screech, like a 1950s melodrama on the wireless set. "And I'll see to it that Terry never, ever has you in one of the productions again," she said, exhausting her tirade.

"Oh, him!" said Roland. "I'd go and see him straightaway if I were you; he's probably screwing your daughter in the dressing room, even as we speak."

"I'll kill you, I really will!" screamed Kara, and a stream of savage and homophobic insults followed, accompanied by the crash of broken crockery, running footsteps, a door banging and then Terry's voice shouting urgently:

"Kara, Kara, the speakers are—"

There was a click, the speakers were silenced, and a second later, Roland burst into the dressing room.

15

"My God!" gasped Roland, hurling himself into the chair. "What a bitch! She actually threw something at me."

"I know," said Leslie, and explained about the speakers.

Roland put his head in his hands in exaggerated anguish. "Oh my god. But what an absolute vixen!"

"What did you expect? That was a terrible thing to say about Terry and her daughter," said Leslie, unable to constrain his honesty. "It's no wonder she lashed out."

"I know, I know," he said, shaking his head regretfully. Then he added, in quite a different tone, "But wasn't it fun? Almost worth risking my stunning looks for, when she pitched that china jug at my face."

It was Leslie's turn to shake his head, unable to think of a repeatable response. Instead, he said, "You're not really going to walk out on the play, are you? I don't think Jim would ever forgive you if he couldn't have his moment of glory."

Roland laughed. "Of course I'd never walk out on a production," he said. "I'm too much of an old pro to let my audience down. But it doesn't hurt to keep Kara guessing. And I'd never leave you in the lurch, dear boy, you can be quite sure of that."

"Oh, good," said Leslie brightly, picking up his comb and turning towards the mirror to avoid the soulful expression that Roland was casting him.

"I really do think we've hit it off, you know," said Roland, and Leslie, looking into the mirror above the counter, found himself staring at the reflected face of Roland who was looking into his own mirror opposite. Roland gave him a most provocative wink, and said, "Are you sure about Bennett? I really think—"

"Absolutely certain," interrupted Leslie firmly. "And I said I'd meet him in the foyer, so I'd better get changed."

Leslie had packed up a basket of food for tea, though with his stomach in a knot, he did not expect to eat much of it until after the performance. He had automatically included enough for Roland, in case he wanted to join them but, by this time, Leslie was sorely in need of a calm atmosphere, and that was unlikely in the actor's company. He was wrestling between an acute desire to escape his companion, and his pathological hospitality, when Roland said:

"I've booked a table for the three of us at The White Bear. It's the only decent place to get a meal in Lymeford and they know me. I've arranged for them to serve us as soon as we get there so we can eat without rushing and be back in plenty of time. I don't want to be all churned up," he added, patting his trim abdomen.

Leslie felt so nervous that he couldn't face even a cheese straw from the picnic basket, let alone a pub meal, but he didn't feel equal to refusing the invitation. Resigned to his fate, he made his way to the foyer with Roland.

The café was open, and a few strangers were milling around, looking at an exhibition of art that had been set up since they arrived that morning. Bennett was seated at a table, idly fingering a menu, and he looked over as they approached, giving Leslie one of his rare smiles. It was quickly replaced by his customary sardonic expression, but not before Leslie's morale had been restored.

"You watched—what did you think of it?" Leslie asked him, though he knew from the smile that Bennett had, indeed, sat in on the rehearsal, and it had not been bad.

"The main event was thoroughly eclipsed by the unscripted scene," Bennett remarked wryly.

Roland threw his head back and laughed but made no comment other than announcing the dining plans. Bennett looked enquiringly at Leslie who gave a resigned shrug of the shoulders.

"You're sure you don't prefer the jacket potato with prawn Marie Rose?" Bennett said, proffering the arts centre menu. "No, I thought not."

"Someone must eat the stuff, I suppose," snorted Roland, "but I'm beggared if I'm risking my life on it. Now let's get the hell out of this place and have an hour's break from it all. They do an excellent selection of spirits at The White Bear. I don't think I can do this evening's performance totally dry, but don't worry, I'll stay as sober as the proverbial."

Roland's plan to get away from it all was thwarted, however, as before Bennett had even risen from his chair, the clarion voice of Gloria could be heard and she appeared, accompanied by Caroline, Tracey, Jim, James and Keith, and enquired about their dinner plans. Leslie, who was no keener than Roland to be sociable before the performance, said vaguely that they thought they might pop out for a bite to eat.

"What a marvellous idea," Gloria enthused. "We'll join you."

In the end, this proved to be a mercy. Gloria's crowd, unsure of Roland, did not dare to discuss the play, let alone the row between Roland and Kara. Roland, making the best of the situation, played the great celebrity, and regaled them with humorous, and highly suspect, tales of his life in the theatre, putting on as much of a performance as he was about to give on stage. Leslie was free to retreat into silence, toying with the bowl of soup which had been all he could manage, while Bennett observed the scene with a quizzical eye.

It was only Jim, as ever oblivious, who said, as they were leaving to return to the theatre, "Back to the battlefield, everyone. Let's hope we get through it without murder being committed."

***

Although it did not sound as bad as a murder, there was certainly an acrimonious row going on ten minutes after they had returned.

121

Leslie had hurried to the stage in search of the button he noticed was missing from his jacket and could not be found in the dressing room, and as soon as he opened the door into the wings, he could hear talking on the other side of the stage. It was obviously an argument, and instinctively Leslie closed the door quietly behind him and stood in silence.

The voices were unmistakeably Kara and Terry's and, although they were speaking at a restrained volume, it was easy enough for Leslie to hear them from the opposite wing where, shielded by the scenery on stage, he could not be seen. At first, he wondered if the row was to do with the scurrilous allegation that Roland had made about Terry and Pippa. However, it was soon apparent that it was another family issue causing strife.

"Look, Kara," said Terry, "you know what our rules are. No one backstage who's not in the production, and certainly not side-of-stage. If we make one exception, it's the thin end of the wedge. We'll have every Tom, Dick and Harry cluttering up the place." Terry's voice was persuasive but less genial than usual.

"You may not have noticed, Terry, but I'm the director of this production. And Franklyn's not any Tom, Dick or Harry. He's my husband and he should have been in the sodding play, after all. If he wants to come backstage, he's coming backstage."

"But surely you can see that it's because you're the director that you need to lead by example. And there's the health and safety angle. I don't think the stage manager will allow someone hobbling round on crutches—far too dangerous."

"You know full well that the stage manager will do whatever you tell her," barked Kara, angrily. "I don't know what you've suddenly got against Franklyn, after all the support he's given over the years. Listen to me, I'm picking Franklyn up from the hospital in the morning, he's watching the matinée from the audience and he's coming backstage for the final performance. It's my show, and as far as I'm concerned, he can go in the wings, the scenery dock or climb up into the ruddy flies, with or without his crutches, if it takes his fancy. You've had your own way in everything else in this goddamned production, but you're not telling my husband if he can or can't come backstage tomorrow night."

With that, Kara stormed off through the door at the back of the wings and Terry uttered several uncharacteristic oaths before leaving through the same door. Leslie looked down at his feet, and there was the button of his jacket. He had plenty to think about as he hurried to the laundry room for Tracey's needlework services.

***

With jacket repaired, Leslie was returning to his dressing room a few minutes later when he encountered Gloria in the corridor. She was emerging from the kitchen, in full costume, with a cloth in one hand and a bottle of washing-up liquid in the other.

"Oh, there you are," she hissed, urgently. "I was trying to find you, but I didn't want Roland to suspect anything. Look at this."

Mystified, Leslie followed Gloria for a few paces where she stopped in front of the framed poster of *The Importance of Being Earnest*. Leslie drew an involuntary intake of breath, for the glass had been defaced by some highly offensive remarks, scrawled in red lipstick.

"Thank goodness, it's coming off easily enough," she said, rubbing vigorously at the glass. "I wanted you to see it, but I couldn't risk waiting, as if it got back to Roland... Well, we don't need anything else upsetting things, do we?"

She darted back into the kitchen to replace cloth and bottle before anyone should come along and make enquiries. They made their way to their dressing rooms and Gloria whispered, "I suppose it must have been her," nodding in the direction of Kara's room as they passed.

Leslie made a noncommittal gesture, trying to calculate if Kara would have had time to deface the picture in the period between her row with Terry and the moment when Gloria had seen the graffiti. It could not surely have happened more than a few minutes earlier, for there were people coming and going all the time. Jim, perhaps, might have passed it by without noticing, but anyone else must surely have seen it and either sought to conceal it by cleaning it off as Gloria had done, or spread the word, which did not seem to have happened.

With great determination, Leslie put this latest crisis from his mind and went into his dressing room to prepare for the performance.

***

Roland was surprisingly tranquil, giving no indication that there was a show imminent until the five-minute call came, at which he fell silent and sat completely still until it was time to go to the stage. His calm demeanour did much to steady Leslie's nerves but as they left the dressing room, he felt sick with stage fright. So much so that when Roland put a friendly arm round his shoulders, it was welcome, rather than disconcerting as it would otherwise have been.

As soon as the lights went up on stage and the curtain opened on act one, Leslie forgot about being nervous. Before he knew it, they were into the final scene, where he and Roland were ostensibly wooing Bella, but were really singing to each other. Roland played it for all it was worth, and with exactly the right injection of subtlety to avoid crass parody, while making the meaning clear to the audience. The rest of the cast all played their parts with great determination, but all eyes were inevitably on Roland Rawlison. The curtain closed for the interval to rapturous applause.

The dressing room corridor was filled with excited and relieved laughter and mutual congratulations, though Kara, Terry and Pippa were nowhere to be seen.

"Marvellous," said Roland, slapping Leslie on the back as he closed the dressing room door behind them. "You were bloody marvellous."

Leslie disclaimed any praise, throwing it back with complete sincerity, on Roland's performance.

"Joint effort," said Roland, peering at himself in the mirror and making some adjustments to his bow tie. Leslie was looking in his own mirror opposite and, once again, Roland met his reflected gaze with a most meaningful wink.

"We were made for each other, you know," he said suddenly, turning round. It sounded like a line from the play, but Leslie was in no doubt that Roland was sincere. "Why don't you think about it? It's not as if you've actually tied the knot with that Bennett fellow, is it? Just think what a couple we'd make."

"Roly!" exclaimed Leslie, and he tried to compose a suitable reply. He had no wish to have a painful scene, especially as they had to go on in the role of clandestine lovers in act two. And, despite himself, he found, to his great mortification that he was flattered by Roland's words.

"I don't ask for a snap decision," said Roland. "I realise you're the loyal type. I know I haven't much to offer you, and I wouldn't say it if I didn't— Well, the truth is, I need someone like you."

By a great mercy, this terribly embarrassing moment was curtailed by a loud rapping at the door and Gloria calling out, "Are you decent? May I come in?"

"I'm never decent, dear lady," Roland called back, resuming his usual flippant manner. "But come in and take your chance, by all means."

Gloria had only come to tell them that there was tea and coffee in the kitchen and, as Leslie followed her in welcome escape, Roland caught him by the arm and said, pleadingly:

"Think about it, please. Promise me that."

"Let's talk about it later, shall we?" Leslie replied, hoping that Roland, fickle and capricious as he was, would let it go and the awkward conversation would never be resumed.

Leslie found Gloria and the others clutching mugs of tea and coffee in the little kitchen, breathless with relief but anxious not to jinx the second half by premature complacency. It was no surprise that Kara did not appear, to congratulate them or give any notes or encouragement before the second half, or that Pippa kept to her dressing room. However, Leslie thought Terry might have joined them, taking on the role of proxy director as he frequently did. He did appear a minute or two before the five-minute call to the stage and, although he made a few hearty comments, he seemed much less affable than usual. Leslie suspected that his unease was the result of the increasing tension with Kara, though perhaps, like the rest of them, he was simply nervous.

It was an onerous responsibility to get the second half of the play off to a strong start with just two of them on the stage. Roland was right, the interval and second act did seem to be in the wrong place. To add to Leslie's anxiety, this was the scene that Roland was most inclined to ad-lib, so Leslie was particularly on edge. But he need not have worried. Roland immediately had the audience eating out of his hand and, as he advanced onto the apron of the stage and paraded up and down, Jezza adjusted the lighting as if their movements had been in the stage directions all along. Roland convulsed the audience with laughter but at the moment when he made the great sacrificial parting from Bancroft, Leslie's character, he managed, without mawkishness, to bring out the full poignancy of the scene, exiting the stage to a storm of applause.

Roland's part in the play was over and he went back to the dressing room. Leslie, however, continued on stage, or was scheduled to help with props in the wings, until the penultimate scene of the play, when, feeling quite parched, he hurried to the dressing room for a quick drink of water. As he got to the dressing room door he hesitated, remembering the awkward conversation with Roland in the interval and he braced himself in case Roland mentioned it or was off hand with him. He did not, however, expect the reaction which greeted him as he entered.

"How could you do this to me? I thought you were—my friend," said Roland in angry accusation. It was immediately obvious he was very, very drunk.

"Oh, Roly!" exclaimed Leslie, looking at the empty bottle of whisky on the counter. Next to it was an old plastic tumbler from the kitchen which added to the horribly seedy ambiance, and the stuffy room reeked of spirits.

"Don't 'Oh, Roly' me," slurred the actor. "If you don't care for me, just say so. There was no need to totally sabotage me."

"What are you talking about?" said Leslie in acute distress.

"Leaving this here," said Roland, waving the empty bottle at Leslie. "You knew what would happen if this was in front of me."

"Where did you get it?" Leslie asked. He was starting to realise that his assumption that Roland had brought the bottle with him, or gone to the bar for it, was wrong.

"It was here when I came back to the dressing room after my last scene." He got the words out with some difficulty. "You know. You put it here. Didn't you?"

"It's nothing to do with me," protested Leslie. "I'd never do such a thing and, in any case, how could I? I went out of here before you, after the interval, remember? And I haven't been back here since."

"Oh God, so you did," said Roland, clutching his head in his hands. "And I thought it was all because of what I'd said to you. I thought you—" His words trailed away, and he leant forward onto the counter with his head on his forearms with a groan. The man's accusation was manifestly illogical, but he was beyond reasoning. Leslie hovered anxiously, loath to alert Kara or Terry to the situation but wondering if it would make matters worse if

Roland simply did not appear for the bow. As Leslie paused by the door, indecisively, Roland looked up and gave him a lopsided smile.

"If you've forgiven me," he said, enunciating the words with great care, "be a good man and get me a coffee. Black. Strong. Four sugars. Always does the trick. Be right as rain in five minutes."

Leslie hurried to the kitchen, doubting that the strongest, sweetest coffee would be efficacious in the short time they had before the end of the play, but glad of something to do. The hot water came from an urn, so there was no waiting for a kettle, and Leslie splashed in some cold water so that it could be drunk quickly.

"An enemy," moaned Roland, staring up at Leslie through glazed eyes, as Leslie put down the coffee in front of him. "Someone's out to ruin me. 'S that cow, Kara. Or the bastard, Terry. Or both of them."

Leslie remembered the abuse which had been scrawled in lipstick across Roland's poster but naturally he said nothing about it.

Roland took a sip of the coffee, shuddered and said, petulantly, "God, what disgusting stuff. Ground-up acorns. Muck. Trying to poison me now as well." He looked up at Leslie, his face full of pathos. "Not you; you're the only friend I've got left here. Everyone else is out to get me. Chucked out of the star dressing room; cut my part down so much it's hardly worth putting on the costume. Cameo role, huh! Bloody spear carrier, that's about the size of it. Second bloody footman. And now they're trying to bloody sabotage even that." He drunk the coffee down in a few large gulps. "But I'll show 'em."

The call to the stage for the bow had just come over the speaker and Roland rose unsteadily to his feet, adopting an exaggeratedly upright posture but swaying noticeably.

"You're not going back on?" Leslie said. He was dubious that Roland could even get as far as the stairs.

"Of course, of course… Always go on for the bow… Never missed one yet… Never let your audience down or your pals down… I'd never let you down." He picked each word with deliberation. "Don't worry, dear chap, I'm only very slightly pissed. I did the whole of *Hamlet* totally rat-arsed once. Word perfect and never missed a cue. Proudest moment of my career."

He waved away assistance from Leslie and, with the caution of a tightrope walker, stepped carefully out into the corridor. Leslie followed, wondering, as he closed the dressing room door, who would play a dirty trick like that on Roland, and why.

16

"What brand was the whisky?" asked Bennett later as they discussed the events of the evening over supper in the sitting room. "Did you notice?"

Gloria had brought them home, chattering loquaciously for the entire journey, but fortunately oblivious to Roland's misadventure and not even hinting at an invitation into the cottage. Leslie was exhausted, but with so much on his mind, he knew that he would not sleep until he had told all to Bennett, as was his unvarying custom.

"Oh yes, it was Bells," said Leslie, taking another crumbly chunk of Cheshire cheese onto his plate. "Why do you ask?"

"I was wondering if Roland had really brought the bottle in himself, and his accusation was a ploy to cover his sins. But I don't see Roland buying a blended whisky to binge on."

"He really does have an enemy, then," said Leslie. "I wonder who. I wonder if it was the person who defaced that poster. Anyone would have had the opportunity in the first scene as only Roly and me are on stage. Everyone else is in the next scene so they should all be in the wings ready, though Terry isn't in it until the end, but it wouldn't take a second to shove a bottle in our dressing room, on the way to the side of the stage, for example. Do you think it was Kara, given that awful row?"

"I wonder if she hates him enough to risk the production," mused Bennett. He sliced a piece of Stilton and topped up both their glasses. "If he'd fallen down the stairs and broken his neck, or if he doesn't show up tomorrow because the bottle of whisky has sent him on a complete bender and he's too hung-over, the whole show would be finished."

"She probably wouldn't think of that," said Leslie. "She's not very logical at the best of times, and she was so angry she might easily have taken leave of her reason. I can't think who else it would be. He made that terrible insult against Pippa and Terry, but I can't see either of them doing something like that. Terry surely wouldn't risk the production, certainly not over one of Roly's offensive remarks. Look how he's kept his patience with him just so that it all runs smoothly. In fact, I can't imagine anyone in LADS would do such a thing." He smeared some butter on a cracker and ate it thoughtfully.

"But what about Brad?" he said. "I heard him say he'd get even with Roly. I wonder if it was him."

***

They woke to a grey drizzling rain the next day and Leslie had a mood of despondency to match. He had, he confessed to himself, thoroughly enjoyed performing again, but the off-stage drama had badly overshadowed it.

"What if they do it again?" he said to Bennett at the breakfast table.

Bennett looked up from his bowl of cereal and raised an enquiring eyebrow.

"What if whoever-it-was puts a bottle in the dressing room again this afternoon?" Leslie poured himself a cup of tea, which was all he could face. "It's all very well Roly bragging that he got through *Hamlet* while totally inebriated, but I expect that was a long time ago, and last night he could barely take the bow. If it happens in the matinée, I wouldn't put any money on him being able to do the evening performance. That's if, as you said yesterday, he hasn't gone off on a complete binge in the meantime. It would be awful for everyone if the show couldn't go ahead. I couldn't care less about Kara or Terry but think of poor Jim who's got his whole family coming tonight for his big moment on stage."

Bennett nodded thoughtfully but said nothing.

"I can hardly post a guard outside his door for the second act, can I?" said Leslie gloomily, but then he brightened. "Actually, there's only a very short time when a bottle could be put in our room unseen, isn't there? That's during the first scene when Roly and I are on stage. After that, it's too late as Roly is back in the dressing room. That's not long to keep watch. What's more, during the scene in question, the whole cast should be on the side of the stage, except Roly and me, of course."

Leslie took a drink of tea and continued, thoughtfully, "I know just the person to help; Gloria. When Roly and I go up for scene one, she could keep an eye out to make sure no one goes into our dressing room until everyone has gone up to the stage—it's only a minute or two before they all get called. And everyone assembles in the wing on the left, so if anyone disappears from the side of the stage, she could make an excuse and follow them."

"What about your suspect, Brad?" said Bennett.

"Oh him," said Leslie, and thought for a moment. "It's alright—he should be on the side of the stage then too, with everyone else, ready to change the scenery and backcloths."

Leslie poured himself another cup of tea and then said, "Damn, I forgot; Terry is in the opposite wing; he's the only one to go on from stage right."

"Could Gloria see him from the other side of the stage?" asked Bennett.

"Impossible. Remember, that side of the stage is set as the wall of the drawing room. You can't see into the wing at all, even from the stage. Still, I suppose it's the best we can do. It does mean confiding in Gloria."

"She'll be delighted to help, I'm sure," said Bennett with an amused smile.

"That's what I'm worried about," said Leslie, thinking of Gloria's propensity for throwing herself into a task with fervour.

Leslie explained the scheme to Gloria on the way to the theatre—fortunately, the hood was up on the car because it was raining, so he could make himself heard quite easily. Apart from commenting that she had suspected Roland to be 'a trifle squiffy' last night, she listened with unusual attention and was clearly thrilled to help.

As they pulled into the theatre car park she exclaimed, "I've got it! During your scene with Roland, I'll say that I feel hot, and wait in that quick change area, where the props table is. From there, I'll be able to see anyone leaving from either side of the stage—Terry, Brad, or any of the cast. Even Keith, though I know the dear man could never do anything bad, but let's leave no one out. I can slip back into the wing as your scene finishes, when it would be too late for anyone to get to the dressing room before Roland. How about that?"

"Perfect," Leslie said. "Can you do it without anyone suspecting anything?"

"Most certainly," she replied with confidence. "Anyway, only a guilty person would suspect something, wouldn't they?"

***

Leslie descended the stairs to the subterranean world which was now so familiar that he felt as though he lived at the theatre and could barely remember life before the play. He quickly scoured their dressing room for any possible hidden bottles and had just risen from the floor when Roland came in. The actor looked surprisingly chipper for a man who'd had to be manhandled into a cab the previous night.

"How dost thou, sweet lord?" was his greeting, and he gave a small Shakespearian bow. "Don't look so worried, I'm as sober as a judge. Depending on the judge, of course."

Leslie's heart sank, fearing that Roland was about as abstinent as the proverbial newt. On further scrutiny, however, the actor seemed to be at about his habitual level of intoxication, which was probably as much as could be hoped for.

"Hair of the dog," said Roland, confidingly, as he sat down at the mirror and smoothed his hair. "Had a spot of lunch in The White Bear on the way in. The landlord's a good fellow; he looks after me."

He prattled on with no further reference to yesterday's episode or his maudlin mood and remarks. In fact, he seemed to have swung to a mildly euphoric state.

"It's a full house for both performances," he said with a note of triumph as he started to apply his make-up, a task he had declined to delegate to 'The Avon Lady', as he called Tracey.

Roland was as calm and assured as he had been the previous evening, which was just as well for Leslie, who was as nervous as ever, especially as he knew that half the village had tickets for one or other of the performances that day. But Roland's confidence was contagious and as he proclaimed that they would 'bring the house down' and 'knock 'em out' it was hard not to feel better.

Gloria seemed to be having a similar bracing effect on the rest of the cast as they waited, chattering excitedly, for Tracey to do their make-up. As Leslie joined them, he was pleased to see that Caroline seemed much more upbeat now that the production was underway, and even young James looked as though he belonged to the cast.

"Do you have to do Kara's make-up?" asked Caroline, looking nervously behind her.

"No, thank God," said Tracey, smearing foundation on Jim's forehead. "She does her own, and Pippa's. Do keep your head still, Jim, or this'll get in your eyes."

"We haven't seen hide or hair of her," said Jim, in a distorted voice as Tracey worked the sponge over his cheeks. "Funny kind of director. I bet she hasn't even looked at the sign-in sheet to check we've all turned up. And you'd think Terry would be out rallying the troops, wouldn't you? But perhaps there was truth in what old Rawlingson said at the dress rehearsal and he's busy in another dressing room. He's certainly not in with us at the moment."

There was an awkward silence—everyone had given up correcting Jim's mispronunciation of Roland's surname, and no one seemed to have a response to his insinuations. Leslie noticed Caroline flush deep crimson at the very mention of Terry's name. Gloria, who was standing next to Caroline and could not have failed to notice her embarrassment, said brightly:

"Talking of Roland, I take it that he's arrived safe and sound this morning?"

Leslie, to whom this was addressed, acknowledged that the actor was on the premises and in the process of getting ready. Jim started to enquire into how sloshed he was, but fortunately his make-up was complete, and Tracey hurried him off to his dressing room to get changed.

17

The first act sped by, once again, and with barely a mumbled line or ill-timed cue. The audience members were clearly in the mood to enjoy themselves; most of them were there in friendly support of the cast, and those who were not connected to the company had come to see their Roland Rawlison. He did not disappoint. With a tiny pause, an almost imperceptible gesture or expression, the slightest change of inflection to a word, he made the humorous scenes side-splittingly funny. This was, somehow, enhanced by the contrast with the outrageous overacting of Gloria and Kara, especially when they were peering through the drawing room window, beaming, pouting and grimacing like a couple of cartoon characters.

The audience loved it and the applause, when the curtain closed for the interval, was very gratifying. The only negative factor for the cast was Kara's extreme ill humour which she made no attempt to disguise, standing angrily apart in the wings with her arms folded and glowering at everyone. Fortunately, it had not impacted on her performance on stage as her hostile mood was quite in keeping with the forbidding character of Lady Charterhouse.

Backstage, the atmosphere was a heady mixture of elation and apprehension. There was palpable relief at getting through the first act with success, but Kara's malignant mood could not be ignored. However, she had become the common enemy, and this united the lesser members of the company. They clustered together in the kitchen, buoying each other up with jokes and words of encouragement, principally led by Gloria who was impervious to hostility.

Terry joined them for a quick coffee again and his bonhomie, as he dished out compliments and encouragement, appeared falser than ever. Leslie felt rather sorry for the man; he had noticed him apparently trying to appease Kara in the wings, unsuccessfully, and the strain was showing through the amicable exterior. Beneath the veneer of confidence, he looked as taut as a bowstring and his presence seemed to heighten the tension among them. Caroline cast nervous and uncertain glances in his direction and reverted to looking ready to burst into tears at any moment. Gloria, Tracey and Jim talked in tones of false cheerfulness, and James hunched moodily over his phone.

There was an audible sigh of relief, anticipation and resignation when Sue's voice came over the speakers, starting the countdown to the second act.

"Don't worry, I haven't forgotten my little assignment in the first scene," Gloria said in a conspiratorial whisper as she parted from Leslie outside his dressing room. "I'll do everything in my power to make sure no one sabotages the performance."

As before, Roland fell into a reverie at the five-minute call, but as soon as they were called to the stage, he was voluble again, extolling their earlier performance and sighing with mock resignation that he mustn't keep his faithful public waiting. Leslie fervently hoped that this euphoric mood would not put a hoodoo on the next act.

As they took their places on the stage, Roland turned to Leslie, suddenly wistful. "I really think we could make a go of it, you know," he said, laying his hand gently on Leslie's arm. His eyes were brimming with apparently genuine tears. "Don't turn me down without thinking about it."

To Leslie's enormous relief, they caught sight of Sue performing an urgent gesture, slicing her hand rapidly across her throat, clearly a signal to shut up as the mics were about to go on. The lights went down, and the curtains opened to agreeably loud applause which banished all thoughts other than of the play.

Roland was certainly on form, and he played as though he was on a West End stage. As before, he had taken the action onto the apron, and in the front few rows Leslie could see people doubled forwards, clutching their sides. He caught sight of Bennett who happened to have a ticket in row C for this performance, and he was gratified to see him mopping his eyes.

Their unaccompanied duet went without a hitch, arresting the audience with this suddenly poignant moment as the two characters were parting for ever. Then, instead of immediately walking upstage and exiting through the scenery door on stage right as scripted, Roland turned to face the audience. Suddenly and imperceptibly, he stepped out of his role as Hugo Merriman the piano tutor and became, for this fleeting moment, Roland Rawlison. He glanced back at Leslie with a stunning smile then said to the audience, "If only…" His perfect delivery and timing brought the house down. Leslie's unguarded reaction, utterly nonplussed, added to the audience's delight. Roland then made his belated exit, glancing back at Leslie again with a look which this time only Leslie could see, and gave him the smallest of winks, provocative, amused, triumphant.

The cast, who were cued to enter from stage left when the applause from Leslie and Roland's scene had died down, had a very long wait and, as they had no idea what had occurred on stage, they were in a state of bewilderment. The audience was now in the mood to laugh even more heartily at every amusing line or comic gesture, however amateurishly delivered or ill-timed. They loved it all, and no one cared when James knocked over a vase or when the garden backcloth did not quite pull all the way across the stage, apart from Brad who had to climb into the flies and crawl across, high above the stage, to unsnag it.

No one even minded when Caroline, flouncing indignantly past Jim, accusing him of treachery and declaring that she would never go near him again, found that her shawl had snagged on his tiepin, and they were inextricably entangled. After some surreptitious yanking, covered by faltering and unlikely impromptu dialogue, they were forced to sidle off stage shoulder to shoulder, to be disentangled by Tracey and Gloria, whereupon they returned to the stage to pick up the thread of the scene as best they could. By this time the audience was howling with laughter.

It was this debacle that delayed Leslie from running down to the dressing room to check up on Roland. The first opportunity to go was when the incident occurred on stage. It was impossible not to wait to see how the thing resolved itself. He ran down the steps, his laughter turning to apprehension as he recalled the possibility of finding Roland clutching a bottle or, possibly, ready to renew his amorous proposals. Wondering what state he would find the man in, he pushed the door open.

18

It was the last thing Leslie had expected. The dressing room was empty. There was no Roly, and none of Roly's things. No costume, no clothes, no bag, no make-up case. Nothing. Leslie gripped the doorframe; it was such a shock that he felt momentarily quite light-headed. He stepped inside, peering into the shower cubicle which contained no clues. None of his own things had been moved, and there was no note of any kind left for him. He grabbed at his phone and checked for a message there, a futile gesture since he had never given Roland his number.

Everyone else was up on the side of the stage, as far as he could recall, and he had a few minutes to spare. He ran along the passage and up the exit stairs that led out towards the foyer, just in case he might catch Roland up. There was no sign of him on the stairs or in the corridor, and the stage door to the car park was firmly shut. He hurried along to the reception desk and asked if Roland had gone by. The middle-aged lady behind the counter looked surprised and rather too interested.

"He hasn't been up here, dear, I'm sure of that. Is there a problem?"

"Oh no, don't worry, I expect he's in the gents' downstairs, or somewhere," Leslie gabbled. "I just wondered if he'd come up to go to the bar, or for some fresh air."

The receptionist looked disbelieving, but Leslie hurried away before she had a chance to quiz him. He ran back down to the dressing rooms, flying up and down the warren of corridors, opening every door that would open, and calling Roland's name. It was a pointless exercise, he knew, for if Roland had taken his things, then he obviously meant to leave the theatre. Presumably, he had come down after his scene, packed everything up and gone out via the stage door into the car park, without going through the foyer.

Wild thoughts ran around Leslie's mind. Perhaps Roland had succumbed to drink again and had staggered from the theatre in a drunken state. He might now be lying outside in the car park or street. Leslie hesitated at the foot of the exit stairs again, but he knew he couldn't really justify such a search outside when he was due back on stage shortly. He pushed away the unwelcome feeling of betrayal that Roland had not only gone back on his promise not to leave him 'in the lurch', as he had phrased it, but had not even left a message. There was another feeling too—that this was all wrong. There was something nagging at his mind, something he could not put his finger on. He knew that he had seen something, somewhere, that had a sinister implication— what was it?

There was no time to dwell on it; at this moment, what he must do was to break the news to Terry. Terry could tackle Kara. He put his head back round his own dressing room door, in a desperate hope that Roland would be sitting there, laughing at the practical joke he had pulled, but it was of course still empty.

Leslie ran up to the stage. He had lost all sense of time and in a sudden fit of panic, he thought that he might have missed his entrance for the final scene. He burst into the wings on stage left, attracting an admonishing glare from Brad and a poisonous scowl from Kara. Ignoring them both, he paused long enough to take in which scene of the play was in progress, and see that Terry was not on that side of the stage or in the scenery dock.

It was much darker in the wings on the opposite side as the scenery completely obscured the stage with its lighting, and it took Leslie a moment to see Terry, leaning against the wall by the stairs and the pass door that led down to the exit corridor.

"You're not saying Roland's gone?" said Terry when he heard the news. "I never thought he'd really do it, the bastard, whatever he said." He ushered Leslie out to the quick change area.

"Come and see," said Leslie, leading the way down the stairs to the dressing room. Terry had not doubted him, but Leslie felt an irrational desire to have the calamity confirmed by someone else.

As they went, Terry muttered some uncomplimentary comments about Roland and asked if Leslie had told anyone else.

"Then keep it to yourself," Terry said. "We don't want to upset everyone while the show's running. They won't know anything's wrong until the bow, and even then they'll probably think he's too pissed, after last night."

It took no more than a couple of seconds for Terry to look in the dressing room and confirm Leslie's discovery.

"What are we going to do if he doesn't come back?" said Leslie, though there was no doubt in his mind that Roland wasn't returning.

"God knows," said Terry. "What can we do?"

Sue's voice came over the speaker system, calling actors for the final scene.

"Let's just get through this performance before we break the news," he added.

This was not to be, however, as Kara appeared at that moment, stomping quickly towards them and barking, "What's going on? Is he in there? I've come to see if that pisshead is fit to go on stage for the bow. I came down earlier to check if he was drinking again, but I couldn't find him. Is he in there?"

"He's gone," said Terry simply. "He's gone and he's taken all his stuff."

"You can't mean it," shouted Kara, pushing past them. "Are you sure?" She barged into the dressing room, stared round in disbelief, then looked in the shower and even behind the door. "My God, what an absolute bloody bastard," she said through her teeth.

142

Her remarks were curtailed by the arrival of Gloria who had just appeared, to find out where Leslie was as he had not responded to the final scene call. Leslie quickly explained and, fearlessly, Gloria stepped past the fuming Kara into the dressing room.

"Are you sure? Surely not," and she looked in the shower and bent down to peer under the counter.

At this moment, James appeared, running. "Didn't you hear the call?" he said. "Sue's doing her nut. She sent me down to find you all."

Despite everyone speaking at once, he quickly understood the cause of the delay.

"No way!" he exclaimed, crowding into the dressing room with Kara and Gloria. "Are you sure?" He looked in the shower cubicle and peered between Leslie's clothes hanging on a rail.

"Get out, get out!" screeched Kara, manhandling James and Gloria out of her way. "For God's sake get yourselves back on stage. I won't have this performance ruined, at any rate."

"Oh, I say!" said Gloria, tripping over a pair of shoes and clutching Leslie's arm to steady herself.

At that moment Leslie realised what it was that had been bothering him, and he let out an involuntary exclamation. This did not escape Gloria's notice, and she looked at him enquiringly, but Leslie shook his head and hurried after the rest of the party, who were following in Kara's wake. They arrived in the wings in time to see the tender reunion between Constance Pennington and her fiancé Jack Gibson, the moment only marred by Jim clutching at his tiepin, like a nervous tic, every time Caroline moved.

There was cheering and loud applause when the actors finally took their bow, but it seemed as though the audience was holding back their fullest appreciation for Roland Rawlison whom they expected to walk onto the stage as the star performer. Bennett reported later that the only topic of conversation as the audience departed was, predictably, the absence of their hero, and speculation about the cause.

Backstage was in uproar. Kara was incandescent, ranting that she knew this would happen. Jim, apprised of the facts, was complaining loudly that he had thirty-five people coming to see him for the evening performance and would they get their money back if it was cancelled. Caroline looked close to tears; Gloria was wondering if she was in time to contact her daughter who was driving from Hampshire for the show, and Leslie heard James muttering that it looked like he'd had his life ruined all for nothing. They were called back to the stage once the auditorium was clear.

As he made his way through the wings, Leslie overheard Brad gloating to Sue, "That's the trouble with amateur companies. They think they can manage without understudies. Thank God I've finished until Thursday—Sanjay's welcome to this nightmare. Whatever they decide to do, I don't envy any of you. I've never looked forward to my days off as much as this."

The cast sat on the scenery sofas and chairs, still in costume. Tracey had joined them and was perching on a small footstool, as had Keith, who balanced his bulk uncomfortably on a chaise longue. To Leslie, it felt exactly like another scene in the play, full of drama but quite unreal. Terry stood up in front of them, hands under his tailcoat, like the squire about to tell the family that the debts had been called in and the estate had to be sold.

"You will all know by now that Roland has done the dirty on us and walked out on the show." Terry raised a hand to silence the outcry. "As the company chairman, I have the unenviable job of dealing with this. As you know, we have no understudy for Rawlison and even if we could find someone at short notice willing to read in the part from the script on stage, there are the songs to consider. The scenes would never work without the song, and we have to have a singer who's also a pianist. We can't possibly re-block the whole play with Rawlison's scenes cut out at this late stage, it's out of the question. I know it will be unpopular, but the only feasible decision is to cancel this evening's performance."

There was another uproar which again Terry silenced with a hand gesture. "God knows what this will mean financially, what with tickets to be refunded and the theatre and the staff who were booked to be paid—I'll have to look at the contract."

Everyone stirred uneasily. Gloria and Caroline looked grave and even Pippa and James looked put out.

"Are you sure he's not coming back?" said Jim. "It's not a prank, is it? You don't think he'll walk back into the theatre two minutes before curtain-up?"

"Don't be so bloody stupid," barked Kara. "Of course he's gone. He's done what he threatened to do. You all heard him." She swung round on Terry saying, "You have tried ringing him?"

Terry replied that of course he had, and had left messages, and Tracey's husband had driven round to his house, but he wasn't there.

"He'll be halfway to London by now," said Terry.

"Or out on a bender," muttered Jim.

"Well, didn't he say anything to you?" Kara said, fixing her eyes accusingly on Leslie, as though he might be an accomplice.

"I'd no idea whatever," said Leslie. "In fact, he assured me that he wouldn't walk out. I'm hoping he hasn't been taken ill, or anything like that."

Kara gave a snort of derision. "What, and taken all his stuff away without leaving a word? He's just a slimy bastard, and he wants to ruin us, but I suppose I can't expect you to see that."

Terry cut in, hastily, "I'm afraid there's little room for doubt that he's left us high and dry. We have no option but to cancel the final show."

This time he made no effort to silence the outcry of disappointment.

"May I make a suggestion?" put in Leslie tentatively, when the noise eventually subsided. "If you would consider running the performance with a stand-in, Bennett knows Roly's, I mean Roland's, part. He's rehearsed it with me hundreds of times and

145

he's word perfect. He can play the piano part and sing, too, and he's got quite a lot of stage experience. It won't be the same as having Roland, of course, but it would save the show."

There was a clamour of excited voices over which Gloria's was the loudest, extolling Bennett's virtues. "And don't forget," she said, "he sat through the dress rehearsal and two of the shows."

Kara seemed to have something negative to say, but no one was listening to her, and Terry dispatched Leslie to fetch Bennett, for a trial. The foyer was still bustling, mostly with friends and family of the cast who were waiting to see them, and probably eager to hear what had become of the star of the show. Bennett was lolling back on a padded armchair near the bar area with an empty glass on a table beside him and he raised his eyebrows when he saw Leslie advancing towards him with great urgency.

"Quickly, come with me," said Leslie, and Bennett, though he rarely moved with haste, unpeeled himself from the chair without question and followed Leslie out of the foyer and into the side corridor. As soon as they had gone through the first pass door, Leslie stopped and said, in little more than a whisper, "Roly's gone—he's vanished and taken everything with him. Everyone thinks he's walked out on the show but it's not right. Something has happened to him."

"Why so sure?" asked Bennett.

"It's the shoes. He's taken all his stuff, everything, but he's gone off in my shoes and left his own behind. I haven't time to tell you any more now because you're needed for a rehearsal. You're on as Hugo Merriman tonight."

Leslie was treated to another raising of the eyebrows, but Bennett offered no resistance. As they were going through the second pass door onto the side of the stage, Bennett put his hand on Leslie's shoulder and said, very quietly, "Have you mentioned the shoes to anyone?"

"No, I've said nothing."

146

Bennett nodded his endorsement and made his way onto the stage with a leisurely gait, seemingly unperturbed by this unexpected demand upon his talent.

There was little for Bennett to do in the play outside the two main scenes which he featured in with Leslie, and the abbreviated rehearsal went through splendidly. The burst of applause and congratulations from the cast members was interrupted by Kara who rounded on Leslie and said, furiously, "Why the bloody hell didn't you tell me he could do this? I'd have sacked Rawlison weeks ago. I only kept him on because I thought there was no one else."

She marched away to the sound of loud protests from the rest of the company which they did not try to disguise, even though Pippa was standing with them. Bennett was escorted downstairs for Tracey to find him a suitable shirt, cravat and jacket from the costume rail. There were no costume trousers as the men all supplied their own, and Leslie was in dismay at the pair Bennett was wearing, which were thin with age and concertinaed at the knees. However, by the time Tracey had gone to work on them with a starch spray and iron, they were no worse than Jim's.

"They'll pass muster from the stage," said Tracey, confidently.

"Let's hope I do," said Bennett, with his usual sardonic expression.

19

"At last!" exclaimed Leslie as soon as they were alone in the dressing room. "I can tell you all about it while we have tea—I suppose we'd better eat something."

Leslie took off his jacket and cravat and put on a dressing gown over the top of his remaining costume.

"I know that it looks like Roland has walked out on the show. Everyone heard what he said when he had that row with Kara, when the speakers were left on." Leslie opened the picnic basket and put the plates and cutlery onto the space which had been vacated by Roly. "But it was all talk. I asked him outright when he came back in here afterwards and he said he hadn't meant it. He said he'd never let the audience down and, I blush to recall it, there was some twaddle about not leaving me in the lurch."

Bennett raised a mocking eyebrow but, ignoring this, Leslie went on.

"And even if I'm completely wrong about his character, misjudged him or he changed his mind, there are the shoes. There they are, by the door. He has packed up all his belongings, every single item, and then gone off in the wrong shoes."

Leslie got out a tablecloth which he spread over Bennett's lap and then unclipped the lids from a couple of plastic boxes. Bennett observed in mute impassivity as Leslie adjusted the cloth to cover every inch of his trousers, and then put two small fig and goats cheese tarts on each of their plates, with some cherry tomatoes and a handful of grapes. Bennett took the plate and ate two of the tomatoes.

"Would your shoes fit him?" he asked.

"Oh yes, they're the same size," said Leslie, "and they're both black leather brogues. But Roland would never take someone else's shoes. I know you're the sort of person who could come home in a pair of women's carpet slippers by mistake, but Roland was the opposite. He was really particular."

"And you think," said Bennett, through a mouthful of tart, "that if he was sober enough to collect up all his belongings and leave the place without being seen, he was sober enough to put on the correct footwear?"

"Exactly," said Leslie. "I feel we ought to be doing something urgently, but I can hardly dial 999 and say that I'm worried about a grown man because he's gone off in the wrong shoes, can I? Especially when it looks like he's done exactly what he threatened to do."

Bennett ate in thoughtful silence.

"But, if he didn't take himself off, I can't imagine what has actually happened to him," said Leslie unhappily. "I wonder if anyone saw anything suspicious. The trouble is everyone's convinced he's just gone off to spite Kara. And if I start suggesting that he's come to some harm based on the shoes, they'll think I'm mad."

"Very likely," said Bennett, reaching for another tart from the box. "Apart from the malefactor, if there is one."

"Yes indeed. There's no way on earth that Roland mistook my shoes for his. My only conclusion is that he left the theatre in costume—in what manner I daren't imagine—and that someone else gathered up his belongings. All his stuff was together on the counter and hanging rail, except the shoes. We had them side by side at the door."

Bennett did not reply, and Leslie stood up restlessly. He took off his dressing gown and put on his outdoor jacket. "I'm going to go and have a look round outside. I know I'm not going to find a trail of footprints leading to his body slumped behind some hedge or parked car, but I've got to do something." He passed his plate of untouched food to Bennett. "I can't eat a thing."

"Just you leave that to me," said Bennett, taking the plate, his appetite clearly unaffected by the events.

"Damn, I've got no outdoor shoes, and I can't wear my stage ones, they'll get filthy out there. I'll have to use Roly's."

Feeling rather foolish, he examined the well-polished shoes closely for anything that might be a clue and, finding no secret note stashed in the toe, or mysterious blood stain on the sole, he put them on.

"I must say, they're a very nice pair of shoes—better than mine," said Leslie wryly as he laced them up. "And they fit perfectly."

"Not a bad swap," observed Bennett.

Leslie went up the exit stairs and out through the stage door, as this could surely have been the only way Roland could have left the theatre. He wedged the door ajar with the large bin that was there for this purpose, to be used, unofficially, when Brad wanted to sneak outside to smoke one of his dubious roll-ups.

It was a dark evening and there were no lights in this part of the grounds, so Leslie switched on his phone torch. He started by looking behind Terry's hire van, which was parked just outside the stage door, imagining a scenario where Roland had staggered out and fallen behind it in a drunken heap. He was not surprised to see nothing there and he set off anticlockwise round the edge of the theatre grounds, stooping uncomfortably to look under hedges, behind walls and around the various structures that comprised the environs of the theatre.

It had stopped raining, but Leslie was glad he had made the effort to change out of costume as dirty puddles, fallen leaves and dripping ledges and trees had to be negotiated. All he found was a depressing volume of rubbish. The bin store was the most unpleasant area to investigate. Four huge wheeled garbage containers were in a low pit, with their padlocked lids at ground level for easy loading. Leslie stepped tentatively down the slippery, leaf-strewn ramp to the base of the pit, a malodorous area into which piles of leaves and detritus had blown, and carelessly unloaded rubbish sacks had spilled. It was impossible for him to poke through the layer of filth, but his flashlight revealed that the bins fitted snugly into the deep recess and no adult, not even the slight figure of Roland, could fall, or be pushed between or behind them. However, it was the perfect habitat for rats and, on hearing a scuffling sound, Leslie retreated hastily from the area.

There were a few cars in the central car parking area, and early arrivals were just starting to trickle in for the evening performance, but if Roland had collapsed out in the open, the departing matinée audience would have seen him. So, Leslie kept to the perimeter, painstakingly searching the boundary of the car park. He was nearing the front of the theatre when he saw two of his Dartonleigh neighbours climbing out of their car, and having no time nor inclination to make conversation with them, he hurried inside.

Leslie shook his head in reply to Bennett's enquiring raised eyebrow and had just started to speak when there was a tap at the door, and a familiar "Yoo-hoo" in the corridor outside. At Leslie's answer Gloria bobbed her head in.

"I've come to see if you want a cup of tea or coffee, since you haven't joined us in the kitchen," she said. She looked at Leslie in his outdoor attire with an appraising eye. "The others said that Bennett must be mugging up on his lines, but I knew you were up to something. It's Roland, isn't it? But don't worry," and she made a little zipper action across her lips.

The beverage order taken, she disappeared, and Leslie quickly clambered back into his costume, exclaiming that Gloria could, at times, be irritatingly perceptive. He recounted the details of his fruitless search. He had no sooner changed than Gloria was back with the steaming mugs.

"I must just tell you," she said enthusiastically, "I've had it from Annie that everyone from Dartonleigh is in the audience tonight, absolutely everyone, and they're over the moon that you're in it too, Bennett."

This was not perhaps the most calming thing to say immediately before the performance, and Leslie gave a little groan, though Bennett appeared unmoved. She continued with even less diplomacy.

"And, I say, you'll never guess what! The whole company, all the deserters who have boycotted the production, are here, too. Can you believe it? Jim says they've come to watch because they think it's going to be a shambles and they want to gloat. Well, we'll show them, that's all I can say!"

On that note of valiant defiance, she left them.

Sue's voice came over the speakers giving them the fifteen minute call, and both men got into their remaining costume. Leslie felt terribly nervous. He had no doubt of Bennett's ability, but he knew that his own success in the last two shows had been because he had hidden in the shadow of Roland's celebrity. He would inevitably be more conspicuous now that he was on stage with Bennett, to say nothing of the fact that their Dartonleigh friends and neighbours would be watching their every move.

The call to the stage came over the speakers and, seized with sudden panic, Leslie said, "I've got The Forgetters again; I can't remember a thing."

"Rot," said Bennett, and he steered him through the door, to join the others issuing from their dressing rooms.

"I honestly thought old Rawlingson would turn up," said Jim, as they made their way up to the side of the stage. "He loves the limelight so much I thought he was just doing it to wind Kara up."

Leslie opened the door from the quick change area on the right side of the stage and stepped into the wings rigid with panic. He was immediately distracted from his stage fright, however, by the presence of a stranger. Though Leslie had never met him before, he recognised the face from the portrait in Kara's house, even in the subdued lighting. Even without that, the large surgical boot and crutches made the man instantly identifiable as Kara's injured husband Frank. A chair had been brought into the cramped space for him, and with his gammy leg and crutches protruding close to the pass door, which was also their fire exit, Leslie could not help thinking that Terry had been justified in his objections. However, since Terry was now chatting amicably with the invalid, it seemed that he had reconciled himself to Frank's presence. Terry beckoned Leslie over.

"This is the man you have to blame," he said to Leslie in a genial voice. "If it wasn't for him, you'd be at home with your feet up now."

"Cheers!" said Frank. "It's me with my feet, or rather foot, up instead. I can't say that it was worth it to get out of the play, but rather you than me on stage. I'm normally backstage helping Keith, or with a bit of a walk-on part. I only got roped in for a main part as a last resort. But you were brilliant this afternoon when I was watching, so at least it's worked out for the best in that sense."

Leslie started to protest but Frank, who seemed more of a talker than a listener, waved his crutch perilously at Bennett who was standing apart, and said, "And that's the chap who's stepped in at the last minute to save the show? I can't believe Rawlison's gone. It's the last thing I'd expect him to do, but I've heard all about the problems, so I guess—"

Whatever Frank was about to guess remained unsaid as they were all ordered to silence. Frank prodded Leslie with his crutch. "Break a leg," he hissed and, pointing at his own injured limb, threw his head back in silent laughter.

As Leslie and Bennett waited in the wings, there was an apologetic announcement over the speaker that Roland Rawlison was unable to appear. This generated an audible murmur from the audience, rapidly eclipsed by loud cheers and applause, presumably from the Dartonleigh contingent, when the substitute was announced. The two men looked at each other and Bennett gave Leslie one of his rare smiles. Leslie was momentarily transported back twenty-odd years when they had first met in a production of *HMS Pinafore*. The audience applause died down, the stage lights went up, the mics went on, and the curtain opened on the final performance.

The audience was everything a cast could hope for, laughing uproariously at the slightest trace of humour, clapping and cheering at every opportunity, and if there was any hostility from the non-participating members of LADS in the audience, it could not be perceived. Bennett was, of course, word perfect and, shunning any foolish attempt to imitate Roland, he made the part his own. It was a great success, and the humour worked as well when understated by Bennett as it had when overplayed by Roland.

Leslie was in buoyant mood at the interval and joined the others in the kitchen again, leaving Bennett to the solitude of the dressing room. It was only as they were going up for the second act that he was suddenly seized with a feeling of doom. He gripped Bennett's arm and held him back in the quick change area.

"You will be all right, won't you? I don't mean the play. It's afterwards I'm worried about. I know it's stupid, but Roly went off the stage and hasn't been seen since, and I'm terrified it's going to happen again. Promise me you'll go back to the dressing room and not move until it's time to come up for the bow."

"Can I have that in writing?" said Bennett. "It's a rare thing coming from you—an order that I'm not to go out."

Before Leslie could reply, they were ushered onto the stage and the curtain opened on act two.

20

The second act went through to loud cheers of approval from the audience and the atmosphere after the final curtain was jubilant. There was unanimous agreement that it had been a triumph and even Kara was sufficiently caught up with the moment that she was able to congratulate everyone in a vague and general kind of way, while conveying the impression that she was exclusively responsible for the success. Terry moved about distributing fulsome praise, but Leslie could see that the successful completion of the play had not removed the anxiety which lurked beneath the mask of joviality. Frank's congratulations seemed completely genuine, and he hobbled about, getting in everyone's way, until he was assisted down the steps to the pass door by Terry and steered out of peril.

As is the lot of amateur performers, they could not bask in glory for long, as there was the set to be struck, props collected up and boxed, costumes packed, and numerous other tasks that everyone had to turn their hand to. Gloria and Caroline shrewdly disappeared below to help Tracey with the costumes, leaving the men to assist Keith and the theatre staff to dismantle the stage. Pippa and Kara were, of course, nowhere to be seen.

Terry was, predictably, in complete control and stood on the ramp of the scenery dock, loading everything into the van. He resolutely refused any assistance with the loading, clearly having a precise method of arranging everything inside the van.

Leslie repacked the props. He could not believe that it was only three days ago that he had first taken them from their boxes—it seem like months had passed. With Keith, he carried them into the scenery dock and left them for Terry to load up.

Jim appeared, dragging one of the backcloth sacks which he left next to the prop boxes, and as they walked back to the stage, he said, "You'd think the bastards would have stayed to help, wouldn't you?" This was surprisingly ferocious language for him, but he did look rather tired.

"Perhaps we're better off without them," suggested Leslie, assuming he was referring to Kara and Pippa. "Kara, at least, has caused quite a lot of bad feeling and everyone is much more relaxed when she's not around."

"I don't mean her," said Jim. "The other buggers in the company. I can't believe it. They never came to help set up and I can't believe that they could sit through the whole production and then not come and help with the get out. There are usually dozens of people helping, and all we've got is a handful of us who are already knackered. God knows what time we'll get to the aftershow party."

Jim stomped off to help with the second backcloth, and Leslie went to find Bennett, who was languidly coiling a roll of cable on the apron of the stage.

"You know I had no intentions of going to the party," said Leslie, looking round to check that he could not be overheard.

He had been planning to sneak off home in a cab with Bennett after the performance, gladly shaking the dust of LADS from his sandals, as it were. He was going to break the news to Gloria only as he was departing, to avoid the inevitable pressure from her to attend, or the risk that she would be deterred from staying and insist on taking them home.

Bennett looked up from his task.

"But after Roly's disappearance," Leslie continued, "it might be a chance to find out if anyone saw anything. It'll probably come to nothing, but at least I'll know I tried. It's the last thing I feel like doing just now, but I'll regret it if I don't go. It's only round the corner, at The White Bear."

Leslie stooped and took hold of a tangle of thick black wire, found the end and started winding. "I'm wondering whether to mention the shoes," he said, lowering his voice even more. "If I do mention it, I guess some people will just dismiss it and think I've gone mad. But anyone who thinks twice about it will realise the inference."

"And," said Bennett, "if there is a guilty person present, they will know that you have realised the inference, which is perhaps more to the point."

"Exactly," said Leslie.

The two men wound the cables in silence. Leslie said, very quietly, "I've just thought of one possible innocent scenario. Suppose Roland got drunk again—suppose he brought a bottle with him or our saboteur eluded Gloria's observation. By the way, remind me to ask her about that later. But suppose Roly was too drunk to go on stage and phoned a friend to come and pick him up. The friend may have loaded Roly into the car and, if Roly gave him the pass numbers, the friend could have gone down and cleared the dressing room. That could explain the mix-up with the shoes."

Leslie paused as Keith came past, puffing under the weight of the heavy crate he was carrying. When he was out of earshot, Leslie continued. "I don't really believe it happened like that, but it goes to show that there may be some explanation we haven't thought of. Or something might yet come up that could shed light on the business. Anyway, what I'm trying to say is that I have an instinct to keep quiet about the shoes for now. What do you think?"

"Best go with your instinct. That's all there is at the moment."

Leslie picked up the final piece of wire and, shaking it to release the tangles, said in an uncharacteristically pleading voice, "You'll come to the party as well, won't you, Bennett? Please say you will, just for once."

Bennett tossed the final coil into a box with its compatriots and sighed. "At least they've got a decent bar at The White Bear," he said.

***

It was nearly midnight when they all trooped over to the pub for the party. Gloria's voice could be heard in cheerful conversation as she led the procession with Caroline and Tracey. Keith, Jim and James followed on, with Leslie and Bennett walking behind them. At the very back came Terry with the three technicians, Sue, Jezza and Sanjay who, during the evening performance, had made himself as pleasant and inconspicuous as Brad had been the opposite. Leslie overheard Gloria commenting on how nice it was that Terry had invited the theatre crew along, but Leslie cynically suspected it was a ruse to maintain his position with them.

They were soon at The White Bear and, to their united astonishment, the little room that had been booked was packed with the non-participating members of the company who, from their merry condition, had obviously been there since the end of the show. On one side of the room a trestle table held the remains of the party food, now consisting of a few dismantled and curling sandwiches, two large bowls containing some cold, limp chips, some chicken pieces abandoned on a large plate smeared with a dark sauce, into which someone had tossed a chewed bone, and a few more plates of party fare in a similar condition.

Kara sat at the far end of the room, champagne glass in hand, talking very complacently to a suave-looking middle-aged man. Frank was evidently telling a hilarious story, waving his crutch about to the peril of the large group gathered around him; Pippa was lounging in the corner with a young man of rugby-playing physique, both of them peering at their phones. This was presumably the boyfriend James had mentioned.

"Bloody hell!" exclaimed Jim, surveying the interlopers.

"I say," gasped Gloria, her eye on the decimated trestle table.

Leslie suddenly realised how hungry he was and wondered if it was worth staying, especially as he would have strongly preferred not to start asking questions about Roland with all these extraneous people around.

Terry came into the room, swore richly under his breath and strode across to the bar which opened into the room. He returned a minute later saying that he had ordered more food and that drinks for the cast and crew were on the house.

They were still hovering on the threshold, when one of the renegade company members spotted them and gave a whoop. Seconds later they were surrounded and being shamelessly congratulated as though these people had never shunned the production and abandoned them to all the hard work.

"Would you credit it?" said Leslie to Bennett, as they extricated themselves. "It's the most dysfunctional group of people I've ever had the misfortune to come across."

"It's a bit thick," said Jim indignantly, from within the crowd. "Coming in here and eating all the grub when you haven't lifted a finger to help."

"Put a sock in it, Jimbo," said one of the men, sloshing beer from an unsteady hand. "Don't you want any congratulations?"

"It'll be the only time you ever get any," called out another voice, and someone else jibed:

"At least you remembered some of your lines."

The novelty of being the centre of attention soon got the better of Jim and, assisted by a pint of beer, he visibly mellowed. Leslie went to the bar for drinks for himself and Bennett, and then the supplementary food arrived, after which he felt in better shape to mingle.

Without mentioning the shoes, Leslie realised it might be hard to explain why he was concerned about Roly's disappearance but he did not have time to worry about it as he wanted to speak to the whole cast and crew, and he had no idea how much longer the party would go on for.

He made a start with Caroline, who was, predictably, glued to Gloria's side. Gloria was delivering a panegyric in praise of Reiki massage, so it was difficult to interrupt the conversation, but eventually she broke off to tackle a sausage roll.

"It was such a relief that the show went so well, in spite of Roland's absence," said Leslie.

Gloria eyed him with interest as he launched into his prepared speech.

"Everyone says he has walked out, but I can't help being a bit worried about him."

"Why?" said Caroline. "What do you think has happened?"

"I wish I knew," said Leslie. "I wondered what time he left. Did either of you see him in the dressing rooms, or anywhere else?"

"I didn't go down to the dressing rooms, well not until after you had discovered he was missing," said Gloria. "I had nothing to go down for and it was far too much effort struggling on the stairs in that long gown. But you did, didn't you, Caroline? You forgot your water bottle, do you remember?"

"Yes," said Caroline defensively. "But I didn't see Roland. How could I have done? Why would I have gone to his dressing room?"

And with this she flushed scarlet and looked uncomfortably about her.

Affecting not to notice, Leslie said, "You didn't happen to notice anyone or anything strange at all? Nothing out of place?"

"No. No I didn't," said Caroline taking a step backwards. "I must... Please excuse me while I... while I get some food." She turned and hurried to the trestle tables carrying her plate which was still full.

"I say," hissed Gloria. "How about that?"

Bennett had been propping up the wall across the other side of the room. He wandered over with an amused look.

"You haven't been making suggestive remarks to the ladies again, have you?" he said to Leslie.

"You are a tease, Bennett," said Gloria and told him what had occurred.

Leslie had not expected to get such a reaction from any of them, certainly not his first target. However, there was no similar response from James who was brooding over the screen of his phone, no doubt agonising over the current goings-on of his girlfriend and her ex.

Leslie did not try leading up to the questions but just said, outright, that he was worried about Roland, and wondered if anyone had seen him in the dressing rooms before he left the theatre, or seen anyone who might have come to collect him. James looked blank. He couldn't remember if he had even been back to the dressing room, thought he'd probably gone down for a slash, as he delicately put it, but that might have been the evening performance on Friday. It didn't matter anyway because he hadn't seen Roland and didn't remember seeing anyone. Oh yes, except Pippy. She was coming out of her dressing room, and they went back up to the stage together. No, he couldn't remember which performance it was, but he thought it was probably the matinée. Pippy had gone down to the dressing room whenever she could so she would be the one to ask, though whether you'd get anything out of her was anyone's guess.

Pippa was still à deux with the boyfriend, and Leslie, lacking the fortitude to butt in, decided to postpone talking to her. Perhaps she would go to the buffet, alone, and he could intercept her.

It was easy to get Tracey and Keith to talk, as the disappearance of Roland was a hot topic. Tracey had been stuck in prompt the entire time and had nothing to say except that Leslie was wasting his time—the old sot had gone on the booze, and it was a pity he couldn't be bothered to change first as he'd gone off with his costume and there would be no end of trouble trying to get it back.

Keith had moved only between the stage and the scenery dock for the whole performance and agreed with Tracey that if Leslie had been with the company a bit longer, he wouldn't be worrying himself. True, Roland had never done this before, but he was gradually getting worse over the years. He would turn up in his own good time, but whether he would get a welcome back was debatable.

Sue, Jezza, and Sanjay were making short work of the food and free drinks, and it was easy enough to introduce the subject of Roland's disappearance. But it was a fruitless exercise. Sue had been at the control desk side-of-stage throughout so had not seen Roland since he went off stage; likewise Jezza was stuck in the sound and lighting box. Sanjay had not even been on duty for the performance, though he knew all about the disappearing actor, of course.

"Brad's the only one who could have seen him," said Sue, 'but he'd obviously have said something if he had. If he'd seen Rawlison leaving the theatre, there's no way he'd have kept it to himself. And if he'd seen someone prowling about, coming to collect him, or whatever it is you're suggesting," she said, with a puzzled frown, "you can be sure we'd all have heard about it. Brad's back on duty on Thursday. I'll ask him if you like and let you know. But don't hold your breath, I'm certain he'd have said something already if there was anything to say."

Sue was very pleasant, but Leslie could see she thought his questions rather odd, and he suspected that the whole thing would have been forgotten by the time Brad returned.

It took ages to get Jim on his own and when he did, Jim had nothing to add. He thought he'd gone down to the dressing room for a drink but couldn't be sure if that was the matinée or one of the other performances. But he hadn't seen Roland, which wasn't surprising as Roland would have taken care that no one saw him if he was sneaking off. To Leslie's dismay Jim turned to a group next to him and said, "Leslie here is worried about old Rawlingson. I've told him that the old tosspot's gone on a bender, but he won't believe me."

To Leslie's consternation he had suddenly become the centre of attention.

"I know he said he was going to walk out on the show, but he told me he wouldn't," said Leslie and instantly realised that he had struck the wrong note.

There was laughter, and among the muttered comments, he was sure he heard, "Better luck next time." Leslie tried to protest, but it made matters worse and the sniggering increased. It seemed they were determined to misunderstand him. Fortunately, Frank interrupted at this point.

"We're used to old Rawlison," he said. "He's done this before. That is to say he's never walked out of a show, but he has disappeared and can't be contacted, sometimes for weeks on end. He keeps his London address a closely guarded secret and even his agent couldn't get hold of him one time when we were trying to tie him down with dates for a show. When he eventually responded it turned out he'd gone off to stay with some friend in Liverpool or Manchester or somewhere up that way."

There was a general chorus, disparaging the poor actor who wasn't there to defend himself, and Leslie took the opportunity to sidle away.

He braced himself and approached Terry who, by now, knew that Leslie was making enquiries. He had seen Roland come off stage after his final scene and head straight for his dressing room without stopping, completely as normal. Terry pointed out that Roland was such a good actor that, if he'd been intending to disappear, you could be sure he wouldn't have given the game away.

"Look, if you're really worried, I'll do my best to track him down." Terry sounded friendly enough but there was another note in his voice, too—irritation, perhaps. "I'll go round to his house again tomorrow and see if he's back. But he'll have gone to London; that's his main address and he gives that out to no one. He never picks up messages at the best of times, but I'll keep trying. And I'll give his agent a call. You're worrying over nothing, though. He's a complete maverick, you don't know him like we do. He may have said all sorts of things to you, and even meant it at the time, but on the spur of the moment he's changed his mind and not even given a thought to whatever he promised."

Leslie fancied he heard all sorts of insinuations in this final sentence and he felt a complete fool. Terry walked past him to join the three technicians, and Leslie was about to creep back to Bennett in humiliation when Pippa walked by, with a plateful of buffet food. To his surprise she stopped and said:

"Why don't you ask her what she was doing snooping about in the dressing rooms during the performance?" She pointed a fork past Leslie's right shoulder. He turned around to discover that the subject of this unexpected accusation was, undoubtedly, Caroline, who was fortunately facing the other way. By the time Leslie turned around again, Pippa was on her way back to the boyfriend.

Leslie was about to go after her when he overheard one of the technicians, standing close by, referring to Bennett's performance in the play, and it was impossible not to pause for a moment and listen.

"I'd no idea that chap who understudied Roland Rawlison would be so good," said Jezza. "I was expecting the worst when they said someone was standing in at short notice, but he was really good."

"It was a miracle to find someone who could do the part," said Terry, "and I couldn't believe it myself when it all went through so smoothly."

"That performance went smoothly," said Jezza. "The other two were a nightmare, from a technical point of view. I think Rawlison put a jinx on us."

"What do you mean?" Terry asked.

"On Friday night the laptop blue-screened on me halfway through act one and I had to run the lights manually. Of all the shows to have to do manually! Then on Saturday, a fuse went in one of the moving spots, so I had to operate that manually as well."

"And don't forget the problem with the backcloth, in the matinée," Sue added. "Brad had to go up into the flies and unhook the garden cloth in the second act; you know that scene where the cloths had to be wiped quickly? The ties got snagged up. He was in a right strop about it."

"I didn't know all that," said Terry sharply.

"Good, that's how it should be," said Sanjay. "Something's gone horribly wrong when the cast or audience knows we've had a problem."

"But I'd expect to be told," said Terry, his displeasure showing.

There was an awkward silence and Leslie thought that Terry had overstepped the mark. Sanjay, who seemed less intimidated by him, said, "Sue was stage manager for the performance. She was the only one who needed to know."

Terry's transient annoyance had disappeared. "Of course, of course," he said affably. "It's just that, as the company chairman, I'm used to having to fix things myself, and there's usually nothing that goes on that I don't know about. Finger on the pulse, and all that. But I know you guys are always on top of everything."

With that he melted away into the crowd, leaving the three technicians staring after him and whispering under their breaths.

Leslie turned to the place where Pippa and her boyfriend had been sitting but it was empty, except for an abandoned plate of food. He looked round the room but there was no sign of Pippa or Kara anywhere, and they were the only two cast members he had not spoken to.

Leslie could have kicked himself for giving into curiosity and not having gone after Pippa straightaway. In truth he was glad to have missed Kara—it was impossible to imagine having a constructive conversation with her. However, Pippa's accusation against Caroline had to be followed up and now he had lost his chance.

21

It was the early hours of the morning before Gloria dropped them off at the cottage. They had left as soon as the party started breaking up, Leslie glad to escape and Gloria keen to get back to her daughter Gina, who was staying with her overnight after watching the performance. Bennett certainly put up no protest about heading for home. Despite the late hour, Gloria put out many feelers on the journey, but Leslie was too tired to satisfy her curiosity and eventually she took the hint, and they drove the last few miles home in weary silence.

***

The men slept in late the next day but as soon as Leslie was up and preparing Sunday brunch, he was impatient to discuss Roland's disappearance. He was preparing scrambled eggs when Bennett ambled into the kitchen with the newspaper rolled up under his arm. Just as Leslie was about to pour forth all his questions, concerns and ideas about the mystery, Bennett pushed a piece of paper across the table.

"Five letters," he said.

"Honestly, Bennett, you might know I'm wrestling with what's happened to poor Roly, and you expect me to look at one of your wretched clues." He turned over the bacon and gave the frying pan an irritated shake. "It's Roly's disappearance that I want to work out."

But he picked up the piece of paper nevertheless and studied it. "They fly off stage," he muttered, giving the frying pan another abstracted shake. "Five letters, you said?"

His rumination was interrupted by a ring at the doorbell. Bennett strolled to the front door and returned, followed by Annie from the tea shop bearing an apple pie, a bottle of wine and abundant praise. No, she wouldn't have a coffee—she could see that they were about to eat, and in any case, the tea shop was open, and she was needed. She would have called earlier but their curtains were shut, and she guessed they were having a late start. This was the problem with living in the centre of the village— sometimes it felt as though their lives were a stage performance.

Annie bustled away, but not before she had made Leslie promise that he would call in during the week to tell her all about what had happened to Roland Rawlison, and how Bennett came to be the star role. She had watched both evening performances and Bennett was just as good as the local celebrity, if not better, in her opinion.

Leslie flipped over the slices of mushroom and tomato which were just starting to sizzle in the frying pan and was about to tip the beaten egg into a saucepan when the doorbell rang again. Muttering something about Piccadilly Circus, Bennett plodded to the door once more and returned this time with the Dartonleigh chess club chairman, Martin, his wife, Sylvia and their wiry grey Lurcher, Cromwell. They had, they said, been walking the dog and had called in to say how much they'd enjoyed the play. No, they wouldn't stay as they could see that Leslie and Bennett were about to eat and, anyway, they had family coming for Sunday dinner. Leslie was relieved—he did not dislike dogs, but Cromwell was far too inquisitive and had once destroyed one of Leslie's favourite milk jugs with his wagging tail. Looking at the hound cavorting about the house now, Leslie feared the disaster may repeat itself.

While Cromwell capered about, snuffling for non-existent crumbs on Leslie's pristine floor, Martin and Sylvia congratulated Bennett on his part in the play, and asked what had become of the famous actor. For the want of something better, Leslie said that

Roland Rawlison had suddenly had to leave, but had not disclosed the reason to anyone. Yes, it had seemed strange to them as well but fortunately Bennett had rehearsed the part with Leslie so could step in at short notice. It was another five minutes before they left.

"If anyone else rings that bloody bell, hide under the table," Bennett said, opening the newspaper, "or we'll starve to death."

Leslie put four thin slices of sourdough bread into the toaster and poured the egg into the saucepan. He picked up the crossword clue again and looked at it while he stirred the pan. The toast popped up and at that moment the doorbell rang again. Both men uttered a similar expletive in unison, and Bennett said, "I'm not answering the door until I've eaten, if it's King Tut himself."

"Better had," said Leslie, who had looked through the window and seen a red open-top car parked in the lay-by. "It's Gloria."

Bennett put down the newspaper on the table with an exaggerated gesture of resignation. "She will not be triumphed over," he declared, which Leslie took to be a quotation.

Bennett was quite capable of discourteously keeping Gloria on the doorstep but, even if Leslie's nature could allow it, he knew that it would still be ages before she finished apologising for disturbing them and took her leave. Taking the line of least resistance, he refilled the toaster, broke three more eggs into a bowl, and called her in.

Gloria sallied into the kitchen, resplendent in her scarlet and gold wrap which she wore over a billowing dress made of a bright fabric patterned with parrots in the jungle. She was profuse with apology for disturbing them and would not dream of interrupting their breakfast—or was it lunch? It was only that she had just seen Gina off and she suddenly felt at a loose end. Gina was such a dear girl and such good company, and Gloria always missed her so when she'd left.

"I've put some toast in for you," said Leslie, pouring coffee from the cafetiere, "and there's plenty of scrambled egg for three, so sit yourself down."

Leslie plucked the newspaper, which was occupying half the table, from under Bennett's nose, folded it neatly, and passed Gloria the milk jug and sugar bowl. He piled scrambled eggs and chopped bacon onto the thickly buttered slices of toast and spooned the mushrooms and tomatoes onto the plate.

"*Oh, I say!*" said Gloria, emphasising each word. "What a feast."

Bennett doused his scrambled eggs with Worcester sauce, much to Leslie's disgust, and Gloria spooned a generous helping of ketchup onto hers, which was not much better.

There were a few minutes of reverent silence, punctuated only by Gloria murmuring ecstatically, "These mushrooms are heavenly," and, "Mm, so delicious."

"Well now," said Gloria, plucking toast crumbs from her impressive decolletage, "what about this business with Roland? What has happened to him? You must have a theory."

There was really no reason to keep anything from Gloria for despite her flamboyant loquacity they knew her to be trustworthy. In any case, she had a knack of wheedling out the information. Still, Leslie felt slightly cautious about what he should share and glanced across to Bennett. Bennett was studiously mopping up a small puddle of Worcester sauce left on the plate with the remainder of his toast and did not look up.

"I heard what you were saying at the aftershow party," she said, leaning forward eagerly, her multicoloured beads rattling against her plate. "And if you think that he didn't walk out on the show, then I'm sure you're right. You're such a good judge of character."

Leslie, who was collecting up the plates, disclaimed this accolade, adding, "But there was a bit more to it than I said yesterday."

Gloria gave a knowing nod and said, "Ah! I thought there was more to this than meets the eye."

"It was the shoes. He went off with my shoes. All his clothes and other belongings were gone, every item, but his shoes were left by the door, and mine had been taken."

There was a pause while Gloria digested the information. At last, she said gravely, "I guessed you suspected foul play, and now I can see why. That natty-dressing little man wouldn't go off in someone else's footwear, not even for a joke. You didn't mention it yesterday?"

"No, and I'm not sure why. I just had a feeling it would be better not to say anything about it."

"Always go by intuition," agreed Gloria. "And if in doubt, say nothing, that's my motto." This was an extraordinary maxim coming from the garrulous Gloria. "You can always say something at a later date, but you can never un-say anything."

"Of course, my feelings might be completely wrong—I hope so. There could still be an innocent explanation."

Leslie repeated to Gloria the scenario he had thought of the previous day, where the drunk Roland was collected from the theatre by a friend.

"I suppose so," said Gloria doubtfully. "But I'd be very surprised if Roland could have given anyone the access codes, even when stone-cold sober. On more than one occasion, I found him waiting by the door for someone to come along and let him through. I offered to write the numbers down for him, but he said the only notes he carried round had the monarch's head on them."

Leslie nodded agreement. Roland had complained bitterly to him about the security doors and said that, although he could recite someone-or-other's soliloquy word perfect and without rehearsal, he couldn't remember a four-digit PIN to save his life.

"And did the dressing room smell of alcohol when you found him gone?" asked Bennett.

"No, not a whiff," said Leslie. "I didn't think of that. The previous evening when he was drunk, the place reeked. Anyway, I didn't seriously think that scenario was true, I was just putting it forward as a hypothetical example."

"Funnily enough," said Gloria, "I've had a few hypothetical ideas of my own. Why don't I tell them to you, and let's see which of those we can dismiss, too?"

She leant down to rummage in her capacious bag, somehow sweeping two teaspoons and a knife to the floor.

"Oh, I say! Oh really! Dear me!" she exclaimed cheerfully, as a phone, a powder compact, and a tube of sweets sprung from her bag to join the cutlery on the floor.

As Leslie grovelled about retrieving the errant items, Gloria unfolded a sheaf of closely written pages. It was obviously going to be a long morning and Leslie suggested they took their coffee through to the lounge. The day was overcast, but it was mild, and with the wide French windows looking out onto Leslie's well-ordered garden, it was always a pleasant place to sit. They settled themselves down for Gloria's discourse.

"First of all," she said, consulting the top sheet of paper, "I discount the idea that Roland walked out of his own accord, for all the reasons that you gave, and now I can add in the shoes as well."

There was a pause while Gloria explored the depths of her bag for a pencil, and then made the addition to her notes. "And don't forget those awful words written across his picture in the dressing room corridor. In lipstick. We know he had at least one enemy."

Leslie had, of course, told Bennett about the defaced poster.

"And if Roland felt ill and went outside for some fresh air and collapsed," Gloria continued, "he would have been found by now, and he wouldn't have taken all his things with him. If he'd been called away for an emergency, he would have at the very least left a note and would have gone off in the correct shoes."

She paused again, this time to drain the coffee from her mug. "So," she said, dramatically, "it looks as though someone had a hand in it and the poor man has come to no good. But who could it be?"

Leslie took advantage of this cliffhanger to top up their mugs from the cafetiere.

Taking a deep breath and, exhibiting her flair for suspense, Gloria started with the members of the cast she thought the least likely. She began by eliminating James, as he was new to LADS, could have no connection to Roland, and no one could imagine that quiet young man harbouring some murderous intent.

She had not seen his face when he thought he was being two-timed, Leslie thought, but he did not interrupt the flow.

Tracey, too, she discounted as she had been stuck in prompt the whole time so, even if Gloria could dream up a reason for her wanting to murder Roland, which she could not, she had no opportunity.

"Now what about Caroline?" Gloria said, darkly. "I rule her out of any direct involvement, of course. She's obviously a poor thing who wouldn't hurt a fly and can have had no possible motive. And as she followed me round like Mary's lamb, I know that she had no opportunity, either. But she knows something. Her reaction when you questioned her was very telling. I believe she saw something and for some reason, she doesn't want to say. She might be shielding someone. But I'll get it out of her, don't you worry."

Having eliminated these bystanders from direct action, Gloria paused to galvanise herself with a drink. It was easy to belittle her approach but Leslie had to confess to himself that, so far, she reflected his own thinking even if he would not have expressed his ideas in the same way.

Gloria continued. Jim, she confided, seemed a very decent man but he had been with LADS for quite a long time so, unlikely as it seemed, he could not be ruled out of having a hidden motive.

He was a big chap who could have physically overpowered Roland with ease.

Leslie asked how, given the demands of the performance, Jim would have had the opportunity. With the triumph of someone who has thought of everything, Gloria replied that he could have had an accomplice.

"I don't really think Jim is the culprit," she clarified. "I'm just not ruling him out completely. It's the same with Keith. He's a perfectly lovely old chap but he does go back a long way with LADS, and he's lived in the town all his life, like Roland. There could be a dark secret. Like Jim, he's a big man. He could make mincemeat of Roland, though of course it's impossible to imagine him wanting to make mincemeat of anyone. But still, he could have secretly slipped away from the scenery dock at some time so, to be scrupulously fair, I won't cross him off."

Gloria turned to the next sheet and spent a moment glancing down the page to marshal her thoughts. Bennett, leaning back in his chair with his fingertips together, stared into space, completely inert. Leslie gazed at the gently waving trees in the garden and was seized by the unreality of it all. Gloria's ingenuous manner made the whole thing seem totally ridiculous, but perhaps it was ridiculous. Perhaps Roland had simply got it into his head to wreck the production, to pay back Kara as he saw it, and had taken Leslie's shoes for a souvenir. Was that any less believable than that someone had abducted or murdered him, and done so without leaving a trace?

"Now to Terry," resumed Gloria. "He is also a local man and has known Roland for a long time, like Jim and Keith. And he and Roland did not always seem to be on friendly terms although it was the wrong way round—it always seemed to me that it was Roland who made himself unpleasant to Terry. Still, like Jim and Keith, we can't rule him out completely."

There was now a change in Gloria's manner and Leslie sensed that they were moving on to her serious suspects. Requesting a short intermission, he went through to the kitchen and refilled the cafetiere to fortify them for the approaching finale.

"So that brings me to Kara and Pippa," said Gloria. She leant forward and the parrots on the magnificent bodice of her dress eyed the two men keenly. "I would have discounted Pippa at the outset, even though she wasn't on stage very much and ran straight down to the dressing room at every available moment. She hasn't got enough go in her to swat a fly let alone murder a man. But being Kara's daughter, I thought she might have been dragged into it by her mother."

Leslie poured fresh coffee all round and awaited the denouement.

"As for Kara, she is surely the most likely. She clearly despised Roland. Those lipstick words on the picture look just her style. Did you know that he once made a fool of her on stage, and she's never forgiven him? And he was very rude and provoking toward her at the rehearsals, you both saw it for yourselves. What's more, she vowed she'd kill him when they had that dreadful row that we all overheard. What more do you need?"

"But that was a reaction to a dreadful thing Roland had just said about Terry and her daughter," Leslie pointed out. "Anyone could have said that. I'm not sure it counts as a serious threat. And people don't really go round killing just because someone makes a fool of them."

"That wouldn't be enough of a motive for murder in a normal person, I agree, but she really is abnormally unpleasant, don't you think? I realise that Kara couldn't have done it alone, but perhaps with Pippa, and perhaps another accomplice, it could somehow have been achieved."

"Surely if it was anyone in the cast who did it, they would have needed an accomplice," Leslie said. "It's impossible that anyone could have gone to the dressing room, done away with poor Roland, packed up his stuff and dragged his body up those stairs and out of the theatre. No one had time for that and a man's body, even Roland's, would be impossible to move any distance without two strong people. I confess I can't imagine how it was done, or by whom. The more I think about it, the less credible it seems."

"The fact remains that he has disappeared," said Gloria.

"Perhaps everyone else is right after all and Roland has simply gone off to spite Kara," said Leslie. "Or there is some factor that we know nothing about, and someone not related to the cast or the show is responsible for his disappearance."

"Yes indeed," agreed Gloria. "I thought of that, too." She turned to another sheet of paper and tapped at a line on the page with her pencil. "Person or persons unknown. Someone from outside, with a past grudge. But that does leave the field wide open—so unsatisfactory." She sighed sadly, as if disappointed by the idea of the crime having been committed by a stranger.

"Anyone coming in from outside would have had to get through the pass doors, all with security codes, and know when and where to find Roland," said Leslie who had already worked through this in his own mind. "If they had inside knowledge, I suppose they could have slipped downstairs and hidden in the showers, say, until they knew the coast was clear. But what a risk; a couple of strangers wandering about backstage would be instantly suspicious. And why would outsiders choose a time when Roland was at the theatre to... to do whatever has been done to him? Led him away at gunpoint after he had gathered up all his belongings, leaving the wrong shoes as a cry for help?"

"Now there's an idea," said Gloria, and added it to her list.

"No, the whole thing is beyond belief," said Leslie, firmly.

They fell into gloomy silence and after a while Gloria said, with uncharacteristic reticence, "Now I did have one final idea on my list, rather different from the others. I don't want you to be cross with me, Leslie, as I'm sure you know me well enough by now to know..." The sentence trailed off enigmatically. "In this scenario, no one else was involved, and Roland took himself off, but not for the reasons Kara and Terry and all the others think." There was a dramatic pause; Gloria pursed her lips and Leslie wondered what on earth she was about to come out with. At last she continued. "I did get the impression that Roland thought rather well of you, Leslie; he was perhaps a little fond of you." She spoke with more confidence now but still blushed a deep shade of crimson. "Now I did just wonder if he'd suffered a disappointment, a personal one you understand, and left the theatre in a state of emotion."

This was the only scenario that had not occurred to Leslie, and he was about to dismiss it vigorously when he remembered Roly's earnest entreaties, even with tears in his eyes. It was a most unwelcome conjecture. He said, reluctantly, "You're quite right that Roland had, for some unaccountable reason, taken a shine to me and that I'd made the position pretty clear."

"I don't know why you say unaccountable," said Gloria. "You'd be such a catch for anyone. If things were otherwise, well I—"

"Really! Gloria!" interrupted Leslie and it was his turn to blush.

"Don't get swollen-headed," Bennett interposed, giving Leslie a sardonic look. "It's only your cooking everyone's after."

"Nonsense!" protested Gloria. "But back to Roland. Of course, I didn't know about the shoes when I compiled my list. If he was too distraught to recognise his own shoes, he wouldn't have gathered up everything else so tidily. And if he'd wanted to take some memory of you with him, it would have been a little keepsake he could put in his pocket, not a pair of shoes. No indeed."

Gloria drew a line diagonally across the page and the theory was scotched.

"There now," she said, "those were my thoughts. What do you think?"

Leslie could find nothing to say. Each of Gloria's suggestions was more improbable than the last, and none of them offered a shred of evidence or plausibility. But the fact remained that Roland had disappeared, unaccountably, and with the wrong shoes.

Bennett looked across. "Why the matinée?" he said.

They stared at him.

"If there was a crime, why did it happen at the matinée?" repeated Bennett.

"Oh, I say!" said Gloria, and she thought for a moment. "I don't know. Does there have to be a reason?"

"Everything has a reason," said Bennett. "Except when it doesn't."

He opened out the newspaper that he had brought through with him, evidently fatigued with the discussion, and resumed his earlier reading.

"Well," said Gloria, taking the hint and stirring herself. "As for reasons, there was another reason I called in. I wanted to invite you to tea at the shop on Tuesday, Leslie."

Leslie eyed her suspiciously. He had got to know Gloria well since she moved into the area, and they had frequently had teas or lunches together, but never at her health store. He suspected an ulterior motive.

"I'd love you to see my little shop now that it's been extended. I've enough space to give you tea there now, and I'd like to after so many wonderful meals here. Not that there will be anything home-made, I'm afraid. I wouldn't attempt to compete with you."

She beamed at him and Leslie waited.

"And Tuesday would fit in so well. You see, Caroline has an appointment with me in the afternoon. She's having a reading done; always such a good opportunity to break down barriers. The crystals are so efficacious, I always find. Then, if I can persuade her to stay to tea as well, we might be able to get to the bottom of her little secret. I'm sure she'll feel so much better to get it off her chest."

Leslie hesitated, but it was certain that Caroline had been concealing something, and this might be their only chance to find out what it was. And he remembered Pippa's extraordinary claim about Caroline snooping. He agreed and, with raptures of joy from Gloria, they made the arrangements.

Gloria stood up to take her leave. She gave a sudden gasp and swept to the French windows. "Well, look at that!" she exclaimed. From the grey sky, a single shaft of sunlight fell on a tub of marigolds outside on the patio, and they were illuminated like fire. "A sign!" she said, breathlessly. "And the first positive one for a long time."

***

Leslie saw Gloria to the door and returned to the sitting room a few minutes later carrying a raincoat. "Isn't this Roly's?" he said. "How come it was hanging up in our porch?"

"It was in the dressing room," said Bennett, glancing up from the newspaper. "Hanging up behind the shower door. I saw it when I was scouting round during act two, after I'd finished on stage."

"Oh yes, Roly put it in there to dry. If you remember, it was raining yesterday when we arrived at the theatre. In fact, that's how come our shoes were together just inside the dressing room door and not with the rest of our stuff."

Leslie held the coat out and looked at it. "I saw it in the car last night, but thought it was something to do with Gloria. I didn't see you bring it in but that's not surprising, given all the clutter we seemed to have. I take it you've checked the pockets."

"No clues," confirmed Bennett.

"So, Roland went without his shoes and his raincoat," said Leslie. "Does that change anything?"

"I shouldn't think so," said Bennett. "Whatever reason his shoes were left probably applies to the coat as well."

"Still, I won't be happy until I've reported all this to the police. Despite everything, I know in my heart that something untoward has happened to Roly and I'm prepared to risk derision."

Leslie's previous experience in reporting issues to the police had not been positive.

"You can stop worrying," said Bennett. "I've already called Charles and he's going to try and drop by tomorrow, meetings permitting."

"Thank heaven for that," said Leslie, and returned to the kitchen to bake a cherry cake.

Detective Chief Inspector Charles Ridgeway was Bennett's chess partner and a friend of both men, but this would not be the first time they had been involved with him in his professional capacity. The chief inspector was amply rewarded for his friendship and services by Leslie's generous hospitality, and the cherry cake, now occupying Leslie's time, was his favourite.

A short time later, Bennett roved into the kitchen, in the hope, no doubt, of a spoon to lick or a bowl to scrape. Leslie was stirring cherries into the mixture, and he looked up.

'Wings,' he said triumphantly, holding up the piece of paper with Bennett's crossword clue on it in his free hand. "They fly off stage. Wings! I don't know if I would have got it if I hadn't just been in the production. I expect I've got 'wings' on my mind at the moment."

Bennett picked up the discarded wooden spoon and licked it thoughtfully.

22

"I'll never be able to hold my head up in the village again!" Leslie burst into the library the following morning, and Bennett looked up from his work, inclining his head in mild enquiry. "It's utterly humiliating," Leslie exclaimed. "We'll have to leave the village."

Bennett rose and led the way through to the kitchen, the proper place in the house for heated discussions. Leslie dumped his shopping bag down and filled the kettle.

"It seems that Gloria's idea that Roly has gone off because I rejected him wasn't Gloria's idea at all. She got it from Tracey who has only gone and suggested the idea to her mother-in-law. And you know what Vera is like—Mouth Almighty. Everyone who has been into the shop this morning has been given the glad tidings and they've spread the word in the post office and The Daffodil. That's how I found out. I went in to see Annie and the place virtually fell silent. She broke it to me—it's been the talk of the tea shop all morning. They're actually suggesting I had an affair with him!"

To Leslie's fury, he saw the corner of Bennett's mouth twitch, though Bennett did have the discretion to take out a handkerchief and pretend to blow his nose.

"It's all very well for you," he said angrily, "you don't have to look these people in the eye, festering in here all day long as you do. How can I face them when I know what they're all saying? An affair! At my age. With Roland Rawlison. It's more than embarrassing—it's completely mortifying."

He slammed the cafetiere on the table and scooped the coffee in moodily. "One of the best things about this village is that I've never felt talked about, or at least no more talked about than anyone is in a village. Even living right in the middle under everyone's nose. We've always said what a civilised place it is."

"Gossip's fine until you're the subject of it," said Bennett.

Leslie could think of no rejoinder to this, and he stomped round the kitchen as he put his shopping away and made coffee. His wrath always subsided quickly, and at last he had to admit to himself the truth of Bennett's observation. Rumours were endemic in the village, and they spread with astounding rapidity, especially scandalous news. Leslie found it just as absorbing as anyone, though he usually managed to maintain the appearance of discreet detachment. But he had never been the focus of out-and-out scandalmongering before or, at least, not to his knowledge.

"It's the Roland Rawlison effect," said Bennett. "Everyone likes a spicy story about the local celeb."

"That's all very well," said Leslie, petulantly, "but I didn't ask to get caught up in it. We'll have to move back to London— there's nothing else for it." He pushed the plunger down in the cafetiere. "It might help if we could find out what's really happened to Roland, but at the moment there seems to be a fat lot of chance of doing that."

This catastrophising mode, brought about by exhaustion from the efforts of the show and fatigue because he could not put it behind him as he had expected, was fortunately interrupted by the sight of a car pulling up along the road and the familiar figure of Charles Ridgeway alighting from it.

The chief inspector seemed taller and thinner than ever and, as usual, scooped three spoons of sugar into his mug and cut himself a giant wedge of cherry cake. Leslie sometimes wondered if he ate between visits to them.

"So, tell me what our local celebrity has been up to now," he said, brushing the crumbs carefully from his fingers onto the plate. "This cake is superb, Leslie."

Ridgeway had the art of listening, and interpolating occasional questions which guided the conversation quickly to the point.

"So," he said, when Leslie had finished explaining, "Roland Rawlison has disappeared in the middle of a local production, wearing the wrong shoes."

"Exactly," said Leslie. "And I'm positive that something's happened to him, that is, until I try to come up with an explanation, and then I start to doubt myself."

"Quite," said the chief inspector equably. "Rawlison took his wallet, keys, phone and cards with him, and there are plenty of men who could put on the wrong shoes. One of my sergeants came to work in a non-matching pair once and didn't notice, even though one of the shoes was his son's, a size smaller."

"But Roland wasn't like that," said Leslie plaintively. "And don't forget there had been rows and threats."

"True, there was animosity towards the man. But apart from the shoes, you must admit that there is precious little evidence that any foul play has occurred. No sign of an assault, and the difficulty of explaining how an abduction, or anything similar, could have taken place."

"Yes," agreed Leslie, miserably. After all, he had dismissed the threats as mere angry talk when Gloria had raised the subject. "It's too ridiculous. I'm sorry I've wasted your time."

"Most people who are reported missing turn up safe and well within forty-eight hours, but I'm here now, and it's worth it for this cake," Ridgeway laughed. "I might as well look at this list of people who were backstage."

He took another bite of the cake as he read the list of names which Leslie had drawn up before his arrival, starting with his chief suspects and with notes beside each of the names. "You suggest that the person with the obvious grudge was the director, Kara Anderton. And Pippa Anderton is her daughter?"

"Yes. And Kara has been utterly vile to just about everyone in the company," said Leslie. "She's one of the most unpleasant people I've ever come across—quite pathological, I'd say."

"Yes," put in Bennett. "And I'm just picturing her coshing Roland with her parasol and carrying his inert body up the stairs, with her lovely daughter, in their long Victorian frocks."

Leslie tried to be annoyed at Bennett's flippant interruption, but he had to smile at the image it conjured up. "Whether or not she had anything to do with Roland's disappearance," he said after a pause, "I wouldn't be a bit surprised if it was Kara who wrote that abuse across his picture in a fit of temper."

"You didn't happen to take a photo of it, did you?" asked Ridgeway.

"Unfortunately not," said Leslie. "It never occurred to me, but of course we didn't know then that Roland was going to vanish. And speed was of the essence to clean the writing off before anyone else saw it, and word got back to him. Do you think it's really connected?"

"It would have been good to have had a look at it," mused Ridgeway, noncommittally, and he took another bite of cake thoughtfully. "What do you think about it, Bennett?"

"Hard to be sure. But whatever has happened to Roland looks carefully planned and premeditated, whereas the graffiti seems more like an outburst of rage. That doesn't mean they're not connected, of course. It might, for example, be a blind, to throw suspicion on a hot-tempered wearer of red lipstick."

"Anyone could pick up red lipstick in a theatre," observed Leslie, "so it doesn't narrow it down very much."

Ridgeway turned back to Leslie's notes. "You've marked the company chairman as a possible suspect: Terry Wiseman," he said.

"Yes," said Leslie. "But to be honest it's probably because I don't much like him, either. There's something very oily about him. There was said to be bad feeling between the two men but really it was Roland who loathed Terry. Terry was forever trying to mollify him."

Ridgeway made a few of his own notes on the page.

"Now, what about this theatre technician, Brad?"

"It's a very long shot, but there was a run-in between him and Roland. It was a silly thing over lighting, but Brad is rather a nasty piece of work, too—quite sinister. He made some threatening remarks, but I can't remember his exact words. He was going to get his own back— you know the sort of thing."

"And what's this cryptic comment by Caroline Tibbs' name?"

With an irrational feeling that he was betraying the poor lady, Leslie described her reaction to his innocent questions, and then Pippa's unexpected comment.

"If you met Caroline," said Leslie, "you couldn't possibly imagine her directly involved in Roland's disappearance. But maybe she saw something. I hate to mention it, but she's got a terrific crush on Terry and if, for example, she'd seen him coming out of our dressing room, or something like that, she might keep it to herself."

"It might be something totally unconnected," said Ridgeway. "Perhaps she was poking about to see if anyone had left a bit of cash lying around in the dressing rooms. The most innocent-looking people have their little peccadillos, and it's surprising how many unrelated crimes come to light in an investigation."

"I might be having tea with her tomorrow," said Leslie, "and if I find out anything relevant, I'll obviously let you know."

"I might have known you'd be on the case already," said Ridgeway, accepting a second slice of cake. "Do feel free to spare me any irrelevant indiscretions or fetishes that might come to light."

"I'll certainly try and steer clear of anything like that," laughed Leslie.

The chief inspector turned to Bennett. "You're looking very thoughtful. Are you about to come out with something profound?"

Bennett was stretched back in his chair. "I don't know about that," he said looking up. "But I think that if I was planning to do away with a well-known actor, and wanting to cover my tracks, I would not have chosen the matinée performance to do it."

"Surely that was to reinforce the idea that he had disappeared in order to wreck the production," said Leslie.

"Why try to give that impression? Why draw any attention to it at all?" said Bennett. "If Roland had vanished during the final performance, then all that he would have been absent for was the bow; everyone in the cast would have said that he'd stomped off, inebriated or in a huff, after he'd said his final lines. He would hardly have been missed, certainly not by the public, apart from some mutterings because he hadn't come back on at the end. A much quieter way and much less likely to cause suspicion or immediate follow up. Instead, the perpetrator must have expected that the evening performance would be cancelled and then Roland's disappearance would have attracted much more attention. Don't forget, it couldn't have been predicted that I was going to stand in for him."

"Could it have been a publicity stunt, then, by Rawlison? I believe he was famous for such things in the past," said Ridgeway. "What are you suggesting, Bennett?"

"I'm suggesting nothing at the moment."

Ridgeway sighed. "There's not much to go on but I'll log it as a missing persons enquiry," he said. The chief inspector folded the sheet of paper into his pocket. "And I can class him as vulnerable, as an alcoholic. If he really has gone AWOL, we can make a start with the people on this list. And I can get someone to check the theatre CCTV; that might give us a clue to his movements. To be honest, I think we'll find Rawlison at home in a day or so with nothing worse than a hangover."

"I do hope so," said Leslie doubtfully. "But if you do, for heaven's sake don't say I reported him missing as a vulnerable person."

"How art the mighty fallen," sighed Bennett.

The chief inspector reluctantly rose to his feet and took his leave, no doubt to go to one of his numerous meetings, and Leslie topped up the cafetiere.

"We couldn't have expected much more than that," said Leslie, "and if we'd reported it to the police in the normal way, I expect we'd have been sent away with a flea in our ear at this stage."

"Charles is a good chap," said Bennett, picking up his mug and heading for the library.

23

The following afternoon found Leslie scuttling, head down, along a track behind The Daffodil Tea Shop. He was making for the bus stop on the main road, to keep his tryst with Gloria at her health store in Temple Ducton. Normally he walked through the village centre and would not consider using this rough and dirty path unless he was late and needed to take the shortcut through the fields. But today, still acutely embarrassed by the gossip about Roland's departure, even muddy shoes were preferable to meeting any of his friends or neighbours. He skulked along the pathway, praying for solitude on the journey.

His wishes were fulfilled and there was no one at the bus stop, nor anyone on the bus that he knew beyond a nodding acquaintance, and he sat on his own at the back. He did his best to enjoy the ride, for the route was very pleasant and he rarely came out in this direction. Temple Ducton was the sort of place one might go for a scented candle or an organic cotton T shirt, or one of Gloria's cures, so his visits were infrequent. The journey took them off the main road here and there into those of the pretty little hamlets where the lanes were just about wide enough to accommodate a bus. He gazed out as they passed thatched cottages and bumped over narrow bridges, crossing bubbling streams and brooks, all typical of the area.

Leslie always viewed the passing of the year in colour and, even though most of the trees were still well leafed with green, there were definite signs of early autumn—the red season. In neighbouring Ilstone, a huge Virginia creeper covered The Carpenter's Arms in brilliant crimson, and in the cottage gardens along the way, rich red dahlias and chrysanthemums nodded their heads. A mile or so further along, they rounded a tight bend in the road, and a beautiful maple flapped its ruby leaves against the bus window. Admiring all these objects of beauty as they trundled along, Leslie fought off the bittersweet melancholy that so often accompanies the onset of autumn. He had anxieties enough without plunging into existential gloom.

Due to the constraints of the bus timetable, Leslie was very early for his meeting with Gloria and, anxious not to impose himself before he was expected, he alighted from the bus just outside the town. It was a peaceful stroll; the river meandered lazily alongside the lane on one side, and on the other stood a row of elegant houses, punctuated by The Heritage Museum and The House of Glass, both shut during the week now that the tourist season was over.

The town was certainly a picturesque place with its narrow streets and stone bridge, and flanked, as it was, by an attractive park, but it had the deserted air of most tourist spots when the visitors have gone away. Leslie came first to a tempting cheese shop. He knew it was scandalously expensive but, happy to support the local economy, he went in. An elderly lady, engrossed in a conversation with the shopkeeper, looked across as the bell on the door clanged and she greeted Leslie with a strong Devonshire accent that was rarely heard in these parts, certainly not in Dartonleigh where most of his friends came from Surrey.

After a pleasant time browsing the shelves, Leslie put a jar of caramelised onion chutney and some thin rye crackers into his basket. He was at the refrigerator, toying between a smoked and a blue cheese, both of which he could get far cheaper even in Dartonleigh's village store, when the elderly lady suddenly exclaimed, "You be in that play at Lymeford on Saturday! I knew I knowed you!"

Leslie expressed astonishment that she should recognise him, and the old lady said that she never forgot a face, especially as she didn't get out much these days.

"My Polly here"—she indicated the lady behind the counter—"she do take me to see her friend who be in it."

"It was very good," Polly said, in a voice which was markedly Devonian but much less idiomatic than her mother's. "We went to see the lady in the health food shop—Gloria's her name. Lovely lady, she put posters up all over the town."

"And she be wonderful in it. It were a wonderful show, wonderful." The old lady sighed.

"But we've been wondering," Polly said, lowering her voice, "what happened to what's-his-name—Roland Rawlison? He didn't take his bow. They do say as how he has a fondness for the bottle. You were in the play so you must know."

Taken off-guard, Leslie muttered that he hadn't been told the reason why the actor had gone, and the two women exchanged knowing glances. Leslie hastily bought a piece of both cheeses and fled the shop, his gloom deepening. Who knew what rumours might be flying round even in this neighbourhood? Not daring to encounter anyone else, Leslie eschewed the delicatessen and the bakers, not to mention the eco-homeware store and the organic jewellery shop, and made straight for Gloria's.

It was a bow-fronted shop with leaded-light windows, full of olde-worlde charm, with the legend *Healing Temple* above the entrance. The shop assistant, a young woman, approached him as soon as he stepped inside. "Are you Leslie?" she asked, politely. "I saw you in the play on Saturday. It was very good."

"Goodness! I know what it's like being a film star now. Never mind," he added, seeing the woman's enquiring expression.

"Gloria's expecting you," she said. "She told me to show you round the shop and then put you in her office if you got here early. She's doing a consultation with a client at the moment." She nodded her head towards a door behind them.

Leslie had been to Gloria's shop before, but it was not long after she had started it up and he was surprised at the changes. He knew that she had since bought the next-door property but was not prepared for quite how significantly it had been upgraded. It was now quite an emporium. There were sections for health foods, natural remedies and cosmetics, but there was also a large area for Gloria's particular penchant—crystals—and other aids to divination. Two doors led into what had been the neighbouring shop, now the consulting room at the back and Gloria's office at the front where, in due course, Leslie was shown in and instructed to help himself to a drink.

It was a large and very comfortable room and, although it was furnished with a desk and computer, there was also a settee and soft chairs, and the ambiance was more like a sitting room. The outlook, directly onto the street, with shops, a small art gallery and café opposite, was perfect for gratifying Gloria's inquisitive nature.

Leslie was just examining the tray of beverages and reflecting that apart from a couple of sachets of fruit tea, there was little evidence of the shop's own products, when he heard Gloria's unmistakable voice. The door swung open revealing the lady herself, resplendent in a scarlet and gold kaftan with a chain of huge gold pendants resting on the shelf of her bosom. Hovering in her shadow was Caroline, in grey trousers and a beige cardigan.

"You really must come in and have a cup of tea," Gloria was saying to the limp form behind her. "I absolutely insist."

"I don't like to butt in," said Caroline.

"Nonsense," said Gloria guiding her into the room. "I know that Leslie's looking forward to seeing you, aren't you, Leslie?"

"I certainly am," he replied, and it was truthful in one sense. "Gloria said you would be here, so I brought enough cakes for three. There's some cherry cake I baked yesterday and some Florentines I made this morning."

Giving in to the invitation, Caroline perched herself on the edge of a high-backed chair. "What a lovely room this is," she said.

"I do like to be comfortable," Gloria replied as she made the drinks and laid out the cakes and little biscuits that Leslie had brought, adding some luxury cookies from a packet.

"Everyone is so kind," said Caroline in a wavering voice, "and I feel I don't deserve it."

"What nonsense," Gloria asserted. "No one has to deserve kindness, and if they did you would deserve it just as much as anyone."

"Gloria's marvellous," said Caroline turning to Leslie. "She's incredible." She looked down at her plate and broke the Florentine biscuit into little pieces. "To be honest, I was a bit sceptical about all this before I came. I did admit that openly, as I didn't want to come under false pretences. But those crystals—they may only look like a few old stones, but they're magic."

Gloria glowed with gratification and said, through a mouthful of cherry cake, "Oh yes, it's all in the stones."

"But it's what Gloria makes of them that is so amazing. It's not just vague ideas like you get in a horoscope. It's as though she can read my mind." Caroline looked admiringly at her mentor and received an encouraging pat on the arm.

"Oh yes, I believe you," said Leslie. Gloria was utterly shameless, but there was nothing for it but to throw himself into the stratagem.

Caroline was getting into full flow now. She put her plate down on the table and leant forward. "The things the crystals told about me, you wouldn't believe. They even—" She hesitated. "They even said I was troubled by a secret."

"Really? And were they right?" Leslie asked, picking up the cue.

"Yes. It's so difficult—I've been worried sick. I haven't slept a wink since Saturday."

"A problem shared is a problem halved," said Gloria, and she cast Leslie a meaningful glance, worthy of her alter ego, Griselda.

"I can step outside if you ladies would like to talk," said Leslie.

"Oh no, it's nothing personal," said Caroline. "That's exactly the problem—it's not my secret to share. But if I don't tell someone then that might cause problems, too. I really don't know what to do for the best."

191

Gloria dabbed her mouth with a napkin and cast another furtive glance at Leslie.

"I'm sure that you promised secrecy in the first place to do good, to be helpful to someone," she said reassuringly, and Caroline nodded eagerly. "Think of it this way. If the circumstances change, and keeping the secret may do more harm than good, then by sharing the secret you are acting with the same motive as you did in the first place. That means that telling us the secret is just the same as keeping the secret. Better in fact."

There was a short pause while they tried to comprehend this novel piece of philosophy, but Gloria's assured manner, if not her reasoning, seemed to give Caroline courage.

"I think I'll go mad if I don't tell someone," she said after a moment, "and hopefully you'll know what to do."

Gloria nodded encouragingly and Caroline continued.

"It's this," she said. "I did see someone in the dressing rooms during the matinée, someone who wasn't supposed to be there. I promised I'd keep quiet about it. That was before I knew you were worried about Roland Rawlison going missing, of course. In any case, I can't believe it has anything to do with the disappearance, but you did seem very concerned, and anxious to know if there had been anyone backstage who wasn't in the cast."

The narrative dried up for a moment, and Gloria, her diplomacy temporarily forgotten, blurted out, "You saw someone? Well, who was it?"

"If we're sure it has no significance," Leslie quickly added, speaking with as much ambiguity as he could muster on the spur of the moment, "then I promise it will go no further. But if Roland doesn't turn up safely, and it does, in fact, become a police matter, it's probably best if you've told someone what you saw. It might look better, on balance."

"The police? I see, oh dear," said Caroline unhappily. "Oh well, it was this. It was during the first act, and you probably remember, Gloria, that I went down to the dressing room to pin my hair. I did it quickly but there was no rush to come back up to the stage as I wasn't in much during the first act. I know this sounds really stupid."

At this the poor woman blushed red to the roots of her hair and buried her face in her hands. They sat in an awkward silence for a moment, and Gloria said, "Do go on, dear, I'm sure it's not as bad as you think."

"I feel so ashamed," said Caroline, still with her face in her hands. "I decided I'd have a look in Terry's dressing room. I knew that Jim and James weren't in there and I just wanted to have a look, to see his things." She looked up and said, almost with defiance, "How pathetic is that?"

"Very natural," said Gloria, cheerfully. "You wouldn't believe how inquisitive I am, especially about people I'm interested in. But do go on, what did you see there?"

"Oh, nothing at all in there," said Caroline. "The silly thing is that I lost my bearings, and I went into Pippa's room by mistake. Imagine my shock when I saw a great big man sitting there, drinking beer. I think I screamed and then I slammed the door shut and ran back to my own dressing room. It was Pippa's boyfriend, of course, and she went mad at me when she found out. All I could think of to say was that I mistook her dressing room for mine, but I could see she didn't believe me. She said that if I told anyone I'd seen him backstage, she'd tell everyone I was a thief and I'd been creeping around all the dressing rooms. It was awful."

Gloria refilled their cups and passed round the Florentines, helping herself to another. She caught Leslie's eye and flashed him a brief but significant look.

"Well, that was very brave of you to tell us, dear," she replied, patting Caroline's shoulder sympathetically. "I'm quite sure it's got nothing to do with Roland Rawlison; it was just Pippa misbehaving herself and trying to avoid getting into trouble with her mother or Terry. Don't you agree, Leslie?"

Leslie murmured an inaudible reply, and Gloria continued.

"The best thing you can do is to put it right out of your mind, dear. The whole thing. No one else but Pippa knows, and she won't say anything since the boyfriend shouldn't have been there. I don't suppose she'll be in another LADS production, so I doubt you'll ever see her again."

"I'm not going back to LADS, anyway. It's too pushy for me. I stayed in it for this production because of Terry; he was so nice to me. But he seems to have changed. When I told him I thought I might not come back after the production, he just said, 'Please yourself'."

She gave a choking sob and buried her face in her hands once more. Gloria passed her a box of tissues and put a comforting hand on her shoulder.

"Put the whole episode behind you," she said. "You're best out of it, it's not a nice organisation. I was completely taken in by it myself, and by Terry, too. Quite the charmer when it suits him. But there are lots of genuine people about; you must come along with me to tai chi, or the choir or the mahjong club in Dartonleigh. I'll give you all their details when I see you here next week, and you can see what takes your fancy."

"You're very kind, I might do that," said Caroline and stood up to take her leave. "But aren't you going to the debrief on Thursday? I've got some bits of costume to return, and I've geared myself up to see it through to the end. If I don't go, I'll always think they said awful things about me, and it will haunt me for ever."

"I forgot about the debrief for a moment, and I do wish you would stop imagining all that nonsense about people saying things about you," said Gloria. "But it might be good closure, for all of us, and you can sit with me. In the meantime, I'll email you some good meditation links, and do keep taking that tincture of valerian."

Promising to take Gloria's advice, Caroline picked up her coat and bag and hastened out. From the vantage point of the office window, they could see her hurrying away down the road.

"Well!" said Gloria, pouring more drinks and putting two more Florentines onto her plate. "I wasn't expecting that. I thought that she was going to tell us something incriminating about someone, most likely Terry. I had her down as an unwitting conspirator— agreeing to shield him in some way."

She sounded thoroughly vexed.

"It does let Terry off the hook as far as that goes," said Leslie. "But it might give us the accomplice we were looking for. That boyfriend, Gareth, is enormous. He's the one person so far who is strong enough to lift Roland. I wonder…"

"So, we're back to Kara and Pippa again," said Gloria, eagerly. "They could be the only ones in league with Gareth."

"And I've just remembered something," said Leslie. "When we first discovered that Roland was missing and I was in my dressing room with Terry and Kara, she said she'd been down earlier to look for Roland and he wasn't there." He paused and finished his cup of tea, thoughtfully. "That would be a perfect cover in case someone had seen her."

"She said that, did she?" said Gloria with a note of triumph in her voice. "Then how come she didn't notice all his things were missing, just tell me that!"

24

When Leslie got home, he found Bennett pouring over the script in the library. He brought the copy through to the kitchen and sat down at the table while Leslie made a pot of tea and recounted Caroline's disclosure.

"At least the poor woman seems to have seen the light with regard to Terry now," said Leslie, speaking to the top of Bennett's head as he continued to read. "But I don't know where it leaves us with Roly's disappearance."

He then raised the observation, made by Gloria, that it was odd that Kara should not notice that all Roland's stuff was missing when she went looking for the actor.

"Do you think Kara would notice something like that?" Bennett asked, without looking up.

"It was the first thing that struck me when I opened the door," said Leslie. He reflected for a moment. "But I suppose that's because I knew what I expected to see. Perhaps if I'd glanced quickly into, say, Gloria's or Terry's dressing rooms, I wouldn't have noticed if one person's things had gone."

"Or maybe his things were still there at that point," Bennett muttered, his eyes still on the script.

Leslie considered this point in silence as he refilled their cups. Then he talked through a scenario that he had thought of in the bus on the way home which involved Kara as the instigator, Gareth taking Roland away at knife point and Pippa gathering his belongings up.

Bennett merely grunted.

"Whatever are you doing with that script?" said Leslie, crossly. "I never want to see it again as long as I live, and I'm trying to tell you about Caroline and Gareth."

"I knew from the outset that the script was all wrong," said Bennett, who was now staring out of the window. "Did you ever see a copy of the original?"

"No, never. I suppose Kara must have it, but I never saw it. Why? Is it important?"

"I can't be sure without seeing the original."

"The script takes us back to Kara again," said Leslie. "She's the one person in the cast I haven't managed to speak to. But I suppose if she's guilty then she's not going to tell me anything useful. She's hardly going to incriminate herself."

Bennett was intent on the page open before him and made a non-committal sound.

"I've been thinking about Gareth," said Leslie, pressing on with his line of thought. "I obviously haven't spoken to him, either. My first reaction was that it would be pointless because, like Kara, if he's involved, he'll just make out he knows nothing. But supposing he's innocent and had nothing to do with Roly's disappearance—he might have seen or heard something. He was down in the dressing rooms the whole time. Someone told me he works in that place that does tyres and clutches and brakes and things, on the industrial estate just beyond Lymeford. I wonder if I could persuade Gloria to drive down there with me and get her tyres checked and I'll see if I can find him. We don't have to betray Caroline; I'm certain that Gloria will have no hesitation in saying that she saw him backstage herself. And it would be interesting to see his reaction."

"He's a big chap if he does react," said Bennett.

"He's hardly going to try anything in the middle of the garage," said Leslie. Then he laughed. "It's a shame that Frank's incapacitated, otherwise we could have implicated the whole family in the abduction."

"Yes," said Bennett dryly, "it's a pity he was sitting in front of me for the whole matinée performance, otherwise we could depict him hobbling stealthily backstage, overpowering

Roland with his crutches and seizing a knife from the side of his surgical boot."

"As it was," said Leslie, "he waited until the evening performance before creating mischief. He sat in the most inconvenient place in that narrow wing on stage right; you were there, you saw him. I nearly broke my ankle tripping over him at one point. I thought Terry was just being finicky when he objected to Frank being there, but he was right and it's a pity he didn't hold out and overrule Kara."

Bennett stared at Leslie. "I think I have been the most infernal ass," he said and stood up, clutching the script.

"What do you mean?" Leslie demanded, but Bennett was already halfway to the library, and he did not look back.

Leslie sighed. Bennett would never think out loud or say anything until he had it all worked out. It was galling and never failed to aggrieve Leslie, but there was nothing he could do about it, so he poured himself another cup of tea and ate up the last slice of cherry cake to spite him.

***

Bennett was still preoccupied with the script the following morning, was silent at breakfast and took little notice when Gloria pulled up outside soon afterwards and Leslie bade him cheerio. Gloria had been wildly enthusiastic about the visit to the garage to quiz Gareth, though apologising profusely, she explained that it would have to be early as she had some consultations booked in.

It was a busy time for traffic, and the backroads which Gloria loved to use were much frequented by the locals who were also avoiding the busier main route. Consequently, the journey was every bit as bad as Leslie expected and they raced through the narrow, twisting lanes, screeching to a halt whenever they came nose to nose with another kamikaze driver rounding a corner at speed. Each time, Gloria uttered an exhilarated, 'I say!' or,

'Well I never!' before scrunching the car into reverse and screeching backwards into a field entrance or passing place. Their destination was on the other side of Lymeford and when they got to the town, the narrow streets were gridlocked. Mounting the pavement, Gloria squeezed through an impossibly small gap between an oncoming bus and the frontage of The Lemon Drop where they had previously eaten lunch and had watched Caroline and Terry emerging separately from the pub along the street.

"What a shame we can't stop for coffee and cake," sighed Gloria. "If only I'd known, I would have kept the morning free. Oh, I say, these roads weren't made for all this traffic."

This last comment was made in response to hooting from a van whose driver had taken exception to Gloria's latest manoeuvre. She waved a cheerful and conciliatory arm from the window and at length they emerged from the traffic jam. It was only a few minutes later that they reached the garage, and it was with a mixture of relief and trepidation that Leslie alighted from the car.

The plan was for Gloria to make enquiries about her tyres while Leslie went in search of Gareth, to whom he would explain that he was taking the opportunity of Gloria's visit there to ask if he had seen anything in connection with Roland's disappearance. It was, Leslie thought, too far-fetched to pretend to encounter Gareth by chance, but now, in the noisy, commonplace environment of the garage, the speech he had prepared, and even the notion of any harm having come to Roland, seemed ridiculously implausible.

Leslie's apprehension was, however, needless as he quickly discovered that Gareth was not at work that day. He returned to Gloria, who was thanking the mechanic profusely and promising to return in a few months to have the tyre he was aimlessly kicking checked again. As they pulled away, Leslie apologised to Gloria for wasting her time and insisted that she drive back along the main road and drop him at the turning for Dartonleigh. Gloria brushed off all Leslie's apologies, but glancing at her watch did reluctantly agree to set him down outside the village.

"I say," she said, "do you think that Gareth has gone on the run?"

This sounded ridiculous when Gloria said it, although the same thought had gone through Leslie's mind.

"It's very fishy that no one would tell you when he's due back," she added.

"I did only ask two people," Leslie pointed out. The first had simply said, 'Dunno', but the second, a weaselly little mechanic, had eyed Leslie suspiciously and asked why he wanted to know. Leslie had given up at that point and now he wished that he had handled the whole thing better.

"If you want to go back again, just let me know," said Gloria cheerfully, ignoring the fact that a repeat visit might be difficult to explain. "But do give me a bit of notice if you can and then we can have lunch again in The Lemon Drop."

A thin drizzle had started and as they approached the Dartonleigh turning, Gloria insisted on driving to the edge of the village. Leslie would have much rather been left at the main road by the bus stop, then he could have got home using the footpath and avoided walking through the village centre, but he was not going to confess his cowardice to Gloria.

He trudged through the rain with legs that felt like lead and a heart that was even heavier. He was suddenly terribly weary; he had become fixated with this case, repeatedly turning over all the possibilities and endlessly talking himself into and out of every argument. It had preoccupied his mind since Roland had disappeared and had even robbed him of his sleep. And to crown it all, it was now, so it seemed, making him a laughingstock in the village. He was genuinely concerned for Roland, but it was not worth all this anxiety.

As soon as he got indoors, he would tell Bennett that he was leaving the problem, if indeed there was a problem, to the police. Roland had been registered as a missing person and could be followed up like any other missing person. His mood lightened a little and he stepped out briskly, pulling his hood further up as the rain came steadily down. But his relief was short-lived, for as soon as he thought of Bennett, another anxiety gripped him. This was the old trouble back again, the terror that used to possess him after Bennett's heart attack, that he would return to the house and find Bennett collapsed and past help. It came less frequently now, and only when he was excessively tired or his nerves were bad, but knowing this, and recognising it, did not eliminate it. He took the deep breaths that he had been taught to use, and tried to keep his steps even and unhurried, but by the time he was in the village, passing the shop and the post office, he was going at a trot.

The porch door was always kept unlocked and Leslie flung it open and stepped in out of the rain. He fumbled with the front door key, turned it in the lock and thrust the door open, with his heart pounding. As he stepped inside the hall he froze—he had the strongest feeling that something was terribly wrong. He shouted Bennett's name, waiting for a response that would have him chiding himself for his foolishness, as had happened on previous occasions. But this time there was silence. Feeling cold and sick he shouted again and again with increasing urgency as there was still no reply. He approached the library and with awful caution pushed the door slowly open. Peering nervously in, he felt momentary relief as he could see from the doorway that the room was empty; there was nowhere Bennett could be slumped unseen, and the patio doors were bolted.

With his heart in his throat, Leslie went through each of the downstairs rooms, looking behind furniture and doors, but none of them, not the kitchen, utility room, lounge nor cloakroom, yielded Bennett's collapsed form. He was beside himself with agitation and shouted Bennett's name at the top of his voice. He must be in the house somewhere. Bennett had never been one to pop across to the shop or drop in on friends unexpectedly and since his heart attack he had become a hermit, leaving the house only very occasionally, and for very specific purposes. And while Bennett was apt to ignore Leslie if he was preoccupied, it was unthinkable that he would not have responded by now.

He mounted the stairs in abject fear. The scenario of Bennett feeling unwell and going to lie down on the bed was now the only possible explanation for this terrible silence and Leslie knew that no one could have slept through his shouting. Whispering Bennett's name, he pushed open the bedroom door, sick at the thought of what he was going to find there.

It was with a strange, perplexed relief that he found that room, and all the others upstairs, empty. The relief was transient, however, for although thankfully Bennett had not succumbed to another heart attack in the house, he was still missing.

With sudden hope Leslie hurried to the French windows; Bennett was not in the habit of frequenting the garden on a rainy day, but it was conceivable that something might have taken him outside. But the windows were locked, as had been the back door, and there was no sign that Bennett was in the garden or ever had been. Leslie went through the house again wildly, flinging open cupboards, peering under bookshelves, pulling back curtains, even though one could barely conceal even a baby in any of these places.

A sudden impulse took Leslie back to the porch. He saw straightaway the thing that he had missed in his hurry to get in the house: Bennett's coat and shoes were missing. His conscious mind had not registered their absence, but it was perhaps this that he had perceived subconsciously and had given him that immediate sense of foreboding.

Utterly baffled, Leslie scoured the house for a note, but none could be found. He now discovered, too, that Bennett's wallet and keys were missing, but his phone was in its place in the library. Leslie checked his own phone but there was no message. He went outside and searched the garden, the shed and the garage without success. Apart from the missing coat and shoes, everything looked exactly as Leslie had left it earlier; there was no indication of Bennett having so much as made himself a cup of coffee, let alone any signs of misadventure. But this gave Leslie little reassurance. Bennett had vanished in a manner as sudden, inexplicable and sinister as Roland's disappearance.

He ran across to the shop which had a good vantage point in the village centre and where Janet always watched the comings and goings with benign interest.

"Have you seen Bennett?" he said anxiously as he burst through the door.

"Whatever do you mean?" said Janet, who was aware of Bennett's aversion to leaving the house.

"I've just got home and he's not in," said Leslie.

Irene came in from the stockroom and Vera, who had been out of sight by the freezer section, appeared at the counter.

"It's not like Bennett to go off, is it?" said Vera, and she gave an expressive look to Irene, who raised her eyebrows.

Leslie was too agitated to take notice of this little exchange between the two women.

"He certainly hasn't been in here," said Janet, "and I haven't seen him go by, though of course I don't see everyone who goes past the shop."

The other two ladies agreed that they had not seen him either and, apart from Janet speculating that perhaps it was a good sign that Bennett was wanting to go out and about again, no one had any suggestions to offer so Leslie left them for the post office. He met with the same negative there and, fraught with distress, he ran across to The Daffodil Tea Shop where Annie was serving behind the counter. Her welcoming smile turned to concern when she saw the wild expression on his face.

"Have you seen Bennett?" he burst out. "I've just come home and he's not there. I've been through the whole house and garden and there's no sign of him. I don't know what to do."

Annie turned and called quietly into the kitchen behind her. "Laura, take over from me here, will you, love? I'm popping over to Leslie's for a minute."

"Are you sure? Aren't you busy?" said Leslie, for the place seemed to be bustling, as usual.

"Never mind that, they'll manage," Annie replied, taking off her apron and grabbing a jacket that was on a peg by the counter. Then she added, under her breath, "Don't say anything more until we're out of the shop."

Annie often remarked that the tea shop was a hub of gossip and Leslie could see that the occupants of some of the tables were looking at him with interest.

Back at the cottage it did not take Leslie long to explain everything to her and, knowing the two men well, she was quick to understand why Leslie was so worried. She was very businesslike and asked if she might check the house in case there was anything he had missed.

"Did Bennett seem normal when you went out this morning?" she asked when she had finished her search. "There hadn't been any misunderstandings or anything?"

"Misunderstandings?" said Leslie. "We're always arguing, but Bennett never takes the slightest notice of a row. I'd be more likely to walk out than Bennett. It wouldn't be anything like that."

"Don't take this the wrong way, but I was only wondering if Bennett might possibly have taken this silly business about Roland Rawlison more seriously than you thought. Don't be cross with me," she added hastily seeing Leslie's outraged expression, "I'm just searching for explanations, however unlikely."

"It's not you I'm cross with," said Leslie, with exasperation in his voice, "but I've just realised that's what those old cats in the shop were thinking when I went to ask in there. So, now everyone will be saying not only that I had a fling with Rawlison, but that Bennett has gone off because of it. Still, what does it matter, what does anything matter? I just need to know what has happened to him. But I can assure you that's not the explanation."

Annie apologised profusely for even raising the suggestion and asked if Bennett had talked about anything or had been doing anything that morning that might give a clue.

"Now I come to think of it, he hardly spoke at all," said Leslie. "He was reading the script of that blighted play. He asked me if I had seen the original and I said I hadn't and that Kara, the director, must have it." He explained about the script being revised for their production.

"You don't suppose he's taken a taxi to Kara's to look at the original script?" suggested Annie.

"That doesn't sound at all like Bennett," said Leslie, though for the first time it gave him a crumb of hope. "I'm the one who does all the running around and I can't imagine what would be so urgent that he couldn't wait for me to get home. And, if it was, why not leave a message?"

Annie put the kettle on and made a pot of tea.

"Gloria has Kara's number. She must be back at her shop by now," said Leslie. "But I know she had a customer coming for a consultation and I don't like to disturb her as I've already taken her on a wild goose chase this morning. I'll message her to give me a ring when she's free." He stared miserably into his cup of tea. "I wish we'd never gone out and then Bennett wouldn't have disappeared."

It was not long before Gloria rang back. "I'll come over straightaway," she said as soon as Leslie had told the story.

"What about your consultations?"

"Never mind them," said Gloria, "I'll reschedule." And with unusual brevity, she rang off.

She pulled up outside the cottage in record time and Annie took advantage of her arrival to return to her duties at the tea shop.

"I'll look in at The Woodman and the antique shop on my way over," she said as she left them, although they all knew that anything said in the shop went round the whole village in minutes, and anyone with any information would already have called round.

"I think I may have dragged you round here on another wild goose chase," said Leslie. "I don't think I'll call Kara just yet. After all, it was just a random suggestion from Annie. It's not as though there's any reason to think that's where Bennett went, in fact it's highly unlikely."

"You don't want to call her so that you know one way or the other?" asked Gloria.

"If Bennett really has gone to Kara's to see the script, he must have gone in a taxi, and he'll be back soon. And in the unlikely event that he has gone there, he might have spun Kara a yarn about his reason for calling in, and if I ring up it might spoil it all. So, as I say, I think I've dragged you round here for nothing—that's twice in one day."

"I'm glad you did ring me," said Gloria. "You're not leaving my sight until Bennett returns."

"Whatever do you mean?"

"Roland went missing, for all we know Gareth has gone missing, and now we don't know where Bennett is. We can't afford to mislay anyone else."

Leslie was beyond any concern for his own welfare, but he was very grateful to have Gloria's company as the time passed with agonising slowness. He made no objection to Gloria hanging a crystal at the front window which she claimed would communicate with the higher energies and give them guidance. In normal times he would have silently scoffed at such a superstition, but at that moment he would have embraced voodoo if it would hasten Bennett's safe return.

Annie popped across at twelve o'clock before the café got too busy with the lunchtime rush and brought them some sandwiches and cakes. Leslie appreciated the gesture though he could not face eating anything, and he would really rather have had the distraction of making lunch for Gloria himself.

Leslie had phoned Ridgeway earlier. He had no hesitation in disturbing him, for as a good friend, he would appreciate how out of character this was, and anyway, Leslie was far too worried to be concerned about whether he was wasting a chief inspector's time. As usual, he could not get hold of Ridgeway directly, and had left a message knowing that he would reply as soon as he was free. However, by the time lunch was over, he was overcome with impatience and agitation.

"I'm phoning the police," he said to Gloria as he poured out yet another cup of tea. "I can't expect them to take me seriously, reporting an adult who has only been missing for a few daylight hours, but I can't help it. Supposing there had been some terrible accident somewhere and I hadn't—"

"Don't start supposing anything of the kind," interrupted Gloria. "But I can't see that it will do any harm to contact the police if you want to."

Leslie was not so optimistic; he had never had much luck reporting anything to the police. Nevertheless, leaving Gloria to clear their plates away in the kitchen, he went through to the sitting room and dialled the non-emergency number.

When, after a very long time, he was put through, he explained the problem and gave all Bennett's details as requested.

"I do realise that it must seem odd that I'm calling about this, but it's so completely out of character," he said. "Bennett simply never goes out; he can go for weeks on end without going out of the house."

"I see," said the operator. "Is he agoraphobic?"

"Oh no," said Leslie. "It's not like that."

"Are there any mental health issues?" she asked, kindly. "Is he a vulnerable adult?"

"Oh no, nothing of that kind. He's fine. He just doesn't go out."

"Is he... a recluse?" asked the operator, in a voice that suggested she was doing her best to understand.

"No, he's not anything," said Leslie. "He's just Bennett."

"OK," she said. "When did he last go out before today?"

"Actually, it was last Friday and Saturday, but that was different," said Leslie feebly.

"So, when you say he doesn't go out—"

The operator was now speaking tentatively, as though she was trying to decide, thought Leslie, whether he was a timewaster or a lunatic. He tried to explain but it made matters much worse and although the woman on the phone was not unpleasant, Leslie sensed that she thought he was the one with the problem.

"It was only in case there had been an accident," interrupted Leslie. "In case—" He left the sentence unfinished, unable to put his worst fears into words. The operator was reassuring on that point, intimating that they currently had no unidentified casualties or corpses on their hands.

As soon as he rang off, Leslie phoned their GP. Leslie and Bennett had known Dr Paul since long before they moved to Dartonleigh. In fact, the cottage which they now lived in once belonged to the doctor and they had, for many years, rented it annually as a holiday home. When the time came for the doctor to sell the cottage, the two men had bought it, retired and come to live in the village. The doctor had now semi-retired, though he still worked part-time at the local practice, and he was a good friend.

"I don't know why I'm calling you, Paul," admitted Leslie when he had explained the situation. "It's so totally inconceivable that Bennett's gone off in this unexplained fashion that I'm at a loss to know what to do."

The doctor asked some questions about Bennett's health and state of mind that morning, confirming that he had not been breathless or confused or showing any other worrying symptoms. He made some reassuring comments, cautioned Leslie against thinking the worst, but had nothing concrete to suggest.

"What's your gut feeling?" he asked. "Even if it sounds ridiculous, what do you think might have happened?"

Leslie considered this and then said, "I honestly have no idea. Even after all these years, I can't predict Bennett or guess what he's going to think or say next. But I've never been as baffled as this. It's what makes it so worrying." He could barely keep his voice steady. "I'm terribly afraid he's come to some harm."

25

The afternoon was agony. Leslie paced about the house, racing to the window whenever he fancied he heard a noise, and refusing to go outside in case Bennett rang the landline. Gloria recounted an endless stream of stories about people, pets and objects that she knew of which had gone missing and all returned safely. The tales varied from the banal to the bizarre, involving misunderstandings, messages that were supposed to be passed on but were not, unlikely coincidences and impossible concatenations of events. Leslie barely heard a word of it but found the endless chatter consoling, if only because it was so well meant.

Janet ran across from the shop to see if there was any news and to bring some chocolate biscuits. Once again, the kindness of the gesture was felt, even if Leslie did recognise the packet from Janet's bargain basket which contained the items about to expire.

"Don't you worry, Leslie, dear," she said, patting his arm kindly. "He'll be back soon, you'll see, and they'll be some perfectly good explanation that you just can't put your finger on at the moment. You'll be laughing about it by this evening, you'll see."

Leslie fervently hoped she was right but could not imagine how such an outcome could come to pass.

Janet added, "You can be sure he's nowhere round the village, though. Everyone's been out looking; they've checked their gardens and sheds and all around the lanes. But he'll be back soon, Leslie, love."

"It sounds like they're looking for a lost cat," said Leslie to Gloria when Janet had gone. "But it's very kind and it's a relief to know the village has been searched. Naturally it's been on my mind that it might be something to do with his heart."

He tried not to think about what they were all saying while they were looking. The doorbell rang and he sprinted to the door to find Paul, the doctor, standing in the porch.

"I didn't want to block the phone line by ringing," he said, "so I thought I'd call by and find out if there is any news and see how you are."

Gloria, showing laudable tact, asked Leslie if he would mind if she had a look around to see if there was anything that might have been missed earlier. She left the two men in the kitchen and Leslie heard her pad off into the sitting room.

The doctor asked if Bennett had been himself that morning, repeating similar questions to those he had asked on the phone earlier. "He didn't seem odd? No confusion or disorientation? No chest pain?"

Leslie answered in the negative to all these questions.

"My guess is that it will turn out to be a Bennett thing," said the doctor in a resigned tone. "Something eccentric that only Bennett would do, something you couldn't guess and won't know until he turns up again."

"I might feel a bit reassured by that," replied Leslie, for this did resonate with Bennett's personality, "if only other people hadn't also disappeared."

Of course, the doctor knew none of the background story and Leslie poured it out, omitting nothing, not even the embarrassing relationship which Roland had been trying to embark on and the rumours which were now circulating.

"It's going round the village now that there was something between me and Roland, and that Bennett has run off because of it. It's dreadfully embarrassing, humiliating, in fact. It sounds like I've been carrying on like a teenager and I feel like a complete figure of fun."

"I don't believe it," said the doctor firmly. "You are liked and respected in the village, believe me. People wouldn't be out checking the highways and byways for Bennett if they thought he'd caught the first train for London with his suitcase. You're overwrought at the moment and you'll feel differently when Bennett turns up again, as I'm sure he will."

Leslie started to exclaim that he hoped to God that Bennett turned up quicker than Roland who had been missing since Saturday, when he heard Gloria calling out.

"Have you a minute, Leslie?" It sounded as though she was calling from the library, and there was an unusual urgency in her voice. "Is this anything?"

"What is it?" said Leslie anxiously, hurrying to where she stood by Bennett's desk.

"It's a note, well not really a note, perhaps. It was slipped in near the top of this stack of papers on the desk."

Leslie snatched the paper from her and saw, in Bennett's unmistakeable hand, the words: *Taken in a strange red car with one.* The sentence seemed to be unfinished.

"What do you think it means?" said Gloria looking quite worried.

"Dear God," exclaimed Leslie, sitting down suddenly. "It sounds to me like he somehow knew he was being taken away and managed to scribble a note and tuck it in the pile of papers hoping it would be seen. What shall we do? I must phone the police. He's in danger."

"Perhaps he saw something outside and went in pursuit?" suggested Gloria.

"Then why would he have hidden the note?" retorted Leslie, clutching his chest which he thought would burst.

The doctor, who was of the old school, appeared carrying a glass of brandy. "Drink this first," he said, "and let's have a look at that note."

The doorbell rang and Leslie leapt to his feet again, and the brandy swirled up to the rim of the glass as he raced to the door. It was Martin, with the dog, Cromwell.

"I just dropped in at The Woodman and they said Bennett has gone AWOL. What's it all about?"

"A red car!" exclaimed Leslie. "Can you find out if anyone saw a strange red car round here today? Ask in The Woodman and the shop and the post office. And The Daffodil, too, and the antique shop. Someone must have seen it."

"A red car? Why has—"

"Never mind why," snapped Leslie with unprecedented abruptness, and impatiently he flapped away Cromwell who was attempting to enter the cottage. "Just find out if anyone saw a red car. A strange one. And hurry."

Leslie slammed the door shut before Martin had chance to delay by asking any more questions and hurried towards the telephone to update the police with this latest finding. As he put his hand to the phone it rang and he snatched it up, to hear Ridgeway's voice on the other end.

The chief inspector already had the bare outline of the circumstances from Leslie's earlier message and Leslie filled him in with the details and then told him of the note they had found.

"I was just about to phone the police again when you rang," said Leslie. "I'm convinced that Bennett is in danger. He tried to leave me a message. It's the first clue we've had."

"Hold on a minute," said Ridgeway. "Can you read out the note again—exactly what it says."

After he read the message out again, there was a pause and Leslie, beside himself with impatience, tried twice to say something but the chief inspector politely silenced him.

"I don't think you need worry about the note," Ridgeway said at last.

"What do you mean, not worry?" said Leslie in exasperation.

"It's a clue, all right," said Ridgeway. "But it's a crossword clue. One of Bennett's. The answer is 'carried'. It's an anagram of 'red car' with an 'I' in it from the letter one."

Ridgeway was a great fan of cryptic crosswords and had often tried to find out from Bennett which papers he worked for and what name he used.

There was a silence while Leslie, staring at the paper, digested the chief inspector's words.

"Yes, I see," he said, sheepishly. "And 'taken' can be the same as 'carried'. I can't believe I didn't realise, after all these years of living with bits of paper like this lying round the house. I can't tell you what a fool I feel."

"At least we can rule out the involvement of the strange car," said Ridgeway.

To Leslie's mortification he was sure he could hear a suppressed chuckle in Ridgeway's voice.

"In my experience, when someone can't be located it invariably turns out to be nothing, but it's certainly not like Bennett to go off like this. And given the funny business with Rawlison, I'll get someone on the case. You should hear from somebody in the next hour or so, with a bit of luck. Get back to me if you don't."

He rang off, leaving Leslie in a whirl of contradictory emotions: both relief and anxiety because the chief inspector was taking it seriously, and utterly idiotic because of the strange red car. He was distracted from these agonies by Gloria.

"I must apologise for sending everyone down a blind alley with that note," she said, looking rueful. "But I shall put it right straightaway. If the dear doctor will promise to stay with you for a few minutes, I'll run around and explain that there was a misunderstanding about the car and tell everyone it's all my fault. Luckily you didn't say anything about the note to Martin, so no one needs to know a thing about it."

Leslie sank into the chair, feeling exhausted, as Gloria went out. Of course, it was a relief that Bennett had not been abducted in a car, strange, red or otherwise, but he was still no nearer to knowing where he was.

The doctor had been in search of the glass of brandy which had been abandoned in the library, and this time he insisted that Leslie drank it. They sat in quietness, both lost in their own thoughts, and Leslie sipped the restoring spirit.

It was a while before Gloria returned, bursting in on their silence and declaring that you couldn't believe how many strange red cars had been through the village that morning according to the locals. Even when she told everyone that it was no longer relevant, they insisted on telling her about them.

"I've heard about the post van," she said, "a red mini that apparently had no numberplate and a scarlet three-wheeler. But it was an old man in The Woodman who told me about the three-wheeler and I think he was pulling my leg. Several of them also mentioned a flash little red sports car which they obviously didn't realise was mine considering what they said about the noise of it and, well, a few other things."

On any other occasion, Leslie would have found the quirks of the Dartonleigh inhabitants diverting, but he was so preoccupied that he barely acknowledged Gloria when she spoke.

"I wonder how long it was since Ridgeway rang. We haven't had a call from the police, and he said to let him know if they didn't get in touch." He looked at his watch and was surprised to see that it was only just four o'clock—it seemed much later. "That must be them now," he said and snatched up the ringing phone.

It connected but instead of the voice of someone from the police, there was a strange buzzing and clicking noise, and Leslie froze, not knowing what was to follow.

"I left my bloody phone at home, and it's years since I've used one of these damn things." It was unmistakably Bennett. "Last time I used one you had to put 10p in and press button B or something like that. And you can't believe how hard it is to even find a phone box these days."

"Bennett, Bennett! Where are you?" shrieked Leslie. "I thought you were dead."

"What the devil are you talking about?" said Bennett, across a hissing line. "Why should I be dead?"

"I've been worried sick all day. Where are you and why did you go off like that?"

"I'm in London. I left you a note."

"London? What note? Where? We looked everywhere."

"I left it on the kitchen table," There was a slight pause. "Oh bugger! It's in my pocket. I think the pips are about to go. I was going to get a train home at three-thirty but I missed it, and the next one is four-thirty-something. It gets in at about half past seven, I can't remember exactly. I'll get a cab home from the station."

With that he rang off.

"That was Bennett," exclaimed Leslie, unnecessarily. "He's in London, God knows why," and he gave them a resume of the brief conversation. "He didn't even say sorry," he added bitterly, but his relief was so great that if Gloria and Paul had not been there, he would have sat down and wept. "God knows what he's been doing in London. London!"

"We're not letting him come back by taxi, are we?" said Gloria. "He might take it into his head to go to Plymouth or Penzance. I'll take you to meet him at the station later."

"I'd rather like to collect him, if you don't mind," said Paul, and there was a menacing undertone to his voice. It sounded as though he was going to make sure Bennett knew what mischief he had caused. "I'll make myself scarce in the meantime," he continued, "as I expect you need a bit of a rest and then you'll want to get the dinner on. I don't suppose Bennett will have thought about food all day, knowing him."

Gloria took the hint and said that she would also go, but Leslie must not mind if she phoned him once or twice to put her mind at rest. "Now that Bennett hasn't really disappeared, I'm not quite so worried, but we are still missing an actor."

The doctor had taken himself away without ceremony but before Gloria left, she said she would go over to The Daffodil and tell Annie that Bennett had been located.

"If she spreads the word around, third hand as it were, it will save a lot of individual enquiries."

216

Leslie was infinitely grateful to Gloria for all her help, but it suddenly felt as though she had been in the cottage for half a year not half a day, and he would have agreed to anything so long as he could get some peace. He watched her hurry across to the tea shop, nimble, as always, for a woman of her substantial physique, and shortly afterwards he heard the roar of her car engine as she shot off.

His peace was short-lived as almost immediately the doorbell rang, and it was Annie. When she confirmed that Bennett had been located as Gloria had told her, she seized Leslie in such a hug that he realised she had been much more worried than she had revealed.

"I didn't want to disturb you, but I had to double-check that you were happy if I tell everyone Bennett's back and that he just forgot to leave a note."

Leslie confirmed that he would be grateful if she did so and was about to embark on the story when she interrupted.

"No, don't tell me anything about it. If I'm going to say that I don't know, then it's better if I really don't know. You can give me all the details another time, over a cup of tea, if you feel like it."

As she was leaving, she looked over her shoulder and said, "I'd better tell you that Gloria's put me on lookout duty over you until Bennett's back. So, if you look out the window and see me peering at you from the café or my flat above later, do give me a wave!"

26

Having left a message apprising Ridgeway of Bennett's restoration, Leslie took himself into the sitting room for a rest as the doctor had recommended. However, despite feeling utterly exhausted, he was unable to relax, and soon found himself prowling around the room and eventually back in the kitchen. It was hours before he could hope to serve dinner, but the kitchen was the place he always felt most tranquil.

Lamb curry had been on the menu for the evening meal, but he needed ginger and chillies for that recipe, and he would have starved sooner than go to the shop just now. He settled on lamb casserole as the ideal alternative; he could rustle up the necessary ingredients, it could be cooked slowly and served whenever Bennett eventually deigned to appear, and it was filling if he had not eaten properly all day.

He felt somewhat calmer as he peeled and chopped and poured and stirred, although he could not quell his impatience to know what Bennett had been up to, nor the waves of indignation when he considered that after incarcerating himself in the cottage for months on end, he had suddenly gone off to London and failed to leave a message. And to ring off rather than apologise! That was Bennett all over and Leslie did not know how he tolerated it. And when he thought of how Bennett's disappearance had fanned the flames of gossip in the village, his previous agitation nearly got the better of him again. However, by the time he slid the casserole into the oven, he had gone over the topics so many times that most of his grievances were exhausted, as indeed was he. He hung up the oven gloves, went through to the sitting room, flopped into his favourite chair and fell asleep.

Leslie's slumber was interrupted by Gloria, ringing to check up on him, and he was inspecting the casserole when he heard a car pulling up and saw Bennett unfolding himself from the passenger seat and shambling up the path, as Paul drove away. Resisting the temptation to rush to the front door, Leslie started to lay the table.

Bennett peered into the kitchen with an uncharacteristically hangdog look about him. "I think I owe you an apology," he said in a voice of unprecedented penitence. "Paul tore me off a strip. In fact, I don't think I've had such a dressing down since the headmaster caught me smoking a cigar behind the gymnasium— it was one of his cigars."

Leslie had prepared a fine speech for Bennett's homecoming but it seemed to have gone from his mind. "Bennett, you are utterly impossible," he said. "If you only knew how worried I've been. What the hell have you been doing in London?"

"Getting hold of this," said Bennett, producing a rolled-up document from the inside of his coat. He spoke with triumph, his remorse clearly short-lived. "It's the original script. I located the publishing company; it's one of those old-fashioned outfits in a road off Piccadilly. I got hold of the old chap who manages the place this morning, by phone. They had the play in their archive but there's no digital version. He offered to make a copy and post it to me but, thinking time might be of the essence, I ran up there to pick it up."

He said this as though it was the sort of thing he might do any day of the week and Leslie shook his head in disbelief. Bennett continued his narrative.

"I spoke to the old gaffer just after you went out and I realised that if I left straightaway, I could get a bus to Horton and pick up the ten o'clock train into Paddington. I was in town by lunchtime."

"How come no one saw you go?" said Leslie. "It was as though you'd vanished into thin air, and after Roly's disappearance you can imagine how I felt."

"I had hardly any time to get to the bus stop, so I went down that footpath behind The Daffodil as it cuts off quite a corner. And I had written you a note."

He produced a crumpled piece of paper as evidence.

"Please tell me that the trip was worth it," said Leslie, taking the casserole from the oven. "I couldn't bear to think that I've had twenty years taken off my life for nothing."

"Indeed, it was," said Bennett. "I chanced on a particularly good exhibition in a private gallery just along from the publishers. There were some very nice interiors by Ron Bone. That put me in a Rembrandt mood. There's not much in that line in the Royal Academy, which would have been convenient, so I jumped on a bus and went to the National Gallery. That's how I came to miss the earlier train. Living out in the sticks like we do now, I'd forgotten what it's like to be able to go and see *A Woman Bathing in a Stream* whenever you feel like it." He had a satirical glint in his eye.

"I warn you, Bennett," said Leslie, brandishing the serving spoon, "I'm in a dangerous mood. Tell me about the script."

"Ah, that," said Bennett, settling himself down in front of the steaming plate. He blew on a forkful of lamb and composed his thoughts.

He had, he said, already concluded that the script had been tampered with for reasons other than that of propriety or to accommodate the vagaries of the cast. And he had marked out all the places in the script which he felt were in some way anomalous, where there was some inconsistency or irregularity. He had spent the journey home comparing those passages with the original and in almost all cases he was correct and there had been an alteration. The script they had used for the play, he said, had been significantly changed, a far cry from the impression they had been given.

"So, what does it all mean?" said Leslie. "Do you know how it's connected to Roly's disappearance?"

"More or less." Bennett went back to his dinner and ate thoughtfully.

"And you're not going to let me in on the secret?" said Leslie, all his resentment rising to the surface again.

"It would be better if you went to the production debriefing tomorrow unbiased," said Bennett.

This had happened before—Bennett declined to share his thoughts on the grounds that he did not want to impose his conjectures on Leslie or influence him. It was true, of course, that knowing Bennett's ideas would have a bearing on how he viewed the situation, that was only natural, so for the sake of impartiality, perhaps it was better to be in the dark. But Leslie could not help suspecting that Bennett also thought he would give something away if he knew too much, and he felt rather hurt. He finished his dinner and cleared away in a grumpy silence.

"I was all for giving up on this case," he said, at last, as he spooned yogurt and fruit into their dessert bowls. "After this morning's wild goose chase, I'd decided that it wasn't worth the worry, and I was going to tell Gloria to go to the debriefing without me. But we've got this far and, anyway, I suppose this changes things." He indicated the script which was lying on the table.

Bennett sprinkled chopped nuts onto his yoghurt and spooned over a generous helping of honey, dripping it everywhere.

"I'd nearly forgotten that I need to talk to Brad," Leslie continued. "He's due back from his days off tomorrow so I'll try to run him to ground while I'm at the theatre. It's a shame he's such an objectionable character."

Leslie drizzled a careful zigzag of honey across his yoghurt and made what he knew to be a futile attempt to wheedle even the smallest hint from Bennett. "Is it still worth me trying to talk to Kara and Pippa?" he asked.

Bennett licked the stickiness from his fingers and shrugged noncommittally.

221

"Oh, damn you, Bennett," exploded Leslie. "Sometimes I don't know how I put up with you." Once more he tried to be rational about Bennett's reticence. Even when he grudgingly admitted that if Bennett told him who and what he suspected, his behaviour towards everyone would probably be altered, it was still infuriating. He collected up the bowls moodily and made the coffee which he took through to the sitting room in silent indignation.

Bennett was already there. "I saw this when I was out today," he said.

Leslie put the tray down and took the little box Bennett was holding out to him. Inside, wrapped in tissue, was a dainty blue and white Wedgwood jug.

"Jasperware," said Bennett when Leslie had opened it and exclaimed at its beauty. "Not a collector's piece but rather pleasing."

Leslie was completely disarmed by this surprise new addition to his collection. He rearranged the existing jugs and added the newcomer to the display with delight. Bennett poured out a couple of glasses of port.

"We'll be the talk of the village," said Leslie, returning to the old topic, but with none of his earlier pique. "Did Paul tell you that everyone thinks you went off in a huff because there was something going on between Roly and me?"

"What?" exclaimed Bennett with unusual energy and gave a guffaw of laughter. It seemed that the doctor had withheld this detail.

"When you weren't here, and there was *no note*"—Leslie said the last two words with menacing emphasis —"I obviously went round the village to see if anyone had seen you. It's set tongues wagging, coming on top of the rumours about Roly's disappearance. And as for the strange red car—"

He paused to drink some of his coffee and it became apparent that Bennett knew nothing about the bogus clue, either. As Leslie started to explain, Bennett hastily put his mug down and collapsed forward in one of his rare outbursts of hysterical laughter.

"I can't tell you what kind of an unutterable dolt I felt when Ridgeway solved it over the phone."

"Stop, stop!" Bennett gasped, clutching his sides. "Please don't tell me that you've disabused anyone of this. It's wonderful. I can just see myself in the role, flouncing off to London in a strange red car after a lover's tiff."

Leslie tried to protest but Bennett's laughter was always infectious and, before long, Leslie was also wiping his eyes.

27

The production debriefing session was scheduled for two o'clock on Thursday at the Lymeford Arts Centre. As Leslie was getting ready, he said, "I don't know whether to mention the shoes to anyone. I know I decided against it before but now I'm not sure."

Bennett was reading the newspaper, and he looked up but made no reply.

"It's impossible," said Leslie plaintively. "If I don't know what you've found out, how can I know what I should do?"

"That's my whole point," said Bennett. "If you know what I'm thinking, the dangers are that you'll be out to prove or disprove my ideas. I might be barking up the wrong tree."

"I suppose so," sighed Leslie. "But that doesn't help me decide if I should mention the shoes or not."

Bennett gave him no help, but after a few moments he said, "If I am right, you would be wise to watch your step."

Leslie looked at him in enquiry.

"Don't forget, there's a dangerous person at large," Bennett said.

"Really!" exclaimed Leslie. "I know you don't want to scupper the investigation but it's a bit thick reminding me there's a dangerous person about without telling me who you think it is."

"I might be wrong," repeated Bennett. "Much safer to beware of them all. You don't want to be watching Cassius, only to find you've turned your back on Brutus."

Before Leslie could respond to this, the loud and cheerful hooting of a car horn sounded outside. Opening the front door, they saw the scarlet convertible with its roof down, pulled up outside their gate. Gloria, resplendent in a rainbow-coloured scarf and enormous sunglasses, yoo-hooed and waved energetically, drawing the attention of three dog walkers, four women going into the tea shop, a couple of men on their way to The Woodman, a young lad with his parents heading for the park, and Irene who came out of the shop for a look.

"One being taken in a strange red car," Bennett announced and, laughing loudly to himself, disappeared into the library.

The journey to the theatre was the usual heart-stopping ordeal, but they pulled up in the car park unscathed if not unruffled.

"I wonder how many will be here," said Leslie, able to hear himself speak now that they were stationary. "It seems a strange time to have a meeting, in the middle of the day, when you have a lot of working people."

"I know," said Gloria, "I thought the same myself. But everyone I spoke to was intending to be here. Look, there's Kara's car, and Jim's." She pointed first to a huge black SUV and then a dark blue estate. "And there's Terry's. Whatever you may say about him, he does have a very nice taste in cars," she sighed.

The vehicle which had drawn her admiration was a small, bottle green classic car, a Triumph, if Leslie was not mistaken. He could easily see how this had added to Terry's attractions for Gloria, before the scales had fallen from her eyes, and had perhaps also impressed the susceptible Caroline.

They found the room which had been hired for the meeting, and most of the cast and backstage crew were already assembled. To their surprise, there were also more than half a dozen other members of the company, just like at the aftershow party. Everyone was chatting as though there had never been any hostility between them.

"I say," said Gloria, "what are these people doing here? Do you suppose that, since the show was such a success, they all want to be associated with it, after all?"

Leslie could think of no better explanation, but he was beyond caring, relieved only that this was the very last occasion that he would ever be gathered with them.

The tables were arranged in a long rectangle, boardroom style, with Kara and Terry seated at the top. They were in lively conversation with a man and woman who Leslie recognised from the aftershow party. Leslie and Gloria took seats well away from them and, as they sat down, Gloria said, in a stage whisper, "I think someone is here under duress."

She nodded towards Pippa who was slumped so far down in her chair that she seemed in danger of sliding under the table, and she looked more than ever like a sulky teenager. In contrast, Frank, seated next to her, was jesting loudly with Jim, Keith and a few others.

Tracey was standing up, across the table from Leslie and Gloria, holding a sheet of paper and chatting with those around. Terry approached her carrying some neatly folded clothes and a jacket on a hanger covered in plastic wrap.

"All washed and pressed, and the jacket's been dry-cleaned," he said, looking pleased with himself.

"You're a pet," said Tracey, taking the items and ticking them off on her sheet. "You didn't need to go to that trouble. I'd have done it."

"Oh, that reminds me!" Gloria exclaimed, and she delved into her bag and produced a jewelled lorgnette. With a loud, "Yoo-hoo, Tracey!" which temporarily silenced the conversation in the room, she slid them across the table. Tracey marked her list and put it in the box of returned costume items.

Terry started to call the meeting to order and those who had been standing around took seats. Just as the general conversation died down, the door opened cautiously and Caroline scuttled in, flustered as ever, and made for the empty seat next to Tracey, tripping over the costume box and causing a commotion. She stuttered an apology and received a sneering look from Kara.

Terry started the meeting with effusive thanks to everyone for attending and gave apologies from James who, he said, was in college. Leslie remembered the boy telling him that he did not have classes on a Thursday, but it was not surprising that he had excused himself.

Terry then proceeded with a catalogue of extravagant praise to everyone who had contributed to what he described as 'an unparalleled achievement'. He gave a fulsome speech, worthy of the Olivier Awards, after which flowers and bottles, which had been concealed under an adjacent table, were produced. He began by presenting Kara with a bottle and bouquet for her 'outstanding stage direction' which Leslie felt had passed way beyond polite courtesy and into rank dishonesty. Tracey was acknowledged for the 'splendid' costumes, Keith for the 'incomparable' scenery and, in a climax of sycophancy, Pippa for 'playing our most beguiling leading lady, yet'. Even Frank was commended for 'getting up from his hospital bed to give loyal support', which was an astonishing piece of falsehood given the argument Leslie had overheard between Kara and Terry. Just when Leslie thought Terry must have exhausted all his adjectives, a final bottle bag was handed to Leslie for 'providing such a capable understudy at short notice'. Leslie took the unexpected gift and applause with a forced smile, certain the bottle would not satisfy Bennett's discerning palate and would be destined for a village fayre or raffle, from whence it may, indeed, have come.

The fantasy continued as Kara gave her director's feedback, which was as meaningless a stream of nonsense as Leslie had ever heard. It seemed to refer to some other production completely. Roland's astonishing departure, and Bennett's phenomenal understudying, were dismissed in the single sentence; "The stand-in for Hugo Merryman on Saturday evening gave a competent performance." Leslie was outraged that Kara, that prize scenery-chewer, dared to judge Bennett 'competent', although Bennett, he knew, would be highly entertained by this appraisal.

Tracey then went through the list of costume items still to be returned and Keith fed back that it was good to have worked with traditional scenery, although the set changes were very tight, especially the backcloths. The whole fiasco concluded with the presentation of a huge bottle of champagne to Terry by Kara on behalf of the whole company, for piloting them through another stupendous success to add to their catalogue of accomplishments.

Throughout all this, Caroline stared down at her fidgeting hands and shot furtive glances at Terry, blushing each time she did so. The poor woman was obviously not cured of the infatuation, and it was regrettable that she could not conceal her feelings a little better. Terry, himself, had a rather strained look about him, and Leslie noticed that whenever he was off-guard, his eyes flicked nervously round.

Leslie was just scolding himself for these fanciful conjectures and admitting that Terry was probably just anxious that this final meeting should go smoothly, when he realised that rather than closing the meeting, another item on the agenda was being introduced. It was a grand announcement about the next production, which explained the presence of the extra company members. The producer and director were named, which were the couple at the far end of the table. They gave a gushing speech expressing doubt at their abilities to adequately follow Kara's spectacular success, and then sat back smugly to lap up the flattering contradictions which inevitably followed.

At last, the meeting was over, but it seemed that no one had any intention of leaving, for they made their way across the foyer to the tables by the bar and the café area. Leslie suppressed his impatience to get home; he had wanted an opportunity to speak to Kara and Pippa and he would not get a better chance than this.

Gloria was making for a table with Caroline and Tracey, and Leslie was about to join them when he saw Pippa peel herself away from the crowd and step behind some display boards which were part of the art exhibition still in progress in the foyer. Before he lost his nerve, he darted behind the display and approached her. She looked up from her phone, surprised; she had evidently come here to make a private call.

"I'm sorry to disturb you," said Leslie, feeling very awkward. "Can I have a quick word? I promise I won't keep you a minute."

"I was about to make a call, but if it's quick," Pippa replied guardedly.

"Yes, of course. I think you heard me asking around at the party because I was worried about Roland Rawlison disappearing like that. I didn't really get a chance to speak to you about it."

"Yes, I knew you were asking questions and no I didn't see anything. And before you ask, neither did Gareth. There's no need to look surprised, I dare say that snoop told you she'd seen him in my room." Pippa flicked her head roughly in the direction of the table where Caroline sat, though concealed behind the board, they could see no one.

"It wasn't very likely that either of us would have seen anything, if you think about it," she went on, with a rather derisive air. "I always went straight into my dressing room, about three paces from the stairs. And Gareth was hardly going to wander about the corridors, was he? He didn't even put his head out of the door. The only odd thing he heard was you charging about, shouting and throwing open the dressing room doors. He had to dive in the shower so you wouldn't see him!" For a brief moment, she looked as though she might smile. The sullen expression quickly returned. "But you can tell anyone you like that he was there, now; it doesn't matter now the show's over. Anyway, neither of us saw anything because there was nothing to see. That pisshead walked out to ruin the production and spite Mum."

Pippa started to move away but she paused. "Oh yeah, do me a favour and don't ask Mum anything about Roland Rawlison. She goes ballistic if she even hears his name. We'd never hear the last of it. You don't know what it's like."

Leslie waited for a minute after Pippa had gone, wondering what to make of the encounter, and then joined Gloria and the others at the table. There was a cup of coffee ready for him, and some giant muffins had been cut into small pieces to share. This must have been Tracey's work, Leslie thought—not Gloria's style at all. He had joined them in the middle of a discussion about the costumes, and it seemed that Tracey was lamenting the loss of Roland's smoking jacket and waistcoat.

"Still no sign of the old sod, then?" It was Jim butting into the conversation from the neighbouring table. "He's probably flogged the jacket and spent the money on booze," he laughed.

Frank, who was sitting next to him said, "You've kissed goodbye to that costume. You won't hear from Roland until he's ready. I've known him for years. I like the bloke, but you can't pretend he's not a maverick. He'll be in London now or down in Brighton, or he might have gone up to Manchester; he's got contacts in all those places."

"But there was an odd thing about it," said Leslie, recklessly throwing caution to the wind. "He took the wrong shoes when he went."

He explained what he meant.

"That is a bit odd," Frank agreed. "But there's no telling what old Roland will do when the fancy takes him."

"So, he's nicked your shoes as well as the costume," said Jim. "I'd have a word with Terry if I were you. He's pretty good and I'm sure he'd give you the money for them, from the funds."

"It's not the money I'm worried about," said Leslie hastily.

"Isn't it? I'd be spitting tacks," said Jim. "A decent pair of shoes isn't cheap. Hey Terry!"

Before Leslie could stop him, he had attracted the notice of the chairman and also the group who were standing with him and told them the story.

"Please!" interrupted Leslie at last, mortified to find himself, once again, the centre of such ridiculous attention. "Please forget about it. I only mentioned it because it seemed strange. It wasn't anything at all to do with the cost of my shoes."

There was a general hubbub of conversation, mostly relating to Roland's drinking habits and his unreliability, and some banter about the missing shoes. Leslie drank his coffee pensively. He recognised, with some misgivings, that he had now opened Pandora's box without knowing what, if anything, was inside. Everyone now knew about the shoes, and if there was a murderer among them, he or she must realise that they had made an error and that Leslie was suspicious. Everyone except Kara who was sitting at a more distant table with another woman, and Pippa who was nowhere to be seen. But word about the shoes must surely get back to them from Frank or Terry or one of the others before long.

"Let's have a look at this exhibition," said a member of the group who was standing around. "You vote for your favourite one and then they enter you into a raffle for a big case of plonk. Not bad either, I've just looked at it—it's been donated by The Wine Seller in the high street."

There was a general agreement, and they started to move away.

"I'll leave you to it, I've got work to do, I'm afraid," said Terry. "The ushers' roster," and he beamed on Gloria before striding off towards the reception desk.

Leslie heard a small intake of breath from Caroline, who Terry had completely ignored. Leslie had been oblivious to Caroline throughout, but he now noticed that she was sitting with a half-drunk cup of coffee and a piece of uneaten muffin on her plate, looking as miserable as ever.

"Come on, let's have a look at these pictures," said Gloria.

"They look like crap to me," said Tracey. "I wouldn't give any of them house room."

"No, dear," said Gloria, "but a case of wine would be rather fun, don't you think? Come along, Caroline, where shall we start?"

"If you'll excuse me for a moment," said Leslie quietly to Gloria, "I'll go and see if Brad's free. I shouldn't be long."

The women headed for the nearest display and Leslie crossed to the reception desk. Behind him he heard Gloria's carrying voice as she said, in reply to a comment from Tracey, "But perhaps the artist actually wanted to make it look like a child's scribble…"

"Can I have a word with Brad, please?" said Leslie to the receptionist.

"A word with who?" she enquired hesitantly. Leslie had never seen this receptionist before and her badge, bearing the name 'Marian', looked brand new.

"Brad, he's one of the technicians," he said. "I only need a quick word with him."

Marian was starting to reply, when Leslie realised that Jim had followed him to the reception desk and was now at his elbow.

"Have you looked at them?" he interrupted and waved his hand at the exhibition pieces. "I dunno what they call art these days. That one over there looks like a tractor's driven over the canvas. Give me a good old Constable *Hay Wain*, any day. Me and Keith and some of the others were thinking about going to The White Bear for an early pint. Are you up for it?"

"Kind of you to ask, but I've a few things to do this afternoon," said Leslie.

"Oh, OK." Jim replied. "What do you want with Brad?"

Leslie hesitated, reluctant to disclose his intentions to anyone here, and especially not to Jim, who was so indiscreet. Before he could think up a response Jim said, with an unwelcome flash of insight:

"You want to stop worrying about that business with Rawlingson. The mystery of the missing actor—ha! That would make a good play for the LADS if someone would write it— *The Mystery of the Missing Actor*. Or how about *The Mystery of the Missing Shoes*?"

He went back to the others and Leslie could hear him share these hilarious titles at the top of his voice to anyone who would listen and announce to them all exactly what Leslie was doing.

Whatever Marian thought of this peculiar exchange, she continued their previous conversation as if she had never been interrupted. "I'll find out if Brad's in. None of the backstage people come in this way, so I don't see them arrive. But I can find out for you."

She disappeared into the back office and Leslie waited, hoping that Jim did not return with any more questions or wisecracks. She soon reappeared.

"I've been told to send you through to the stage," she said. "Apparently that's where the technicians are at the moment."

"Are you sure?" said Leslie, certain that his appearance backstage would be unwelcome.

"It's all right," she said, "there's no live show on tonight, it's only a film, so I don't suppose they're too busy. You'll need the pass numbers."

She referred to a sheet, copied them down and handed the paper to Leslie who could see that they had not been changed from the previous week. He took the now familiar route down the side corridor, through the two pass doors, entering the key codes as he went. As he climbed the half dozen stairs onto the side of the stage he felt like an imposter again, just as he had the first time he had entered the backstage area, just over a week ago.

There was no sign or sound of anyone and, as he ventured onto the stage, calling out a tentative, "Hello there," he was struck, not for the first time, by the emptiness of an empty stage and auditorium. If ever a place was meant to be full of activity, it was surely a theatre. He searched for the word for it—hollow, came closest. It was a lonely, hollow, empty shell. There was clearly no one here, but he started to walk across the stage just to make sure when he heard the smallest of noises from the back of the auditorium; it sounded as though someone was in the sound and lighting box. In the moment it took him to turn to the front, and before he could call out again, the stage and auditorium, the whole theatre, plunged into darkness.

Leslie froze. Rooted to the spot and hardly breathing he tried to tell himself that whoever had switched off the lights, thought that the theatre was empty. But it was a vain hope—he knew that his presence, centre stage, could not have been missed by anyone in the lighting box, and every instinct told him that there was ill intent behind this.

He turned cautiously round, looking for a glimmer of light from a doorway, a futile action since the venue was designed with the purpose of eliminating outside light. Worse still, by turning he had lost his bearings and now did not know which way he was facing. He did not dare move for fear of what, or who, he might walk into. Screwing up his courage he called out, in a voice as level as he could manage, "Hello there, can you put the lights back on now, please?"

A blinding spotlight hit him full in the face, and he threw his forearm across his eyes. At least he knew which way he was facing, and he took a few tentative steps to his right. The spot followed him. He moved again, and the same thing happened. Every time he tried to edge out of the beam, it moved with him, keeping him blinded. He tried turning his back, but although there was relief from the glare of the light, he could see nothing, and it was very unpleasant to have the perpetrator of this mischief behind him.

Suddenly, for all his fear, Leslie felt very angry and turned directly into the beam. "Hoy, cut it out, will you?" he shouted and, as he did, the spot went off and once again he was plunged into pitch darkness.

He fumbled in his pocket for his phone and switched on the torch, cursing himself for not thinking of it before, but his eyes had been so dazzled by the light that it was still difficult to see where he was going. He blundered along, stifling panic at the thought of someone coming after him silently in the darkness. Having found the pass door, it was still a slow process to feel for the door handle and escape.

He made his way along the corridor as quickly as his dazed vision would allow and, nearing the foyer, he stopped and leant against the wall to give himself time for his heart, which was beating with painful ferocity, to steady. Just then he heard a familiar voice and, stepping forward, he saw Gloria at the reception desk.

"Gloria!" he called out, with relief.

She broke off her conversation with Marian, the receptionist, and rushed across to him. Leslie was glad that they were out of the receptionist's line of sight, as he did not feel equal to anyone's enquiring gaze.

"Whatever has happened?" she said, grabbing his arm, and escorting him to some seats in a quiet spot. "We finished going round the paintings and then I suddenly thought that I should never have let you go and find Brad on your own. That new lady at reception said she hadn't seen you and I thought, for a minute, that you'd disappeared like Roland. Thank goodness you're all right."

"I've just had the most awful experience," said Leslie, and quickly recounted what had happened.

"Who do you think did it?" said Gloria. "Surely it must have been one of the technicians. But I can't believe any of them would play a prank on you."

"I really don't know what to think," said Leslie. He looked round the foyer. "Where is everyone? Have they all gone?"

There were a dozen or so strangers viewing the exhibition and a handful at the café counter and bar, but no one from LADS was anywhere to be seen.

"I think they must have," said Gloria. "Caroline and Tracey were with me most of the time, but they've left now, and I didn't notice anyone else. I think the rest of them went to the pub, but I didn't see anyone leave. I wasn't paying them any attention, I'm afraid. What do you want to do now?"

Leslie had an overwhelming desire to go home. He could think of no way of identifying the perpetrator. There was no point going to the lighting box which would surely be empty, and the person could be anywhere inside the theatre or out, by now. However, he still had not seen Brad and, since he was the only one of the technicians who he could imagine playing an unpleasant trick on anyone, he felt compelled to find him. Brad was hardly going to admit to it, but Leslie wanted to see how he would react when he told him what had happened. Leslie explained this to Gloria.

"But I'll see him out here, or you can come with me this time, if you don't mind," he said

"Just leave it to me," said Gloria. She fumbled in her bag and pulled out her theatre lanyard and usher's badge. She slipped them on and then strode up to the reception desk with Leslie following at a distance, wondering what she was up to.

"Hello there, Marian, dear, can you ask Brad to come up to reception? I need a word with him."

"I'm sorry," said Marian apologetically, "I just heard one of the others, Jezza I think they call him, saying that Brad's taken an extra day off as they've got no show on tonight. Actually, they were trying to get hold of him for something, I don't know what, but he wasn't responding to messages. I'm sorry, I didn't know earlier."

"Ah, not to worry," said Gloria. "Can you have a look at the roster for me?" The receptionist looked blank. "It's that black folder there, on the shelf. Just pass it to me, will you?"

Marian obediently passed the folder over and Gloria turned the pages. "Oh, yes, I see Brad's been crossed off for today," she said. "But he's in tomorrow, I'll catch him then."

"I'm sorry, I didn't know anything about this roster. I only started on Monday. And I didn't realise that was the gentleman you were looking for when you asked earlier," she said, looking towards Leslie. "I do apologise."

"Don't worry, you're doing a great job, Marian," said Gloria magnanimously, and moved away as the receptionist dealt with a customer who had just appeared.

"I went through all that for nothing," groaned Leslie.

"But Brad's on the roster for tomorrow," Gloria said. "So come back to the theatre with me then. There's a show on and I'm ushering. We ushers have to get here early, so I'll go and find Brad and make sure you speak to him. Then you can either wait for me here in the foyer or get a cab home. I would suggest that you got a ticket to watch the show, only—"

She was interrupted by a voice calling Leslie's name. It was Frank approaching them—he was now quite adept on his crutches.

"I didn't realise you were still here," said Gloria. "Everyone else seems to have gone."

"Everything takes a bloody long time with these things," he said with cheerful resignation, indicating the crutches. "Even going to the gents."

"Really," sighed Gloria, in one of her stage whispers, but Frank was oblivious.

"I'm glad I caught you, Leslie," he said. "I thought you'd gone. You don't fancy a theatre ticket for tomorrow night, do you? I was going with old Rawlison but of course he's let me down. I can't get anyone else, a few of them already have tickets for it and the others are either busy or it isn't their thing. It's definitely not something I could drag the wife along to. I was banking on Terry but he's already here ushering. The theatre has a no returns policy unless it's a sellout, and old Rawlison hasn't even paid me for the ticket."

"What's it for?" said Leslie, cautiously.

"It's called *Queens of the South*," said Frank, and waved a crutch towards a poster on the column opposite them.

It depicted a group of impossibly buxom characters in clinging lurex costume, with exaggerated make-up on their heavy features and curling false eyelashes. It was a crass-looking drag act.

"You'll love it. I saw their previous show—it was hilarious." He chuckled at the recollection.

"OK," said Leslie on an impulse. Since he was coming to the theatre anyway to see Brad, it would not kill him to sit through it, and there was always a chance he might find out something from Frank. "I'll give it a try."

"That's fantastic," said Frank. "Thank God they've installed a lift; I'm getting better on the crutches, but I still wouldn't fancy all those stairs. Our seats are halfway back, I think it's row K. Thankfully one is an aisle seat; Roland always sits at the end of a row to get a quick exit to the bar, or so he says." He laughed heartily again. "I'll see you in the theatre just before seven-thirty. You can settle up with me then. I'd better go and find the wife and daughter," he added looking round. "Did either of you see them go? I expect they're waiting in the car park."

He swung himself off on his crutches towards the door.

"I wonder where Kara and Pippa are," said Leslie but, as Frank did not reappear, he assumed that they had been waiting in the car as expected.

Leslie looked at the poster for *Queens of the South* and shuddered.

"It might not be as bad as it looks," said Gloria, but even her indomitable optimism sounded hollow.

As they passed the reception desk on their way out, Marian said, cheerfully, "I'm glad you found your hubby after all."

"If only he'd have me," said Gloria over her shoulder, and she linked her arm through Leslie's as they left the theatre.

28

"I've let the cat right out of the bag now," said Leslie to Bennett, when they got back to the cottage. He had taken a pot of tea through to the sitting room and he gave Bennett a full account of the afternoon's exploits, with Gloria adding interpolations.

"Why did you mention the shoes at that moment?" she said when Leslie had finished telling the saga. "Were you hoping to get a reaction?"

"I don't know," said Leslie truthfully. "I think I suddenly got fed up with everyone writing off Roland's disappearance as one of his eccentricities, and having no concern at all for his welfare. Especially Frank who's known him for years and seems to like him."

"Or says he does," said Gloria darkly.

"When I mentioned the shoes to Frank, I knew that it would get around to everyone eventually, but I didn't reckon on Jim who's like the town crier."

Leslie poured tea for them all and handed round the cups.

"Yes indeed, it went round like wild fire," said Gloria. "The only ones who weren't within earshot were Kara and Pippa, but I expect Frank or one of the others would have mentioned it to them."

"That's what I thought at first," said Leslie, "but now I'm not so sure." He told them what Pippa had said to him about Kara's reaction if the actor was mentioned. "Anyone who knows Kara might think twice about relating a story connected with Roland." He sighed. "I don't know what to make of it. And as for that incident on the stage today! Was I being warned off? But perhaps there was no connection, and it was just a prank."

"You don't really think it was a prank or a joke, do you?" said Gloria. "You said, yourself, that the only one nasty enough for that was Brad, and he wasn't there."

"I've got to a point where I doubt my judgement about the whole thing," said Leslie. "Bennett going off unexpectedly yesterday didn't help; I feel as though anyone might do anything."

His accusing glare was wasted as Bennett had gone into sphinx mode, his gaze fixed somewhere beyond the wall.

"Whether it was a prank or a warning, it would need to be someone who knows how to operate the lights, which can only be the technicians," said Gloria. "Or Terry—he knows about the lighting."

"It's not as easy as that," said Leslie. "Lots of the LADS company had worked on the lighting desk over the years so they can't be ruled out completely, though I don't know how difficult it would be to pull that stunt on the spur of the moment. No-one could have planned it, and I'm baffled as to how anyone knew I was going backstage."

Leslie passed around the plate of biscuits and said, "But I don't know why we're speculating. Bennett's got it all worked out."

"I say, Bennett, do you really know who did it?"

"Well-timed silence hath more eloquence than speech," Bennett replied and dunked a digestive in his tea.

"That means he won't say," explained Leslie.

Gloria nibbled a shortbread and said, casually, "The most likely person behind it, I think, is Kara, with Gareth and Pippa as accomplices."

Leslie could see her eyeing Bennett for a response.

After a moment she added, with a sigh, "But I suppose that would mean that Kara or Pippa worked those lights today, and we don't even know if they knew that Leslie was worried about the shoes." She popped the remains of the biscuit in her mouth and washed it down with a gulp of tea. "Of course, it could still have been Brad," she said.

Once again, she watched Bennett for a response and once again was disappointed.

"We know that Brad didn't like Roland, and he might have rushed down when he had a free moment, done away with Roland and... I know! He could have opened one of those spare dressing rooms and put Roland in temporarily. Then perhaps today he came back secretly because he remembered he had left a clue, and you disturbed him, Leslie."

"It's a good point about those vacant dressing rooms," said Leslie, ignoring the rest of the absurd scenario. "But Brad could hardly have removed the body, as he went straight home after the matinée for his days off, remember? I can't see him leaving a corpse in the dressing rooms until today, though perhaps we'd better make sure those rooms have been checked."

"Ah!" Gloria burst in. "Then it was Terry! He got hold of the dressing room keys, dragged Roland into one of them and then crept back to dispose of the body at a later time."

"He must have crept back before the evening performance," announced Bennett.

They looked at him in surprise.

"When I came off stage in the second half," said Bennett, "I had a prowl around and when I found those locked rooms I went in search of the house manager to open them up. But she had already looked in them. She explained that when she was told that Rawlison had gone missing after the matinée, she had a thorough scout round the whole theatre, including the vacant dressing rooms. She was 'concerned for his welfare', as she put it. She thought that Rawlison might have found an unlocked room, shut himself in for a secret drinking binge and come to grief. She put it a bit more tactfully than that."

"I should have guessed that Louise would have thought of that," sighed Gloria. "She's such a nice person, and so thorough."

"It puts paid to the empty dressing room theory," said Leslie. "But it's good to know that someone took his disappearance seriously and that he hasn't fallen down in some boiler room somewhere."

He got up and walked restlessly to the French windows. He was suddenly irritated by Gloria's well-meant but insensitive efforts to get information out of Bennett, and the glib way they were talking of Roland's murder, for he felt sure that was what had happened.

"If you know who did it, you're very naughty keeping Leslie in the dark," said Gloria to Bennett, her efforts evidently exhausted. "I don't mind for myself, but I don't know how you can keep it from Leslie."

Leslie found himself springing to Bennett's defence, even though he had complained to Bennett about the very same thing.

"Bennett doesn't tell me, so that I don't alter my behaviour towards anyone," he explained. "People are more likely to give themselves away if I know nothing. Or something like that."

"Ah well, you always have a reason for everything, Bennett," sighed Gloria, sounding unimpressed. "But if you do know, can't you do something?"

"Knowing isn't the same as having evidence that will stick," said Bennett. "But I think things are coming to a head, especially now that Felix is loose."

On this enigmatic note, he put down his cup and headed off to his library.

***

"I'm dreading that awful show," said Leslie. "*Queens of the South*, I ask you. From the poster, it looks a hideously low budget affair."

It was dinner time. Gloria had gone and Leslie was carefully sliding an omelette onto Bennett's plate from the pan. He took his own out of the oven.

"I don't know why I agreed to go to it," he said.

"When left to your own devices, your instincts are usually right," said Bennett.

"What do you mean?" Leslie took a small helping of salad onto a side plate.

There was a pause while, to Leslie's disgust, Bennett went into the pantry and returned with a bottle of brown sauce and daubed it liberally onto the omelette. A blob found its way onto the handle of the fork and Bennett licked it off. The bottle lid left a brown ring on the table and Leslie was glad they were eating in the kitchen.

"There are a couple of things, the final clues you might say, that Frank should have the answer to," said Bennett. "In fact, I'm hoping he will give us the key to the whole unfortunate episode when you see him tomorrow night."

"Frank?" said Leslie in surprise. "What has he to do with it? As far as I'm aware he hasn't had anything useful to say."

"No one has asked him the right questions," said Bennett. "I hope I'll know what those questions are by tomorrow."

They ate in silence. Unlike Gloria, Leslie knew it was futile to pester Bennett; he would never be tricked, cajoled, flattered, shamed or manipulated into anything. It was maddening. He cleared away their plates and while he was waiting for the kettle to boil, he picked up the two scripts that Bennett had left lying on the table: the original and the LADS version. Although some scenes were unmarked, many others were heavily annotated with the alterations that had been made.

"And to think that we were led to believe that there were just a few amendments to avoid causing offense to a modern audience," said Leslie. "And to fit in with the peculiar requirements of Roly and Pippa."

He poured the boiling water into the cafetiere and sat down at the table again with the scripts. "So, they did move the interval," he said peering at the end of act one in both copies.

"Roly suspected it had been changed. He thought it was to deter him from bunking off at half time. And that scene with all the stunts in it—that's not in the original at all. I can't believe it. And Roly's character is in it to the end in the original. All these changes, so much effort. But why? I can't believe even Kara would murder because someone once made a fool of her on stage. I wish I knew what it's all about." He poured the coffee and, as he expected, Bennett made no reply. "You do believe that the worst has happened to Roly?"

"Unfortunately I do," said Bennett.

Leslie suddenly felt overcome by sadness. It was easy to discuss it as if it was just a mystery to be solved, but now he remembered Roly as a real person, outrageous and offensive, but also genuine and very funny. There was no doubt that his overtures to Leslie, though highly inappropriate and unwelcome, had been sincere and it was impossible for Leslie not to have been a little flattered.

"And what does Charles make of this? I presume you've taken the chief inspector into your confidence?"

"I've not long had anything worth telling him—I've been painfully slow on the uptake. But I've left him a message now. Unfortunately, none of what I told him is hard evidence and I don't suppose he can start arresting people based on an altered script, especially as much of it could be accounted for by the explanations we've been given. He messaged me back to say he'll call round tomorrow evening, so I'll find out what he makes of it then."

"I wonder if he got the theatre CCTV checked, like he said he would."

"That won't come to anything," said Bennett. "When I was talking to Louise, I asked her if she could look at the recording. But there are only two cameras which cover the area that we need to know about, the stage door and other back entrances, and neither of them is working. She bemoaned the fact that the front of the theatre was refurbished and there are new security lights and cameras everywhere, but the rear area, which the staff use, was ignored."

"You didn't tell Charles that?"

"He can find out for himself," said Bennett. "Anyway, I expect they'd want to look at footage from all the cameras."

Leslie put the cafetiere and coffee mugs on a tray and they went through to the sitting room.

"I'd advise against creeping about backstage on your own tomorrow," said Bennett.

"I definitely won't be doing that again," said Leslie. He poured out coffee and handed a mug to Bennett.

"Apart from anything else, you might meet one of those artistes in a dark corner," Bennett laughed. "But seriously, if Ridgeway wasn't coming over, I'd have come to the show with you."

"Good God!" exclaimed Leslie. "Is it that dangerous?"

"It might be," said Bennett. "But that wasn't my reason. I'd just like to see your face when that show is running."

29

The following morning crawled for Leslie. Bennett was in the library and, as far as Leslie could tell, he was trying to find out some additional information. Leslie messed about in the kitchen then pottered into the garden, but he could not settle to anything. He took a cup of camomile tea into the sitting room and thumbed through the script again. On the revised version, the one that LADS had used, Bennett had struck through the interval and marked it instead after the second scene of act one, with the word *Why?*. In the margin of scene two, he had written, *P, K, G, C, J & J = stage, Les & Keith = props, Brad = cloths. Why?* It was as cryptic as one of his crossword clues.

Leslie made a sandwich lunch which they ate in near silence in the kitchen; Bennett was preoccupied with his own thoughts and Leslie was not in the mood for futile questioning or idle chat. Bennett returned to his room and Leslie heard him making some phone calls. However, when he put his head round the door a couple of hours later to see if Bennett wanted a drink, he was sitting back in the chair staring at the ceiling and he looked like he had been in this position for some time. He followed Leslie through to the lounge for coffee.

"I've been thinking about tonight," he said. "Given that unpremeditated reaction you got when you mentioned the shoes, it's probably not a good idea to be seen asking any more questions."

"But that's the whole point of me going," protested Leslie. "I'm not sitting through that show for nothing. We must get to the bottom of it now, and if you think Frank can tell me something vital, this is the best chance we've got."

"I wasn't thinking of dropping it. But it'll be best if you can get Frank talking and slip a couple of things into the conversation, without sounding too inquisitive."

"There'll be no trouble getting him talking," said Leslie, thinking wryly of Frank's garrulous nature. "But I don't know how good I'll be at finding anything out without sounding like I'm asking. Still, I've got more chance with him than with most people; he's not a suspicious type."

"Good man," said Bennett. "Keep a low profile and remember not to creep about in any lonely places. With a bit of luck, you'll be OK."

This was far from reassuring and Leslie was about to complain when he remembered something. "What about Brad?" he said. "I was going to speak to him and find out if he saw anything."

"You don't have to worry about that," said Bennett, "He's not in."

"What do you mean? He was due back at work today after his days off."

"I know. I rang the theatre, but it seems he hasn't turned up for work."

"What on earth made you phone?" Leslie asked.

"I wondered if he would be there. I wondered if he might be another disappearing act."

"And is he?" exclaimed Leslie, thoroughly perplexed.

"I really don't know," said Bennett.

Leslie could see that he would get nothing further from Bennett on the subject so he did not waste his breath asking. Instead, he said, "You haven't told me what it is I'm supposed to be finding out from Frank in a roundabout way without asking any questions."

"Get him talking about Kara rewriting the script," said Bennett. "See what he says about that. And see if you can get onto the subject of that strange marriage of Roland's, years ago.

Then call me or message me the answers as soon as you can, and I might catch Ridgeway with them while he's here."

***

Gloria arrived at five-thirty. Although the performance did not start until half past seven, the ushers were required early for a pre-show briefing before the public were allowed in. She had also given time for them to find Brad first, not knowing, of course, that he would not be there.

"Another disappearing act," she said, when Leslie told her, echoing what Bennett had said. She had the car roof up, so they were able to hold a conversation. "I don't suppose Bennett hinted if he thinks that Brad's been spirited away like poor Roland, or if he has done a runner? I say, do be careful. If he's guilty he could be lurking around outside the theatre; it's awfully dark and creepy out the back."

Baseless as was this suggestion, Leslie felt goosebumps appearing on his skin, and he shivered. "Bennett suggested I keep a low profile," he said, "so, if you don't mind, I'll wait in the car while you have your briefing and come in when the audience starts to arrive."

Gloria drove round and round the empty car park looking for a parking spot that she deemed satisfactory. She spurned the staff parking area, which was near to the stage door, although the ushers were entitled to use it, stating that she never left her beloved vehicle in such a nasty, dark place. Terry obviously had no such scruples as his green Triumph could be seen there already, with a couple of others.

Eventually Gloria selected a bay. "This will do nicely. Not too many people need to walk past you here, but it's not isolated when you get out later. But ring me if there's the slightest issue—I'll leave my phone on even though we're not supposed to."

They chatted for a while until it was time for Gloria to go in, and when she did, Leslie locked the car doors, feeling rather foolish but remembering Bennett's warnings. He had brought the newspaper along to pass the time but apart from the fact that there was no room in the car's cramped interior to comfortably open the pages, he was not in the mood to read. He had vowed to stop trying to fathom out the mystery—if Bennett had worked it out there was no point—but it was impossible to think of anything else. There was nothing on his phone that could distract him, so he stared through the window, involuntarily turning over every detail in his mind and becoming increasingly irritated with Bennett. It was all very well to say that better results were achieved when he kept Leslie in the dark, but he could have no idea of the strain it caused.

Eventually the evening audience began to arrive. Gloria had chosen this parking spot well as Leslie had a good view of all the arrivals without being conspicuous himself. The Queens of the South seemed to have an eclectic following. A party of young women, chattering and laughing, was followed by a group of much older people and Leslie even saw a couple with a teenage boy.

Just then, he heard a familiar voice and was disconcerted to see Jim arriving, talking loudly to some friends, followed soon after by another group from LADS. This added a fresh challenge; if Jim saw him, there was no saying what gossip about Roland would be shouted abroad, and he could be sure the missing shoes would be broadcast at full volume. The time went on and more cars pulled in, but not in any great number and Leslie guessed that the auditorium would be half empty. There was no sign of Frank and eventually Leslie wondered if he had somehow missed him, so he made his way to the foyer.

He could not see Frank, but Jim's party was in the bar area, holding a noisy conversation. The scanty number of people standing about offered little cover, but Leslie could see Gloria at her station at the top of the main steps by the door which led into the back of the auditorium. He hurried up as stealthily as his age and physique would allow and, remembering to hand over the car keys, begged to be let in without a ticket.

"Of course," she said in a conspiratorial whisper, "and I'll look out for Frank and tell him that you've gone in. Here take this, compliments of the house." She thrust a programme at him, refusing payment.

There was only five minutes to go, and the auditorium was not even half full. Remembering what Frank had said about the tickets, Leslie took a seat by the aisle in row K, keeping an eye on the opposite door in case he had picked the wrong side. He could see glimpses of Terry in the lower right corridor on the opposite side, selling programmes and directing the patrons in. He was struck by the unwelcome thought that Frank might not turn up and that he had been dragged away from the safety and comfort of his home for no good purpose.

There was still no sign of him when the duty manager, a man today, made the customary announcement forbidding filming and photography, and the house lights went down. Then, into the momentary silence, a banging and clanking announced Frank's entry. Just as the people around Leslie started to crane their necks to look, the overture struck up and everyone's attention was taken to the stage.

The show was not to Leslie's taste. The four drag queens, each well over six feet tall, were accompanied in their routines by four men in male costume, all the size and physique of flat race jockeys. They appeared in a variety of outfits to suit the scene, Parisian, military, gladiator, lifeguard, all of them, of course, in exaggerated parody. There were some clever costume changes and effects, and Leslie grudgingly admitted that the singing and dancing were much better than he had expected. But he was very uncomfortable with the commentary and banter between, and he found himself cringing at the humour.

Despite this, Leslie felt quite sorry for the performers who were working very hard for what must have seemed a lukewarm response. Even though each new stunt was greeted with laughter and applause, it echoed around in the half empty theatre and the show was not good enough to create an atmosphere with such a small audience. Frank laughed, clapped and caterwauled heartily throughout, and Leslie felt obliged to force a smile and to applaud from time to time, to avoid remark.

Gloria had taken a seat near the door behind him once the show had started and Leslie glanced round at her once or twice and each time she gave him a long-suffering look. Terry was seated by the door near the front, and he was throwing himself into the humour with gusto.

"Great stuff, great stuff," laughed Frank, when the interval finally arrived. "Are you going to get a drink? I'll never make it to the bar with this leg, so I brought my own." He produced a hip flask from his pocket and took a swig.

"I don't think I'll bother," said Leslie. This was the only chance he had to raise the topics which Bennett wanted to know about. He had lost the opportunity he had been expecting before the show started, so there was no time to waste.

"Look at old Terry down there," laughed Frank, nodding towards the front of the auditorium where Terry was selling ice creams from a trolley.

Jim was in the queue and, even from this distance, Leslie could hear him shouting to his companions, who were still seated, "We'll have to call him Mr Whippy from now on."

"Such a shame about your leg," said Leslie, plunging in. "Though lucky for me, of course. It was such a good play."

Leslie, never a very good liar, spoke with a forced enthusiasm, but Frank did not seem suspicious.

"Getting out of that was the only good thing about the accident," Frank laughed. "I could never have carried it off, not like you did, anyway."

"It was a great play. I'd never heard of it before," said Leslie, trying to sound natural. "Wherever did Kara find it? I understand that she had to rewrite some of it. That must have been a lot of work for her."

"She had nothing to do with it, to be honest," said Frank. "I'm not supposed to tell anyone, actually. It was all Terry's idea. He came across it on one of the playwriting courses he did. Apparently, it was an example of how a good play can fail because it was written at the wrong time, or something like that. He'd seen the potential in it, so he got permission to make some changes and gave it to Kara to direct. Terry thought it would be better if everyone thought that it was Kara who'd rewritten it, since she was in charge of the production, and she was quite happy with that. She likes a bit of kudos."

He laughed, evidently unconcerned that he had betrayed his wife's deception and conceit, and obviously unaware that he had disclosed the person behind the alterations which was, if Bennett was right, related to Roland's disappearance. Leslie had no time to waste in trying to make sense of this astonishing revelation.

"You go back a long way with Roland, I believe," Leslie said, hoping that Frank would not notice the abrupt change of subject.

"Oh yes, donkey's years. Awkward bloke at times but I've always liked him," he said. "No good letting him rub you up the wrong way. That was the trouble with the wife, she let him get to her."

"That didn't bother you? You still got on with him?" Even though this was wandering from the subject, and rather rude, Leslie could not resist asking. He wondered how Frank could be friendly with a man who belittled his wife and who was despised by her.

"If I fell out with everyone old Kara doesn't like..." He laughed flippantly. "Kara's not a bad old stick when things are going her way, but she can be very touchy."

"I read somewhere that Roland once got married," said Leslie, abruptly bringing the conversation back on topic. "Married to a woman. I couldn't make that out—what was it all about?"

"How did you get hold of that story?" exclaimed Frank. "I hope you didn't ask about it at LADS— it's never mentioned. I'll tell you, but it's off the record. Don't quote me whatever you do."

"I won't breathe a word," said Leslie, brazenly lying.

"It was all years ago," said Frank. "I hadn't been married long, myself. I got involved with LADS to please the wife, as you do." He gave his familiar glib laugh. "She was already a member. Terry and his wife were the leading lights, he was a good looker and she'd been an actress before she got married. They looked like the perfect couple, but old Terry always had an eye for the women. Actually, he was a regular tom cat, and they used to joke that there wasn't a woman in Lymeford that he hadn't had his wicked way with."

Frank said this as though he was commenting on the vagaries of the weather. Leslie was disgusted but this was no time for honesty.

"Rumour had it that he knocked his wife about if she complained," Frank continued. "What was her name? Steph, that was it. Anyway, not long after I joined LADS, I happened to meet old Roland in the pub. I used to run into him from time to time if he was down this way; there's some old family connections so we knew each other a bit. On this particular evening, he had a few too many to drink and he started pouring out his troubles. He was right down on his luck, with no work and no money and, to cut a long story short, I got him involved in our next LADS production, for a fee of course.

"When he came to rehearsals it turned out that he knew Steph—they'd been in the same production at one time. They hit it off together, a couple of pros with a bit of shared history. They got very pally and she ended up telling him how miserable she was with Terry and what a regular bastard he was. Terry realised what was going on and he wasn't pleased. He called Roland a lot of things which, even in those days, were near the knuckle."

Leslie was desperate for Frank to get to the point before the interval was over, but there was no way of speeding the thing up without the risk of missing something. Terry was still selling his ice creams and Leslie had a strange sense of disconnect between the man performing that most innocuous of tasks, and the odious subject of the story that was unfolding.

"Well to cut to the chase, it was Roland who persuaded Steph to divorce Terry. That would have been bad enough because, I didn't mention it before, she was the one with the money. Terry was on the brink of opening his own professional theatre company, and it was on the back of her money. That all fell through, of course, with the divorce. And, to make matters worse, Roland and Steph only went and tied the knot, even though she must have been half his age, and he was… well, you know! It was a real slap in the face for Terry and I couldn't help feeling sorry for the bloke. At the time, some people said Roland did it to get her money and others that it was to make a fool of Terry— Roland's way of putting two fingers up at him for all his abuse.

"I got a lot of the story from Roland himself—I only had his side of it, of course, and he only ever talked when he'd had a skinful. I once plucked up the courage and asked him why he married Steph. He told me it was for love. He said it in his joking way but actually, when she got cancer, he really did look after her and he was shattered when she died. It's sad when you think about it."

It was an astonishing tale, but Leslie had no time to dwell on it. "After all that, how could Roland and Terry both stay with LADS?" he asked.

"You have to remember that Terry wasn't chairman in those days, so he had no say about whether Roland was hired or not.

If Terry didn't like it, he was the one who would have had to walk. He's not the type to creep off with his tail between his legs, and LADS was pretty much his life, so he had a lot to lose. And don't forget, Roland has never been in all the LADS productions and, when he is in one, he only ever comes in for a few rehearsals beforehand, so they've never had to see each other often.

"As for Roland, he had no reason to step back, he saw himself as the victor. There was a lot of animosity between them at first, but it's pretty much died off—twenty years is a long time. Terry seems to have let it go, water under the bridge, and all that. Not that anyone would dare to talk about it; luckily there aren't many of us left who go back that far.

"Roland makes out he's doing us all a favour, but he needs the money, and he loves the stage. He's spent everything Steph left him—the booze took care of that. He claims for absolutely every expense from LADS, every taxi fare, train fares to and from London, and he gets paid a fat sum to stand on stage for a couple of scenes in each production. But he gets bums on seats, so they carry on using him."

Leslie had heard enough. "I think I will go and get a quick drink, after all," he said, leaping to his feet.

He glanced down to see if Terry was still there and, to his consternation, saw that he was staring intently up at them with an inscrutable, but very attentive, expression. Leslie had a fleeting realisation that Frank had been nodding and indicating in Terry's direction as he had been speaking, but Leslie had been too preoccupied to grasp the significance that this might have to someone with a guilty conscience.

However, there was no time to worry about it, and he clambered over Frank's lame leg and crutches and rushed past an astonished Gloria who was selling ice creams at the top of the auditorium. As he ran down the stairs into the foyer, he pulled his phone out and rang Bennett. He answered straightaway.

"It was Terry who wrote the script," said Leslie quickly. "Kara had nothing to do with it. And the woman who Roland married was Terry's wife. It left Terry humiliated, hard up and with his hopes and dreams shattered. It was Terry, wasn't it?"

"Where are you now? Can you keep an eye on him without being noticed?"

"I'm in the foyer. Terry's in the auditorium selling ice cream at the moment but I should be able to watch him—the ushers come in for the show."

"Keep him in your sight if you can and—"

The connection broke up and was lost, so Leslie hurried back towards the auditorium. As he mounted the steps, he saw Gloria returning her tray of ice creams to the kiosk in the foyer and he debated whether to wait and alert her, but the second half was about to start, and he wanted to get in without drawing attention to himself. As he went through the door, there was no sign of Terry, and Leslie paused, not sure whether to take his seat or not, but then Terry appeared through the bottom door.

As Leslie climbed back into his seat, he accidentally kicked the crutch, which clattered, and landed on Frank's broken foot, resulting in a loud expletive from the injured man. It happened at the moment of quiet before the music went up for the second half, and every head in the auditorium turned their way. Leslie looked involuntarily in Terry's direction, and across the rows of seats, their eyes met. Terry's face was a picture of hostility and Leslie knew that his own expression had completely given the game away. Bennett was right, once he knew something, it was impossible to conceal it when caught off-guard.

He struggled into his seat, bleating a distracted apology to Frank and almost oblivious to the attention he had drawn from everyone else. To his chagrin, Terry did not sit in the same seat at the front, but moved much further back, a few rows behind Leslie and where he was not in Leslie's direct line of sight. Leslie was forced to cast furtive backward glances but each time he did so,

Terry was watching the performance as though there was nothing untoward.

The second half of the show was on much the same lines as the first. A brief Busby Berkeley spoof moved on to a mystical number with the drag queens dressed in gold angel costumes and the backing dancers as scarlet demons. The smoke machine was working overtime and Leslie was briefly transfixed by some pyrotechnics on the stage. When he looked back to Terry's seat, it was empty. Uttering an oath, he leapt up and clambered over Frank again, who uttered a bewildered, but apt, "What the devil?"

Leslie rushed out to the gallery at the top of the stairs and looked down, where he saw Gloria hurrying towards him.

"I was coming to find you. Terry's just run outside," she called up. "It's very odd, I don't know what he's doing."

"Which way?" said Leslie, flying down the stairs, and Gloria indicated in the direction of the staff car parking area round the back of the theatre.

"I was out here as I couldn't face the second half of that show when—"

"Phone Bennett," interrupted Leslie as he ran past her to the outside door. "It's very urgent. Tell him what's happening."

As soon as he rounded the corner of the theatre, Leslie could see Terry ahead of him. He had reached his car and was fumbling to find his keys. He had just pulled them from his pocket when Leslie, putting on a final burst of speed, shouted:

"Hoy, Terry, stop."

The man spun round, and as he did so, the keys flew out of his hand and onto the gravel path. With a reaction and agility he did not know he possessed, Leslie sped forward and, barely breaking stride, he stooped for the keys and carried on running. As he passed Terry, he caught sight of the glint of metal and knew that he had pulled a knife from his pocket.

In desperation, Leslie pounded forwards, knowing that he was heading round to the back of the theatre, which was a dead end; with Terry pursuing him, he had no choice. It was pitch dark but as he turned the corner, there was a light shining down the scenery dock ramp and he could see that the shutter had been left partially open. He stepped onto the ramp, giving a quick glance behind him, and Terry, who was only a few feet away, hesitated. A second later there was a loud wail of sirens and the blue light of a police car skidding into the car park. As Leslie ducked under the shutters and struggled into the scenery dock, he heard Terry breathing hard and cursing, and knew that he was barely an arm's-length behind him.

He stumbled through into the wings of the stage. A massive figure whipped round and Leslie found his way barred by a colossal sequined policewoman, in fishnet stockings and stiletto heels. With Terry's knife behind him, Leslie had no escape route but the stage itself and oddly, even in mortal danger, he was aware of breaching an important convention as he ran on from the wings.

In terror, he dodged between a masked robber and a bandit holding a smoking bomb, with Terry inches from his back and the drag policewoman hard behind him, and the audience erupted into the loudest laughter and applause of the evening. Leslie heard someone nearby shout an expletive-laden instruction to close the curtains but it seemed that everyone had joined the chase on stage. As Leslie ducked under the arm of another six-foot tall policewoman, the auditorium lights came up and four uniformed police officers burst in through the doors, followed by Bennett and Ridgeway. The audience cheered and stamped.

At that moment, Leslie was grabbed from behind and wrestled to the ground where he fell with a sickening thump onto his shoulder. The curtain shut in front of his face, and he heard the audience calling for an encore.

30

"You'll be pleased to know he's safely under lock and key," said Ridgeway, spreading a generous layer of butter onto a hot croissant. "At the moment it's just for the possession of an offensive weapon with intent, but he'll be charged with the murders before long."

"So, it was Terry, after all," said Leslie. "But murders? Tell me the worst. I know nothing more about it than when I was being pinned to the stage floor by a cross-dressing Amazonian."

Leslie had been spirited away in an ambulance after the fiasco on the previous evening and, although he had suffered nothing more serious than a nasty wrench to his shoulder, he had been at the hospital for hours and it had been so late that Bennett had refused to discuss it when he finally got home. This morning Ridgeway had called in early, on the way to one of his countless meetings, and he joined them at the breakfast table. Leslie, arm in a sling, was now supervising Bennett's inadequate attempts at serving breakfast.

"I regret to say that there have been two deaths: Roland Rawlison and the theatre technician, Brad." Ridgeway looked grim. "Neither has been confirmed as murder yet, but it's only a matter of time."

"I knew from the start that something had happened to Roland," said Leslie with dismal triumph. "But Brad? Whatever has been going on?" He shook his head in bewilderment.

"When he didn't turn up for work yesterday afternoon, one of his colleagues drove round to his place. His car was there but they couldn't get an answer at the door. They were obviously worried, not least because it seems it was no secret that he was a drug user. He wasn't on the hard stuff like heroin or cocaine—he used what they stupidly call recreational drugs, ketamine, ecstasy and the like. But they were worried all the same, as not turning up for work was so out of character. They reported him missing but didn't mention drugs so, of course, it wasn't dealt with as a priority. As the day wore on, they got more and more concerned, and they rang back. This time they admitted he might have OD'd. Once that was mentioned, it was easy to justify breaking in. By that time, I'd had Bennett on to me. Again." He looked across at Bennett and said, ruefully, "Next time you alert me to a crime, Bennett, I'll pull the suspect in straightaway, no matter how many rules I break."

"But you could hardly have arrested Terry on the basis of the wrong shoes and an altered script," said Leslie, taking pity on the chief inspector.

"I will next time," said Ridgeway, grimly, and drank up the last of his tea.

"So, what happened to Brad?" asked Leslie.

"Officially it's an 'unexplained' at the moment," said Ridgeway, "but it does look like a drug overdose. It could have been self-inflicted but, if Bennett's right about the whole scenario, then it's murder. I'll let him tell you his thinking. But there's one thing that Bennett may not know, unless he's guessed this, too. None of the theatre staff knows who took the message that Brad was taking an extra day off on Thursday. It was none of them that wrote it in the book."

"Terry's smart, you've got to give him that," said Bennett.

"Most of what I've said so far will be in the public domain very soon," said the chief inspector, "but I'd better not speculate further. And now, much as I'd like to drink tea and eat croissants all morning, some of us have a job to do."

"But what about poor Roly?" said Leslie. "You can't go before you tell me what happened to him."

"Bennett can fill you in on the background to that, too, since he'd worked it out ahead of us." Ridgeway stood up to take his leave. "But just so that you know, I hadn't ignored your concerns about Rawlison, and I'd had a couple of chaps looking for him. In fact, we'd started questioning the people on your list; that's probably why Terry got the wind up. And we had an anonymous tip-off yesterday." Here, Ridgeway looked suspiciously at Bennett.

"It's amazing how powerful the anonymous call is," observed Bennett.

"Be that as it may, on the basis of that, we tracked this week's waste disposal from the theatre and found the bins at a sorting depot en route to landfill. On searching they found a body, well wrapped in plastic and tarpaulin. It hasn't been formally identified but I'm afraid there's no doubt it's Rawlison. I'm very sorry, I know you were friendly with the chap."

"Thrown away with the rubbish," said Leslie in disgust. "No one deserves that. Do you know how he died?"

"Not yet, we'll have to wait for a postmortem report. You can be sure I'll do my damnedest to see justice is done."

When Ridgeway had gone, they took their mugs through to the sitting room where the autumn sun was shining in as brightly as if all was well in the world, and murders did not happen.

"Go on," said Leslie, "let's have it. I've got half the story but I can't even guess the rest."

"Very well," said Bennett, settling himself in his favourite chair. "You know from Frank," he said, "the background history and the basis for the hatred that Terry had for Roland, although he disguised it so well."

"Before you go any further," Leslie interrupted, "when you told me to ask Frank about Roland's marriage, you obviously suspected the truth, and just wanted it confirmed. How did you know?"

"It was like this," Bennett replied. "When I knew that the culprit was Terry, and we'll get to that in a minute, I started looking for a motive. I began digging up as much background as

261

I could about him and that included his divorce—the fact that it was not to be spoken about made it an object worth investigating. I had no clues to dates or other details and, without asking around and potentially giving the game away, it was tricky to find out anything. In the end, our good friend the doctor made some discreet enquiries among his friends in Lymeford, and came up with the lady's first name, Stephanie, but nothing else.

"This rang a bell, and I looked up that article the you found about that unlikely marriage of Roland's, and it named the bride as one Stephie Sweetcroft. Nothing to link her to Terrance Wiseman, but the coincidence of names was too strong to ignore. From the article I could work out the rough date of the marriage to Roland and I managed to obtain a copy of their marriage certificate, a perfectly legal process," he added seeing Leslie's enquiring look. "The marriage certificate named the lady as Stephanie Ballard and it gave her status as a divorcee."

"I suppose Stephie Sweetcroft was her stage name—she was an actress," said Leslie. "A bit more theatrical than Ballard."

"Quite. Despite neither surname connecting her with Terrance Wiseman, I felt certain she was his ex-wife and had reverted to her maiden name for marriage. That's where I'd got to when you had the invitation to the drag show with Frank. By then, Terry knew about the wrong shoes, and we knew that Ridgeway was going to question the people involved in the production. I was afraid Terry would be nervous and do a runner, so it seemed time to find out about Stephanie, for sure. I guessed that Frank would know the story."

There was a pause while Bennett drank some coffee and Leslie digested this information.

"As you now know," Bennett continued, "by the time Terry became chairman of LADS, he had developed a pathological grudge for Roland. Not only had Roland publicly humiliated him by the divorce and marriage, but he had snatched away the one chance that Terry had to make it in the theatrical world as a theatre company director. It must have really rubbed salt into the wound coming from Roland, who was, in his own way, a successful actor, Terry's unfulfilled ambition.

"So, Terry kept Roland involved in the company, and behaved as though all was forgiven and forgotten, until such time as he could take his revenge. And that revenge he planned in meticulous detail."

At this tantalising moment they were interrupted by a lively ringing at the doorbell. Uttering an uncharitable oath, Bennett rose in mock weariness, and went to the door. Moments later, Gloria made a grand entrance into the sitting room, clad in a vast royal blue cape, and bearing a basket.

Luckily, she did not seem to hear Bennett mutter, "What big ears you have, Grandma," as he took the cloak, draped it unceremoniously across the back of a chair and disappeared in the direction of the kitchen. Gloria placed the basket triumphantly on the coffee table.

"I've brought you some fruit," she said, and with the panache of a conjurer producing a rabbit from a top hat, she drew out a huge and bulging paper bag. "To keep up your vitamin levels and— Oh I say!"

The additional benefits of the gift remained unspoken as oranges, nectarines, a small melon and a mango erupted from the bag and tumbled to the floor. She stood, holding a single pineapple in the wreckage of the paper bag, looking astonished.

Bennett chose this moment to come in, holding a very full cafetiere. "Lady Curzon and a pineapple," he said. He made an exaggerated study of the floor and enquired, "Has there been a typhoon?"

Leslie was exhausted by the previous days' events and irritated beyond measure by the untimely interruption to Bennett's exposition, and now the sitting room carpet had been turned into the floor of an ape house with tropical fruit strewn about and a brown trail where Bennett had spilled the coffee as he walked.

He stomped off to get a cloth and returned to the sight of Gloria's very ample posterior as she stooped to gather the errant fruit.

She rose from the floor and clambered into an armchair, puce in the face and gasping, but quite unperturbed. "I've also brought you a tube of arnica and some turmeric ointment to rub into your shoulder and some lavender oil for the bath. You'll be right in no time, just follow the instructions on the labels," she said cheerfully. "But now, do tell me all about what has been happening, because I'm sure you must know everything. All I know is that they took Terry away in handcuffs last night after that, well, that most extraordinary exhibition!"

It was tempting to tell Gloria that it was all top secret and send her on her way, and then settle down to listen to Bennett's account in peace. But he looked at her eager face and beheld the evidence of her abundant kindness, and he was filled with remorse.

"You've come at the right moment," he said, giving in. "Bennett was just about to explain it all to me, so you might as well hear it too. After all, you've been involved. Just make sure you keep it to yourself for the time being."

"Oh, I'll be the soul of discretion," she said, and drew a pinched finger and thumb across her mouth in a zipping gesture. "But I can't wait to hear it all. Don't leave anything out."

There was a short pause while Bennett composed himself, Leslie went to the kitchen for a plate of biscuits, and Gloria filled her coffee mug and topped up the men's.

"To begin at the beginning," quoted Bennett, and he repeated everything he had just told Leslie.

"So, Terry had cultivated a consuming bitterness for Roland ever since," Bennett continued, "and he planned his revenge meticulously. He rewrote the script of an unknown but excellent play he had come across on a course and used his position as chairman of LADS to select Kara to be director, knowing that he could thoroughly manipulate her."

"It was clever of him to arrange things so Pippa could be leading lady," said Gloria. "That was sure to hook Kara in. I heard that she'd been pushing for Pippa to get a starring role in a production. She couldn't seem to see that Pippa wasn't a bit interested; I suppose that Kara was trying to live out her own dreams in her daughter, something I've observed so often. I wonder how they persuaded the girl to do it."

"Money, I should think," said Leslie. "If she was willing to pay young James to be in it, I'm sure that she'd have had no hesitation in bribing Pippa with a substantial sum."

"Did you know it was Terry from the start?" said Gloria.

"I should have done," said Bennett, "but I was initially sidetracked by the fact that it happened at the matinée. I began by suspecting that someone wanted to sabotage the production. It seemed the obvious line to take, especially after the episode with the bottle left for Roland to drink the previous day. Terry seemed to be one of the least likely to ruin the play, in my mind. What motive could he have? It was stupid of me, and I missed what was under my nose."

"What was under your nose?" asked Gloria eagerly.

"A manipulated script, an elaborate stage set, an artfully complicated scene," said Bennett, "and an actor vanishing into thin air in the wrong shoes."

Leslie refreshed their coffee mugs and Bennett continued.

"As I say, I was very slow witted. From early on I had a shrewd idea that the rewriting of the script was connected with Roland's disappearance, and it was a fair assumption that whoever rewrote it needed more ingenuity than Kara had ever shown."

"I had to get hold of the original script," said Bennett, "and when I did, it was evident that the alterations were designed to keep everyone busy in act two, scene two. The only person with any time was Terry; Terry who I knew all along was the most obvious person to have rewritten the script and could have manipulated Kara into directing it his way, but who seemed such an unlikely candidate to sabotage a LADS production.

"Then light dawned. Sabotage had nothing to do with it. The plan had originally been intended for the Saturday evening performance. Roland would go off stage after his final lines, the show would finish, and Roland would not appear for the final bow. Everyone would curse him and put it down to the booze, especially after Friday's incident when he got drunk. His disappearance would not be reported until someone from his private life missed him. But something occurred to change Terry's plan."

There was a pause worthy of Pinter. Gloria gaped in rapt attention, poised with a biscuit above her mug, ready to dunk. Leslie waited in stoic silence, reflecting that it was lucky one of his arms was immobilised, or he might strangle Bennett. Normally succinct, once Bennett started soliloquising there was no saying how long he would take with a story.

"On Friday," said Bennett, at last, "Kara announced that Frank was going to be backstage during the Saturday evening performance, and Terry was unable to prevent it. It was impossible for Terry to carry out his plan with Frank at large backstage. Terry must have been planning this crime for years, he'd gone too far to turn back, so he moved it forward to the matinée, sacrificing the evening performance and the potential effects it might have."

"Of course!" exclaimed Gloria. "But how did he do it? Even though Terry wasn't in scene two until the end, we already decided there wouldn't be time for anyone to go down to the dressing room, do away with poor Roland and dispose of the body. Did he have an accomplice."

"There was no need for an accomplice," said Bennett. "Roland never got as far as the dressing room. At the end of his final scene, as Roland left the stage into the wings he was met by Terry. I firmly believe that Terry lured Roland outside through the pass door and then the stage door, to the van that was parked just there. Undoubtedly alcohol would have been involved— a story about a special bottle of Laphroaig in the van, or something like that. Roland would have gone off with Hitler, Stalin and Vlad the

Impaler if he thought he could get a drink out of them, especially after that bender on Friday. Forensics will confirm how he died, but at a guess he was hit over the head and then strangled or suffocated."

"What a wicked thing to do," said Gloria, with feeling.

"Barbaric!" hissed Leslie at the same time.

"Then I think he was wrapped and hidden in that unnecessarily huge props trunk. It can't have been easy lifting him, but Roland was a small man and Terry is strong."

"Hang on a minute!" exclaimed Leslie. "It was easier than that. The trunk—I remember noticing that it had hinges. I bet it had been specially made, or adapted so the side could drop down. I nearly asked Keith if it had been an old stage prop."

"He certainly thought of everything," said Gloria.

"Including stealing Sue's keys weeks earlier, no doubt," said Bennett, "so that he could access the bins in the bin store and at some point, perhaps after the aftershow party, dispose of the body."

"I can't bear to think about it." Leslie shuddered in revulsion.

"Do you mean that poor Roland was in the van all the time we were doing the evening production, and when everyone was clearing up, and when we were at the party?" said Gloria, in a low voice, clearly horrified.

"I think so," said Bennett. "Remember how Terry stood guard in that van, supervising everything that went in when we were packing up. No one would have noticed that nothing was put back in the trunk."

"No wonder there was a lock on it," said Leslie. "And I suppose that if anyone had commented about those props not being replaced into the trunk, he could easily have said the key was missing, or something like that."

"Surely the police will find forensic evidence in the van," said Gloria.

"He did his best to cover his tracks, forensically," Bennett answered. "That broken bottle of turps will explain why the inside of the van has been scrubbed meticulously, which I'm certain it has. And it's a hire vehicle so I dare say Terry hoped that subsequent users would have masked any residual evidence, if investigations ever got that far. He was banking on Roland's disappearance being unnoticed for much longer."

"He cleaned his costume, too," said Leslie. "But I expect the police have got that in a plastic bag by now."

There was a melancholy silence for a while and then Leslie said, "Do you think that Terry disabled the CCTV equipment at the back of the theatre? He was an electrician after all."

"I don't know," said Bennett, "but he would certainly have been able to check that the cameras weren't working that day."

"That reminds me, Leslie," said Gloria. "I rang Marian in the box office this morning. She said that it was Terry who told her to send you onto the stage when you were looking for Brad on Thursday. He was in the office behind her doing the usher's roster. I suppose he ran round and shone that horrid spotlight at you."

"A spontaneous attempt to distract you from looking for Brad and frighten you off," said Bennett.

"He didn't realise that it would have the opposite effect," said Gloria. "Anyone who knows you both would know that you wouldn't be deterred by something like that."

"I very nearly was," Leslie admitted.

"But, Bennett, on the subject of poor Brad, you haven't explained what happened to him and why?" said Gloria.

"He was, unwittingly, a potential witness," said Bennett. "Obviously it was essential that no one must see Roland going off with Terry, which is why he had designed the cumbersome scenery and made sure everyone was occupied throughout the scene, including the technicians. Sue was acting as stage manager watching the screen, and Brad was busy with that ludicrous backcloth change. Terry didn't account for the backcloth getting jammed causing Brad to go up into the flies. That was the only place where someone could see over and beyond the scenery and directly into the wings. Terry knew that Brad could easily have seen Roland going through the pass door with him, instead of going off to the dressing room."

"Surely Brad would have said something at the time, when everyone was talking about Roland vanishing," said Leslie.

"He probably would," said Bennett. "But Terry couldn't risk the fact that Brad may not have realised what he had seen; remember, no one was talking of foul play at that point. In actual fact Brad may have seen nothing at all, but to Terry the possibility was enough."

"Terry was very pally with all the technicians, so I suppose it was easy for him to call round to Brad's place, maybe even on the pretext of asking about Roland," said Leslie. "I suppose he managed to spike Brad's drink."

"Quite a risk," said Gloria, "but he must have been desperate."

"Desperate times breed desperate measures," said Bennett.

"You don't suppose Brad did see, and tried a spot of blackmail, do you?" exclaimed Leslie suddenly. "Perhaps he saw Roly going off with Terry, and when Terry pretended to know nothing about it, he realised that there had been foul play. He was a nasty piece of work and it's not hard to imagine him trying to make something out of it."

"Possible, but on balance I think not," said Bennett and, annoyingly, he sounded as though he had thought through this scenario. "Brad would have been completely on his guard against Terry if that was the case and would hardly have let Terry get into his flat and administer drugs to him, however it happened. But I dare say it's one of the police lines of enquiry."

Leslie hoped that for once Bennett's conjectures were wrong. Nothing justified murder, of course, but he felt the blackmail scenario did sweeten the pill a little.

"Whatever would Terry have done," said Gloria, setting off at a tangent, "if most of the cast hadn't boycotted the production? He couldn't have orchestrated that, surely, but it was very convenient having such a small number of people backstage. Everyone said that there would normally have been far more people around, so much harder for Terry to guarantee no one wandered onto his side of the stage."

"He'd have found a way to keep everyone busy," said Bennett. "The scene in question was entirely of Terry's composition, and he could have put as many people on stage as he liked and written in as many gimmicks as he liked to keep the backstage crew occupied. And remember, they never allow random people, those who haven't been signed up to help, backstage."

They were interrupted by a ring at the doorbell. Bennett levered himself out of the chair and ambled to the door leaving Leslie to speculate over which of the village well-wishers had chosen this inopportune moment to call. Some unfamiliar male voices could be heard and a moment later Bennett returned accompanied by two enormously tall men, one of whom was bearing a bouquet of flowers. Leslie was utterly bewildered.

"Oh, I say! It's the Queens!" squealed Gloria.

"Queens of the South, it is, love," replied the one with the bouquet, in a broad Scouse accent. He turned to Leslie and seemed to notice the sling for the first time. "Mother of God, what have I done? It was me who rugby tackled you to the floor. But you can't blame me, I thought we were about to be assassinated. I didn't know you were being chased by a madman with a knife."

"Oh no, I don't blame you, I quite understand, and I'm not really hurt. Nothing more than a strain," said Leslie and urged them to take a seat.

"Thank you, but we won't stay. We're on the road—Torquay next stop," said the other man. "But Chris here was so worried when you were taken to hospital, so I said we'd better come and beg forgiveness."

"It's very kind of you, you really don't have to apologise, but it's much appreciated, and I love the flowers," said Leslie, taking them awkwardly in one hand. "However did you find me?"

"The hospital told us you'd been sent home, which was a relief and, to be truthful, I heard you give your address to the paramedic yesterday. All I could remember this morning was the name of the village, but we came on the off chance that someone would know who you were. It was easier than I thought—I asked in the shop, and they knew straightaway."

They exchanged a few more pleasantries and they all made their way to the door.

"We get a bit of harassment now and again, but no one's ever charged on stage before," said the Scouser. "Mind you, it brought the house down—best gag of the night. Your timing was perfect. If you're ever looking for a job..."

After some final good-humoured banter, and with a "Bye, now," and a "Tarra, love," they departed.

They watched the two towering figures pass through the gate in quest of their car, wherever they had parked it. Vera was standing in the shop doorway, a couple of ladies were coming out of the post office and Sylvia was passing with the dog, Cromwell. Leslie retreated indoors, his mind boggling at what shape the rumours would take after this.

"I can't believe they took the trouble," said Leslie, when he came indoors. "They seemed like really nice chaps, but I'm glad they've gone."

"Me too," agreed Gloria. "I was just about to ask Bennett something, when they rang the bell. Now what was it? Ah, yes! That massive argument between Roland and Kara, surely Terry couldn't have set that up. And yet that seemed to be the thing that clinched the fact that Roland had walked out because we all heard him say that he might do."

"The row was just luck," said Bennett. "You're right, that couldn't have been engineered but it played right into Terry's hands."

"I remember now what Roland really said," interrupted Leslie. "It was something like, 'I might walk out, like everyone

271

says I'm going to'. I remember it because I asked him about it when he came back to the dressing room."

"It struck me at the time, too," said Bennett. "It was as though the suggestion of deserting the production had never originated with him. But of course it seemed to have no particular significance then, as nothing untoward had happened."

"It's amazing what effect a rumour can have," said Leslie, pensively. "But I knew he wouldn't walk out, and not just because he said so. I do so wish we could have averted it—Roland's murder, and Brad's, too. We just weren't quick enough."

"But I think you both solved it miraculously quickly. The police wouldn't have even started looking by now without you."

"Quickly? I should have got onto Terry straightaway," said Bennett. "I had enough information before the final curtain, but I let myself be distracted by the fact that the disappearance happened in the matinée."

A hint of remorse was just detectable in his voice, but Bennett was never greatly troubled by guilt and Leslie had heard him express more regret when one of his puzzles did not work out.

"But you didn't even know a crime had been committed by then, surely," said Gloria.

"I certainly did. Leslie knew some ill had befallen Roland, and I wouldn't doubt him on that."

"Because you knew for sure that he wouldn't walk out on the production?" Gloria asked.

"I knew he wouldn't walk out anywhere in the wrong shoes," said Leslie. "By the way, Bennett, when do you think Terry cleared the dressing room."

"Most likely," said Bennett, "during your final scene with Roland, immediately after the interval, and before the murder was committed. He would have had time to run down and scoop everything up then."

"It wouldn't have taken long to do," said Leslie. "Roland's things were all neatly in one place."

"I say!" interrupted Gloria with great excitement. "It couldn't have happened like that. Remember, that's when I was on watch in the quick change area to see if anyone went to plant another bottle in Leslie and Roland's dressing room. With everything that happened after, I forgot to tell you about that. I kept my watch and the only person I saw was Terry—he looked out of the door in the wings on the opposite side to me, saw me, waved and went back in again."

"Ah," said Bennett. "Terry was on his way, not to plant another bottle, but to collect up all Roland's belongings while Leslie was safely on stage. But you scuppered him, Gloria. He must have made a successful attempt at some other point in the second half, after he had dealt with Roland, no doubt in great haste. All the more reason why he grabbed randomly at one of the pairs of shoes, and missed Roland's coat which was hanging in the shower."

"Now I can understand why Terry was so angry that Roland was sharing a dressing room with me," said Leslie. "It was lucky for him that we were both so tidy or he would have had an impossible task identifying Roland's belongings. But he ran out of luck with the shoes."

"Yes," agreed Bennett, "the shared dressing room, and Frank's appearance backstage were the two things he hadn't planned for."

Eventually Gloria got up to leave. "My omen came true," she said, darkly, as she put on her cape and gathered up her basket. "The black diamond prophesied that some evil would come upon the play. It's one time I'd have been glad to have been wrong."

She spotted the crystal hanging in the window and added, "At least my white quartz helped to bring you back safely, Bennett. Shall I take it away?"

"Leave it there, if you can spare it," said Bennett, unexpectedly. "A reminder that there are more things in Heaven and Earth, Horatio…"

"Oh my!" said Gloria. "Have I got a convert? Or are you teasing me? I'm never quite sure with you, Bennett."

"Believe me," said Bennett in a voice of sincerity, "your insights played an important part in coming to the truth."

Leslie was still not sure if Bennett was lampooning her, but Gloria was highly gratified and moved towards the front door in a mood of elation.

"Oh, I say!" she exclaimed, "I nearly forgot to give you these." She pulled out two bottles of wine from the basket and handed them to Bennett. "I won that case of wine from the art exhibition draw."

***

"What was that about Gloria's crystals?" said Leslie, when he had waved Gloria off. "You'll only encourage her, which is hardly fair, since you think it's all bunkum."

"The bits of glass and stone are, indeed, unadulterated hogwash, though this one is not unpleasing to the eye." The quartz twinkled in the sunshine and split the light into a very pretty rainbow on the floor below. "But the bad omen came, not from a crystal, but from Gloria's own sense of what was going on. I expect that over the course of the week she had pulled out any number of stones from that little velvet bag of hers, but when she produced the black diamond, or whatever it was, it was the LADS production that she thought of and applied it to. For me, that reinforced what you had observed, that there was something sinister going on from within the cast. It helped exclude 'person or persons unknown' from the enquiry and focussed me on the LADS members involved in the play."

Bennett peered at the two bottles of wine, declared them to be pretty decent and honoured them with a place in the wine rack. The two men went back into the sitting room and sat down.

"I'll leave the omens and forecasts to Gloria, I think," said Leslie. "After all, I remember thinking that it wouldn't kill me to sit through that drag show and it very nearly did."

Bennett had the copy of the original script with him, and he was putting it into a large envelope.

"Whatever are you doing with that?" said Leslie. "Surely you're not returning it to the publisher—why would they want it back?"

"I'm sending it to Ambrose at Magdalene," said Bennett, referring to a colleague from his time at the university. "I want his advice about it."

"Advice?" said Leslie. "Connected with the murders?"

"Oh no, nothing to do with that," said Bennett. "You haven't worked out the author's name?"

"Worked it out? I can't even remember it." He took the envelope from Bennett and pulled the script out. "Cora D. Lewis. What of it?"

"It's an anagram."

"Just tell me," said Leslie, wearily. "I've no intention of sitting here for hours, trying to solve it."

"Oscar Wilde," said Bennett. "There's a possibility it was written by him under a pseudonym, maybe while he was in prison. It's in his style and parts of it, at least, are certainly good enough."

"No!" exclaimed Leslie, in great excitement. "Don't tell me you've discovered an unknown Oscar Wilde play!"

"Don't get too hopeful," said Bennett, "it could be an elaborate hoax—that's why I want Ambrose to look at it."

"Before anyone undeceives me, I'm going to celebrate," said Leslie. He took off his sling cautiously and rotated his shoulder. "We'll have souffle and salmon, and I'll make my Aunty Jeanne's lemon cream for a special treat. You can crack open one of those bottles of wine that Gloria just gave us."

He trotted off to the kitchen in happy anticipation.

Epilogue

It was later that evening, and a pleasant piece of Berlioz had just finished as Bennett brought through the supper tray. Leslie's shoulder had survived long enough to make a splendid meal, but the sling was now back in place and Bennett had resumed his temporary domestic role.

There was a plate containing a large brick of Cheddar cheese, a whole camembert still wrapped and some irregular chunks of crumbling Stilton. Another plate bore an untidy heap of crackers, and the pickle was still in its jar. Cutlery was nowhere to be seen. Leslie sighed and decided that perhaps his shoulder was all right, after all.

Bennett put the tray on the coffee table and went for the bottle of port and some glasses.

"What's this?" said Leslie. In addition to the tray, there were two items on the coffee table.

The first was a very old theatre programme for *When We are Married* at the Aldwych Theatre, the production which Leslie had seen Roland in and enjoyed so much. Across the front was written in a neat hand: 'To Leslie, it's been a privilege to work with you. Affectionate thanks, Roly x.'

Totally baffled, Leslie looked at Bennett.

"It was in the raincoat pocket," said Bennett. "Roland was obviously going to give it to you on Saturday."

Leslie held it between thumb and fingertip, as though it was a piece of evidence. "Shouldn't the police have it?" he said. "Come to think of it, I don't think we ever mentioned the raincoat to Ridgeway, did we?"

"No," said Bennett, "I didn't trouble to. What could it have told anyone that the shoes didn't? Evidence that someone other than Roland had packed up his things? Evidence that he didn't leave of his own volition? If they didn't believe the shoes, they wouldn't have believed the raincoat and programme."

Leslie did not think that Ridgeway would see it like that, but he did not bother to argue.

"Anyway," said Bennett, "I was blowed if the police were having that programme. They'd have taken it away in a plastic bag for no good purpose and I doubt you would ever have seen it again."

"Thank you," said Leslie. "Fancy Roly digging this out for me. And signing it. How touching." He flicked through the pages. "It was such a long time ago, before ever I met you; it feels like another lifetime. I could never have imagined then— now I'm getting melancholy."

He put down the programme and picked up the second item from the table, a photograph in a simple silver frame. It was of Leslie and Roland, the one which Bennett had taken before the dress rehearsal. It was a heart-warming picture; Bennett had captured them smiling, natural and unaffected, a couple of good friends.

"I printed it off in the week and I went over to the antique shop when you were out, for the frame," said Bennett.

Leslie raised his eyebrows in wonder at this excursion but decided not to comment. "It really is a lovely picture," he said, holding it up. "Did you ever send a copy of it to Roly?"

"Yes," said Bennett, "I'll read you what he replied." Bennett scrolled down his messages and read, "'Thanks, B, I'll treasure it. You're a lucky sod'."

Too moved to speak, Leslie took the picture across to the mantlepiece where the important photographs were on display: a picture of him and Bennett at an award ceremony, one of Bennett's daughter, Molly, and her family, some grainy shots of various ancestors. After a moment he moved across to the dresser and instead assigned the photograph to a space between a holiday snap and a photo of his prizewinning roses. The death of Roly was tragic, but Leslie had only known him for a few weeks and really he was a terrible louche.

"It's gratifying to have been solicited by a celebrated actor," said Leslie. "But if he hadn't been famous, or once famous I should say, would I really have been flattered? When it comes down to it, I was propositioned by an old soak, who was just after me for my cooking."

Bennett laughed. "There's some small consolation in thinking that he walked off stage to rapturous applause and was probably knocking back a glass of whisky when he was struck down. With luck, he knew nothing about it," he said.

They sat in silence over their cheese and port for a long time. Leslie cast his mind back to the first time he met Roly, in the village hall, which now seemed more like five years ago than five weeks. He thought about the enjoyment they'd had rehearsing, of Roly's shameless attempts to lure him from Bennett, and of his outrageous behaviour in the theatre towards Kara, Terry and Brad. He remembered his consummate skill on stage, his timing, his ability to woo the audience and create humour with the slightest gesture or pause. He really was very funny. And finally, he pictured Roly the last time he had seen him as he left the stage, warm, mischievous, and in his own way, totally authentic and full of life.

"Shall we sing?" said Bennett, suddenly. "Are you up to one last blast of the song from the play?"

"Why not?" said Leslie. "I'll probably cry, but what the hell!"

They went through to the library and Bennett sat down at the piano. "Roland wasn't the only old has-been that loves you for your cooking," he said, looking over his shoulder at Leslie and smiling. "And he was right about one thing, I am a very lucky sod."

He struck up the introduction and they sang the song through for one last time, in honour of Roly, of each other, of life.

Postscript

Tomato Puff Pastry Tart

- Tomatoes – enough to cover the size of pastry base you want (and allow for some shrinkage)
- Ready-rolled puff pastry – 1 pack
- Anchovies – 1 jar or tin
- Dark brown sugar – 1 teaspoon (or more according to taste)
- Olive oil – for drizzling
- Garlic clove, finely chopped or crushed (optional)
- Sprig of rosemary (optional)
- Parsley, Parmesan, olives (optional toppings)

1. Pre-heat the oven to 160°C/140°C (fan)/gas mark 3.
2. First prepare the tomatoes:
   - If cherry leave whole
   - If small slice in half
   - If large or giant beef tomatoes slice thickly
3. Put them on a baking sheet (use non stick baking paper on the sheet if preferred).
4. Season with ground black pepper and salt, drizzle with olive oil (you don't need much) and sprinkle with the dark brown sugar.
5. Add the garlic and a sprig of rosemary if using.
6. Slow roast 160°C/140°C (fan)/gas mark 3. to release the juices and dry them slightly for half an hour or more.
7. Remove tomatoes from oven and set aside.
8. Switch oven up to 220°C/200°C (fan)/gas mark 7.
9. Take the ready rolled puff pastry and roll or cut it to size to fit the baking sheet.
10. Put it on fresh baking paper on the baking sheet and stab it a few times with a fork.
11. Put it in the oven and bake for about 5-10 minutes keeping an eye on it.
12. When it starts to rise take it out and insert a sharp knife into it in a couple of places to let the steam escape. Be careful not to scald yourself.
13. Pat it down and turn it over - it should be nice and crisp on the base.
14. Arrange the tomatoes on the pastry and add the anchovies in a pattern on top of the tomatoes.
15. Add toppings if using (eg parsley/Parmesan/olives)- don't forget the anchovies are very salty.
16. Put it in the oven and check after 20 minutes. Give it a bit longer if you need to.
    It will be very flakey when cut!
    Serve with new potatoes and tenderstem broccoli or salad.
    Bon appetit!

Lemon Cream

- 4 tablespoons of water
- 1 level tablespoon of gelatine
- 225g castor sugar
- Finely grated rind and juice of 3 lemons
- 250ml double cream or whipping cream
- Single cream to serve (optional)

1. Measure water in a small pan and sprinkle in gelatine.
2. Set aside to soften, then dissolve over a gentle heat.
3. Draw the pan off the heat and allow to cool (don't leave it too long or it will solidify).
4. In a mixing bowl combine sugar and lemon juice.
5. Stir in the cream and whisk until thick.
6. Gradually whisk in the cooled gelatine, pouring in a steady stream and whisking continuously.
7. Stir in the grated rind (you can add this earlier, with the juice and sugar, but it tends to stick to the blades of the whisk).
8. Pour mixture into a serving dish and chill in fridge until set.
9. Serve with single cream (optional).

With thanks to Jeanne Newman

Dartonleigh Parish Magazine
Double Crossword

2 sets of clues (Cryptic and Quick), 1 set of solutions

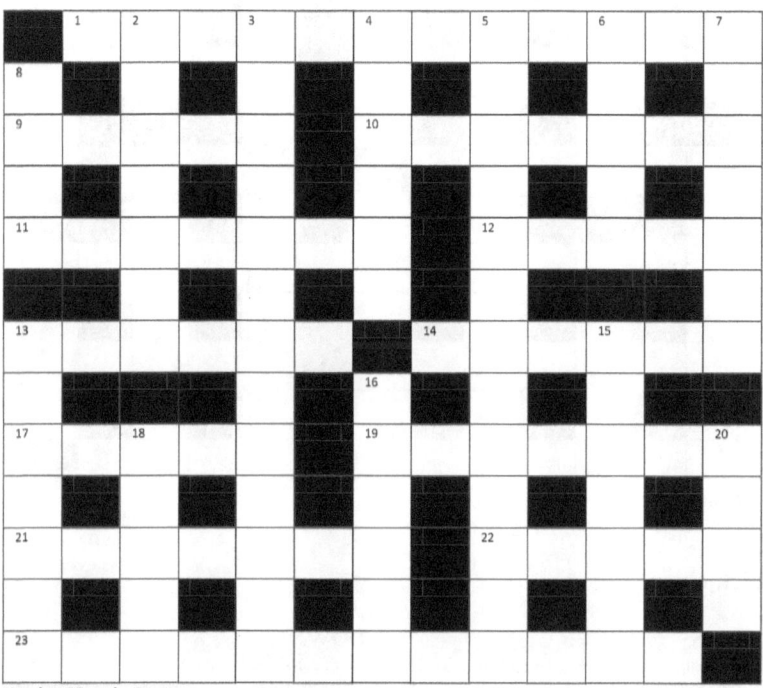

Number 27 set by Bennett

Cryptic Clues

ACROSS

1 I scooped lake for polychromatic view (12)
9 A jester, going backwards, becoming distant (5)
10 German car and rocky outdrop for financial verification (7)
11 Beloved deals a fine ace (7)
12 Roman style villa (5)
13 Out with the commanding officer – strange! (6)
14 Meets back at starting point for good value (6)
17 Somewhere to put something down (5)
19 Sharp ironic point (7)
21 Keepers draw three points badly (7)
22 What I give out is perfect (5)
23 Stresses me as I make a review (12)

DOWN

2 Retail company with digital capability delivers a fruit (7)
3 Success from very loud city in the seventies (13)
4 Trader becomes bad leader (6)
5 Nothing amid chasms is so punishing (13)
6 Frequently less than a dozen (5)
7 Slip-up by Maud creates auditory cannister (7)
8 One of two needed to complete (4)
13 Authorise leader with grass cutting machine (7)
15 Oriental points to the rear of the ship (7)
16 Doesn't score with the young ladies (6)
18 Make a rota for the vessel (5)
20 Instruction to draw the line (4)

2 sets of clues (Cryptic and Quick), 1 set of solutions

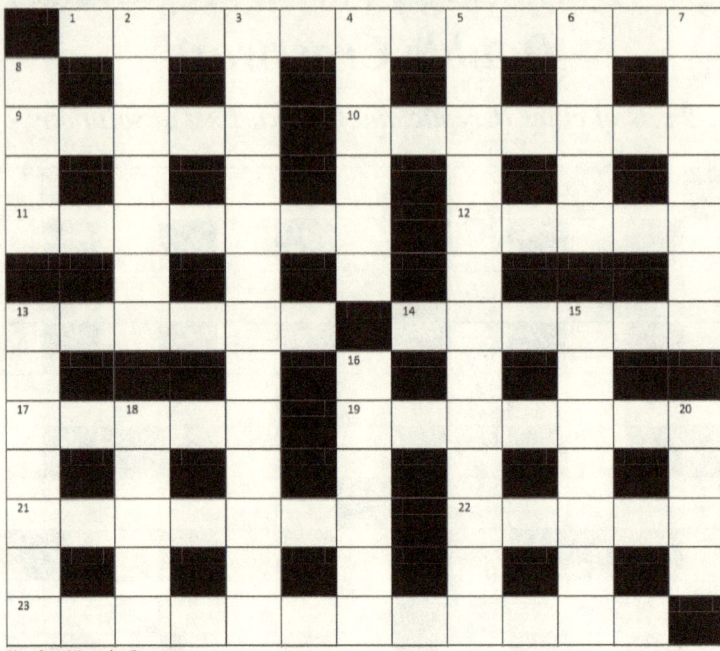

Number 27 set by Bennett

Quick clues

ACROSS

1 Toy containing coloured glass and mirrors (12)
9 Detached (5)
10 Type of accountant (7)
11 Betrothed (7)
12 Mansion (5)
13 Strange (6)
14 Admire (6)
17 Position (5)
19 Tooth (7)
21 Keepers (7)
22 Perfect (5)
23 Reexamination (12)

DOWN

2 Pear-shaped fruit (7)
3 Efficacy (13)
4 Trader (6)
5 Enjoyment of pain (13)
6 Frequent (5)
7 Part of the ear (7)
8 One of two equal parts (4)
13 Authorise (7)
15 From the orient? (7)
16 Fails to hit (6)
18 Large artery (5)
20 Regulation (4)

Preview

Where There's A Song

The fourth novel in J Wilcox's *Leslie and Bennett* series.

"That was Molly," said Bennett putting down the phone. "She's asked us to go up there. It seems there's been some trouble."

"Trouble?" Leslie was seized with foreboding. "Nothing to do with the children, I hope?"

"No, it's Molly's friend. They're saying it was suicide but Molly thinks not."

Leslie is astonished at this unexpected appeal from Bennett's daughter, who Bennett had barely been in contact with these past twenty years. Unable to turn down a request for help, however, and intrigued to meet Bennett's family for the first time, Leslie braces himself for the formidable circumstances, and they set off for the Yorkshire Dales.

Trying to get at the truth, Leslie goes undercover in a local choir and at the foodbank, and before long, he finds himself in situations way outside his comfort zone. But perhaps none of it is quite so daunting as being thrown into family life with a houseful of teenagers.

For the release date and other book news, follow me on -
Facebook: J.Wilcox
Instagram: J.Wilcox_author